THE
ELECTRIC
KINGDOM

DAVID ARNOLD

VIKING

VIKING
An imprint of Penguin Random House LLC, New York

First published in the United States of America by Viking,
an imprint of Penguin Random House LLC, 2021
First paperback editon published 2022

Visit us online at penguinrandomhouse.com.

LIBRARY OF CONGRESS CATALOGING-IN-PUBLICATION DATA IS AVAILABLE.

Paperback ISBN 9780593202241

Manufactured in Canada

1 3 5 7 9 10 8 6 4 2

FRI

Design by Opal Roengchai
Text set in Century MT Std

For my grandmother Jean, whom I have loved in this life.
And my grandmother Lakie, whom I will love in the next.

Those who know the future don't talk about it.

—Ted Chiang, *Stories of Your Life and Others*

Under all these lives I've lived, something else has been growing. I've evolved into something new.

—Dolores Abernathy, *Westworld*

L ife began with a snowstorm.

"The absolute *nerve*," said Theresa Underwood, speeding down the highway. It was nighttime; snow hit the windshield, covered the road in a white blanket. "I could see a slap on the wrist, but firing me is a shameless power play, am I right?"

The only other sentient being in the van was her faithful bird, a budgie named Wilma, whom Theresa had begun bringing with her pretty much everywhere. Wilma sat perched in a cage buckled into the passenger-side front seat, staring out the window as if contemplating where things had gone wrong.

"I mean, *shit*," said Theresa. "It's not like I was jacking *twenties* from the till."

"*Jacking!*"

If the sign of a devoted listener was word repetition, Wilma was world-class. He was also, despite the name, a male budgie, something Theresa's husband had once pointed out, to which Theresa had responded, "Gender is a social construct, Howard. Also, it's a fucking bird."

Theresa lit a cigarette with one hand, negotiated the steering wheel with the other. "Like that place is gonna miss the pocket change I took. My boss, ladies and gentlemen. Forever trying to prove his balls."

"*Balls!*"

And so it went: Theresa Underwood drove through snow like a bat out of hell while Wilma the budgie yelled "*Balls!*" (his own testes having remained dormant so long as to be presumed dead).

And whether because of the snow or Theresa's blind rage—or, as she would claim weeks later, having emerged from a coma, "I'm telling you, Howard, the kid appeared out of thin air"—she did not see the girl standing in the middle of the highway until it was almost too late. At the last second, Theresa swerved hard right, tipping her sagging-rusty van onto its side, where it skidded some thirty yards before ramming into the barrier wall.

Before long, a traffic jam wound through the woodsy New Hampshire terrain like a great luminous snake in the night. Somewhere in the middle, from the warmish interior of a small hatchback, a young man called Ethan said, "I cannot believe this."

His wife Alice said nothing. Secretly, she believed the traffic was karma, the poetic revenge of a universe that did not abide man's irresistible urge to utter the phrase *we're making incredible time*.

"Check the app again?"

Alice raised her phone. "Still no service."

"Can't remember the last time we had so much snow this early in the year." Ethan sighed. "We were making incredible time, too."

She loved him. She did. But five years in, Alice couldn't help wondering if her list of Minor Husband Annoyances wasn't a bit longer than most. As if on cue, Ethan pulled out a plastic bag of peach gummies, made an ungodly amount of noise opening it, popped one in his mouth, and leaned his seat back as far as it would go.

"So long as we're just sitting here. May as well be comfortable."

She tilted her head toward his flannel pj's. "Any more comfortable, you'd be comatose."

"I'd think someone in your condition would be more chill about casual wear."

"My *condition*?"

"You know what I mean."

"First off, I almost never do. Second, that's not *casual* wear, hon. It's *sleep*wear. And third"—she pulled the elastic waistband of her maternity pants, couldn't help noticing they didn't give as much as they used to—"these are actually pretty comfortable." A lie; she hadn't known comfort in months. "Incognito pj's. Whereas yours are just . . . *cognito*."

"That's not a word. Also, how dare you?"

"Yes, how dare I live my life in pants." She reached over, pulled a gummy from the bag; it tasted like dirt and chemicals. "I apologize on behalf of all humans in pants."

"Maybe your mother could've given you more *incognito pj's* instead of a lifetime supply of monogrammed baby towels."

In the back seat, no fewer than two dozen washcloths and bath towels—with hoods of raccoons, elephants, foxes, and a variety of Disney characters—were stacked and buckled in like the tiny human they would soon dry off.

"It was a *baby* shower, Ethan. For the *baby*. Not me." Her hands went suddenly to her stomach—a familiar achy clench.

"You okay?" Ethan stopped chewing, sat up. "Is it the . . . Braxton thingies again?"

Braxton thingies. For a scientist, he could be really stupid. "Braxton Hicks," she said, and the feeling passed, and she forced a smile because she knew he was trying, but God save him if she didn't have this baby soon, and God save them *all* if this traffic didn't start moving.

Time to take matters into my own hands. Alice rolled down her window.

"Hon?" said Ethan. "It's *freezing.*"

Shortly after coming to a standstill in this mess, the truck driver in the lane next to them had rotated through an assortment of evocative eyebrow-raises and quick-winks, all of which she'd pretended not to see. Now Alice motioned for him to roll down his window. "Hi," she said; the snow was heavy, the flakes thick.

"Hey, sweetie."

She gave him a smile that lasted a blink. "You have a radio, right? You know anything about what's going on up there?" She pointed ahead, into the eternal demi-glow of taillights.

"Van tipped on its side."

"Oh God."

He nodded. "Fucking-A."

"How far up?"

"Not a mile, even. But in this weather . . ." Quick Wink shoved a large wad of chewing tobacco into the space between his bottom lip and teeth.

Alice smiled, rolled up the window, put her hands in front of the vents to warm them.

"Now we know," she said.

Ethan nodded. "Fucking-A."

"Stop."

"That guy's staring at you."

Alice switched on the radio: a classic rock station, warbly Beatles, the early years. She and Ethan were silent for a few minutes, each wanting to spare the other their current question, neither knowing the other was wondering the same thing: What *exactly* did it look like, getting snowed in on the highway, miles of humans buried alive in their own cars?

Ethan shook the image, popped a peach gummy. "You could have thanked him."

"What?"

"The truck driver."

"Come on."

"You asked for information and he gave it to you. In this weather, you asked him to roll down his window."

"Tell you what. You trade in those pj's for a pair of big boy pants, and I'll climb on top of this car with a bullhorn and let everyone know just how grateful I am."

"I'm never getting rid of these pants."

"One morning you'll wake up, and they'll be *gone*."

"If they're gone, I'm gone *in* them."

"Ethan."

"What."

She pointed through the windshield to a roadside billboard thirty yards ahead:

NEXT EXIT

BLESSED CHURCH OF THE RISEN SAVIOR

"SEEK AND YE SHALL FIND"

But it wasn't the sign she was pointing to. Someone had climbed up there, was standing on the ledge with what looked like a can of spray paint.

"What's the windchill up there, you think?" Ethan chuckled. "That's some serious commitment to the defacement of public prop—"

Alice inhaled sharply, held her stomach again, only this time her breath quickened, her eyes focused on the small but widening patch of dampness in her lap. "Ethan—"

"Oh shit. Okay. It's okay, right? We have time, I mean. They said in class, we have one to two hours from the time—"

"*Fuuuuuuuuuuuuuuuuuuuuu—*"

"Okay, okay, just breathe, like we practiced."

"*Please* don't use the corporate *we*—mother*fuck*, I cannot believe this is happening now."

Ethan looked at the car ahead of them, tried to measure the distance between it and the median. But snow was piled on the side of the road, and *I could maybe inch around one or two cars, but one slip and we're in a ditch.* "Okay," he said. "You're going to be okay. We're okay."

"Stop saying that word."

Ethan turned from the window, looked around as if something inside the car might present a magical solution—

"Not like this, Ethan, not like this . . ."

His eyes landed in the back seat, where a monogrammed stack of woodland creatures and Disney characters were buckled in, patiently waiting to be put to use.

Seven car lengths back, Dakota Sherouse sat alone in her car wishing she'd never left the house that night. She wasn't sure what was worse: this traffic jam, or the date that had preceded it. At least she'd insisted on meeting Bob at the theater. Imagine being stuck with him now.

Bob.

Perhaps unfairly, Dakota had always assigned value to a person's name. Her mother's name was *Zoe*; her lifelong best friend, *Estelle*; her only long-term relationship, with a man named *Pieter*. Though credit where it was due: Bob had found the cutest little movie theater. It was kind of a drive, and the date was a bust, but you could hardly fault the venue for either.

Phone unresponsive, Dakota turned on the radio to search for a traffic report, when ahead, she saw a young man exit the driver's side of a hatchback, sprint around to the passenger door, and help a very pregnant woman get out.

"What on earth?"

Seconds later they both climbed into the back seat of their car.

Trancelike, without knowing what she was doing, Dakota

opened her door, the shock of cold barely registering. She walked between cars, through a fog of exhaust, until reaching the hatchback. There, she saw the woman lying in the back seat on a pile of animals and Disney characters—*baby towels*.

She tapped on the window; inside, the man turned, looked up at her, eyes full of panic.

"I'm a midwife," she said.

Gladly surrendering his spot in the back seat, Ethan did what he could from the front (next to nothing): he held his wife's hand when she wanted, left her alone when she wanted, offered nervous encouragements. "Ethan," said Alice, her sweaty hand squeezing his. "*The heat.*"

He spun around, adjusted the temperature, and was about to turn back when something through the windshield caught his eye. The roadside billboard, now defaced . . .

NEXT EXIT

BLESSED ~~CHURCH OF THE RISEN~~ SAVIOR

NOW VOYAGER

"SEEK AND YE SHALL FIND"

. . . and there, high on the ledge, the girl who'd defaced it was looking down—right at him.

She was young, a teenager probably. As the wind whipped her hair around, she smiled at Ethan, eyes blue and fiery. Her lips moved, and he found that whatever she'd said had filled him with hope. And then the girl turned, descended the ladder, and disappeared into the woods.

Hours later, and in a different place, their angelic midwife swapped for a team of tired-eyed nurses and doctors, Alice held a healthy baby girl swaddled up tight. "I didn't think she would be this calm," she said.

It was true: their baby was awake, quiet, staring right back at them. And though Ethan could not explain it, he felt it was not the first time tonight he'd seen those eyes.

PART ONE

IN
THE
UNTOLD
WANT

NICO

Etymologies

Years ago, long before the narration of her father turned unreliable, dissolving like one of those Sweet'N Lows in his favorite stale black tea, Nico would climb into his armchair and sit in his lap as he read *The Phantom Tollbooth* or *Tuck Everlasting* or any one of the hundreds of books in the cozy-dank Farmhouse library, and even now, even here, she could smell her father's beard, feel the glow of flames from the fireplace, hear the soothing salivary tones of his reading voice, and Nico wondered if perhaps *that* was life after life: not a physical place, but a loop of some former time in which a person, after death, was allowed to relive over and over again. There, in a story, in her father's armchair—in her father's arms—Nico hoped that was the afterlife.

She supposed she would know soon enough.

Constellations

Nico stared into fire. Beside her, Harry's breathing had long ago fallen into time with hers, and she thought that one could hardly call them two separate entities, that at some point between yesterday and today, she and her dog had consolidated into a single, cosmically connected creature of survival. Maybe this telepathic bond had been there all along, lying dormant below the surface; maybe it took leaving the Farmhouse, entering the wild, to coax it out.

All around, the trees were thick: every few feet, the base of a trunk exploded from the earth, rose up into the sky where branches reached like arms to hold hands with other branches, tree-sisters and tree-brothers seeking touch, listening for words of comfort in the dark night. *I am here. You are not alone.*

The thought of trees talking to each other warmed Nico's stomach.

She pulled a pen from her bag, held the back of her hand up to the firelight. There, in the space between her thumb and forefinger, was a single line in ink. Carefully, she drew a second line beside it. According to the map, the Merrimack River ran over a hundred miles from New Hampshire to Massachusetts before spilling into the Atlantic Ocean. It helped to think of the woods on a large scale; by contrast, their walk in them seemed minuscule, their destination much closer than it actually was.

She stared at the lines on her hand: two days down. At the rate they were going, she hoped to reach the river by the fourth tally, leaving her with four more to get to Manchester.

Not the *Kingdom of Manchester*. Just Manchester. She could still hear her father's voice: *The Waters of Kairos are real. Manchester is a real place . . .*

She knew Manchester (or what was left of it) existed. Outside of that, she wasn't sure what to believe. Her father had seemed lucid enough, though the line between lucidity and opacity had blurred considerably these past weeks. The problem was, there was no protocol in place, no books on the shelf, nobody in the wide empty world to help her answer this question: *What do you do when the person you most trust hands you a fiction and calls it fact?*

On her back now, tucked into the sleeping bag, Nico looked up at the stars and thought of her parents. How quickly her memories of them had come to resemble a place more than a person: a permanent imprint in the armchair, a dusty seat at the dinner table, the empty mantel by the fireplace, her mother's dog-eared Bible. So long as they lived in the Farmhouse, the Farmhouse lived. It was the body and they were the heart. But it was quickly becoming a ghost, every nook and cranny a whispered reminder that her mother was gone, her father wasn't far behind, the beating heart was winding down.

The fire popped; beside her, Harry shimmied in his sleep, his front and back haunches lurching in a running motion, chasing the squirrel or rabbit of his dreams.

Winters in the Farmhouse were cold, but Nico found comfort in them: cozy spots, always a fire, an extra blanket or two. It was late October now, what her mother called *pre*-winter, when the year skipped fall altogether and the sun went to bed early. Out here, she felt she was seeing the true nature of cold, a bitter-bleak affair. At least once, probably twice in the night, she would wake up freezing and add wood to the fire. Still, bitter-bleak or not, here was the truth: part of her—a small part, buried under the threat of woods and Flies, the loss of her mother, the fear of reaching Manchester to find nothing at all—down there, burrowed in, was a part of Nico that was *glad* to be out here. That she'd made the unknowable horizon known, reached out and grabbed it, turned it like a glass doll in her hands.

Around her, the sounds of the wild undulated, rolled in loudly, flowed out softly; a circular pattern took shape in the sky, the stars themselves a cosmic connect-the-dots. Soon she would be asleep in Harry's musky scent, dreaming of herself in a little boat at sea, being pulled by an orca, guided by a large bright eye in the sky.

For now she looked to the stars for answers. "How can I fight this darkness?"

The stars were cold and uncaring as ever.

Furies

"What do you get when your dog makes you breakfast?"

Having finished his strawberry granola, Harry looked up at her expectantly.

"Pooched eggs," said Nico.

A single tail wag; it was the best she could hope for.

Breakfast today was the same as it had been yesterday: one

serving of strawberry granola crunch and a strip of rabbit jerky apiece. It would be lunch and dinner, too.

Blood was the stuff of lore. A long lineage of logic she would never understand, but which her parents had locked on to in the early days of the Flies, when she was still a baby. They maintained live traps along the Farmhouse perimeter, mostly for rabbits, the occasional gopher, but never doing the killing outside. The cellar was for slaughter, skinning, dressing.

Whatever the logic, it had apparently imbedded itself in her.

She could not bring herself to hunt.

Luckily, her dad had been economical in his packing, raiding the food supply buckets for lightweight items. Most of the freeze-dried dinners were out; they required too much space, weight, preparation. There was no chili mac (her favorite), but plenty of strawberry granola (palatable), and a good amount of her dad's homemade jerky. Aside from food, her backpack contained a water-filter bottle, sleeping bag and bedroll, two gallon-size ziplocks of lighters, a compass, folding knife, map, extra socks, a small first aid kit, and packs of ground cinnamon. So long as strict attention was paid to rations, their meals would be taken care of, and they had enough Fly repellent to last weeks.

Nico sat with her back against a tree, savoring the jerky. "Why aren't koalas actual bears?"

Harry tilted his head as if to say, *Go ahead then*. It was a look inherited from his mother, Harriet, whose death would have been unbearable were it not for those same humanoid eyes she'd passed on to her pup. (As for the breed of Harry's father, there was really no way to know, given Harriet's propensity to disappear into the woods for days at a time.)

Harry was a medium-size two-year-old, perky ears, dark black fur. Like his mother, he was playful without being needy, more intuition than simple smarts.

"So now *you* say, 'I don't know, Nico, why *aren't* koalas actual bears?' And I say, 'Because they don't meet the koalafications.' "

Not even a wag this time.

Nico stood, kicked dirt on the remains of the fire. She wrapped herself in her coat, pulled on the backpack, and was about to set out when a deer appeared, and it began to snow, and it felt like the one had been waiting on the other.

Her mother had often complained how much of the wildlife had been wiped out by Flies. Squirrels had survived, and rabbits, all things rascally and quick, animals that knew how to live in claustrophobic places. Nico had seen a moose once: enormous, mythical, like something from a storybook. But that was years ago.

They stared at the deer, and it stared back, two dark orbs inside white eye rings, and time slowed to little wisps, gliding like one of these thousand snowflakes to the ground. Grayish-brown skin. Antlers. "A whitetail," whispered Nico. A buck, though it had been in a fight or suffered some sickness, as the antlers on one side of its head were gone, and a back leg was bleeding.

Sunk in the animal's glow, she didn't hear it at first.

Then, in the distance, a low hum . . .

Swarms had a way of conjuring sounds she'd only imagined: a fleet of trains, a collapsing skyscraper from one of the old cities, the cyclone in *The Wonderful Wizard of Oz*. From the Farmhouse cellar, it was hard to tell whether a swarm's volume was due to size or proximity.

She put a hand on Harry's head, felt him trembling. "Easy," she whispered, scanning the area for places to hide. "Easy . . ."

The whitetail raised its lopsided head to the sky, its nostrils flared . . .

It happened fast: the humming burst from the trees, a deafening roar now, and the Flies came down like holy thunder, a celestial arm from the sky. She jumped behind a tree, yelled for Harry, but he'd run off somewhere, *where, where*, she couldn't see him, and now she was on the ground, couldn't remember falling, heart pounding against the quaking earth. From where she fell, she saw the whitetail covered in Flies, and for the first time in her life, she understood the fury of the swarm.

By the tens of thousands they worked as one until there was no visible grayish-brown fur, no broken antlers or red blood, no deer at all, only a deer-shaped thing, black and pulsing. The deer barked, a nightmarish screech, and as the Flies began lifting it off the ground, Nico buried her face, covered her ears, and did not move until she felt Harry's warm breath and wet nose against the back of her neck. And even though it was quiet again, the thunder in her head lingered.

Optics

Underfoot, a mix of leaves and snow, fresh and old. After the swarm, the day seemed to go on forever, all the noises of the forest a potential threat.

Eventually they fell into an accidental game where Harry would run ahead, never too far, but far enough for them to feel the underlying suggestion of aloneness. They'd go like this for a minute, not biting into the solitude, just nibbling at it. Inevitably, Nico would break first. She'd whistle for Harry's return, count to five under her breath, and he'd come bounding back. (It never took longer than a five-count.) When he returned, she would tell him what a good dog he was, and he would wag his tail, and she would tell a joke or two until he decided to play the Game again—run ahead, nibble of solitude, whistle, five-count, triumphant return, verbal affirmation as to the quality of Harry's petsmanship, and so on.

A few hours in, they found a narrow stream that hadn't yet frozen; they stopped long enough for Nico to refill her filter bottle, and for a quick bite, and by the time they'd started the second leg, their moods had lifted a little.

"Mom used to say the only thing worse than not being educated about something was pretending not to be." In addition to the paranoia of Flies around every rock and tree, the whitetail had stirred something unexpected in Nico. "In the interest of not pretending, I have to admit—I had not considered the possibility of other people. A deer? Fine. And we knew Flies were a danger. But people. That's a whole other deal."

Honestly, the thought of seeing another person scared Nico less than the thought of another person seeing her first. She was stronger than she looked but couldn't help wondering if this wasn't a bit counterintuitive. Appear strong and you never have to prove it. Appear weak and you're constantly disproving it.

Harry ran ahead (all hail the Game!); watching him go, Nico played a different sort of game. She found a tree in the distance and imagined a stranger's eye peeking out from behind it.

What would this person see?

Two outliers headed east, little dots on a map inching toward the Merrimack River: a dog, medium-size, breed unknown; a teenage girl with watery white skin, hair yellow as the sun, blue hoodie, long black coat, backpack.

Maybe they wouldn't even see a girl and a dog. Maybe they would see only meat.

Ahead, Harry stopped dead in his tracks, stared up into a tree. As Nico neared, she followed his gaze, and at first she wasn't sure what she was looking at. Some droopy animal hanging from the branches, furry but flat, strangely indefinable, something that belonged in the ocean, if anywhere. Whatever it was, its colors blended into a tree whose leaves waffled between shades of fall and winter. Then, slowly, a shape took form: twiggy legs, a belly ripped open like a too-full sack, the absence of insides, of eyes, of life. The antlers—a single set only, its beam and tines camouflaged among the branches.

"The whitetail," she said. Hollowed out now, not a carcass so much as a sagging hide and bones. This morning the deer had commanded their attention with nothing but its theatrical presence; it commanded attention now, too, though this was a different kind of theater.

Nico had always possessed a natural capacity to feel what others felt. She could close her eyes and live there, be them, feel this, do that. Now, eyes closed, she tasted lead and panic, felt the wave of Flies behind her like a tracking tsunami as thousands of feverish nips burrowed into the innermost Nico, her body slowly filling as she lifted off the ground, emptied of muscle and organ until, nothing left, the Flies dropped her back to the earth a discarded shell, the saddest of fallen stars.

At her feet, Harry dug a hole. Nico couldn't help being proud of her dog's aptitude, how quickly he had learned what follows death.

KIT

spacedog & computer #611

In the beginning, there was nothing.

Then the world.

Then people, but no art.

Then people made art.

Then people died.

Now there is art, but no people.

Kit set down the chalk, wiped his hands, and turned to the empty classroom. "And that's how it went. A brief history of art in the world. By Kit Sherouse. Your professor. Amen. Goodbye, or whatever."

Even at twelve, Kit felt a many-reasoned sadness at his little playact. Not because he was the one teaching, but because no one was there to learn.

Which was a shame.

Because Kit knew a lot.

Oil paints, for example. He knew all about those. How they were made of natural pigments from heavy metals, e.g., cadmium red, titanium white, et cetera and so forth. It was for this reason, Kit knew, that oil paints could last decades without going bad.

(Also, he knew about *e.g.*, which was an abbreviation for

the Latin phrase *exempli gratia*, which meant "for example," for example.)

Kit stood alone in the art classroom of William H. Taft Elementary School, staring at the blank page on the easel in front of him, stewing in the adrenaline of artistic possibility.

"I could make anything," he said aloud, knowing full well what he would paint, having painted the same exact thing the last 610 mornings.

He stepped forward, put brush to paper, and out it came. *First the moon, big and bright.* He painted that moon, bigger and brighter than he'd painted it yesterday, and around it, a swirling navy night sky. *Now, at the bottom, the dog.* He started with the head: snout up, looking toward the moon, perky ears, *and now the body*, which he outlined first, and then filled in with black. Once the dog was done, he turned his attention to the blank space in the middle of the paper where the giant key would go.

The key was similar to the one his Dakota wore around her neck.

Maybe it was the exact one, who could say.

Yesterday it had occurred to him too late that if he mixed a little glitter into the gray paint, he could make the key shimmer. He did that now and felt a rush of excitement when it worked: a shimmering key in the sky, like cosmic space dust. Whatever it was, this was the closest he'd gotten to an accurate rendering of the vision in his head.

He stepped back, took in the painting. The dog, the moon, the shimmering key.

"Okay," he said, wondering if today was the day. Maybe he could stop here. Maybe he could be done. The three images worked well together; there was no space on the page begging to be filled.

And yet . . .

Stepping forward, as always, he allowed the brush to take over. In the sky, around the moon, where stars might have been, Kit painted a computer from the olden days. Big and boxy. Now a keyboard with a cable. Now a computer mouse, like the one he'd found tucked in the back corner of the maintenance closet, beige and ugly and hanging in the sky as if that were its most natural habitat.

This time, when he stepped back to take it in, the piece didn't just *look* done—it *felt* done.

Strange, how a person could create something they didn't understand. But maybe that was what made art great: *Who cares where it comes from, so long as it comes from you?*

The walls and ceiling of the classroom were plastered in various versions of this same painting. Covered and recovered, as Kit had run out of space long ago. He signed the bottom of this one, and beside the signature, a title: *Spacedog & Computer #611.*

After removing his smock, Kit crossed the hall to the library.

Because William H. Taft had once been an "elementary school," and because, in the olden days, "elementary schools" were populated by younger children, the library was mostly filled with kids' books. Kit was twelve, which, according to Monty, meant he would soon be spending more time in the old person library down the road.

And look. It wasn't that Kit didn't like the old person library. It was the insinuation that a library for old people had more wisdom than a library for children.

It only took a few afternoons in the old person library for Kit to debunk this theory. (*Debunk* being a word he knew that meant "remove the bunk.") The stories were different, yes. Most of the covers were bigger, and some even had print so large, Kit could have read the pages from across the street. There were "books on tape" and "audiobooks," which, so far as Kit could tell, had been nothing more than very long grown-up versions of bedtime stories. But there was no more or less wisdom to be found in the old person library.

Plus, the William H. Taft Elementary School library was *way* cozier.

Here, his books were arranged by genre, and then alphabetically by author, because Kit had a brain in his head.

He'd finished reading the nonfiction shelves years ago, and was currently in fiction, halfway through the *L*s. Not bad considering he usually only had about an hour before he had to be back at the Paradise Twin for high sun curfew.

Kit curled into the orange beanbag chair, opened *The Call of the Wild*, which was about a bunch of snow dogs who wanted to be boss, and picked up in a chapter called "The Dominant Primordial Beast."

This was where Kit waited for his paintings to dry.

This was where he became a Knower of Things.

oh sarcophagi, cacophonies of catastrophe!

William H. Taft Elementary School belonged to Kit, just as Pharmacy belonged to Monty, Sherriff's Office belonged to Lakie, and Garden on the Roof belonged to his Dakota.

It was just the four of them in all of Town, so they got to do things like that, pick out their own buildings.

When picking a building, one had to take into account two things: that building's proximity to home (the Paradise Twin Cinema), and the amount of hollow bones and leftover people-bits that would need removing. Schools and businesses were a safe bet, as they'd mostly been evacuated before things got really bad.

Houses were tricky. In the olden days, houses were where people had lived, according to his Dakota. People would save up their cash-bucks to buy a house. They would spend a bunch of time picking one out. What people in the olden days didn't know was that no amount of time or cash-bucks could keep a house from becoming a sarcophagus (which was a fancy word he knew that meant "tomb").

Houses were cacophonies of catastrophe.

He'd been inside a few, during scavenges. They were dark and smelled like a woodstove casserole of death and farts. The worst cases were the ones where the Flies hadn't gotten in to clean up the job. These houses had people-bits galore, rotten skin, cartilage, and, everywhere, the crumbs of humans.

You knew where the Flies had been. Flies left nothing but hollowed-out bones. Little piles all over the place, once people, now a heap of strange flutes around an empty skull.

Once, when Kit asked why all the bones they found were hollow, Lakie said, "Flu-flies mine them for marrow," and Kit felt bad for the people who used to live in Town. These silly people with their pockets of cash-bucks and dead dreams and houses full of marrowless bones.

Marrow was the fatty substance inside the bone, which Kit later confirmed with a number of literary sources in his very convenient library for kids.

what lay beyond

He hung his latest painting on the wall beside *Spacedog & Computer #610* (covering up *Spacedog & Computer #403*), and then stood at the open window.

Because the art classroom was on the second floor and the school was on Main Street, and because Main Street ran through the heart of Town, Kit could see everything from up here. It was warm but not too warm, the perfect weather for standing in an open window.

A breeze blew in his face, and he held it like a wish, imagined where in the world this breeze had been born. The middle of the ocean, maybe.

The ocean was one of the places he knew about but would never see. Like the moon.

Or Texas.

Or a jazz club.

It was a long list.

Across the street was his home, the Paradise Twin Cinema. Two stories tall, it was one of many old connected buildings on Main Street, all of them with history and things to say, though Kit loved the Paradise Twin most. It was stone and brick and had large iron letters across the top that read PARADISE TWIN, and below, a white-and-gold marquee that had once read WELCOME TO PARADISE, though a lot of the letters had fallen off.

For security purposes (i.e., to keep Flu-flies out), they kept a large semicircle of cinnamon spread on the street in front of the entrance; after high sun curfew, once they were all safely inside, the doors were barricaded.

Safe and sound. Tucked away. Home sweet home.

One of the reasons Kit had chosen Taft Elementary was its convenient location. Twenty-two seconds from here to the Paradise Twin.

Yeah.

He was fast.

There was Lakie now, walking home, rifle slung over one shoulder. She spent her mornings in the field behind Sheriff's Office at a shooting range she'd set up years ago.

Kit knew nothing of guns. Lakie, on the other hand, was about as efficient as you could be in most gun-related areas (e.g., shooting them, cleaning them, safety protocols, terminologies, and so forth). What Kit lacked in the weaponry department, he more than made up for in the observation department. Most days, as high sun curfew approached, he stood like this in his window, watching over his little world.

A few doors down, Monty emerged from Pharmacy, where he spent his mornings on his crystal radio, or studying the Downfall of Society (DOS, as Monty called it). Where the shelves in Pharmacy had once stocked a variety of medicines, it was now home to hundreds of well-organized newspapers and magazine articles from the early days of the Flu-flies, as well as whatever books Monty could find in the adult library on the subjects of radio and communication.

He was what you'd call "obsessed."

Here's how that happened: a couple years ago, Monty found some kind of specialized earphone during a scavenge, and then spent months searching for the rest of the materials for his homemade radio. Apparently, a "crystal radio" required no batteries or electrical power of any kind, although its reach was limited.

Still. Any distance seemed impossibly distant.

"Hey!" Directly across the street, at eye level, his Dakota stood on the roof of the Paradise Twin. She was super-dirty, which meant today was for planting or harvesting. (Canning days were just "sweaty-dirty.")

It was no secret where Kit got his complexion: pale white skin, freckles dotting his nose and cheeks. His mother was the same. *Theater tan*, she called it. *The palest of Paradises*. But he had to admit, recently, she was looking more flushed than usual.

She pointed at the sun, then held up five fingers. *Five minutes.*

"Dakota Primavera tonight!" she yelled.

He gave a thumbs-up. Dakota Primavera was her homemade potato pasta, plus crushed tomatoes and a seasonal rooftop vegetable.

There had been a time, Kit knew, when some people's convictions or diets or preferences had compelled them to forgo the consumption of meat. Here in Town, they were vegetarians because, as his Dakota said, "When the majority of the world has been wiped out, you don't kill what's left."

Kit didn't mind. He had no memory of meat. Not to mention, his Dakota's garden was an overturned cornucopia of variety, and she was basically a culinary genius.

Until a few months ago her garden had been in an old park down the road. But a swarm had come, fast and strong, and she'd barely made it back to the Paradise Twin in time. His Dakota had taken an extra-long bath and they'd burned her clothes, and the very next day she'd started transferring the garden to the rooftop.

Up there, she had the best possible vantage of the surrounding mountains. She kept a large handheld bell with her, and they ran weekly drills with no warning. She would ring the bell, and each of them—Kit from his classroom, Monty from Pharmacy, Lakie from behind Sheriff's Office—would drop what they were doing and *run* to the Paradise Twin.

Standing in his window now, he let go of the breeze, imagined it floating down Main Street, up into the endless mountains that surrounded Town. He thought of a book from the nonfiction shelves about the solar system, and how someone had written in the margins of a page, *THE FINAL FRONTIER.* From this book, Kit learned that there had once been some very smart people who knew an awful lot about space. Some had *gone* to space, flown rockets *into* space, explored regions and documented their findings. *However*, the book said, *outer space is an infinite ocean in which humans have only yet dipped the corner of a toenail.*

Kit thought back to that day of their very first drill. After his Dakota had rung the bell from the rooftop and they'd all run to the Paradise Twin, she'd looked them in the eye and said, "We will *not* be caught off guard."

"*Again*, you mean," Kit had said quietly.

As far as he knew, they had been caught off guard exactly twice: his Dakota's recent close call, and years before, when Kit was very young, the swarm that killed Monty and Lakie's biological parents.

He hadn't meant anything by it. But the looks they'd given him that day taught him something. There was a code. A right way, and a wrong way, to speak of the Flies. Surviving, running, fighting, preparing, defending—these were part of the code. Reminding everyone of a time when the Flies had taken something from them—this was not.

How to be human, it seemed, was an infinite ocean in which Kit had only yet dipped the corner of a toenail.

PART TWO

IN
THE
HOUSES
OF
LIGHT

THE DELIVERER

I find the house in my 7th Life, according to the Red Books.

The only thing more exquisite than its architecture—all sharp angles and natural wood and enormous triple-pane windows—is its ingenuity. To say it was built on top of a mountain is only half correct, as the entire back half of the house is actually set *into* the mountain, immersed in mineral, rock, soil. Where architectural designs had once attempted to bend the will of nature, my house bends to nature's will.

And with such grace.

Survival really is the cleanest aesthetic.

The mountain itself is a scripted *V* flipped upside down: on one side, a steady, incremental climb; on the other, a steep drop, uncounted hundreds of feet to the bottom. During my 7th Life, according to the Red Books, I saw this upside-down *V* from miles away, and came up here to jump.

Imagine my surprise.

Not only in finding the house (and its many miraculous amenities), but at the decomposed body dangling from the upstairs walkway, greeting me upon my arrival. No identification, no note, hardly any sign he'd actually lived in this place so meticulously designed to withstand Flies and the darkened world.

The Architect, I call him, though I can't be sure he was the one who designed the place.

Whoever *had* designed it had done a spectacular job.

My house has no hallways, and few walls. On the ground level, the suggestion of a kitchen nook with an island counter. Beyond that, an open area with a couch facing an enormous wall made of glass. Such majesty in a snowstorm! Thunderstorm! Any storm! Those are my favorite nights, sipping wine, reading a book, listening to records by this glass wall, while outside a storm rages.

Upstairs, a loft space with a bed to end all beds. Four-poster. Mattress you could swim in like a pool. Most mornings, I wake in the cupped palm of this mountain to find the clouds outside my bedroom window. I usually lie in bed for a while, if the Red Books allow, and stare at the photograph on my nightstand until my heart hurts.

Onward now, through the house.

Out back, beyond the chickens in their fortress-coop, through the vegetable garden (a harvest calendar in the kitchen, which veggies for which season), beyond the ten-thousand-gallon rainwater harvesting tank, twenty more steps: here is the edge of the cliff, the tip-top of the upside-down *V*.

Here is the true source of ingenuity, survival, life . . .

The entire face of the cliff is covered in solar panels.

Countless hours I've spent here, sitting on the edge of the world, contemplating the manpower, machinery, or magic involved in attaching so many panels in so many unreachable places. It seems impossible, yet there they are, tilted just so, unfettered access to the sun.

Who were you, O Architect, O man of mystery? Military? Government? The ultimate wealthy survivalist? You, who'd gone to such great lengths to preserve your life, considered every possible angle but your own mind—who were you?

Chilled eggs in the refrigerator. A stovetop to cook and heat water. An AeroPress and beans for coffee. Vinyl spinning in the living room, lounging by the glass wall.

I am not complaining.

I push buttons, flip switches, my own little kingdom in the clouds. And when that godlike power swells inside me, I remind myself that *light begets light*, that my power to create it is only the subset of a greater power, perhaps the greatest: the sun, that beautiful burning orb.

Here, in the earth's song of ruin, my House by the Solar Cliffs is a reprise of survival. In it, I have learned to be grateful for repetition. And while summers are hot and winters are long, and while aloneness is itself a presence in the room, *loneliness* is nothing but pure absence, a reaching down and hollowing out. I have learned to love myself, my own company. I have learned that you can hate a house only so long as you avoid a fundamental truth: that you are the one who calls it home.

Even now, in my 160th Life, I am learning new things.

I write all these things down in the Red Books, so that I might never forget.

NICO

Holes

Three days before Nico found the skin and bones of a deer hanging in a tree, she sat in the Farmhouse library, staring at the dwindling flames in the fireplace, feeling herself dwindle right along with them.

"You okay?"

She looked up at her father, the usual hollowness of his pale white cheeks filled with dirt and dried sweat. Her face was probably just as filthy. "What?"

"I asked if you were okay," he said.

There was no telling how long they'd been sitting like this. She would have wished for sleep or unconsciousness if she'd had the energy to wish for things, and now she couldn't remember if she'd answered the question—but no, she was not okay.

"How long have we been sitting here?" she asked, looking back to the fireplace.

"I don't know. A while."

From the ratty couch, Nico reached out a hand to rest on Harry's head, but felt nothing. She was an empty vessel now, this was her life. A room for hire, an unfillable ditch.

"Should we have buried her outside?" asked her father.

Nico looked at the ceiling, imagined the cluttered attic above, the little door that led out to the deck and the Bell tower: It was Nico's favorite spot in the Farmhouse. She'd spent countless hours up there, staring out across the miles of New Hampshire forest in all directions, pretending their Farmhouse in the middle of the woods was a lighthouse in the middle of the ocean.

Her mother had often referred to the house as if it were an old woman. She'd step on a squeaky floorboard and say, "Her arthritis is flaring up," or when it was drafty in the winter, "Her blood's running thin." Old woman or not, the house was bent on protecting its inhabitants from the outside world: every window was boarded up; the back door had been bricked off; the bathroom was gutted, hollowed into an elevated outhouse. Nico had been allowed once-a-day monitored outdoors time in the confined clearing between the front porch and the tree line. Occasionally she helped plant or harvest the family's corn crops behind the house, climb the apple tree for the out-of-reach fruits, or set traps along the perimeter, but other than these instances, and her time on the attic deck, she did not go outside.

"No," said Nico. "She would have wanted to be in the house."

Suddenly, a piercing alarm rang through the house; her father stood, limped across the room to where a small flashing-red box was affixed to the wall. He flipped a switch on the box and the house went quiet. "Holes are the opposite of electricity," he said.

"What?"

He was quiet a moment, just staring at the box. Powered by a single rooftop solar panel, the Electronic sounded an alarm twice a day: shortly after the sun came up, and sometime after it went back down. Long ago, the alarm signaled that the time had come for someone to trek up to the attic deck and ring the Bell. As a young child, Nico had never questioned the Bell's purpose, just as she'd never questioned the purpose of the fireplace, the cellar shelves, the water pump in the mudroom. And then one day it occurred to her that the fireplace kept them warm, the cellar shelves kept them fed, the water pump kept them hydrated. What did the Bell *do*, exactly? But whenever she asked her father, he would mutter maddeningly vague answers about it having something to do with his work, but that it no longer mattered, and so she was left to her imaginings: maybe the Bell was a method of communication among other Farmhouses in the area; maybe it was some sort of survivalist call-and-response; or, her favorite, maybe every building on Earth had a Bell, maybe there had once been a great choir of Bells the world over, maybe people everywhere used to clang and sing in resounding harmony.

Whatever its purpose, no one had rung the thing in ages. Nico suspected the reason her father hadn't disconnected the Electronic was because it reminded him of the old world, a time when there were so many Electronics, each had their own name.

"*Opposite* isn't the right word," he said, still staring at the device on the wall. "But the absence of electrons . . . or rather, the electrons go one way, holes go the other. I forget."

It was happening all over again.

First her mom. Now him.

"I should fix dinner," he said, turning from the Electronic, his eyes landing on the bright red bag by the front door.

If he thought she hadn't noticed the covert packing, the muttering under his breath about some cryptic trek south, he was wrong. Not that it mattered now. There was no way he was leaving her here alone. Not to mention the sudden onset limp in his left leg, and a usually drum-tight mind that was now leaking in several places. What little Nico knew of the woods had been taught to her by a man who currently had no business being in them.

Whatever his trip was, it was off. She would put her foot down if she had to.

"I should fix dinner," he said again, like some glitchy robot.

"Okay, Dad."

Light from the fire flickered off the bookshelves lining the walls, as if the flames were the sun and the spines were tiny insignificant planets. Nico closed her eyes and tried to remember the feel of her mother's hugs, the crinkled flipping of that old Bible's wafer-thin pages, those eyes the color of kindness, but already these feelings were fading, each memory of her mother a grain of sand in an hourglass nearly expired.

"I should fix dinner."

Nico opened her eyes, found her father standing there staring at the Electronic on the wall, and she wondered how long before his sands slipped away too.

"Okay, Dad."

Homes

Dinner by candlelight. Just the one candle, as always.

Mouth full of rabbit and corn, her father said, "Hey."

"What."

A little smile. "Happy birthday."

An image: one year ago, the three of them smiling around this same table. Her mother had concocted a sort of cookie out of water, smashed apples, and the Metallyte brown sugar cereal. The result was pasty, but sweet, and Nico had blown out a candle, knowing she was supposed to make a wish, but not knowing what to wish for.

"October twenty-eighth," he said. "Still your day, honey."

She stared at her plate, trying to fathom a world in which she could think of nothing to wish for.

"Plus, now you're eighteen. Legal adult in the eyes of New Hampshire."

"Guess I can buy beer now."

"Nah, that's twenty-one," he said.

"I can wait three years."

"Oh, I've got it all planned. Got my sights set on a nice six-pack of single-malt vodka-beer down at the booze shop." He took a sip of water, smiled over his cup, and it would have felt good, this old banter of theirs, but the ease and speed with which he transformed from the loving, wisecracking father she knew to the empty-eyed robot from the library moments ago was all too familiar. "Thought I might pick up a bottle of butterwine while I'm at it," he joked.

She smiled a little, took a bite so she wouldn't have to say anything.

"Nico." He set down his fork and knife. "Listen—"

"Can this wait?" Whatever conversation was about to happen—whether it involved the packed bag by the door, or the fact that her father was showing the same early symptoms of whatever illness had killed her mother—Nico needed the night air, the woods, the calming presence of the Bell at her back. "The attic deck," she said. "After we clean up. I'll make tea."

That small smile again. "The way I like it?"

The way he liked it was with four Sweet'N Lows.

"I wasn't aware there was any other way," she said.

After dinner Nico hauled buckets of water from the mudroom pump to the kitchen, where her father washed dishes. They bagged the rabbit bones, jarred the fat, hung the skins. Chores were robotic and function and unthinking—Nico was grateful for them.

"Almost out of dish soap," said her dad.

"We're due for a Delivery Day soon." She tossed a bone to Harry, who trotted off to his hidey place under the stairs. He'd be there, content to gnaw for an hour or more.

"You know what I was just thinking about?" Her dad had moved from washing to drying, setting the dishes on the counter. "Right after we got married, our first place, that little apartment on Westlawn. You wanted a dog, remember? But the super wouldn't allow pets, so you smuggled in that tiny thing—what was it? A terrier? Only it was so yappy, the whole place knew what was up."

"Dad?"

Even as part of Nico wanted to let him finish the story, to go along with it, *Yes, of course I remember,* she couldn't do it. In his eyes now, the realization of his error. More than sadness or confusion, it was the look of someone who'd stepped inside their own house only to find themselves at the bottom of a hole.

"Nic."

"It's okay."

"Oh my God. I'm so sorry."

"It's *okay.*" She took the towel from his hands, was about to lean in to hug him, when they both heard it—out of nowhere, a deep rumble in the distance.

Water dripped from a half-washed plate.

Fire popped in the woodstove.

Harry was back in the kitchen now, bone in his mouth, ears perked.

"I can't tell if it's getting closer," Nico whispered.

Her dad put a finger to his lips, eyes on the boarded-up window over the sink. "Okay," he said, holding out a hand. "Let's go."

She took his hand, and together, they descended into the cellar.

Lights

It was a rule. Like the Farmhouse boundaries or limited outdoors time or not slaughtering animals outside: the sound of a swarm dictated they hunker down in the cellar as a family, sing songs that had outlived their creators, listen to Nico's mom read the Bible in the hushed-pure tones of a true believer. Bleak moments made a little lighter by the presence of each other. Now, whatever brightness Nico had once found in the cellar was buried right along with the woman who'd brought it.

She sat with her father in the far corner, their backs against the cold cement wall. Overhead, the swarm was close, the Farmhouse pulsing and moaning under its weight.

Occasionally, growing up, her parents had offered glassy-eyed accounts of swarms crashing over cities like waves, drowning houses, buildings, crowds. Whether you died from the Flu the Flies planted inside you, the process of their planting it, or were simply consumed in midair, nothing could make a warm body cool so fast as a Flu-fly.

Or so she'd been told.

She pulled her knees up under her chin, let her long hair fall in her face like a curtain. In the candlelight, the fresh mound in front of them was easy to see, like a bulging tumor in the middle of the dirt floor.

"I was her?" Nico's voice was just loud enough to be heard over the droning outside.

"What?"

It had gone just like this with her mother, too: she'd be acting normal one minute, and then, with no warning, they were someone else to her. In those moments, Nico always had her dad as her true north.

Now her true north was suddenly pointing south.

"The apartment on Westlawn," she said. "Your story in the kitchen just now. You thought I was Mom?"

A beat, then: "Yes."

Eventually the droning dissipated, all was quiet. And even though the swarm had moved on, they stayed in the cellar awhile, staring at the grave, which was part of the earth, which was, allegedly, still spinning.

"Of course she smuggled in a terrier," said Nico.

They both smiled a little, and it felt like second and third candles in the dark. And when she put her head on his shoulder, she realized it was the first physical contact since their three had become two.

"I miss her," she said.

At first he didn't say anything, and she thought maybe he was confused again, but then he said, "Me too," and she understood.

He'd always had trouble talking and crying at the same time.

Birds

On average, the Deliverer came to the Farmhouse once a month.

Drop-offs were downright celebratory, given their shortage of visitors through the years. (In Nico's darkest moments, she wondered if there was anyone out there *to* visit.) And so, the evening of a Delivery Day usually called for a feast, a break from corn and whatever sad rabbit or gopher had been caught in one of the traps along the perimeter. They would boil extra water and crack open five, sometimes six or seven Metallyte pouches of cheesy lasagna or tortilla soup or chili mac, and stuff themselves silly.

She'd read enough books to get the gist of Santa Claus, and even though they didn't celebrate Christmas, she thought the Deliverer was probably a lot like Santa. She'd never seen the Deliverer's face; so far as she knew, no one had. The Farmhouse had a specially designed slat, a square-cut hole with a plank that opened and shut guillotine-style, through which the Deliverer dropped food, tea, salt and sugar, soaps, lighters, candles. Before canned foods gave way to freeze-dried, she had vague memories of slippery-sweet peaches, pears, rings of pineapple—but that was a long time ago. The only items not passed through the door were the five-pound tubs of cinnamon (once doled out by the US military, when there was such a thing); these, the Deliverer left on the porch. And because the front door opened directly into the library, it was not uncommon for Nico to hear the slat in the door slide up, to see those gray-gloved hands slip through the opening and drop the rations on the floor. The process lasted seconds. The slat dropped, the Deliverer's footsteps descended the front porch, and it was over.

When Nico was young, she'd believed those hands to be magical little birds fluttering through the door bearing exotic foods from far-off lands. She'd pick up a pouch (or before that, a can) and dream of a place where the culinary horizons had expanded beyond the simple sweet treat, a land that could produce such glories as *Italian-style diced tomatoes in tomato juice* or *savory stroganoff* or *chili mac.*

This belief held steady until she was nine. She was in her room, attempting for the fourth time to read her father's favorite sci-fi novel, *Dune.* (Even then, her desire to connect with him knew no bounds; the book was a monumental chore, bordering on impossible to read.) Just as she was about to throw in the towel *again,* she heard the familiar sound of the slat in the front door sliding open. Quickly, she blew out the candle and crossed the bedroom. At her boarded-up window, she pressed one eye against a sliver of light between the planks, just in time to see a figure walking off into the woods.

Later that night, wide-awake, Nico stared into the darkness of her bedroom ceiling, replaying those few seconds over and over again. And she couldn't help thinking that what she'd seen—a person wearing a shiny black-and-gray suit, with gloves, boots, a helmet—looked like something straight out of her dad's favorite mind-numbing novel.

Times

They sat on the attic deck, legs dangling through the railings, drinking hot tea from mugs.

"Have you ever tried to eat a clock?" asked her father.

She eyed him nervously.

"It's a joke, Nic."

"No," she said. "I have never tried to eat a clock."

"Probably for the best. It's pretty time-consuming."

A rare thing, this: a joke she hadn't heard. "Good one, Dad."

He took a sip of tea, smacked his lips: "Especially if you go back for seconds."

The view was stunning and endless as ever, miles of treetops spread in all directions, large mountains made small by the size of the sky. Here was the place where Nico had spent the most time with her dad: the stories, the jokes, the way he raised one arm through the railing, reached out, as if simply seeing the view wasn't enough—he wanted to touch it.

They liked it best at night, this view. They called it the Great Green and Navy Unknown.

"I don't know how you drink this stuff." She winced as she swallowed. "It's like an old shoe, even with four Sweet'N Lows."

He looked at the mug in his hands, and she wondered if it was a *normal* look, or if he seemed surprised to be holding a mug. "I never get it quite right," he whispered, and then drank deeply. "No one brews it like you."

The woods had yet to turn white, though it would happen soon enough. Winter could be brutal, but Nico liked it. Or rather, she liked winter in the Farmhouse library, by a fire with a book. Or like they were now, bundled up, a panoramic view of the world. It was a special warm, winter warm.

"We need to talk," he said, and even though he continued

looking out over the woods, there was a definite shift in the air.

"You can't leave, Dad."

He turned from the woods to her.

"You packed a bag and set it by the front door," she said. "You've been mumbling about this trip for weeks, you didn't think I'd notice?"

"Nico—"

"You can't leave."

"I'm not leaving."

Looking at him now, she was reminded of when she was younger, how she would say to one of her parents, *I hear your voice in your eyes.* She couldn't explain it, but throughout her life, there had been moments when she could hear what her parents were about to say in the split second before they said it.

You are.

"You are," her dad said.

"*I am* what?"

Leaving.

"Leaving."

He stood, walked over to the Bell, put a hand on its cold bronze, gently, as if attempting to tame some magnificent beast. The Bell was twice his height, at least three times as wide, and it had a featured role in all her father's stories: *The Misadventures of Hicklebee Swift*, all dozen *Tales from Faraway Frozen Places*, and her favorite, *Voyager in the Water*.

"I saw you," he said, staring at the Bell.

"What does that mean?"

"The angel . . ." And here it came, the thing she'd been dreading: the quiet, verbal spiral. "She was an angel, Nic. She appeared when and where we needed her, when and where we needed an angel," and on and on, a frenetic, mumbled chant about some angel, until Nico stood, put a hand on his shoulder—

"It's okay, Dad. It's okay, I'm here. You're safe."

The sudden confusion, the sporadic hallucinations, it had been just like this with her mom. Soon he would turn in on himself like a perverse cocoon, not a withering so much as an *un-blossoming*. He'd be reading or eating or sitting by the fireplace, and all the while, the un-blossoming would do its work, and eventually the petals of her father would retract into the bud, the stems would retreat into soil, until there was nothing left of him but a seed in the ground, small and buried.

Only this time, there would be no one to help her dig the grave.

"You have to go to Manchester." Still his eyes were fixed on the Bell. "You should leave soon. Tomorrow."

"Come on, Dad. Let's get you to bed."

He shook his head and the mumbles returned, the appearance of the angel, and Nico wasn't sure which was more exhausting: the anticipation of these spirals, or the spirals themselves.

"It's okay. I'm here." She couldn't think of anything else to say. "I'm your daughter and I love you."

"You have to go."

"Dad . . ." Her voice was gentle, as if waiting out a passing storm. "No one's going anywhere."

"I saw you, Nico." He turned from the Bell, and she saw in his eyes that the storm had already passed. "I saw you before you were born."

KIT

dinner theater

"**K**it."

Kit looked up from his dinner plate, untouched. "Hmm?"

"Honey," said his Dakota.

Monty, mouth full: "You zoned again, bud."

Monty and Lakie Mackenzie were fraternal twins, a full five years older than Kit. They were Black, with dark hair and brown eyes. Each wore a daily tribute to their parents: the red bandanna in Lakie's hair had once tied back her mother's; the yellow plaid shirts, which Monty wore every day, had come from a box his father had brought back on one of his final scavenges.

"Morning's Events," said Dakota, handing Kit the brass apple. "Your turn."

He told them about today's painting, his idea to mix in the glitter for a shimmery effect. "Over six hundred versions, and still, so many ways to make them new." Even though the computers in the sky were probably weirder, he never told them about the shimmering key. Something about verbalizing its existence made his bones woozy.

He passed the apple to Lakie, who said nothing, handed it to Monty.

Dakota leaned over, pushed the apple back. "Doesn't have to be much."

A year ago Kit found a brass apple on a desk in one of the school classrooms, and at some point, it had become a conversational torch passed around the dinner table. None of them loved the practice of forced conversation, but Dakota insisted. "I'm now officially a better shot than the range I built," said Lakie. "Outdistancing my current targets, and not by a little."

In accordance with Dakota's law about not killing what little life was left in the world, Lakie never hunted. But being proficient in weaponry seemed to go hand in hand with her self-reliance. It was also one of the main reasons Kit felt safe in Town.

"Spent most of today extending the range," she continued. "Took out a fir that had been getting in the way. Or I think it was a fir."

"Took it out?" said Dakota.

"Chopped it down."

"You chopped down a tree."

"Yes."

"With *what*?"

"The hatchet. Or whatever it is. That we found in Abe's."

Kit recalled a Town scavenge in which Monty had found a small ax below the cash register in Abe's Sporting Goods.

"You stole my ax?" asked Monty.

"Borrowed it. Thanks, by the way."

"You chopped down a tree," said Dakota. "On your own."

"Wait"—Monty side-eyed her—"haven't we had this conversation before?"

"About my borrowing your ax?" asked Lakie.

"You *stole* my ax, but yes."

"I did not," she said. "And we have not."

Dakota took a bite, chewed in that sort of crooked way she did whenever she was feeling big things. "Lake, *please* let me know the next time you decide to chop down a tree."

"Why?"

"Does it need saying? How about because I don't know how to sew a finger back on? You guys are *it* for me, and I'm not going to be here forever, and when that day comes, I need to know you'll be ready."

Living with Monty and Lakie, the reality of a parent dying was very real. But hearing his own mother talk about it—this was new.

"I'm sorry," said Lakie. "I'll be more careful."

. . . not going to be here forever . . .

Some things you know are true, and you still can't believe them.

Monty cleared his throat, set the brass apple beside his plate, stood from the table, and pulled his radio out from under his chair. "On the surface, this may seem like poor timing. But I think this is the perfect segue into what I'd like to share for Morning's Events."

"Monty," said Dakota. "Please, not again."

Monty set his radio on the table. Even though it was called a crystal radio, there didn't seem to be any crystals on it. When

Monty talked about it, he used words like *diode* and *high impedance* and *resistor*, but basically, it looked like this: a wooden plank at the bottom, with a spindle of copper-colored coils and a mess of wires running this way and that.

In the olden days, when humans roamed the earth, one of the reasons they wanted stacks of cash-bucks was so they could purchase "smartphones." The way Dakota explained it, humans invented a phone to be smart so people wouldn't have to be. Now dead "smartphones" were everywhere, the bane of scavenges.

In a world of "smartphones," Monty's radio was probably a heap of crap-junk.

But in a world where Flies ate humans, and the closest you got to communicating with What Lay Beyond was daydreaming about the origins of a breeze, Monty's radio was nothing short of magic.

"Just hear me out." He held the earphone to his ear, tinkering with the settings. "I found a recorded loop."

"What else is new," said Lakie.

"This one's different. There's a place. You guys have to hear this . . ."

Kit had heard snippets of loops Monty had found, tinny messages from strange voices. A woman reading the Bible. A man reading the same set of (seemingly) random numbers over and over again. A monotone dictation of someone's grandmother's cake recipes. Kit imagined some sad person hunched in front of their own crystal radio, desperate for human connection.

"What place?" asked Lakie.

"A safe zone." Monty offered her the earphone. "Go on."

As Lakie listened, Kit wondered what this scene might look like from the little window in his projection room upstairs. Instead of a magic light producing moving pictures, one would see only a dark and cavernous room, six hundred empty seats below, and a stage at the far end with an enormous white screen. On the stage, in front of the screen, four people eating at a table with a few flickering candles.

Lakie removed the earphone.

"Right?" said Monty. "It's perfect, right?"

Lakie, just above a whisper: "Maybe."

"What's it say?" Kit asked.

"Here." Monty leaned over, was about to stick the device in Kit's ear, when Dakota reached out and grabbed Monty's wrist.

"Mom—"

"I don't want your head filled with nonsense fantasies about *safe zones*. Our zone is as safe as it gets."

"Until it's not," said Monty.

"We run drills. We are vigilant about high sun curfew. And cinnamon."

"This place"—Monty pulled his hand out of Dakota's grip, and then offered the earphone to her—"it's a cluster of islands, small and secluded. Run by legit preppers. Well stocked, well guarded. It's perfect."

Kit watched his mother calmly set down her fork and he thought of how much he loved her motions, the way all the pieces of her moved as one. He loved that necklace she always wore, a long chain looped through a key, and how, the more she meant what she said, the more she moved, and the more she moved when she talked, the more that key swung from side to side. These were the things that made his Dakota his. But something had changed in those movements and smiles, something had slowed and dimmed, as if her wick had burned too long. And for the first time, Kit allowed himself to put a word to his thoughts: *sick*.

His Dakota looked sick.

"I know you blame me," she said. Out of nowhere, tears started welling, and she looked from Monty to Lakie. "You should know, no one blames me more than I do. But I promised your parents— we promised each other that if anything happened, whoever was left would raise the kids like they were our own. I've done all I can to honor that promise. I love you both so much. Believe it, don't believe it, that's the truth. And because I love you, please hear me when I say—there are no safe zones. The Paradise Twin is it. And we are not leaving."

Dakota climbed down offstage slowly, gently, as if made of glass. Her back to them, she said, "We're doing baths tomorrow, it's starting to look a little too *Lord of the Flies* in here," and then she walked off, disappearing into darkness down the aisle.

They ate in silence for a while, the sibling kind, where the air was stuffed with a history of words, too full for new ones.

Eventually Lakie said, "Tuesday tomorrow."

Pushing food around his plate, Monty said he would switch

out rainwater and change the filter. Kit said he would do cinnamon, knowing full well Lakie had taken care of both chores the past few Tuesdays.

Suddenly Lakie was chuckling.

"What," said Monty.

"Nothing," she said. "Just—Lord of the *Flies*."

A few laughs, but they turned half-hearted and eventually broke to dust, evaporated into the high ceiling of the Main Theater. Kit still remembered finding the book in his library, those mean eyes and curly blond hair peering up from the green cover. He'd read it, hoping to find out how, exactly, one *became* Lord of the Flies. Ultimately, he was left with more questions than answers, and couldn't tell if the book was supposed to be funny or tragic or what. He couldn't tell if he saw himself in those wild kids, or if he was just hunched over a homemade radio, desperate for connection.

what wondrous magic, the Paradise Twin!

In its heyday, the Paradise Twin was quite the spectacle. People with fancy dresses and fancy suits and big fancy cars came and waited in line under the marquee for a movie called *Gone with the Wind*, which Kit could only assume was a film of suitable fanciness, and not just because of the clientele, but because under the title on the marquee were the words BOTH SCREENS SOLD OUT.

He knew about these things from the old black-and-white

photo. And photographs, unlike book covers, never lied.

A lit candle in one hand, Kit stood between the lobby restrooms—one labeled GUYS, the other DOLLS—and stared up at the photo. His Dakota told him it had been taken in the thirties or forties. She said back then, people got themselves "all dolled up" to go to the movies. He tried to put himself in a pair of those fancy shoes, tried to see his home the way these blurry images might have seen it: an avenue of entertainment.

The grime of years had certainly taken its toll on the old theater. Even so, it was in decent shape. The high-ceilinged entrance and marble floors, the extensive crown molding, the murals of masks and ribbons, the glass chandeliers and light-bulb movie posters and concession shelves made of mirrors, all of it fit for the fanciest of people.

It was called the Paradise *Twin* because it had two separate theaters: the bigger one was called the Main Theater; the smaller one was the State Theater. Kit's bedroom was upstairs, in what had once been the Main Theater's projection room. The projector was still there, dormant in a corner, the ghost of movies past. There were nights when Kit was grateful for that ghost. Surrounded by cases of old reels, he'd walk to the thin window where the projector had once conjured magic tricks with nothing but a little light.

Once, digging through the boxes of old reels, his Dakota had found her favorite movie. "It's called *E.T.*," she'd said, her face lit up like the sun. "It's about this gentle alien with healing powers who befriends a boy on Earth."

She'd told him more of the story, and as she talked, she held the reel in her hands like it was the baby brother he never had.

Her face was almost too bright to look at.

"What was the kid's name again?" she asked this reel, eyes in another world. "Evan, I think. No. Elliott."

Upstairs, aside from the Main Theater projection room, there was also the State Theater projection room, where Monty slept, and a little lounge in between, where Lakie slept. Downstairs, a door behind the lobby concessions said MANAGEMENT, and this was his Dakota's bedroom. Behind that, a kitchenette with a woodstove and pantry. The State Theater, they'd converted into a storehouse for Dakota's canned foods and medical supplies and whatever they brought back from scavenges.

They were lucky, Kit knew this. Not just that they had a place to call home, but that they were alive to call it anything at all. But recently he'd taken to standing here between GUYS and DOLLS, staring at this old photograph, wondering if this was it. The feeling was new. He hadn't quite wrapped his brain around it yet. The notion that what his life had been up to this point might very well be the rest of his life forever—this stirred something inside him. And so he stood and stared and thought, *This photograph unleashes my psyche.*

Psyche was a word Kit knew, which embodied that vague, down-deep compartment where a person kept the soul of their truest self.

He'd read that somewhere, he was pretty sure.

When it came right down to it, Kit wanted this photograph to come alive. He wanted it to turn into the very thing it could only now represent: a *motion* picture. But it wouldn't. Those fancy shoes were probably scattered all through the surrounding mountains, filled with nothing but marrowless feet-bones.

"Both screens sold out," he said quietly, standing in a daze.

He'd counted the seats in both theaters. He knew the maximum capacity of the Paradise Twin.

It was 946.

For all the things Kit knew, one thing he did not know was how it felt to be in the same building as 946 people.

He turned from the photograph, climbed the narrow staircase to his projection room, and thought back to that day his mother found the movie about the gentle alien. She'd spent that whole afternoon rigging an old solar-power strip to the projector; that night, her face full of sunlight, she'd ushered Kit and Monty and Lakie into the theater. "Pick a seat," she'd told them. "And get ready."

Kit still remembered the quiet of the dark theater, as if whatever magic was about to happen might be scared off. A few minutes later a clicking rattle came from behind them, and the giant screen flickered with electric light, and Kit felt the sun of his Dakota in his own heart as he prepared to *watch a movie*.

It lasted maybe three seconds.

In his room now, he walked to the corner, put a hand on the old projector. The reel of *E.T.* was still stuck in its teeth. He never knew what went wrong, if the power strip blew, or if the projector just didn't have any life left. But that night, in the dark stillness of the theater, they'd heard Dakota descend the narrow staircase, cross behind the concession counter, enter her room, and shut the door behind her.

It was the last time Kit saw that particular sun in that particular face.

genesis, a bedtime story

Dakota Sherouse moved into the Paradise Twin when she was three months pregnant.

Kit had heard the story often. "So many times, it feels like I was there," he said.

His Dakota tucked him in cocoon-style, just like he liked; she pulled the covers up under his chin, just like he liked. "You *were* there, my little Kit."

"Inside your uterus."

"*Kit.*"

"Can't see much in there."

She did that little chuckle-sigh he loved, and then asked where he'd learned about uteruses.

"*So Your Mom's Having a Baby, Fifth Edition*, Kate Mendelsohn, MD. Found it in your box marked *old stuff*."

"There were a lot of books in that box."

"I read those, too. Most were about pregnancy."

"Well, I was a midwife," said Dakota.

"You practiced midwifery." If there was a better word in the English language, Kit hadn't found it. And he'd found a *lot* of words. "There were also books about making babies. So I pretty much know all about sex and that sort of thing."

"Okay. Well. Okay."

Kit was born in the Paradise Twin, well after the Flies hit. He'd never asked who his father was. The introduction of some random-faced, lumbering oaf would only serve to ruin what was otherwise a perfectly good story. His mother had once lived in a commune in the mountains, and so Kit assumed that was where it had happened. Where *he* had happened.

The genesis of him happening.

Genesis, which was a word he knew, basically meant the beginning of a thing.

"Did you want to eat dirt?" he asked.

"What . . . in the world?"

"The book said that happens sometimes. When you're pregnant. Possibly linked to an iron deficiency. You crave dirt, clay, laundry starch, charcoal—"

"They're called pica cravings, and no, luckily, I never had those. Now, would you like to hear the story or not?"

Dakota told him how the thought of having a child had always made her nervous, how helping so many women deliver their babies had made her think she might never want her own.

"But then the angel came," said Kit.

Dakota smiled like a true-believing breeze. "In the commune, in the middle of the night, long before I was pregnant with you—an angel came to me in a dream. *Don't be afraid*, said the angel. *One day you will have a son, and he will be one of a kind, a pure soul, and a friend to those in need.*"

Kit reached up, touched the key around his Dakota's neck. "The next morning . . ."

"The next morning, when I woke up, I found this key in my hand. I still have no idea where it came from or what it opens."

"A supreme mystery."

"It is. But I decided to wear the key as a reminder of that night. And as a monument to you."

Kit simultaneously loved and hated this part of his genesis: the appearance of the angel always made him feel special; the angel's prophecy, however, seemed unlikely given he would never leave Town. But the story was far from over, and so he pushed these doubts away and listened as his Dakota explained how, years later, when she was pregnant with him, a large swarm wiped out more than half the commune.

Under the covers, he pressed his feet together, tried to get the blood flowing.

"The Mackenzies and I were planning to leave the commune anyway," said Dakota. "After the swarm attacked, everything was in total disarray. It was the perfect time for a fresh start. Joanne was my best friend. We were both—"

"Why?"

"Why what?"

"Why were you and the Mackenzies going to leave the commune?"

In the calm sea of this conversation, the question was an unprecedented ripple; for some reason, until now, Kit had never thought to ask it.

"Well . . ." Dakota seemed to consider. "Remember our talks about how the world ended for everyone, but how the means to that end was different for different people, especially people of color?"

"Because of structure racism."

His Dakota smiled in a way that somehow made Kit sad, and she said, "*Structural* racism," and she was about to say something else, but her eyes landed on the door to Lakie's room, and she grew suddenly silent.

"What?" asked Kit, following her eyes to the closed door.

"I think . . ." Lost in memory, she stared at the door a moment longer before looking down at him. "I think you should talk to Lakie or Monty about this."

"They were still little, though. When you guys left."

"They remember enough. And they were old enough to have conversations with Joanne and Elias about what happened."

"Can't you just tell me?"

She smiled at Kit. "It's not my story."

Such a den of secrets! His Dakota wasn't normally so enigmatic. This was all highly unusual for the Paradise Twin.

"Where was I?" Dakota asked.

"Joanne was your best friend . . ."

Dakota explained how she and Joanne were both midwives in the commune, how they spent tons of time together. "She loved the mountains. Her husband, Elias, loved the water. And so they named their children after the things they loved."

"The mountain and the lake," said Kit.

"Monty and Lakie were old souls from the start. The names suited them. When it was time to set out for a new home, the five of us were ready."

"Six, if you count me. I was in your uterus."

"Tell you what. Let's leave my uterus out of things from here on, shall we? But okay, when the *six* of us left, we wanted to find a place where we could settle down, and where I could get ready to welcome you into the world."

"Nesting."

"Oh my God, yes, nesting. What else did this Mendelsohn clown teach you?"

"You don't want to know. Continue."

"We needed a place that could be easily barricaded, but nothing too suffocating. Someplace safe, but a place that was about more than just survival. I prayed for a sign."

"And then you saw one."

Dakota nodded. "I hadn't expected a *literal* sign, but that's what I got. A large billboard by the side of the road. Billboards were mostly advertisements, trying to get people to buy things they didn't need."

"Why would someone buy something they don't need?" asked Kit.

"Back then, some people had more money than they knew what to do with."

"Like billionaires."

In the olden days, there had been a breed of human known as "billionaire." To qualify, you had to have at least a billion cash-bucks. One billion! But the real mind-boggler was that billionaires kept on being billionaires even when they knew there were people who had zero cash-bucks.

What a zany place this world had been.

"This particular billboard stood out because it advertised a church," she said. "But here's the wild part."

"*You'd seen that billboard before.*"

"Who's telling this story?"

"Proceed," said Kit.

"*I'd seen that billboard before.* Before the commune, before the Flies hit, back when lights were electric and ice cream was cold. I was on my way home from a date when I got stuck in a traffic jam."

"Too many cars in one place."

"That's right. It was snowing hard, I remember. I was sitting in my car, not going anywhere, when I looked up and saw someone spray-painting words on a billboard."

"What did the words say?"

"I don't remember. But a minute later, this couple in the car ahead of me needed my help."

"Your expertise in the field of midwifery."

Dakota smiled a big one. "The woman was in labor. Stuck in traffic. I remember thinking, *This is why I left the house tonight. Not for a date. I'm here for this woman and her baby.* So then, years later, pregnant with you, traveling with the Mackenzies, looking for a sign—"

"You saw the billboard again."

"And it reminded me of that night stuck in the snow. Of the woman, whose name I never knew, and her baby, which made me think of you. And it reminded me of the date I'd been on, how the man was a bust, but the *place* he took me—"

"An old movie theater in a little mountain town."

"It was *perfect*. And so the five of us—sorry, *six*—moved in. We spent those first weeks scavenging, storing up the State Theater, packed the place so full of water jugs and cinnamon and seeds and matches, you could barely see straight. And when the time came—"

"For me to emerge from your—"

"*When the time came*, we were as ready as we could be. Joanne had this little box she'd prepared for your delivery, which she'd labeled—"

"*Dakota's kit.*"

Dakota looked around the projection room as if witnessing the glories of what it once was, those ghosts of a thousand movies spun like magic yarn. Kit was proud to have been born here, proud that the spool of magic had come to an end at his beginning.

"Until the moment you arrived," she said, "it didn't

occur to me that you would need a name. I don't think I'd let myself go there. I didn't believe it would actually happen. But there you were. Actually happening. With no name."

"And then you saw the box."

"And then I saw the box. *Dakota's kit.* And I thought, *Yes, this child is mine.*"

Kit repositioned himself so his cheek rested in her hand, and the silver key that hung from the bottom of her necklace brushed his forehead. "Do you miss her?" he asked.

"Who?"

"Joanne."

He had vague memories of Joanne and Elias Mackenzie: the blurry image of a woman playing trumpet; a man with a tattoo of a cherry on his leg. Kit was only three when a swarm took them both. Monty refused to talk about it. What little Kit knew, he'd pulled from Lakie late one night in the kitchenette. He'd gone downstairs looking for a midnight snack and come back with the source material for years' worth of nightmares.

"I miss them both, every day," said his Dakota. "But I still see them."

"In the mountain and the lake."

"Monty and Lakie have so much of their parents in them."

Kit often thought how glad he was that they were old enough to have more than vague memories of their parents. But still—more than a little, in this case, wasn't nearly enough.

"Mom."

"Kit."

"Are you okay?"

A pause. "Of course I'm okay. Why would you ask that?"

He decided to answer a different question. "If the Flies came and carried you off—if you were gone—I'd want to leave Town too."

The room was quiet, the brush of a hand in his hair. Kit debated whether to tell her what he really thought: that when he stood at the open window of his art classroom, held a breeze in his face, he had long ago resigned himself to the reality that he would never know where that breeze came from, or where it was going. Instead he said, "If you were dead, I'd build a radio out of high-impendence resistor diodes, and I wouldn't care how sad the voices were on the other end, I would try to find them. If you were dead, I'd want to leave too."

mountains & lakes

That night, Kit had two dreams.

In the first, he was a Fly, buzzing and angry, soaring from town to town. *When you were little, you had night terrors*, said Lakie, her voice coming from the sky. *Dakota was up all hours trying to calm you. She was constantly exhausted.* Kit flew high for a while, then dipped low to the ground, always keeping close to his swarm. *Your mom was in the garden that day, only back then, it wasn't on the roof, it was in that park down the road*, faster and faster Kit flew over trees and towns, lakes and mountains. *We heard the swarm, kept waiting for your mom to run back, but she wasn't coming.* Kit buzzed angrier now, flew faster, hungry and ready. *Dad ran outside to find her. Mom waited by the barricade, ready to latch it as soon as they were inside.* There! Just ahead, the place called Town, that small, insignificant part of the world. *We finally saw them coming—your mom and my dad running toward us. And then the swarm came over the mountain like a tidal wave,* fluid and free, Kit crashed down the mountain toward Town, sights set on two little running things. *I don't know what Dad tripped on, but he fell.* Kit went for the one on the ground . . . *Your mom made it inside. My mom ran out to get Dad. And the swarm swept them up,* up into the sky, Kit carried his prey toward the full, bright moon . . .

She fell asleep, said a new voice in his dream, quiet and familiar. *My mom. She fell asleep in the garden.*

It's not your fault, said Lakie.

And lo! as Kit flew, he saw a computer and a keyboard where the stars had been, and a small silver key swung from the bottom of a celestial chain.

Yes, it is, he said, such a small voice. *She fell asleep because I was such a handful.*

The key grew until it was bigger than the moon, shimmery and glittering.

Your parents are dead because of me, he said.

Carrying his prey, Kit flew for the key, but no matter how fast he went, or how much ground he covered, he never reached it.

The dream ended there.

It always happened this way.

His second dream that night was new. In it, he sat at a table in a bright room. A strange woman sat across from him. *Speak to me and I will listen*, said the stranger's eyes. They had a full conversation, but when Kit woke up, he remembered none of it. And his bed reeked of urine.

NICO

Acts

Like the night's first star, his words hovered alone in her mind, blazing and far-off: *I saw you before you were born*.

When Nico asked what this meant, he said he should start at the beginning, and before she knew it, he'd fallen into a different kind of spiral: "It started as an experiment to fortify the honeybee against colony collapse." His speech was fast but not frantic, quiet but not whispered. "Russian scientists used a virus to genetically modify the honeybees, but—something went wrong. Both the virus and the bees mutated."

"Wait. So—"

"Technically, the Flies aren't flies. Global panic drives misinformation, so people *thought* they were flies. Of course, they aren't really bees either, not anymore."

They sat on the edge of the deck, staring out over miles of treetops as he painted a picture of swarms crossing oceans and continents, scaling mountains, mining the depths of the earth, and Nico watched his words float like little souls through the attic railing, into the cold night air.

Stories of the old world were variations on a theme: how the Flies were too much, too fast, too many, how quickly they pushed humans to the brink of extinction. How governments buckled, hospitals overflowed, and how a dwindling workforce leads to a devastating domino effect: no fuel, no transportation; supermarket shelves looted or simply bought out, nothing to restock; when the electrical grids shut down, one by one, each pocket of the planet was plunged back in time, a Revolution not of Industry but Atrophy, and when this global rewind was complete, the world was back where it had started, the Darkest of Ages.

"I used to think of it as a two-act play," her dad said. "Act One. Those first few weeks, we didn't even know there *was* a flu. The Flies were more than enough. Billions of people wiped out. Those who survived thought themselves cunning to have outlasted the apocalypse."

She'd heard most of this before, but this time felt different, as if she'd only heard the variations, and now, for the first time, the original theme.

"Act Two," he said. "The Flu spread quicker than the Flies, quicker than science or medicine could catch up. Plenty of theories, but no . . . real certainty. Very few people survived Act Two. Those of us who did thought ourselves cunning to have outlasted the apocalypse."

Nico had consumed enough story in her life to feel its cadence in her bones. "You think there's a third act," she said, searching his eyes for signs of himself. "You're saying what Mom had—*what you have*—you think it's the Flu."

"I know it when I see it."

Lucid or not, what he was saying made no sense. "But we haven't been exposed."

His voice flattened, and he turned back to the tree line. "There was a study once that theorized that most humans had herpes, but in latent form."

"Latent form."

"Viruses rely on the host cell for replication. Some viruses, though, instead of replicating, go into a form of hibernation. *Hit and hide*, they called it. Viral latency. A state in which the virus lives but does not replicate. Until something causes it to reactivate."

Hard as it was to believe the content of what her father was saying, his communication was quite clear. She tried to let the information sink in, that even now Fly Flu might be inside her, lying dormant. "Like what?" she asked. "What would cause it to reactivate?"

"Could be any number of stress factors. Physiological changes. Could be another illness—a different, unrelated virus might act as a sort of diversion, so while the immune system is busy fending *it* off, Fly Flu has its moment. Could just be . . . time. Or maybe I'm wrong. Maybe it's nothing to do with reactivation. Maybe it took this long to find its way into our food and water supply. We don't get certainty. Only theories." He paused for a moment, and then: "There was this study once that theorized most humans have herpes, only in latent form . . ."

Nico wanted to cry. Instead she stared blindly at the dark horizon as her father explained for a second time about viral latency and reactivation, as if their conversation were a script he was rehearsing. As he talked, Harry scratched at the door behind them; Nico let her dog out, and the three of them sat together, Harry's head in her lap while she tried to process not only what she was hearing, but how quickly her dad swung from clarity to fog and back again.

"Nic."

"What."

"*Voyager in the Water*." He reached one hand through the railing; moonlight reflected off his wedding band, and she felt the urge to both hug and slap him. "The story is true," he said.

"What?"

"I know it sounds crazy, but the Waters of Kairos are real. Manchester is a real place."

For him to talk about her favorite story like this—a story she'd grown up hearing, begging to be told again and again—for him to ruin it this way, to claim it as anything other than the glorious fantasy it was, felt like the perfectly awful ending to what was easily the worst birthday of her life.

"Dad, we should go to bed. I can't do this."

"You have to listen." He put a hand on her shoulder, soft but urgent, and he told a new story, how, years before she was born, he'd been recruited by the government under the guise of a company called Kairos, Inc., to study a geological phenomenon that had appeared in a flooded riverside mill, and as he spoke, she watched the cold breath of his impossible words, and she felt her soul was one of those wisps, as if it had exited its shell and was now floating in the air in front of them, free to live its brief, bright life. "When activated, the anomaly becomes the Waters of Kairos from my story. Or not—*from my story*. I mean I told the story . . ." His eyes fogged, and he grew visibly frustrated before breathing, calming, continuing: "The anomaly appears in the water. It's a kind of door, we think. We were still figuring out how it worked when the Flies hit."

Over the years there had been many mysterious conversations between her parents, times when she'd come close to learning more about what their lives had looked like before the Flies. Nico knew her dad had been a geophysicist, and while she'd love to think *this* was what he'd been working on, it felt like trying to spot an eagle on the horizon: she was suspicious of her own eagerness to believe.

"The anomaly is activated by sound." He pointed to the Bell behind them, said the right frequency flipped it on like an electrical switch. He explained how Kairos had once needed someone from the team they could trust to man the switch, how in the days before the Flies, he had climbed up here once in the morning, once at night to ring the Bell. "Just like Bellringer."

It was like dreaming your house was at the bottom of the ocean, and then waking up underwater. One minute, it was her dad talking: storyteller, scientist, true north. The next, it was a man she barely recognized. "So this—*anomaly*," she said, swimming for the surface, struggling for air. "You said it's some kind of door. Where does it lead?"

"We don't know. A few volunteers went through—" He stopped, the implication glaring: *We never saw them again.*

For a moment they simply looked at each other. She felt him search for understanding in her eyes, while she searched for the haze in his.

"You have to go," he said.

"I'm sorry. I have to go *where*?"

"To Manchester."

"Dad—"

"We buried your mother in the cellar." His eyes welled and, haze or not, she saw truth there. And she knew that the promise of love was also the promise of pain. That grief was a root: the deeper it reached, the stronger it grew. "We buried her in the cellar," he said again, shaking his head, and she heard what he'd left unsaid: *And I'll soon be beside her, and at some point in the future, you will die alone in this house in the middle of the woods.*

Nico leaned into his shoulder, felt the full weight of their combined love. And suddenly her head was full of shadowy images she couldn't explain, pictures of the woods from deep behind the borders of the tree line, as if she were there already, as if she'd gone a hundred times before. He wiped his eyes, ran through the list of things he'd packed for her trip, said they'd review the map in the morning. "Shouldn't take more than a week to get there. Let's call it eight days to be safe. On the night of the eighth day, I'll ring the Bell. We can't coordinate times, exactly, but I'll wait until a couple hours after sunset."

"Dad, I can't do this. Not alone."

He looked down at Harry. "Who said anything about you going alone?"

Harry's ears perked up as if he knew they were talking about him. Nico rubbed the soft fur on the side of his neck while she tried to calm her own nerves, slow her thoughts. Most fiction was laced with truth, she knew this. But if she were to believe her father now, the most impossible elements of *Voyager in the Water* were also the truest.

If she did go, there was no telling what she would find in Manchester, or any guarantee of even getting there. The question was, if she stayed, could she do anything to curb his sickness? If not, those unsaid words would come to fruition: she would bury him in the cellar beside her mother, and eventually she would die out here.

"I can't just leave you." It was the most honest thing she could think.

He put one arm around her, and when he spoke, his words mimicked the moon: gentle, bright, immovable. "The unknown can be scary. But when the known is death itself, you enter the unknown. Wherever it leads, it's better than what's waiting for you here."

Her head on his shoulder, he held her in silence. He was dying just as her mother had, and no, there was nothing she could do about it. And maybe there was nothing in Manchester. Maybe his un-blossoming was complete, his mind a swampy fog. The truth was, she had no idea what to believe. But she'd spent her whole life believing in *him*, and she wasn't going to stop now.

"Earlier," she said. "What did you mean—you saw me before I was born?"

"You know why your mom called you her snowstorm girl, don't you?"

"I was born in a snowstorm."

"And almost in the back seat of a car. We were stuck in traffic. And then—a few hours before you came into the world, I saw you. As you are now. Or—a vision of you, I guess. Up on a billboard ledge. I can't explain it. But it gives me hope."

"Hope . . . ?"

He kissed her forehead. "That we'll see each other again."

Bathed in that gentle light, the forest seemed a painting, some dripping-new watercolor, and Nico felt the specific adrenaline that accompanies fate, when you're about to enter a time and a place, and you know deep down that this time and this place have been waiting just for you.

"We'll tally the days on our hands, to be safe," he said quietly. "On the evening of the eighth day, I'll ring the Bell. You know what to do, right?"

Of course she knew.

She'd heard the story a thousand times.

Mythologies

Once upon a time, said her father—on the attic deck, in the library, in the kitchen doing dishes, the Farmhouse was rampant with the echoes of those four words—*there was a girl named Voyager who lived in a lighthouse on a tiny island off the coast of the Kingdom of Manchester. Here she lived with three others: Lightbringer, who was in charge of the lamp in the lighthouse; Skykeeper, who made sure the moon, stars, and sun didn't slip and fall from the sky; and Bellringer, who, twice a day, rang an enormous Bell from the top of the lighthouse.*

Voyager's job was to communicate with the creatures of the seas. She spent her days rowing the open waters, offering advice on everything from how to end the Hundred Year Anglerfish War to the best way to handle dolphin smugness. Occasionally Voyager dreamed of life in the Kingdom—the noble King and Queen who lived in Kairos Castle, the bustling markets, the circus that performed every evening at dusk. But then, *she wondered,* if I lived there, who would tend to the smugness of dolphins?

In Voyager's opinion, hers was the most important job on the island.

Bellringer's was important too: once every morning and once every evening, he climbed to the top of the lighthouse and struck the mighty Bell. Its toll flew over the sea like a cormorant before diving into the water, where it swam like a sailfish all the way to the Kingdom of Manchester, emptying into a great fountain and activating the Waters of Kairos.

If Bellringer was to be believed, the toll of his Bell did nothing less than turn a simple water fountain into a door to another world.

"Yes," said Voyager to her best blowfish friend. "*I suppose Bellringer's job is quite awesome.*"

The blowfish said, "*Bppphhhhhmmmphhhtttt,*" *which was blow-*

fish for, "*But nothing so lovely or awesome as you, my dear Voyager.*"

("Can you skip to the good part?" said Nico.)

("It's all the good part. My stories only have good parts.")

("Dad.")

One night, quite suddenly, the stars went out. Poof. *The sky, the seas, all of it, covered in complete darkness. Lightbringer scurried up the lighthouse to switch on the lamp. Skykeeper ran around in circles, screaming,* "*All is lost, all is lost!*" *Bellringer took Voyager by the hand, led her down to the shores of the island where her small rowboat was kept.*

"*Take thy boat,*" *said Bellringer.* "*Row thyself to the Kingdom, thus to Kairos Castle take heed, perchance, milady, and there inquireth as to what the heck is happening!*"

(Nico laughed; her father smiled. It always happened this way.)

So Voyager looked out across the darkened seas. "*I can't see a thing. I'll get lost.*"

Bellringer pointed to the shallow part of the ocean where the blow-fish awaited. "*Yyyysssssssuuuuuuuuuburt,*" *said the blowfish, which meant,* "*I will lead you through the darkness!*"

Voyager said, "*But even if I get to the Kingdom, how will I know where to go?*"

Bellringer explained that the castle was surrounded by a cluster of brick mills. "*Findeth the mills, milady, and you've found Kairos. Now, Voyager, sail thou forth to seek and find!*"

("Wait. That's Whitman," said Nico.)

("Shh.")

So, Voyager sailed the seas for days, followed her trusty blowfish, wondering aloud what was happening in her world. "Hrrrrrrphhhhh- hizzz," said the blowfish, which either meant, "A great darkness has descended upon our land," or "I could really go for some cake right now." Blowfish is an ancient language, there are varying theories among scholars vis-à-vis this particular interpretation—

("Dad.")

Days passed at sea, until one afternoon, with no land in sight, an orca swam by. "Where are you headed?" asked the orca.

"None of your business." In Voyager's experience, orcas were scheming and untrustworthy creatures.

"Wherever you are going," said the orca, circling her boat, "it will take you a long time with nothing but oars. Why not tie your line to my dorsal fin, let me pull you to your destination?"

Voyager considered this. "How do I know you won't bite my hand off?"

The orca dipped below the surface. When he came back up, he said, "Yes. It would be a gamble."

Voyager looked around: nothing but dark water in every direction. "Very well. We're headed to the Kingdom of Manchester, as fast as you can, please." The orca swam up alongside the boat, and Voyager tied the line to his dorsal fin. "Thank you," she said.

"For what?"

"For not eating my hand, I suppose."

"The day is young," said the orca. "And I am hungry."

Things went much faster tied to the dorsal fin of an orca, and by evening the following day, Voyager found herself standing on the shores of Manchester—this Kingdom she'd so longed to see—now totally obliviated. She walked its empty markets, passed the shadow of what had once been a circus. Inside the walls of Kairos Castle, it was only worse. She found no King, no Queen, just more of the same dark emptiness.

There was, however, a sound. She followed this sound to a great hall, and there she found an enormous fountain. "The Waters of Kairos," she said.

"Indeed," said a nearby voice.

Voyager spun to find a nameless, faceless witch standing in the corner. "Oh."

"Indeed," said the witch again, stepping a little from the shadows.

Voyager was scared but determined. "What has happened to our world?" she asked.

The witch took another step closer. "A darkness has chased away the sky. It has erased the Kingdom of Manchester, and all great Kingdoms of the world."

"Oh," said Voyager.

"Indeed," said the witch.

At that moment, the waters in the fountain began to bubble and spin, and Voyager knew that Bellringer had done his duty, that the toll had activated the Waters of Kairos.

The nameless, faceless witch pointed into the heart of the fountain whose waters now spun furiously. "In you go, my dear."

"What? I'm not going in there."

The witch said, "The door is open. You must enter."

Voyager was tempted, but only for a moment. Thinking of Bell-ringer back home, and Lightbringer and Skykeeper, she said, "I will not abandon my friends."

The witch took another step from the shadows. "You asked what was happening to our world. Now ask the question you came to ask."

Voyager stood at her tallest and asked the question that suddenly burned in her heart. "How can I fight this darkness?"

The witch pointed to the spinning Waters of Kairos. "In you go, my dear."

THE DELIVERER

Into the shower, the revelation of water on skin.

I like to imagine the cycle of water, gathering in the sky, bursting and falling into my ten-thousand-gallon cistern. I picture it running through the downstairs filter, the heater, before flowing through pipes in the walls, and for the briefest of moments it is on my face, before returning to the pipes, the earth, the air.

Sometimes, instead of clouds outside my bedroom window, I see eternal life.

I see myself.

Shower complete, I stand over the sink, rub fog from the mirror, run the blade under water. I cannot remember when I first decided to shave my head. Long enough ago to have forgotten what hair feels like.

More than just the absence of hair, my reflection has become incrementally less familiar to me. "Where did you come from?" I ask myself in the mirror.

It's called aging, the mirror says back. *First you are young, then you are not.*

I get a good froth going. Slowly, blade against skin, from the back of my neck, plotting a course from pore to pore, I keep the shave close, right down to the scalp. Strangely, there is enormous comfort in the process, and while I will never fully acclimate to the way the world looks through the visor of my helmet—that deep green tint, unnatural, sapping, and sickly—I cannot deny a curious pleasure in the sensation of its soft rubber foam against my skull.

As I shave, I consider what the Red Books have in store for today. Entries from the last few weeks have been nothing but gastric lavage instruction manuals, my bedside table stacked with every book the Hooksett Library had on the subject. I've been up to my elbows in intubation equipment, endotracheal tubes, jelly lubricants, and activated charcoal. So far as I can remember, this is the first time the Books have dedicated so many pages to one thing.

And now the day is here.

I towel off and get dressed. Back downstairs, over a second cup of coffee, I put on a record and stand in front of the map that brought me here years ago. Trace a finger from the bottom corner, follow the line of red ink through woods and mountains, roads and towns, finally landing in the top corner, and the words written here that had once been so daunting, so mysterious . . .

This house will save your life, it reads.

The map is in a frame.

It won't be for much longer.

I drain what's left in the mug, pour a third coffee, and by the time I return to the couch, rain is pounding the window. I watch this collision of clouds and earth—the cycle of life unending— and with this frame of mind, I open the third Red Book.

DATE: October 2, 2043

ACTION ITEMS:

—*Pack all gastric lavage tools, suction and intubation
equipment, large-bore OG tubes, endotracheal tube–stabilizing
devices, jelly lubricants, saline, and activated charcoal.*

—*Follow purple route west to Pin Oak Forest.
Northernmost peak. Cluster of campers.*

INCIDENTAL NOTES

Life 13 here: Get there by sunset or they die.

*Life 43: Southwest of Hooksett, we hear a person yelling for help.
Circumnavigate. He is not in need.*

Life 76: Gear up. Mountainous terrain.

I return the mug to the kitchen and head upstairs for my
biosuit.

"Here we go."

KIT

uninspired signage

KNOW YOUR ENEMY
(quick tips on Fly Flu and spotting its carrier)

1. *THE MULTITASKING KILLER: As with prior strands of influenza, Fly Flu is believed to pass from person to person, though little scientific evidence of this has been verified. (Wash hands thoroughly and regularly!) Unlike prior strands, the primary carrier also acts as killer.*

2. *BUSINESS TIME: The Flu-fly prefers to travel in a "business" (the technical term for a group of flies).*

3. *TEMPER, TEMPER: Leading theories suggest the Fly is not a product of nature, but a botched experiment. If true, this might explain why the Fly acts as a fearless aggressor, more closely resembling an angry bee than the common housefly.*

4. *BLINK OF AN EYE: The Flu-fly moves fast. (See: angry bee!)*

5. *FEED AND BREED: It is widely believed that*

Flu-flies stick together for two reasons: to breed with rapid frequency and to feed on their own dead. This stunningly effective evolutionary twist allows a business of Flu-flies to survive in isolated spaces for years at a time!

The sign was clearly homemade. Just a plain white sheet of paper with black type.

No artistic sensibility at all.

Kit found it on the floor behind the library help desk and then hung it in his corner, in the window over his orange beanbag. As he waited for his painting to dry, he reread the sign, and wondered about the brain in the head of the person who'd cooked it up.

Maybe the person was still alive! Maybe this was their life's work, climbing mountains, roaming the countryside, sailing the high seas in search of small children in need of basic education via sad homemade signs.

No, probably not.

Probably, the head of the person who'd cooked it up had no brains left.

Hollowed-out skull and whatnot.

Later, back in his art classroom, he pulled *Spacedog & Computer #632* from the easel. It had been weeks since the breakthrough painting (*#611*), in which he'd mixed in glitter to create the shimmery key. Since then, each day's painting seemed duller than the day before.

He hung today's effort on the wall and spent what was left of his free time gazing out the window. Even from a foot away he could feel the cold radiating off the glass. Soon there would be snow and he would be forced to live months on end in a coat and that knit cap his Dakota had made for him.

He hated that knit cap. It made his brain itch.

Right on time, there was Lakie, returning from the woods behind Sheriff's Office. He looked toward Pharmacy now, waiting, wondering if today was the day Monty's crystal radio would reappear. It had been weeks (the same day Kit first mixed glitter with paint) since Monty's announcement of a possible safe zone.

Thunder sounded in the distance; behind the theater, the mountains loomed large. Kit looked at them now and wondered why he cared so much about the radio. He was safe here in Town. Anyway, his Dakota had made it clear she didn't want to leave, and he'd always wanted what she wanted.

And yet . . .

Staring at the mountains, Kit felt the full weight of his unleashed psyche, and he knew he wanted to do more than *look* at those mountains, he wanted to *be in* them.

He wanted to see the ocean.

And Texas.

He wanted to see What Lay Beyond.

But he couldn't tell his Dakota this. Which meant if Monty didn't convince her to leave, they would stay here forever.

This stunningly effective evolutionary twist allows the burgeoning young artist, a Knower of Things, to survive in isolated spaces for years at a time!

"I should make a sign," he said, and was about to turn from the window when he saw it. At first he figured it must have been his Dakota all dressed up, or maybe Monty, but just then, both his Dakota and Monty crossed the street toward the Paradise Twin.

He stepped nearer to the window, opened it, not feeling the cold at all, his heart pounding in a way it never had, not even with the swarms.

There, high up in the mountains: a person.

the mysterious astronaut

Dinnertime conversation came in spurts around Dakota's coughing fits.

And it wasn't just the coughing.

These last couple weeks, Kit had noticed a permanent sheen of sweat on her face. She'd already cut back on her time in Garden on the Roof, instead spending hours alone in her room. At night, when she climbed the stairs to the projection room to tuck him in, he heard the mighty struggle of her lungs to get air.

"I'm worried about you," said Lakie, stating the obvious.

Dakota tried to muffle another cough, got out an unconvincing, "I'm fine," and then ate a spoonful of corn as if to prove she was.

But she wasn't fine, not even close, because the symptoms of mononucleosis included, but were not limited to, extreme fatigue, sore throat, and fever (*Humphries & Howard, 2006: A Beginner's Guide to Infectious Diseases*). Mononucleosis would be bad, but not as bad as Hodgkin's lymphoma, cancer of the lymphatic system (*Humphries & Howard, 2008: A Beginner's Guide to Cancer*), which affected the lymph nodes, which filtered out foreign organisms from the body, which certainly sounded like an important job. The thought of his Dakota's blood full of foreign organisms made Kit want to walk out onto Main Street and scream at the sky. Whooping cough was the best-case scenario, according to his research in the William H. Taft Elementary School library. (Research that was, admittedly, limited to two men whose burning passion was to introduce people to ways in which they might die.) Still, this was a hope-for-the-best, prepare-for-the-worst situation.

Kit would hope for whooping cough but prepare for Hodgkin's lymphoma.

"Morning's Events," said Lakie, trying to change the subject. She grabbed the brass apple and offered a brief account of the day's target practice. It was conspicuous, to say the least, her choosing to speak when she didn't have to.

She's as worried as I am.

When Lakie was done, she passed the apple to Monty. "You guys don't want to hear what I have to say."

"Go on," said his Dakota.

"Really?"

"We're not leaving Town," she said, holding off a cough. "But you should have your say."

To his credit, Monty was concise. He said he'd done all the legwork, had the exact location of the Isles of Shoals, that it would be a trek, but doable.

"Isles of Shoals?" Kit asked.

"The safe zone is a cluster of islands called the Isles of Shoals." He turned back to Dakota. "For what it's worth, I've combed through enough of these recordings to know a legit opportunity when I hear it. This place—it's as close as you get to a pre-DOS existence. Once you're feeling better, I vote we pack up and go."

"It's not a vote," said Dakota.

Monty looked at his sister, then Kit. He didn't have to say anything; the words hung in the air like a giant question mark over the table: *If we took a vote, where would we land?*

Kit would side with his Dakota, of course. Monty had to know this. Which meant even if Lakie voted to go, it would be split.

But what if I didn't? he thought. *What if I voted to follow the breeze?*

The silence was broken by Dakota's coughing. She leaned forward, grabbed the brass apple from Monty, and handed it to Kit.

"Okay." Kit set the apple beside his plate, wiped his mouth on his napkin, and cleared his throat. "*Spacedog & Computer #632* turned out okay, I guess. Also, I saw someone today."

Whatever tension had weighed down the table during Monty's share time now tripled in volume.

Dakota set her fork by her plate. "What do you mean, honey?"

"Just before curfew. I was standing by the windows in my classroom. I like looking out across the mountains. Thinking about breezes and the Final Frontier."

"The what?" said Monty.

"Shh." Lakie smiled at him. "Go on."

"I saw something. Some*one*. In the woods." Kit reached below his chair and pulled out a book. He thought back to earlier, the shock of seeing a person in the mountains. But that shock turned to something else when he realized the person looked sort of familiar. In the library, he'd found the book he was looking for in the younger kids' section, a picture book called *You Will Go to the Moon*. Because it had been published in 1959, ten years before anyone actually *went* to the moon, the people who'd made the book had no idea what going to the moon would actually look like, or how it would work.

"The person I saw wore a mask. Or, like—a helmet, I guess. And a suit and gloves." Kit opened the book to the first page, where two people in comical-looking spacesuits lunged through the air. "Like this. Only the suit was shinier. And gray and black."

Part of Kit was afraid they wouldn't believe him; the other part was afraid they *would*, which would confirm he'd actually seen something so entirely unexplainable.

"So like . . . an astronaut," Monty said in a whisper.

"Sort of," said Kit. "Not as puffy."

After Kit finished a painting, there was always a moment of assessment, of looking the piece up and down and calculating its value. Until now, he'd never wondered how his assessment of their value might make *them* feel.

But before anyone could think of anything to say, Dakota stood in a quick, erratic motion that rattled the table, and then stared straight up into the darkness of the high ceiling. "Look at that," she said, but the light of the candle did not reach very far, so they found themselves staring into inky nothingness. "What is that?" Dakota said. "Like a—it's a circle. Look at that. What a beautiful thing."

And she collapsed.

PART THREE

IN
THE
FINAL
FRONTIER

NIC

Lullabies

Air was chilled. More than a nip, it was the kind of temperature that joined snow, leaves, and sun on their way down. The hollowed-out whitetail in the tree, miles and hours behind, still hung over them in a sense, and whether from this or the cold, Nico was dreading the night.

"Last stretch of the day. One more good haul, then we'll call it."

Harry, sensing the impending finish line, ran ahead, disappeared through a row of hedges some fifty yards up. All day, and he had not tired of the Game. Still—if she had to row in the dark, she was glad to have a blowfish at her side.

She whistled him back.

"One. Two. Three. Four. Five."

Nothing. She stopped walking, held her breath.

Around her, the woods seemed softer, the snow quieter. She whistled again, the note echoing. Under her breath, she counted: "One. Two. Three. Four . . ."

There. A snout through the hedgerow. But only for a second before disappearing again.

Nico ran ahead, ready to scold him for not keeping up his end of the primordial agreement. (*When Human calls, Wolf responds.*)

But, pushing her way through the hedges, any thought of repri-
mand melted.

A road.

Aside from a dirt road leading to the Farmhouse, and a narrow
one-lane deal they'd crossed at one point yesterday, Nico's entire
understanding of true roads came from books. But if those fictional
roads were pictures of a small child, this road—with its pavement
of cracked skin and weeds growing like unruly hair through every
accessible crevice—was the picture of an old man breathing his last.

Harry wandered up and down the road, nose to the ground,
until boredom or satisfaction kicked in, at which point he pawed
across it with utter familiarity.

Running alongside the road in both directions was a symmetrical row of tall wooden poles, as if an endless line of branchless
trees had been planted to keep the road company. In the back of
her mind, flashes of the old world took shape and dissolved like a
photograph coming out of the dark into candlelight, and then, too
close, melting. She had no name for these tree-poles. But she had
an impression of electricity, and its methods of transportation.

Kneeling, she ran her hand over the gravelly pavement. Maybe
twenty yards up, two automobiles—not on a page or in her mind's
eye, but physical objects—sat in the middle of the street, rusted
over, as dead as the road on which they'd died. She walked to the
closest one, a smaller black car. At the front driver's seat, the window had either been smashed out entirely or rolled down years ago.

She reached inside, unlocked the door, and climbed in. Both hands on the steering wheel, she asked, "Where to?" and couldn't help smiling a little, until she saw the bones in the back seat, a small frame the size of a child, wrapped in a coat, lying sideways on the bench as if taking a nap.

Fun while it lasted.

She was about to climb out of the car when movement ahead caught her eye. She leaned over the steering wheel, squinted through the layer of grime on the windshield . . .

"Shit."

Instinctively, her hand went for the door—but the car was in the middle of the road, no way she could exit without being seen.

She crouched lower in the seat, peered over the top of the dashboard, and counted.

There were eleven in the group. Genders and ages were difficult to say: on the bottom halves of their faces, each wore a metal mask, crude and clearly homemade; a few had scraggly beards poking out underneath the masks; most carried a weapon. Large knives and machetes swung at sides, clubs on shoulders, a couple of guns. As they neared, she sensed an ease and carelessness, laughter devoid of goodwill, eyes with little light, and she understood that neither this road nor this world were new to them.

In a matter of seconds, they would be right on top of her.

Harry.

Low in her seat, she managed a cursory scan of the road but

didn't see him anywhere. He'd never been around other people. She could only hope he'd make himself scarce, though scarcity didn't seem a very doglike instinct.

Closer now. Forty feet away, maybe.

She pushed down the door lock, *as if that's helpful*. Nothing she could do about the wide-open window.

Thirty feet.

She opened the glove box, *some kind of weapon, anything*, but it was empty.

Laughter and voices outside, muffled by the masks, and she imagined how it would go: they would spot her (if they hadn't already), drag her from the car, and whether from knife, club, or gun, that would be that. She spun, looked in the back seat, *something to fight with*, but she found only the sad outline of bones . . .

Fifteen feet.

. . . a small child who went to sleep and never woke up . . .

Ten.

At the last second, Nico pulled the hood of her coat over her head, tucked her hands into her pockets, and lay sideways across the console, facedown in the passenger seat.

She took a deep breath and held it.

Animals

"I don't know, man. It don't feel right."

"It is the fucking way of things, Herm."

The first voice sounded like a small bird; the second, like a slowly squeezing fist.

"It just don't seem very—scien-*tific*."

The car shook as someone jumped onto the hood, scaled the windshield, and now the hollow thumps of footsteps on the roof. "Y'all hear this? Herm's leaving the group so's he can pursue higher-minded, scientific endeavors."

Laughter, cruel and shrill.

Up top, the footsteps stayed put.

They've stopped. Why have they stopped?

A different sound now, a dull thrumming against the roof, as if someone were pouring out a bottle of water. "Who wants to remind Herm what we are?"

A new voice, from the ground: "Dogs!"

"And you know why dogs piss on everything, don't you? Let people know, *This shit is mine*. Humans went and domesticated themselves into oblivion. You wanna make that same mistake, Herm, go right ahead." The sound of a zipper, and then the car shook again as whoever it was climbed down the back. "Survival is gruesome work. You wanna live, you gotta find out how far the body can go before it dies."

Pulses

All was quiet.

Slowly, by inches, Nico sat up, looked through the rear windshield.

The road was empty.

She waited a few minutes, just in case, eyes to the west. When it was clear the group had passed, she climbed out of the car (watchful for any rogue streams of urine off the roof), made for the cover of woods, and gave a quick, clear whistle.

Eyes scanning the trees . . .

"One," she whispered, only now realizing she was physically shaking. "Two. Three. Four. Five . . ."

Cold and quiet and silence.

And it suddenly hit her, the difference between a *sense* of panic and *true panic*, the stone-cold dread that settles in the stomach, slowly rises through the chest, chases the heart, tingles and spreads through the arms until the body accepts the fact of death.

"Harry!" she yelled, not even caring if the Metal Masks heard her. "Come on. Okay."

She breathed. Closed her eyes.

Be the Listener.

"One." Breathe. "Two." She opened her eyes. "Three . . ."

There.

Across the road, Harry emerged with a large squirrel in his mouth. And when he reached her, as she hugged and good-dogged him, their consolidated pulse restored, only then did she truly understand the value of his companionship, and how much she loved him. "Good boy," she said through tears, offering a silent thank-you to God, to the universe, and above all, to that entity who, in giving its life, had most likely saved theirs: a limp, hapless squirrel.

Stations

The road appeared to go for miles, dipping into a shallow valley before running up the length of a mountain on the other side. Nico wanted no part of it, but the road ran east, and a little south, and because that was their direction also, they could not avoid it entirely. And so they walked, keeping to the woods, eager to put some distance between this evening's campsite and the cars.

As they went, she considered the correlation between the awfulness of a memory and the length of time it lodged itself in one's mind: *You wanna live, you gotta find out how far the body can go before it dies.* Violence, in stories, had always eluded Nico, both its purpose and the people who seemed to take joy in it, make it an art form. But for all the creative ways she knew people could be violent, there was something about the functionality of that line that she found truly unsettling—and that she would never forget.

Before long, they were in the heart of the valley. The trees gave way to a wide-open field, and in the middle of that field, just off the road, was . . . what . . . not a house. Not unlike one, though. A structure of some kind. Nico stopped at the edge of the tree line and scanned for signs of people, anyone who might call this place home. Moving forward, there would be nowhere to hide until they reached the other side of the valley; the grass grew tall in places, but small patches of snow had tamped it down, so if anyone were watching, she and Harry would be spotted for sure.

One knee on the ground, she put a hand on the back of Harry's neck, and took comfort in the knowledge that she did not have to tell him to be quiet, just as she did not have to tell herself to be quiet.

It was: *Be quiet*. And they were.

The structure had large windows in front and on both sides, though they appeared mostly broken. Out front, a tall sign read TEXACO, and huddled like small children around the foot of this sign were four smaller structures.

"A station," she said. "Fuel. For cars and trucks."

They stayed at the tree line for a few minutes, watching, waiting. Nico might just as well be contemplating the wardrobe to Narnia, the hole to Wonderland, or any number of fictional fantasies.

This could be home to the Metal Masks. Might be more of them inside.

Or maybe not. Still, the place had a roof and walls, and while it had not been built as a house, someone might now call it home. In which case, walking inside could be seen as an invasion with who knew what consequences.

Dusk was close. A cold fishgray sky crept over their heads. Soon the sun would be gone completely.

From her backpack, she pulled out a folding knife, a back-bladed family heirloom. "We should check it out. Could be supplies."

Technically true, though far from the real reason, which was that Nico simply had too much Lucy and Alice in her to pass up such a curiosity.

They emerged from the woods together, low and fast, and as they neared, she noticed a number of solar panels attached to the top of the TEXACO sign, cords running from there to the roof of the station. She made her way to one of the shattered windowpanes and poked her head inside.

Waiting, listening. All was quiet.

Around to the front door now, knife out, she opened it and stepped inside. Head down, listening.

Not a sound.

Breathe in—now move. She went fast but lightly across the floor, a quick glance up each aisle as she passed. All were empty. Bathrooms in the back: empty. Now retracing her steps to the front, she leaned over the counter to check behind it: empty. "No one's here," she said. Harry's nose was on the ground, and as with the road, he walked the floor of the station, familiarizing himself with the smorgasbord of new scents.

Content they were currently alone, Nico walked the aisles again, more intentionally this time. The shelves had been ransacked, a giant pile of discarded wrappers and empty cardboard displays in the middle of the center aisle. "Like the opposite of Midas," she whispered, standing in awe at the foot of this strange monument. "Everything humans touched turned to garbage."

And for the first time since entering the station, she noticed something else: a soft hum.

At her feet, Harry whined.

"We should leave." She stood where she was though, looking around for the source of the hum. And when she saw the sign on the metal door at the back of the station, she knew she'd found it. "'Cold beer,'" she read.

Refrigeration. The hum was the sound of electricity, which meant the solar panels on the TEXACO sign outside were still operational. And what had only been a theoretical understanding of her world was one she now felt in her bones: that where power was, people were also.

Knife out, she walked to the metal door. It was cold to the touch.

Someone had jammed a crowbar into the door handle, effectively locking it from the outside. "Locked in or locked out?" she said quietly, putting a hand on the crowbar.

Harry whined again, but Nico had made up her mind. She pulled the crowbar out of the handle, let it clank to the ground, and pushed open the door. With all the busted windows, the station was already cold, but the air that rushed out of this room was a different, manufactured sort of cold.

"I have a weapon." Nico stood in the doorway, trying to sound stronger than she looked. "It's a big gun. With lots of . . . gun bullets."

Behind her, Harry turned in circles, a look in his eyes that said, *This is all you.*

"Wimp."

As with the rest of the station, the goods in this room had been pillaged. Silence reigned. Unlike the rest of the station, blood was everywhere. On the walls and floor, like a child had slung a paintbrush around, covered everything in deep red and maroon.

In one corner of the bloody room was a bucket. In the opposite corner, a blanket covered at least one human shape, maybe more.

Fossils

When the entirety of one's universe is an old boarded-up farmhouse, there is no greater treasure than a dusty shoebox full of photographs. All smiles and kisses and travels and meticulously positioned foods on butcher blocks. Nico's favorites were the ones from her parents' honeymoon in Italy. And while plenty of food had been documented, these photographs revealed a shine in her mom's eyes like Nico had never seen, and her dad's, too. Beyond happy, their lives together just beginning, they stood on cobblestone streets, in front of old statues and churches, inside museums full of art Nico could hardly believe had been created by human hands. But her parents had *been* there, had seen these things with their own eyes.

They'd also seen the ruins of Pompeii, an ancient town that had been covered in lava and ash from the eruption of Mount Vesuvius. In her parents' photographs, Nico saw the mummified castings of Pompeian citizens in their final moments, mere seconds before being engulfed in lava: how they sat, stood, or crawled; how they burrowed together like birds in a nest; how they held out their hands or covered their pregnant bellies or—and these were the ones etched into Nico's memory—how some looked as though they were screaming into the void.

As if screaming would stop the fire-wave speeding toward them.

But when she asked herself how one *should* respond in such a situation, screaming into the void seemed as good as anything.

There were three bodies under the blanket: a grown woman and man, bent in Pompeian fashion around a small girl between them, as if to protect her from death itself.

Screaming into the void.

The man's eyeballs were gone, plucked out, dark and empty sockets. His ears were gone too, his whole head a mess of dark blood and indefinable abrasions. Both of the woman's arms (wrapped around the young child) ended just above the wrist, frozen blood on bone, the skin raw and far from healed. Between them, the young girl stared up with marble eyes, dollish and horrible. She appeared to be whole, and Nico tried not to guess how she'd died.

There was no telling how long this family had been like this—the temperature in the room had prolonged, if not stunted, the process of decay, turning each of their lips blue—but she had a feeling she knew who was responsible.

You wanna live, you gotta find out how far the body can go before it dies.

She pulled the blanket back over them, pausing before reaching the little girl's dollish eyes. "If there's another life," said Nico, "I hope it's better than this one."

A blank sheet of a face stared back at her, and she thought of the people of Pompeii, how their final moments had been fixed in time, put on display for history, for anyone, for her, even.

"No one else will see you like this."

Nico covered the faces of the blue-lipped family, and then left the room to fulfill her promise.

Rainbows

Like the fires of Mount Vesuvius . . .

She stood over the trash heap in the middle aisle of the station and flicked her lighter. One aisle over, Harry paced up and down, the consolidated pulse quickened, and she said, "It's okay, we'll just need to move fast," but Harry was already gone. She flicked the lighter again and, in its quick flame, felt genuine potential— not for justice, that was impossible, but for *cleanliness*. Maybe this place had been home to the Metal Masks, maybe not. But it had been home to their evil, and while she could not undo what they'd done, she could wipe its evidence from the face of the earth.

At the foot of the trash pile, she found a good, dry box. On the side of the box were the words *Taste the Rainbow* with a picture of someone who appeared to be doing just that. She held her lighter under this box, flicked it once, twice, three times—it caught—and Nico watched the rainbow ignite.

KIT

purple flowers

It burned quicker than he thought it would.

All that old magic, probably. Whatever material those reels of tape were made of. Projectors and screens, ancient fabrics, cloth chairs and carpets. No matter how ornate the carvings in the crown molding, wood was wood, food for flame, et cetera and so forth.

Kit stood with Monty and Lakie in the middle of Main Street—backpacks on, coats and hats, Lakie with her rifle, Monty with his ax—and watched the Paradise Twin go up in flames. At first the smoke seeped, filtered through cracks in the front door in little spurts. Before long, those spurts were full-on plumes, and where there were no windows, the fire formed them, crumbling brick and ash and pops of light, all that history—the fancy shoes and dresses and suits and smiles, now free to float up into oblivion.

He just didn't think it would burn so fast.

"Kit."

He turned to find Lakie and Monty staring at him.

"You okay?" asked Lakie, and he opened his mouth but couldn't be sure anything came out. Monty put an arm around his shoulders, and as Kit turned back to the smoke and fire, he thought about that word—*okay*.

Certainly, he was not okay now, nor would he ever be okay again, that much was obvious. But when had he *last* felt okay?

It would have been five days ago, probably. He'd just finished a pretty decent *Spacedog & Computer*, hung it on the wall, feeling not great, but exactly *okay* about things. He'd continued feeling okay as he made his way back to the Paradise Twin, where he'd found Monty and Lakie . . .

"Where's Dakota?" he'd asked.

No one knew.

And his okay-ness was gone, dissolved like a short breath in the winter air, never to be seen or heard from again.

At first their search for Dakota had not felt urgent. They'd climbed up to the roof, checked her garden. On the makeshift terrace, the potted plants and soils in which she'd spent all those mornings, they'd found nothing but wilted vegetation. There was one flower in a pot in the back corner of the roof, a little purple thing that refused to die. (Kit knew why: His Dakota had taken care of it. And while all the other plants had moved on, that purple flower was stalwart, which was a word Kit knew that meant stubborn as all get-out.)

After that, they'd checked her room behind concessions, both projection rooms, the kitchenette and bathrooms. While Lakie had gone to check the State Theater, Monty paced the top of the concession counter, saying the same things over and over. "I knew this was going to happen. The way she's been seeing shit, the endless coughing and mumbling. Passing out. She hasn't been the same since the attack."

Kit had said nothing. He stood in the lobby, holding the pot with the little purple flower, staring up at the old black-and-white photo.

She hasn't been the same since the attack.

Was that true? He tried to think back. Her close encounter with the swarm had happened this past summer. Or was it late spring? Regardless, she'd been fine, hadn't she? If it had been an overnight thing—if one morning she'd woken up with a flushed face, sweating profusely, babbling nonsense, hallucinating—it would have been much easier to pinpoint.

He'd swallowed a lump down his throat, pulled the potted flower close to his chest, and tried to let the old photo stir him. Tried to let it unleash his psyche, to get lost in the magic of how things used to be.

It wasn't happening.

After clearing the entirety of the Paradise Twin, they'd broken curfew and extended their search for Dakota to various pockets of Town, checking the old market down the street, the little public park with its overgrown weeds running up and down the swing set and merry-go-round and slide. They'd checked dumpsters filled with decades-old plastic, stores and buildings they'd combed through a hundred times on scavenges.

In the end, they'd found Dakota at the very edge of things, where Main Street ran out of Town before winding up into the mountains. She was alive, but barely conscious, babbling the same thing over and over again: "Just sit there. Just stay where you are."

It had taken all three of them to get her back to the Paradise Twin. Once inside, they'd helped her to her room, gently laid her in bed. They took turns feeding her (or trying to). Kit had moved into her room that night, hauling blankets from his room upstairs to the floor beside her bed. Monty and Lakie checked in regularly, tried to send him away to get some rest, but he refused to leave her side. Soon a halo of sweat had expanded around her body like a pupil dilating in slow motion, until the mattress was completely soaked through, and as she slipped in and out of dreams, always, she came back to the same set of instructions.

"Just sit there, Kit. Please. Just stay where you are."

"I'm not going anywhere, Mom."

He'd probably said it a thousand times—holding her head in his hands, recounting histories and geneses he'd never lived, stories of fancy shoes and breezes off the ocean and fantastic adventures in exotic locations like the moon or a jazz club or Texas. Kit had unleashed his psyche, hoping right down to his feet-bones that it might unleash hers. And just when he'd catch a glimpse of his old Dakota—just when he'd think, *Maybe it's passing*—she would say, "Just sit there. Just stay where you are."

And always, he would respond: "I'm not going anywhere."

Two days later she was dead.

They'd used the wooden barricade as a stretcher, carried her to the old park. Lakie and Monty had said a few words. Kit closed his eyes and imagined the soul of his Dakota transformed into a breeze, free to float and wander and drift from town to town. He wished he knew where breezes went, so he could go too.

He'd transplanted the little purple flower from its pot to the soil beside her grave—*She took care of you*, he thought, *now you take care of her*—and then stayed in that park long after Monty and Lakie had left, until the high sun was low again. He'd told stories and cried and talked about his paintings well into the night. And when he'd finally returned to the Paradise Twin, he found Monty and Lakie upstairs in the lounge between the projection rooms.

They'd clearly been talking about him, their silence heavy and suspicious. The crystal radio was in Monty's lap. Without a word, he held out the earphone.

"Hang on," said Kit. He went back to his room, dug out the old knit cap his Dakota had made for him, the one that itched his brain. And from his pocket, he pulled out the chain necklace and key his Dakota had always worn, which he'd taken before they buried her.

He understood now. Lakie's red bandanna, Monty's yellow plaid shirts: They were more than reminders. They were monuments.

He put on the necklace and knit cap, thinking he would never take them off again. *My brain will just have to get used to being itchy.*

Back in the lounge with Monty and Lakie, he'd held out his hand for the earphone. "I'm ready now."

After listening to the recording twice, he'd handed the earphone back and looked around the room. "I wish we could bury this place, too."

"Well," said Lakie. "We can't bury it, but . . ."

They'd spent the next three days planning their route east, packing bags, and telling nostalgic stories of old. Occasionally Monty or Lakie would laugh at a memory and Kit would pretend to smile, but the stories felt like someone else's life, the Paradise Twin like someone else's home. Without his Dakota, the place had no soul. Whatever thread had tied him to Town had been cut, and he wanted out. In that sense, for Monty and Lakie, the Isles of Shoals were a destination; for Kit, they were just a means to an end.

Now, walking side by side down the middle of Main Street, the three of them left Town for good. Behind them, the Paradise Twin went up in flames. Ahead, the mountains loomed. And when they passed the spot where they'd found his Dakota in the road, Kit reached under his coat for her necklace, the cold silver key pressed against the skin of his chest.

"We're gonna be okay," said Monty.

A small but loud collection of crows flew high in the sky. Looking up, Kit thought of the buzzing-black fog from his nightmare, a swarm that consumed Town and everything in it. "If you say so," he said.

greetings from the Isles of Shoals

"... *42.9880 degrees N, 70.6135 degrees W ... Isles of Shoals, Carl Meier, radio and communications. Repeat ... 42.9880 degrees N, 70.6135 degrees W, Isles of Shoals, six miles off the coast of the Maine–New Hampshire border. If you're hearing this, you are capable and alive, two things in short supply. We're a cluster of islands, well stocked and organized. Solar power, mostly. Early stages of a tidal power station. One hundred and eleven residents. Maybe the only real community left in the whole godforsaken world. If being part of something like that sounds good to you, come on out. Though be advised ... we are heavily armed and on guard twenty-four seven. Peaceable entries only. Carl Meier, signing off. May our numbers rise ...*"

"... *42.9880 degrees N, 70.6135 degrees W ... Isles of Shoals, Carl Meier, radio and communications. Repeat ... 42.9880 degrees N, 70.6135 degrees W, Isles of Shoals, six miles off the coast of the Maine–New Hampshire border. If you're hearing this, you are capable and alive ...*"

NIC

Ideologies

S he was six and the radio was a miracle.

"But how does it *work*, Daddy?"

"I'm trying to explain. See this antenna, here? It catches radio waves in the air, and then transforms those waves into electrical signals, which the radio then, sort of, reads."

These were the last days of batteries and generators, and while Nico's parents had always remained calm and collected, looking back, she thought there must have been a wild-eyed panic under that demeanor, the feeling of clinging to the bottom rung.

But at six years old, it was all miracle and marvel.

"Can I turn it?" she asked, and he answered by smiling, scooping her into his lap, and she turned the knob slowly, not wanting to mess things up, knowing if she did it right, she would achieve the miracle. "Is it like the Electronic?"

"A little bit," he said, but explained how the Electronic was powered by the sun, while the radio was battery powered.

Batteries. That such little things could rival the power of the sun . . .

Her mother joined them in the cellar, and Harriet, too, and they all gathered around that little table, turning knobs, holding breaths, waiting for whispers of news from faraway lands. As they waited, her mother told stories of the old world—movie theaters with friends, professional sporting events, restaurant after restaurant after restaurant.

"Did they have chili mac?" asked Nico. "Or taco seasoning?"

Her parents laughed at first, but she couldn't help noticing their smiles always turned a little sad. "Yes, honey. Some of them had those things. And other things too. Even more delicious than chili mac and taco seasoning."

Now she *knew* they were lying.

Suddenly a man's voice came through, tinny and staticky, and they listened for a minute, until her father changed the channel, declaring that the voice belonged to a "prepper fanatic" and that he was "clogging up the airwaves with half-assed conspiracy theories."

Airwaves, prepper fanatics, tinny and staticky interruptions— Nico welcomed all of it. Miles away, maybe on the other side of the world, a strange man sat at a desk and spoke into a box, and now, here in their cellar, his voice came out of a different box.

Miracle of miracles.

One night, weeks after the tinny prepper fanatic, Nico was in bed when she heard the clunking of her father's boots climbing the cellar stairs. Urgent whispers emerged from the kitchen, where her mother had been, followed by both of them descending into the cellar.

Quietly, Nico got out of bed, crept through the hallway, and sat at the top of the cellar stairs. Right away she could tell this particular radio voice was different from any of those she'd heard before. Whereas the other voices spoke quietly, in secretive tones as if communicating *just with you*, the tone of this voice felt big; Nico imagined an actor on a stage, projecting, making sure everyone could hear.

She understood very little of what the man said. There was a lot of talk about "rebuilding infrastructure" and "hope for the future," and every couple of minutes, a very light scattering of applause in the background. From her spot atop the cellar stairs, she couldn't see her parents—but she could hear them.

"What a joke," her father said. "I mean, I get it, hopeful message and all. But how about some practical application, or updates from labs? Surely we've learned *something*."

"It's not like he *asked* for the job," her mother said. "No one becomes Secretary of Agriculture thinking the line of succession might reach them."

The voice on the radio encouraged a levelheaded approach to the Flies and the Flu. "*In time*," said the voice, "*this struggle will be cast in the same light as all those that came before. It is an obstacle, no doubt, but not an insurmountable one. Through grit and determination, we will clear this hurdle with room to spare.*"

A slam, as someone's hand met the table.

"Honey," said her mother.

"Sorry. It's just—"

"I know."

"He's using sports metaphors."

"I know."

"The world has gone dark, most of the population is dead, and he's encouraging levelheadedness and using sports metaphors."

The radio voice kept talking, but it was just background noise now.

"Where do you think he is?" asked her dad.

"Raven Rock, probably. Or Mount Weather. One of those underground bunkers built for nuclear fallout."

"Far cry from the House Chamber."

"Wait, shh. I think he's wrapping up."

"*It has always been the American spirit that perseveres, and I believe that spirit is alive and well.*"

"He better not go where I think he's going," said her dad.

"*We've walked the moon, explored the oceans, defeated every enemy that has come our way.*"

"Don't do it."

"*And because of this unyielding and unprecedented spirit, I can stand before you now—*"

"In an underground bunker."

"*—and declare that the state of our Union is strong.*"

A sudden click, and the voice went silent.

Nico never heard the radio again. Later, when she asked about it, her mother said, "Oh, that. The batteries died."

Plausible as this was, Nico still heard the echo of her father's hand hitting the table, and she wondered if her mother had answered truthfully.

KIT

"This place is strange," said Lakie.

Kit agreed, but silently, as his tongue seemed to have frozen to the roof of his mouth.

His tongue wasn't the only part of him having troubles: his psyche had shriveled, and his lips seemed to have chapped their way to the back of his throat.

Life in the Final Frontier was a vast and mysterious existence.

They'd been out here for two days. Aside from walking and freezing, it was a lot of sleeping on the ground, listening for Flies, watching Lakie take to the woods like a fish to water, while Monty navigated their easterly course to the Isles of Shoals. There was a lot of hiking up one mountain only to find another, and just when Kit had started wondering if maybe What Lay Beyond wasn't simply _more_ Beyond, they saw it: in a little valley tucked between mountains, a town.

"Eyes open for any and all consumables." Lakie swung the strap of her rifle around as they stepped onto the street. "Might even sleep indoors tonight."

Monty held his ax out, at the ready.

Good thing I brought my artistic sensibility.

They entered the town slowly, cautiously. He suddenly thought of a crude model of Town he'd once constructed from old reels and cardboard. His model had everything: a Main Street, a theater, a rooftop garden—he'd even colored little green mountains on the outskirts. But no matter how many details he included, it always felt like something was missing.

This town was like that.

Also, there were people-bits everywhere. Marrowless bones galore.

They walked through a little town square, passed shops with broken windows, and a bar, which was where people had once paid cash-bucks to drink old corn liquids that made them forget their names and problems. Whenever Kit got down about being born in a world where Flies ate humans, he reminded himself that even in the world before Flies, things made little sense.

The road eventually passed into an area of houses only, strange structures made of synthetic-looking pastels.

"This is . . . interesting." A little way ahead, Monty had stopped beside a rusty car. Inside, behind the steering wheel, marrowless bones had miraculously retained the shape of their former person. "You ever see one so intact?"

Lakie circled the car. "Windows aren't broken. Must have gotten in through the vents."

"Or the person somehow died of the Flu?"

"While *driving*?"

While Monty and Lakie discussed their find, Kit stood in the middle of the road, turned slowly, stared back the way they came. He felt something. It wasn't new, this feeling, but until now it was a feeling he had no words for.

All these piles of marrowless bones in tall-grassed yards . . .

The cars that once went places, now statues lining roads and driveways . . .

Above it all, the cold mountain sky . . .

"Kit." Lakie put a hand on his shoulder. "You okay?"

"Do you feel it too?" he asked, but he barely heard his own words, and everything from the road to the synthetic houses, from *that* peculiar chirping bird to *that* gust of wind—even Lakie's response . . .

"Do I feel what?"

. . . all of it was part of the feeling, which he now had a name for: *familiarity*.

"I've been here before," Kit said.

Far off, there was a rumble of quiet thunder, low and steady.

"What?" asked Lakie.

He looked up at her. "It's coming."

Just then, far down the road, a person appeared out of no-where. He was yelling something, running right for them.

"Get behind me," said Lakie; she started to raise her rifle, but Kit reached out, pushed it down. "*Kit.*"

"Just wait," he said.

Monty was by their side now, ax at the ready, and only when the person tripped and fell, an armload of supplies scattered everywhere, did they even notice he'd been carrying anything. He got up again, holding his arm, and kept running, content to leave his supplies behind.

"What's he saying?" asked Monty.

As the person neared, the rumbling thunder grew, and they realized it wasn't thunder at all.

"I told you," said Kit. "It's coming."

And in that place on the wide horizon, where the road wound up into the mountains, the low rumbling twisted and turned into form: a black tidal wave crested the peak, rose high into the air, almost paused as if in slow motion, before crashing down the mountain-side toward them, a great droning aliveness descending on the earth like a breathing blanket.

Kit caught his breath—*Look at it*, he thought, tears in his eyes, only vaguely aware that he would be dead in less than a minute.

And now the stranger was with them, so much shouting, and Lakie had him by the wrist, pulling him, dragging him backward. He stumbled, half ran to keep up, but it didn't matter, his feet were no longer his own, they belonged in the calmness found on the other side of terror, when you've made peace with your fate.

It was beauty and discord at once. Nature unleashing her global psyche.

Kit pulled his wrist out of Lakie's grip, content to stand and witness this wave in the final moments before being swept up in it. "*Look at it . . .*" The swarm was darkest in the middle, where the Flies gathered like a coiled octopus before exploding outward, filling his entire field of vision, tentacles flailing, regrouping, flailing, accelerating forward, always, toward them. *"Just look at it."*

Monty picked him up, slung him over one shoulder, and followed Lakie and the stranger in a sprint toward the nearest of the pastel houses, where a second stranger held open a door, yelling for them to move their asses.

they bring the night

They crouched on the carpet of the empty basement. No candles, no sounds, no motions, nothing that might give them away.

Linked through his, Lakie's arm shook.

A small window at the top of the wall (ground level outside) was boarded up, but through the cracks, where sunlight should have been, there was only darkness. And Kit found himself thinking of the homemade sign back in the library of Taft Elementary.

Know your enemy . . .

He knew enough. In the archives of the grown-up library, he'd seen the photos, read the reports from those first weeks. He knew how swarms operated as one, could carry you off into the sky like some enormous mythical crow, devour you in midair, and when he imagined this, he saw Flies filling his mouth and stomach, eating him from the inside out until he had evaporated *into* them, had become part of the crow's mythology.

Bad as that was, it wasn't even the worst-case scenario.

The Flies' other method, far more common, was to burrow

into their prey, plant their own feces into the skin like a seed, and the disease right along with it. Fly Flu developed at different rates in different people, a little embryo of death content to incubate for a while. According to those same reports, the incubation could last anywhere from days to weeks, and symptoms ranged from the more common—hallucinations, dementia, severe fatigue, blindness—to things Kit had to reread, reports he wasn't sure he understood, and then, once he *did* understand them, wished he didn't.

Inexhaustible hunger. Accounts of people trying to eat their own arms, hands, and feet.

Extreme rectal prolapse. Accounts of people passing their own organs, effectively emptying themselves, *So yes,* Kit thought now, staring at the boarded-up window, *being eaten in midair by a giant cloud of Flies is terrifying, but not the worst of the worst.*

There were other theories about how the Flu was contracted. Some said indirect contact did the trick. People had sealed themselves up in their homes, boarded up vents and windows, when nine times out of ten, someone in the house already had the Flu and didn't know it.

But then—his Dakota may have had the Flu. And he'd touched her.

The problem, as best Kit could tell from these reports, was that the very scientists and doctors whose jobs it would have been to research theories surrounding the contraction of the Flu had all died before they'd had a chance to do so.

"It's good to be scared." Across the room, three new people

huddled in the corner. One of them, the girl who'd let them in the house, was eating dried fruit from a bag. All eyes were on her, the sudden newness of a voice in a quiet, dark place. "Scared means you're not dead yet."

Outside, the swarm raged.

similar fates & strange encounters

When it was clear the Flies had passed, they emerged from the basement and stood in the kitchen, each group waiting for a member from the other to speak first. The girl who'd been eating dried fruit pulled a roll of bandages from a cupboard, tossed it to the kid who'd been sprinting up the street. "Your elbow's bleeding."

"Shit." He removed a scuffed-up army jacket, inspected the wound. "Must've happened when I fell."

"You find any?"

"Yeah, but I dropped it all." He unwound the roll, started wrapping his elbow. "You wanna go get it?"

"Later." The girl turned her attention back to them, squinted, and sighed. "Okay, well—we've been here longer than you, and I definitely just saved your lives, but I'll blink first. I'm Loretta."

Loretta was older than the others. *Maybe even in her twenties*, thought Kit, trying not to let this impress him too much. She was white with long dark hair and bangs just over her eyes. "That's Pringles," she said, pointing to the kid wrapping his elbow in bandages. "And Lennon."

Lennon stood quietly in the corner, twisting what looked like a wristwatch. Kit didn't know anything about watches, other than the broken ones he'd found during scavenges. Reminders of a time when time mattered.

And yet—

Something about this watch mattered to Lennon. *It was a gift*, thought Kit, unsure how he knew, but knowing it was true. He took Lennon in—tall, brown skin, dark hair that went in waves like a sideways S, a large birthmark on one cheek—and under it all, he saw a boy who'd cared deeply for a person. Only now, in place of that person, Lennon cared deeply for a watch.

"I was three when the Flies hit," said Loretta; she nodded toward Lennon and Pringles. "They were still babies. Our families all happened to be vacationing on the same campgrounds. Just before the attack, apparently, a group decided to go hiking. Two women volunteered to stay behind and babysit. Lucky them."

Loretta explained how, after the initial attack, when it was clear everyone else had been killed, those two women—Jean and Zadie—had loaded the kids into a camper and driven to a secluded spot in Pin Oak Forest, where they began stockpiling from a nearby town. "This one, actually. This place used to be a tourist stop back in the day. Mountain homes for rich people. Shops with gear and survivalist equipment, and a parking lot full of campers. Those early days, when fuel was still a thing, Jean and Zadie drove a few of those campers right off the lot. Parked seven of them in a circle in the forest, front to end. Planted a garden in the middle, couple of firepits on either side. That was our life. For years. And then Jean and Zadie got sick."

"Sick how?" asked Lakie.

"Shit," said Pringles. "How *weren't* they sick?"

Loretta put up a hand. Pringles's cheeks, already a ruddy white, turned a deeper shade of red. "We'll talk more after you guys take a turn," she said.

Guess we know who's in charge.

Monty outlined the bare bones of their story, how his and Lakie's parents had been killed by a swarm, how Kit's mother had raised them in the Paradise Twin. Kit waited for the inevitable, *It was all Kit's fault, see. His mom was exhausted trying to take care of him as a baby, so she was asleep outside when a swarm came, can you believe that? And then* my parents *died saving her, and now I can't look at Kit without seeing their faces* . . .

But it never came. Monty ended by explaining how Kit's mother recently got sick.

"Extreme confusion?" asked Loretta. "Hallucinations?"

Monty hesitated, looked at Lakie, who nodded. "Yes."

"Fever, sweat, constant babbling?"

"Yeah."

Kit thought of his Dakota's grave in the park, that little purple flower standing guard, and he realized he'd been gripping her necklace under his shirt.

"When was this?" asked Loretta.

"Few days ago. We burned the place down and left."

"You burned it down?"

Monty's eyes were acting weird, Kit noticed. Like they were trying to communicate something on the sly. Like his eyeballs had a message for Loretta, something secret, something they didn't want Monty himself knowing.

"We'll talk more after you take another turn," said Monty.

"After we buried Jean and Zadie, we assumed we'd stay in Pin Oak. But then . . ." She pushed herself up on the counter, boots dangling, and turned to Pringles. "You wanna take it from there?"

Pringles looked like a balloon someone had let the air out of. "I was just trying to make Zadie's chutney. She used to mash up cherries and fresh-squeezed lemons from that tree. Mix it with onions and garlic, then rub it on any kind of meat, really. *Delectable*."

"It was," said Lennon. "Assuming you use *cherries*."

"They *looked* like cherries, dude."

Apparently, Pringles had spread his concoction on their dinner one night, only it wasn't long before they realized something was very wrong.

"Whatever they were," said Loretta, "they weren't cherries. Pretty potent, too. Pringles passed out first. I don't remember much after that, but—"

"I'm not the only one who saw him," said Pringles, staring at Lennon.

Lennon kept his head down, fidgeting with his watch.

"Sorry," said Lakie. "Saw who?"

Loretta rolled her eyes. "Pringles thinks we were abducted."

"Not *abducted*. But yes, I do think we were the product of . . . some kind of experiment."

The kitchen was quiet for a beat, until Monty cleared his throat. "Like—by aliens?"

Pringles described the experience of struggling to breathe, then not being able to breathe at all, and eventually blacking out. "And then at some point, this—*spaceman*, I don't know what else to call it, was leaning over the top of me and had something jammed down my throat."

"You didn't see a face?" asked Lakie.

"Whoever—*whatever* it was, they had this black helmet with, like, a tinted visor. They saved our lives, I know that." He looked over at Lennon. "You got anything to add here?"

"I'm good."

Pringles shook his head in frustration. "Loretta didn't come to until whatever saved us was gone. But *you* saw it, Len. I know you did. Why can't you just admit you saw this completely unexplainable thing?"

"I thought I was dying. I don't know what I saw."

Another few seconds of silence passed before Loretta cleared her throat, slid down off the counter. "We're going to Boston. That's where Jean and Zadie were from before the Flies hit. They always talked about going back someday, but it just . . . never happened. Whoever or *whatever* saved us, the near-death experience made us realize there was no future for us in Pin Oak. We're hoping to find one elsewhere."

"We buried my mom when she died," said Kit.

Throughout this conversation, he'd begun to feel a bit like Pluto, in that he wasn't sure the rest of them knew he was there, and even if they did know, they weren't sure what to do with him. *Is he a planet? Nah, too small, too peripheral, not gravitationally dominant. Don't pay him any attention, he's just a* dwarf *planet.*

Dwarf planet or not, Kit could spot an unleashed psyche a parsec away.

"That's what you do when someone you love dies," he said, and suddenly, slowly, the room shifted until he felt each of them in his orbit. "The Paradise Twin was our home. We loved it. And we couldn't bury it. So we burned it down."

Loretta smiled, looked at Lennon, who nodded—and then Pringles, who nodded too. "Okay," she said. "I'm gonna go retrieve the toilet paper Pringles dropped in the street, and when I get back, I want to hear where you guys are headed. Also, am I the only one who's starving?"

oh, humanity's indulgent spirit!

In the olden days, humans required an entire room to clean their clothes. In this room, one machine (the "dryer") dried the clothes after the other machine (the "washer") was done washing them. Kit could only assume these wacky humans of old, having invented such machines, were too tuckered out to name them. He also assumed, given the enormity of the machines, that humans had once walked around in six or seven layers at a time.

The whole thing was a ginormous cacophony of unfathomable luxury.

The owners of this house, however, had put their machines to more practical use: the hiding of freeze-dried ice cream. Back in Town, during early scavenges, they often found rotten foods in odd places. People stored things away like squirrels, looking for imaginative ways to keep their stuff safe from looters. But food in a washer and dryer? Kit had to commend the brain in the head of the human who'd thought that up.

"It's good," said Lakie between bites.

"Yes," said Monty. "Thank you for sharing."

They sat around a table in the dining room (humans of old and their separate room requirements!), slowly eating the freeze-dried ice cream. They'd already eaten one jar of Dakota's beans, one of pears, plus a smorgasbord of dried fruits and meats, which Kit had approached hesitantly, but too hungrily to deny, and which wound up being quite good. The other group seemed to have dried foods in droves.

"You guys hunt?" asked Loretta.

Lakie eyed Kit. Shortly after entering the woods, she'd mentioned the idea of *possibly* hunting for dinner, to which Kit had flat-out refused. He didn't put his foot down often, but when he did, it was a thunderous clap. "When the majority of the world has been wiped out, Lakie, you *don't* kill what's left," he'd told her. And that was that.

"We're vegetarians," he said now, taking a very large bite of dried deer meat, chewing loudly.

Loretta smiled. "Well, I'm a pretty good hunter, so lemme know if you change your mind."

They talked about the house itself, and why it didn't smell like a woodstove casserole of death and farts when so many others did. Apparently, since this was a vacation town, lots of the houses weren't in use when the Flies hit. People owned them. Kept furniture and nonperishables in them, et cetera and so forth. But only lived in them for a couple weeks a year. (Some humans needed more than separate rooms. They needed whole other houses!)

When talk turned to the Isles of Shoals, Monty pulled a rip of paper from his pocket, handed it to Loretta. "This is the message I picked up. It's six miles off the coast of the Maine–New Hampshire border. Based on my research, once we reach the shoreline, there should be plenty of transportation options. They were tourist towns too, like this one. Only instead of campers and tents, it's kayaks and fishing poles."

The ice cream was strange. Fine, but not the drippy-sweet, legendary treat Kit had imagined. "I wonder how they made these," he said quietly.

No one answered. No one said anything at all until Lennon pulled out a map, spread it across the table, and showed them a highlighted route from Pin Oak, east to a river, and then south to

Boston. "It's not the most direct walk," he said. "But sticking to rivers gives us a constant water supply, and fish. How long it takes depends on any number of factors. We're more concerned with getting there in one piece."

"We're headed east too," said Monty. "Basically, the same route all the way to the river."

Kit knew Monty well enough to know what he was getting at. And while he liked these new humans (and their unleashed psyches) just fine, he wasn't sure about traveling with them.

Also, was it possible to fall in love ten minutes after you met a person? The way Monty and Loretta kept looking at each other made him wonder. In books, people seemed to fall in love instantly, but then, books were mostly better than real life.

"What are you thinking?" asked Pringles. "You wanna join up?"

Monty shrugged. "I mean, it's whatever. But we've probably got a couple of days where we'll all be walking the same direction. At least as far as"—he pointed to the spot on the map where Lennon and Loretta and Pringles would turn south for Boston, while Monty and Lakie and Kit would continue east to the coast—"here. The Merrimack River."

The table was quiet for a second, each considering.

"More people," said Lakie. "Bigger target for Flies."

"Maybe," said Loretta. "Maybe not. Unless you guys know more about how they operate?"

Kit was reminded of a moment around a different table, in a different town, in what now seemed a different life. *It's not a vote,* his Dakota had said, and her words had hung in the air like a question mark, each of them wondering . . .

"What if we took a vote?" he asked now.

Everyone looked at him.

"A vote," said Loretta.

Monty nodded. "Like people did in the days before DOS. I like it."

"DOS?" asked Lennon.

"The Downfall of Society." Lakie rolled her eyes.

Monty cleared his throat. "In the spirit of human perseverance, I vote we travel together while we can." He raised his hand in the air. "All in favor?"

"Fuck it." Pringles raised his hand. "Why not?"

Kit stared at the freeze-dried ice cream pouch, and suddenly felt cheated by it. He'd stayed in Town because that was where his Dakota had wanted them. But now she was gone, and he was in the Final Frontier with new kids and new ideas and no one to explain the mysteries of things like mediocre freeze-dried treats.

He put his hand in the air, not knowing if he really meant it, but 100 percent sure he was tired of just going along with things. "Yes," he said. "I vote yes, we join groups. I think that's best."

Monty looked at him as if waiting to see if he was finished. "Okay, that's three."

"I vote no," said Lakie. Then, to Loretta: "No offense."

"Lake," said Monty. "Come on. Solidarity."

"It's a *vote*, Monty. The expression of individual opinion."

"Can I put my hand down now?" asked Kit.

"Yes, Kit. Okay, so that's three votes yes, one vote no."

It was down to Lennon and Loretta. Both seemed to be considering when Lennon said, "Somewhere, long ago, someone invented a machine to freeze things and then remove the ice." He held up his half-eaten pouch. "Only now it's not ice *or* cream. It's just a shadow." Dropping the pouch on the table, he said, "I vote no."

The table turned to Loretta as Kit considered the system: if she voted yes, the two groups would combine; if she voted no, it would be a tie, meaning they'd essentially done a dressed-up version of nothing.

If Kit remembered correctly, this was the system America had once used to choose its leaders.

What a wacky bunch.

"In the spirit of human perseverance . . ." Loretta raised her hand. "May our numbers rise."

Given the current look of elation on Monty's face, Kit had his answer: ten minutes was plenty of time to fall in love.

we've been here before

"Kit."

"Yeah."

"Can I ask you something?"

After dinner, the group had dispersed to various rooms throughout the house. Even though Kit found this nursery to be creepy as all get-out—a dusty crib in one corner, unread board books everywhere, a sad painted circus on the wall—he'd followed Lakie here because she took sleep seriously. She even had a special sleeping bag called Big Alma, which she'd found during a scavenge, and which, according to her, could withstand the most ferocious of wild animals.

Kit wasn't sure about that. But he hadn't been sleeping well and was hoping an overnight in a room with someone who did might help.

"Earlier today," Lakie said. "Before the swarm came. We were in the street and you said, 'I've been here before.' You didn't mean déjà vu, did you?"

"No."

"You meant literally. You'd *literally* been on that road before."

Since leaving Town, Kit had taken to sleeping in the knit cap. It was his most luxurious item. His brain's second skin. Now, pulling it all the way down over his eyes, he could almost see the outline of his Dakota's face in the darkness.

"Why did you guys leave the commune?" he asked.

"What?"

"When you and Monty were little. When my Dakota was pregnant with me. Why did you leave the commune?"

It was quiet for so long, Kit was starting to wonder if Lakie had fallen asleep when she said, "You wanna hear a story?"

"Okay."

"Once upon a time, there were three little kids. A brother

and a sister and a third kid, a boy who lived nearby. They hung out every day, played games in the summer, built snowmen in the winter, did all their chores together. Thick as thieves, these three. They lived in a camp that had strict rules. Where you could go and when. How late you could stay out, that sort of thing. One of the off-limits places was a nearby water tower. Must have been over a hundred feet tall, this tower, with a ladder that went all the way to the top. Since it was off-limits, of course, those three kids snuck off to it all the time. They'd stand at the foot of the ladder, shield their eyes from the sun, and wonder what the world looked like from way up there. Occasionally one of them would climb a rung or two, they would giggle nervously, and then go running back to camp. One day, the third kid climbed a couple rungs, only instead of hopping off, he kept going. 'You'll get in trouble,' the other two said, but he just kept giggling and climbing, giggling and climbing. Just when the brother and sister decided to run back and get someone—the boy slipped and fell. They'd never heard a sound like that. The way his body hit the ground."

"Did the boy die?" asked Kit.

"Broke his back and his legs. Camp doctor said he'd never walk again. After that, the little boy stayed in his own family's tent. Days went by. Devastated for their friend, the brother and sister decided to make him something. Giraffes were his favorite. They found a good, sturdy stick. Their dad whittled the long neck and legs. They spent days decorating it, painting it just the right colors, and when it was ready, they brought it to their friend's tent.

The boy's father came outside. He was this big, hairy white guy, the kind of eyes that always look hungry. The little girl was scared but tried to tell herself that the man was probably just sad for his son. Trembling, the brother and sister held out the giraffe.

" 'We made this for him,' they said.

"The boy's father spat in their faces and called them a name they'd never heard before. 'Should have known better,' said the man, 'than to let my son play with—'"

Lakie suddenly fell silent.

Kit slid his knit cap off his eyes, turned, and looked at her. "What was your friend's name?"

"Shawn."

"Shawn's dad sounds like a real *a-s-s*-wipe."

A small smile disappeared as quickly as it came. "Mom used to say, so long as there are people on Earth, there will be willful ignorance and hatred. She said we should stand up for ourselves, protect ourselves, without letting that hatred define us. I was only five, but that business with Shawn's dad—that was when I started to get it."

"Did he hurt you guys?" asked Kit.

"There were threats. I think he would have." Lakie kept her eyes on the ceiling. "It's like Loretta said about leaving Pin Oak. There was no future for us there."

When it came to futures, Kit had always thought of his as something fragile. Like a sick bird. Or a pouch of freeze-dried ice cream. Just a shadow, really.

"Earlier," he said. "In the road. What I meant was, all of us have."

" 'All of us have' what?"

"Lake."

"Yeah."

"We've done all of this before. We've been here before."

THE
DELIVERER

I stand at the top of the ladder, chiseling, chiseling. The rock wall is hard, the work slow going, but I am resilient. My circle is a little smaller, rougher, a little less *alive* than the original, but the heart of the thing is intact. Eighteen years and nine rotations later, I am now entering the homestretch.

As for *why* I've spent years chiseling a massive circle into the rock wall of the basement—I am not sure. Maybe because it feels like an artifact to unearth, embedded in rock for untold years, just waiting for someone to come along and let it breathe.

The circle is more archaeology than art.

I spend thirty minutes a night on it.

I used to chisel for hours. But in the book of the body, age is setting, always happening, always growing. And my back isn't what it used to be.

Though even if I was the picture of perfect health, another truth hovers in deeper places I visit only in dreams: that with each passing year, as the circle looks more like the original, I am uncomfortable in its presence, as if I might get sucked into its infinite center. Or, worse: that the circle is nothing more than a self-portrait.

Thirty minutes over, I climb down the ladder, step back, and admire my progress. The bottom of the circle touches the floor; the top ends where the high ceiling begins.

Not bad. For a replica.

I grab my clipboard, my glass of red wine (*one glass to make it last*), and sip as I take inventory. My basement, the deep yawn of the mountain: cavernous, unfinished, well suited to its purposes. Aisles upon aisles of shelves snake from one wall to the other, buckets of freeze-dried foods, lighters and butane torches and candles, medical supplies, five-pound tubs of cinnamon, a dusty armory, all of it a testament to the ambition of the Architect. Not to mention the forethought it must have taken to design such a place.

It really is something.

Pace each aisle, sipping wine, checking items as I go. There was a time when this process took two or three hours a week, when the clipboard had dozens of spreadsheets. There are only four pages now and, according to my watch, the process has taken all of eight minutes.

While the circle in the rock wall is not art, *inventory*—making things last—is nothing if not an art form. In its medium, I am a master.

There is more than enough to finish this cycle of deliveries, plus three years' worth of rations for a single person.

He'll need to be smart about it. Spread it out over time.

When he arrives, I will show him how to make things last.

Nighttime routine complete, I carry the clipboard and empty wineglass up the spiral staircase, each step an echoing clank. At the top of the stairs, before closing the door, I look down on my cellar, mostly empty now.

"*We've been here before . . .*" The words reverberate off the rock walls; I savor them, allow a moment to soak them in, knowing this daily ritual is the closest I will get to actual conversation.

When the echo of my voice ends, I switch off the lights and close the door as I leave.

KIT

so your body is changing: NOW WHAT?

The medium-size rock was no second-story window, but it would do. Kit sat on top of it, observing the group: Loretta carried her rifle like she knew what she was doing; Lennon's navigational prowess outstripped Monty's by a good bit; Pringles had no prowess, no weaponry to speak of, but when Loretta had returned with two large rabbits for lunch, he'd had a crackling fire going pronto.

Maybe most telling was what had happened during lunch. They'd heard a swarm in the distance, and while he and Monty and Lakie hit the ground, Lennon and Loretta and Pringles had all sprinted in opposite directions. After the swarm had passed, when they'd returned to the campsite, Loretta noticed their questioning looks. "They may get one of us," she'd said, calmly going back to her rabbit. "But they won't get us all."

Verdict: the faction from Pin Oak was not messing around.

"Hey." Lakie sat down next to him on the rock.

"Is for horses."

The woods seemed thicker here, every inch of landscape covered in a light snow or brush. It reminded Kit of his earliest paintings, when he'd felt the need to pack as much punch as possible into every corner of the page. This was before he learned the value of letting the painting breathe, of the ways doing less over here added more over there, et cetera and so forth.

Good grief, he missed painting. And his Dakota.

Also, warmth. He missed being warm.

"What do you think he's doing?" asked Lakie.

At the base of a nearby tree, Monty and Loretta, who'd been having their own whispered conversation, suddenly burst into giggles.

"I don't know," said Kit. "But it's gross."

She followed his eyes. "No, not them. I mean Lennon."

The reason they were sitting here in the middle of the woods—their third time today—was because Lennon had suddenly thrown a hand up, and then made them all wait so he could run ahead to check on something.

"I don't know," said Kit. "Tracker stuff?"

"What does his birthmark remind me of?"

"It's shaped like Alaska."

"Wow. That's it exactly."

"There was a myth in the olden days that birthmarks were a sign of how someone had lived or died in a past life."

"You think Lennon's past life lived in Alaska?"

"Or else Alaska murdered him."

"Hey." Lakie turned his chin toward her, looked him in the eyes like she was reading his secret thoughts. "You look exhausted."

Kit returned the look with what he hoped was an equal

intensity. "I've had the same dream every night since we left Town."

"What's the dream?"

"I'm in a room, sitting at a table. Blinding brightness in every direction. No walls or ceilings or floors. Across the table is a woman. We talk with our thoughts. I don't know what about, I never can remember. And that's it."

"That's . . . rather chilling."

"Tell me about it."

Over by the tree, Monty said something that lit up Loretta's face. Kit had never seen anything like it. But it reminded him of something.

"I read this book once," said Kit. "In the Taft library. *So Your Body Is Changing: NOW WHAT?* by Emil Johansson, MD."

"Okay."

"It was about puberty and how kids start seeing other kids differently."

"Why would you read that?"

Kit shrugged. "It was there?"

"Okay."

"You and Monty are seventeen. You guys went through puberty like forever ago."

"Kit—"

"I'm saying—"

"Please don't."

Kit waited a second, and then: "It's all very healthy and normal, according to Emil Johansson, MD, only you guys didn't have anyone around to . . . you know. Be healthy with."

Currently, Loretta was laughing at something Monty had said, only she laughed so hard, it had turned to coughing.

"They have, sort of . . . gotten lost in each other," said Lakie.

"It's like they forgot how to use their eyeballs. But I guess they like looking at each other."

"I mean—I like looking at her too. You don't see me ogling."

Just once, Kit wished he had a healthy balance of feelings and words. Instead he usually felt things he couldn't articulate or else said something he wasn't sure he felt. "Remember last Christmas, when my Dakota wrote you a play? *The Life and Times of*—"

"*Stephanie Silver*. The girl who traveled the globe—"

"Looking for the perfect slice of pizza."

"Of course I remember. I also remember it was pretty terrible."

"She worked on that story every night for six months," said Kit.

"Really?"

"Started it that summer. Barely finished by Christmas. I remember, early on, I told her it was good enough. But you know what she said?"

"What."

" 'It's for Lakie. It needs to be perfect.' "

Kit turned his eyes from the spectacle of Monty and Loretta to face this girl who was not his sister, but as good as. And whether it was the woods, or the addition of new people, he felt a little clingy in a way he didn't entirely understand. As if all the comfort in the world had been transferred to whatever three-foot radius of ground Lakie happened to occupy at that moment.

"I read this terrible book once, where one character said to another, 'Try to be the best *you* you can be.' That's what you do, Lakie. You inspire people to be their best. Of course you don't ogle Loretta. Ogling inspires no one."

Later, after Lennon had returned and they'd gone back to walking, Lakie put one arm around his shoulders. "You know, sometimes I wonder if you're the most perceptive twelve-year-old in the world."

"Just wait until I hit puberty."

She laughed, and Kit was glad he hadn't responded with his first thought: *Sometimes I wonder if I'm the* only *twelve-year-old in the world.*

nothing is ever only one thing

Dead towns galore.

Kit was amazed at just how many, small and tucked away.

These days, he felt more breeze than human, floating in and through all these little towns, on the lookout for dreamers, Knowers of Things in open windows, observing their little worlds, wondering What (if anything) Lay Beyond.

Some towns were synthetic, like the old cardboard model town.

Others were more like Town: stone and brick, gardens and parks, ancient souls with fancy shoes and stories to tell. One town even had a road that was a bridge! Not half road, half bridge, but fully both.

As a distraction from the cold, Kit made a mental list of other things that were actually two things, not 50 percent one and 50 percent another, but 100 percent both:

Beautiful humans were disgusting. (*Secretion* was a word he knew.)

Refreshing breezes were sad.

Full bellies were uncomfortable.

Deadly storms were life-giving.

As they crossed the bridge-road, Kit looked over the edge and saw the road running beneath him, and he wondered if anything was *ever* only one thing.

Frozen ears and wet socks, maybe. He was tired and cold and tired of being cold.

The problem was, even though snow came and went, the ground stayed muddy and wet, the air thin and bitter. He'd pulled his knit cap down so many times, it was all stretched out.

"Quite the sleeping bag you've got there," said Lennon, nodding to Lakie's pack.

"I don't play around with sleep," said Lakie.

Kit raised a hand. "I can vouch for this."

"Looks pretty heavy, though."

Lakie shrugged. "It's a Big Alma. Found it on a scavenge a few years back. Seventy-five-denier ripstop nylon shell with Insotect Tubic construction."

"Well, sure, one of those."

"Make fun. But in a battle between a bobcat and Big Alma, I'm not saying Big Alma would win, but it would be close."

"See, that's good, 'cause we're entering primo bobcat territory."

Kit looked at him. "Really?"

"He's kidding," said Lakie. A few steps later she looked at Lennon. "You're kidding, right?"

"Let's just say I wish *I* had a Big Alma."

"He's kidding," said Lakie.

Lennon winked at Kit in a covert way, which Kit found surprising. Given Lennon's tracking skills and overall demeanor, Kit had assumed he wasn't the joking type.

Maybe people could be more than one thing at once too.

qualities miraculous and mysterious

At sunset they found themselves in a place that might generously be called a town, but was basically a strip of houses, an old baseball field, and the ruins of a bank. They tried a few houses first, with the idea of sleeping indoors. But these were not the synthetic pastels of a touristy mountain town whose residents had lived elsewhere when the Flies hit. These residents had clearly hunkered down for the long haul. Whatever was left of them—a decent amount, given the smell—was still in there.

The bank was a heap of bricks and two walls, both of which looked like a good strong breeze might take them down at any moment.

Most of the baseball field was covered in patches of mud or large swaths of weeds and overgrown grass, but near the back, along the border of a chain-link fence, they found a more manageable area where they dropped their stuff and got to work making camp: Loretta took her rifle into the woods, and this time, Lakie joined her; Pringles and Lennon went off in search of twigs and leaves for kindling; Kit helped Monty sprinkle cinnamon around the site.

Kit understood cinnamon the way he understood sex: he had been told by those he trusted that it worked a certain way, and so he believed it; its qualities, while supposedly miraculously effective, were a complete mystery; its implications were terrifying.

"You think this stuff actually does anything?" he asked, imagining that giant flailing octopus-swarm, climbing down out of the mountains only to turn around at the smell of the *dreaded cinnamon.*

Monty shrugged. "It's not just us. Loretta—the other group, I mean—they use it too. Had it spread all over the front yard of that house."

For all the good it did.

"Maybe for the smaller swarms," said Monty, reading his mind.

Or maybe it's just a trick, thought Kit. A comforting hoax. *Yes, human, you are still in control of things.*

Maybe sex was a hoax too. Maybe the reason his Dakota had never talked about Kit's dad was because he didn't *have* a dad. He'd once read a book from the nonfiction shelves about certain hammerhead sharks whose female eggs could self-fertilize. Another one said whiptail lizards were an all-female species, and they seemed to be doing just fine, thank you.

Maybe science was in his corner! Maybe the reproduction of humankind didn't really *require* men, after all!

He needed to think about this.

Later, when they had a good fire going, they changed their socks and shirts, hung the damp ones to dry. Pringles removed the bandage from his elbow, and even though it hadn't been that long since he'd last changed the dressing, his skin was beginning to change colors. Blood and some kind of ooze was seeping from it.

Infection was a word Kit knew.

"Damn, Pringles." Loretta and Lakie had just returned with a large dead turkey. They hauled it to the fire, dropped it on the ground. "Does it hurt?"

He shrugged, began wrapping the elbow in new bandages. "Nice bird."

Loretta pulled her eyes from the blossoming rainbow that was Pringles's elbow to the turkey. "Lakie was asking if I'd show her how to breast it out. Lennon, loan her your knife?"

Kit watched in a cacophony of horror as Loretta and Lakie bent down, flipped the turkey on its back, and proceeded to slice into it. "Breasting it out is way easier than a true field dressing," said Loretta, guiding Lakie through the steps. "Cleaner, quicker. You don't have to mess with feathers or innards." Loretta said Jean and Zadie had kept rigid sanitary practices, and even had a camper designated for the dressing of carcasses. "You're doing great," said Loretta. "You sure this is your first— Whoa, maybe slow down around the—"

Just as she said this, the inside of the turkey spilled out all over the place, intestines, and a good spray of blood.

"*Shit*." Lakie stood, blood all over her pants from the knees down.

"Yeah." Lennon smiled, took the knife back from her. "Probably some of that on you too."

After Loretta finished the job, it took quite a long time (in Kit's stomach's opinion) for Pringles to roast the thing, but eventually, they all dug in, and Kit promised himself that once they reached the Isles of Shoals, he would reclaim his vegetarianism.

Later, as everyone began spreading out sleeping bags and bedrolls (giving the wild turkey entrails as wide a berth as possible), Kit had an idea. He walked over to Pringles, who was still nursing his elbow. "Where did you find the sticks for the fire?"

Pringles pointed toward a cluster of trees back behind home plate. "Don't wander too far, little man."

Beside them, Lennon stood from his bedroll. "I'll go with him."

Belittling was a great word inasmuch as it meant exactly what it sounded like; it was, however, a frustrating thing to feel.

"I understand that I am small," said Kit. "But I am *lightning* quick."

Lennon's smile changed; Kit couldn't tell if he liked it or not.

"I don't doubt that. But I helped Pringles earlier, and I saw some good sticks. Plus, I like to walk before bed."

"Okay." Kit pulled the stretched-out edges of his hat over his ears. "Let's go, then."

As they walked, Kit explained the sport of baseball, how humans used to smack a ball with a stick of wood, and then run around the diamond-shape from one rubber base to the next. "At the end of the match, whichever team circles the diamond-shape more frequently wins."

"You know a lot about baseball."

"I read about it in *Play Ball, Amelia Bedelia*. I used to have a very convenient library in my building."

"Your building?"

"William H. Taft Elementary School. By the way, why do you wear a broken watch?"

Lennon held up his wrist. "Not broken."

"Don't watches need batteries?"

"Most do. This one's a windup, though. See? I just have to wind it every night."

For the first time, Kit got a good look at the watch, at the two hands slowly rotating in front of . . . "Is that a city?" he asked.

"Boston skyline. My mom—not biological, but one of the women who raised me—"

"Jean or Zadie?"

Lennon looked impressed. "Lightning quick *and* a good listener. Jean. We were close. She gave it to me."

Something in his tone made Kit wonder if Lennon had a purple flower somewhere too.

They passed a cement structure with the word DUGOUT painted across the side, and through a gap in the fence until they reached the cluster of trees Pringles had pointed to. Kit paced, eyes scanning the ground for the perfect stick. He needed a pointy end. Thin enough to hold like a brush, but sturdy enough it wouldn't break in the snow and mud. "Cool name, too," he said.

"Hmm?"

"*Lennon*," said Kit. "I feel like I've heard it before."

"Ever heard of a band called the Beatles?" Lennon started singing a song about hiding love away, and then said, "John Lennon. One of the greatest songwriters who ever lived. Zadie used to play guitar, knew all the Beatles' stuff. Jean and Zadie had a few days with my birth parents in Pin Oak before the Flies hit. They even ate dinner together once. I know it's—sad and weird, probably. That the only things I know about my biological family, I learned from the memories of a single dinner."

"It is sad," Kit said. "But not weird."

Lennon smiled. "My parents were immigrants from Jordan. I guess doors had been closed to them based on who they were, where they'd come from. Not like a name was going to open all those doors, but they hoped it would help. My biological mom was obsessed with the Beatles. Jean said they could hear her carrying me around the campsite at night, quietly singing me to sleep . . ."

He picked up in the song where he'd left off, and Kit added it to the list of things that were two things at once: 100 percent heart-hugging; 100 percent heartbreaking.

"Sometimes," Lennon said. "I know it's silly, but—"

"You still hear her."

At night, alone in his sleeping bag, Kit would close his eyes and turn his head to one side, and he could swear he felt his Dakota's hand under his cheek, that silver key dangling from her necklace, brushing his forehead. He remembered his beginning, how he was born in the upstairs projection room of an old theater to a mother who had yet to pick a name. *And then I saw the box,* she whispered at night, *and I thought,* Yes, this child is mine.

"I still hear my mom too," Kit said.

Before Lennon could respond, the earth groaned.

A pulsing buzz in the distance, and Kit was full of fear and relief, both in full, both at once: fear that the Flies had come; relief that he could now stop wondering when they would.

gone

Lennon grabbed his hand. "This way."

They ran back the way they'd come, through the gap in the fence, only instead of heading for the outfield, Lennon pulled him to the right, and into the dugout. *If tonight's the night, I'll see you soon*, thought Kit, the buzzing louder, nearer, *though I have no one to plant my purple flower.* From inside, the dugout felt like an elongated closet, equal to the area behind the concession counter at the Paradise Twin, *and behind that, the room where I watched your soul pass from this life to the next, save a place for me, please and thanks, as close to you as possible, please and thanks*, and to their right, a long bench lined the back wall of the dugout; to their left, between them and the field, cement blocks to the waist, chain link above that.

Lennon crouched, pulled Kit down so they were both hidden from view. "Okay, okay," said Lennon, looking around, and even though they were right up next to each other, Kit could barely hear him, the buzzing was so loud now. "There." Lennon pointed to the space under the bench, said something else Kit couldn't hear, and in the air around them, Kit thought he could see the molecules of sound, vibrating, dancing this way and that. Lennon pushed him under the bench, his mouth took the shape of words, "Now, quick, get under," *and what will it be like, I wonder, to live as a breeze forever, traveling time and space? Whatever it's like, it will be better, because we'll be together*, and Kit got on his hands and knees, shuffled under the bench until he was as tucked away as a human could be.

Keeping low, Lennon peered out over the top of the cement blocks.

Seconds passed unaccounted for, as if time had stopped dead or sped up, *is there time where you are? I'll know soon enough.*

Kit could only raise his head by inches before hitting the underside of the bench, his vantage narrow and restricted, and it seemed fitting, but so unfair, that his view of the world would be as limited in death as it was in life.

From here, neck craned, Kit saw: a dirty, snowy cement floor; the boots of a boy whose mother had loved the Beatles and only wanted good things for her son; the boy himself, the side of his face, eyes wide with a fear lit by the moon; and then, slowly, the fear blurred, its source came into focus, the sky and the moon and the wave, the flailing tentacles . . .

Kit closed his eyes.

In that nothingness, he saw his projection room, *your footsteps coming up the stairs, you bring the story of my beginning—now let me tell you the story of how it ends,* and he saw her face coming in the room, her necklace, her eyes so full of soil and mountains and a past he would never know, *now tuck me in cocoon-style, just the way I like . . .*

That face.

In a world so impossibly big.

Places he would never see, tiny islands in a vast ocean.

Like Texas.

Jazz clubs.

She smiled at him.

And shook her head.

Not yet.

Kit opened his eyes and saw Lennon's lips moving, but couldn't hear the words, and then his eyes refocused on the sky behind him, and at first he didn't register what he was seeing. Slowly, he came out from under the bench, crawled over to Lennon, and as he got closer, under the great buzzing drone, he could hear Lennon's voice now: "Oh my God, oh my God," over and over again, and together, they stared up into the night, "Oh my God," watched the enormous swarm fly higher and higher, "Oh my God," and framed in the light of the shimmery moon, grasped at the end of a flailing, soaring Fly-tentacle: the outline of a human. Below that, in another tentacle, something else—another human maybe, hard to say. "Oh my God," said Lennon, and they kept their eyes on the sky until the swarm was gone, and they wondered which of their friends were gone with it.

his anchor too

Not Lakie or Monty, not Lakie or Monty . . .

Kit and Lennon ran toward the campsite in the outfield, the cold anticipation of *who's left?* All Kit could see was that human shape in the sky, the swarm surrounding it, enveloping it—

Not Lakie or Monty, not Lakie or Monty . . .

As they neared the campsite, there was a moment of horror when it looked like *no one* was there, like he and Lennon were the only ones from the group to survive. The swarm had been large, teeming; for most of the attack, he'd been stuck under a bench in the back of a dugout, he could have missed other human shapes in the sky . . .

But then Loretta emerged from the woods on the other side of the fence, and Monty with her, their faces with the same sobering shock, a look that required more than one word, or that a new word be invented.

They hopped the fence and Loretta attacked Lennon in a wide-eyed hug. "*Holy shit*, Len."

Monty ran to Kit, dropped to his knees, and Kit could not remember the last time they'd hugged like this: tight, vulnerable, real. Like they were brothers.

"Was Lakie in the woods too?" Kit asked.

Monty pulled out of the hug; his face was the only answer Kit needed.

"We saw them take Pringles," said Loretta. "He tried to run, but . . ."

The four of them stood there, looking around the campsite. It was in complete disarray: sleeping bags and filter bottles, backpacks ripped open, charred wood from the fire scattered all over the place. Near where the fire had been—where there were now only glowing embers—Monty bent down, picked up Lakie's rifle.

"We don't know they got her," said Loretta. "She may have survived."

"There were two shapes," said Kit, thinking how heavily he'd relied on Lakie to be his anchor—to the Paradise Twin, to his mother, to whatever fragile future lay ahead. "In the sky, there were two shapes."

"We don't know it was her," said Lennon. "I mean, look at

this place. Half our shit's gone, it could have been anything."

"It was her," said Monty, turning Lakie's rifle in his hands. "She never would have left this behind."

Neither Lennon nor Kit asked what Monty and Loretta had been doing in the woods to begin with. It was obvious enough. And the truth was, whatever their motivations, being out there had most likely saved their lives.

They tried cleaning things up, but their hearts weren't in it. Eventually Loretta picked up her sleeping bag, her backpack, and walked off toward the infield. One by one, they each did the same, carrying their stuff to the dugout, a silent understanding that tonight, if they slept at all, it wouldn't be under the open sky.

Later, from a cold, quiet dugout, Kit cried silently. And he felt the field turn to a vast, empty sea, the weight of his Dakota's key against his chest, a reminder of her absence. With Lakie gone, his anchors had been lifted; he was a ship floating aimlessly into the horizon.

"It's my fault." Buried in the sleeping bag beside him, Monty's voice was barely audible. The words came again between sobs, "It's my fault," and Kit knew: she'd been Monty's anchor too.

missing things

Next morning—after much stalling and yelling their lungs out in the woods beyond the outfield fence and gathering and repacking what provisions the Flies hadn't shredded or tainted—Loretta and

Lennon, Monty and Kit walked out of town, and even though their numbers were fewer, their bags less full, each felt heavier than they had walking in.

"I never found it," said Monty.

Kit had been admiring his new stick. He'd gone back to the cluster of trees this morning, determined not to let the Flies take this away too. It was pointy, but not too pointy. Sturdy enough to use for walking *and* drawing in the mud and snow.

"Never found what?" asked Loretta.

"Big Alma." Then, quietly: "She loved that sleeping bag."

There was a lot Kit wanted to tell Monty, things he knew from personal experience: that while it certainly wasn't Monty's fault, the feeling that it *was* would never go away; that when you lost someone, the best thing you could do was plant a purple flower; that looking for signs where none existed—say, in the absence of a sleeping bag—would drive you crazy.

But Kit didn't say any of this. Monty's eyes were already shells anyway.

On the outskirts of town, they walked across a bridge that was also a road. Kit didn't bother looking over the edge.

THE DELIVERER

There are days when I wonder what happened to ambition. It was valued, at one point or another. Maybe not by the world, but by me.

Before the Red Books, before the House by the Solar Cliffs, my life was confined and my mind free; I understood less, but wanted more, and so maybe a prerequisite for ambition is ignorance.

A sad prospect.

And yet sad logic still holds.

According to the Red Books, some of my Lives have been more ambitious than others:

My 7th, for example. Immediately after discovering the house, I went out, rounded up those I loved, and brought them here. I tried this again in my 23rd Life, and once more in my 100th (the spirit of the centennial celebration being too much to pass up, apparently). In all three Lives, I watched from different places—through the upstairs bedroom window; from the garden out back, running to stop them; once, even, from the bottom of the cliff—as they jumped to their deaths. The entries that followed these occurrences were, in all three Lives, a bizarre and only partially recorded account of motherhood.

It was very, very fucked-up.

By my 9th Life, I was ready to take on the world. Literally. The cycles began four months prior to the arrival of the Flies, and so I'd decided it was on me to stop them from ever coming. Recalling vague memories, and going off vaguer information, I attempted to locate and travel to the Flu-flies' country of origin. The idea being, I suppose, if I could somehow contain or eliminate the first Fly, voilà, apocalypse avoided. Alas, traveling from one point to the other, apparently, required all sorts of paperwork and documentation, of which I had none. Nor did I have the time to acquire or forge such documents. It was an enormous waste of time.

I never made it out of New Hampshire.

My 10th Life had been slightly more realistic, though not by much. It involved a few *strongly worded letters* to the Centers for Disease Control and Prevention, which, when left unanswered, compelled me to tackle the problem on a regional level. "Tackle the problem" here meaning "low-key harass a half dozen federal agents at the Department of Health and Human Services in Concord." With no phone, I tried making an appointment at the front desk, and when that didn't work, I camped out in the parking lot and waited for the employees to leave, and when no one listened, I waited until after dark and then climbed a drainpipe into their offices, setting off a silent alarm and getting myself arrested.

I was in the Merrimack County Jail when the Flies hit. Luckily, a nice guard named Warren released me once it was clear the world was ending.

There are a few other accounts in the Red Books, Lives where I've attempted to flex my omnipotent muscles. None of them work out.

And so, I have learned that it takes living in a circle to think in one. I have learned to trust my own handwriting. I have learned how to help people help themselves. And on those days when I wonder what happened to my ambition, I reread the accounts of my 9th and 10th Lives, my 7th and 23rd and 100th Lives, and I am content with my place around the foggy edges of fate.

The Law of Peripheral Adjustments, I call it.

It is my code.

NIC

Voids

The boy in the road had a large birthmark on his cheek in the shape of Alaska, with the tip of the state's tail ending at his chin. He wore no mask, metal or otherwise. Light brown skin, dark wavy hair, he was taller than Nico but not by much. He stood there, maybe twenty feet away, and they stared at each other, neither speaking nor moving.

The whitetail and Flies, the road, the Metal Masks, the station: it was, all of it, eclipsed by the simple act of standing in front of a person. Of seeing them and letting them see you.

"You don't want to be near here when that goes up," said the boy, pointing to the station and the swelling fire inside.

His voice broke the spell, and slowly, Nico pulled her knife from her coat pocket, opened it, held it in front of her. "Fuel went bad ages ago."

"It's still a building. In a field in the middle of the woods." He took a step closer; Nico raised her knife, and when he stopped, she felt surprising power at his lack of weaponry.

"Was this your place?" she asked.

"No."

There was a look her parents used to get when the swarms came. The three of them would hunker in the cellar, and while her parents' mouths could hide their fear, their eyes could not: it was the fear of experience, of having seen something and not wanting to see it again.

"You know what draws them," she said to the boy.

At first he said nothing, just the cellar-look in his eyes. And then: "No. But there were six in our group. And there are only four now. They took two. And I watched it happen."

An image: the hide of a whitetail hanging in a tree, emptied of life.

"Do you?" he asked, the cellar-look turned to feverish curiosity. "Do you know what draws them?"

They come like a thunderstorm, she wanted to say. *Gathering in far-off places and for reasons we will never know.*

"No," she said.

Beside her, a low growl rose in Harry's throat.

"Listen." The boy backed away, pointed to the station. "That fire will be visible for miles. I'm going now. You should too."

They nodded a strange goodbye, and the boy turned and ran. Nico watched him until he disappeared into the woods, and at her feet, Harry's growls turned to whines. Behind them the flames were fed, growing brighter and hotter, and now, in the absence of the boy with the Alaska-shaped birthmark, the truth of his words sank in.

She checked the compass. "Okay. Let's go."

They ran. Across the clearing, back into the woods, headed

east toward the Merrimack, away from fire, garbage, tomb. She half expected the ground to shake, half expected a deep *boom* to rumble at any moment, as if the very guts of the earth had ruptured, and maybe they had, maybe whatever sludge of underground fuel had survived evaporation and oxidation all these years was still capable of *boom*—or maybe, as the boy with the Alaska birthmark had pointed out, it was just a structure on fire in the middle of a field. Either way, they ran, putting distance between themselves and the station. They ran because he'd said he was part of a group, and a group was more than a harmless whitetail. They ran hearing the old stories whispered in their ears, of bandits and ruthless villains, people turned animal by loss of money, purpose, loved ones. Some of those villains, Nico knew, were fluent in the language of tracking, understood the subjects and objects, how where a person went was punctuated by where they'd been. They ran because the station was Vesuvius, and while Nico had no problem screaming into the void, she would not suffer the same fate as the people of Pompeii.

Audiologies

"The Flies spread overnight," her father had told her many times. "But not the darkness. That was a process, a spiraling down."

Nico's father called the earth a balloon, and the darkness a slow leak. He spoke of overpopulated hospitals, riots in the streets.

He spoke of rusty pipes and leaky tanks and no one there to repair them. Whole cities going up in flames, craters where buildings once stood, ash-snow, mountainous piles of soot and metal, stone and bone. It wasn't the first virus the world had seen, but it was the most enduring—and the first whose carriers were somehow strengthened by the virus they carried. He told her about a global economy that hadn't collapsed so much as imploded, dead leaders replaced by the less qualified, dead replacements replacing them, and so on, and all those invisible cables (so impossible to imagine) bridging oceans and continents and history itself, cables that pulled together the widest corners of the world until everyone's pocket *was worldwide*—those cables were severed, history shattered, pockets gone dark.

"But again," her father would say, gazing out over the treetops. "Not overnight. *Things are fine*, people said. *The state of our Union is strong. Keep calm. You'll scare the children.* That's the thing about slow leaks, Nic. Some deny any leak at all."

There were those, like her parents, who understood the true price of blind consumption, of humankind's predilection to swallow and digest, to take a shit and declare it gold. "We were Listeners, from the beginning," her parents told her, and Nico would imagine what a world her world had been: a place of transportation, of people going where they wanted, living where they pleased, all under the grand illusion that geography was meaningless, that humans were untouchable, that the world was small.

"There was anger, in the early days," her mother said. "Finger-pointing and Band-Aid policies. But there was also a strange sense of community. The world was a sinking ship. Like it or not, we were going down together."

In time, roads became wild, the frontier all over again. Horses were a currency people killed for. Food, clean water, medicine, solar panels, things people needed to survive became the things that cost them their lives.

Things are fine, the leaders said.

Keep calm.

You'll scare the children.

"When you were a baby," her father said, "I kept one hand on your back as you slept. I called you 'my Voyager,' and stayed awake long into the night, listening, thinking of ways to survive."

"When you were a baby," her mother said, "I prayed over you as you slept. I called you 'my snowstorm girl,' and thanked God for our survival, listened closely for word of His will."

Here, in the Listening—somewhere between the science of her father and the faith of her mother—Nico ran, Harry beside her, the fires of Vesuvius at their backs. The woods were thick and unforgiving, the darkness multiplied, breeding one on top of the other until she could see almost nothing, and though details of her parents' stories changed each time they told them, the endings were always the same: "Will you be a Listener, Nic?"

She imagined her father standing on the attic deck now,

looking out across the wooded world, wondering where Nico was in all of it, and she could almost hear him say, "Eight days, Nic," could almost hear him ask, "Can you do it?"

"Yes," she said, running as fast as she could. "Yes."

Rituals

That night, they made camp at the base of a fallen tree trunk. As Nico shook a generous portion of cinnamon around the site, Harry trotted off into the woods, and at first she was concerned, called out for him, whistled. He came back, but only briefly before trotting off again. Something about the look in his eyes was trusting, and she suspected that his earlier squirrel hunt was no fluke, that his primordial instincts had kicked into high gear.

While he was gone, she rolled out her bedding, and briefly considered going without a fire. Everything was wet—there would be no shortage of smoke, announcing their location for miles.

They took two, the boy had said. *And I watched it happen . . .*

Still. An overnight with no fire in this cold was unthinkable. She would light a fire and hope for the best, or maybe pray to the trees, *Dear brothers and sisters, may the smoke of our fire be tapered, the tracks of our feet be hidden, amen.*

She built a little house of twigs, tucked the driest leaves she could find underneath, and crouched on hands and knees with her lighter. The wind and cold made it difficult; with all the wetness, the fire kept starting, then extinguishing. By the time she got it going, she'd used up almost a whole lighter's worth of butane. Plenty of lighters left, but still, it was a special kind of frustrating, wasting finite resources in the middle of infinite unknowns. Even after the kindling caught, it was a while before the larger twigs got in the game, and—as predicted—smoke.

Just as she was finished with the fire, Harry returned. "There you are." She dug the granola and jerky out of her bag. "Where'd you go, bud?"

He sniffed the rations in her outstretched hand, then turned away, uninterested. And her question as to his whereabouts was answered, her suspicions as to his primordial instincts confirmed: Harry was providing for himself now.

She shook her head like a proud mother, good-dogged him, and then settled into the sleeping bag with her own dinner. "Why did the lady sing lullabies to her purse?"

Already, he was tucked beside her, in a particular space she hadn't realized was cold until he'd warmed it up.

"Because she wanted a sleeping bag."

Later she would wake in the cold to prod the fire, but for now it was warm, and it was comfort, their consolidated pulse a winter cradlesong. Nico drew a third tally on her hand, and nearly fell asleep before recapping the pen.

PART FOUR

IN

THE

DARK

●RB

NIC

Fins

She woke to voices, and somehow had the presence of mind not to move.

"Should we let her sleep?" a girl whispered.

"Why wouldn't we?" A boy's voice.

Under the cover of her sleeping bag, Nico gripped her knife.

Be the Listener.

"What about the dog?"

Harry. The spot at her side was cold. He was gone.

"What *about* the dog?" asked the girl.

"Can we keep him?" This third voice sounded younger, like a kid.

"Kit. Be serious." Nico recognized this fourth voice as the kid with the Alaska birthmark.

"I like him," said the kid.

"We're not keeping the dog. Just leave him, let's go."

"Wait." The older boy's voice.

"What?"

"I think she's awake."

She tried to stay as still as possible, breathe in and out, up and down—but then Harry's warm breath was in her face, his tongue on her cheek, and it was no use. Slowly, pretending to wake, she kept her hand on the grip of the knife under the sleeping bag, sat up, and looked around.

"Good morning." The girl looked older than the others, with dark hair and bright blue eyes peeking out from under her bangs. "Smart, isn't he?" She bent down, pet behind Harry's ear. "I can always tell with dogs."

A younger kid with freckles and a dirty-looking knit cap joined her, the two of them lavishing her dog with praise, while between them, Harry lapped it up.

Real ferocious there, bud.

"What's his name?" asked the younger kid.

Nico didn't move. Gripped her knife under the bag.

"Harry," she said.

"Hiya, Harry. I'm your new friend, Loretta." She looked at Nico, and then went around the group. "This is Kit. Monty. And Lennon."

All four of them had some version of the cellar-look in their eyes.

The kid with the Alaska birthmark—Lennon—said, "This is the one I told you about. Lit up the gas station."

"Oh, you mean the reason we had to get up two hours early to circumnavigate the giant fire in the field?" Monty nodded toward Nico. "What's your name?"

She whistled for Harry, who trotted over, head down, all, *If I must.*

"Nico."

Monty pointed to Nico's sleeping bag. "Whatever you've got under there, you can let go. We're not going to hurt you."

Given the small ax in his hand, Nico remained on edge. But there was no use hiding anymore, and so she emerged from the sleeping bag, still holding the knife, unopened.

"You live around here?" asked Loretta.

"Not too far," lied Nico. "You guys?"

Lennon said he and Loretta had been headed to Boston when they ran into Monty and Kit. "We're all going the same way for a while, figured we'd join up. There's a river not far from here. One day, maybe two. Rett and I head south from there—"

Monty tossed the ax into a nearby tree.

"—Monty and Kit go east."

Visibly irritated, Monty pried the ax from the trunk. In the short amount of time they'd been standing here, Nico sensed some brewing irritation on his part, not even at her, necessarily, but something had him riled up. "What about you?" he asked.

Nico began rolling up her sleeping bag. "What about me?"

"For starters, why'd you set that place on fire?"

Because covering the blue-lipped family with a blanket wasn't enough. "I was keeping a promise."

Monty was about to toss the ax again when Loretta stepped closer, laced her hand into his. The effect was immediate: Monty's shoulders lowered, his eyes warmed, and Nico could almost see the frustration seep out of his pores. If they really were a day or two from the Merrimack River, from Monty going one way and Loretta going another, the catalyst behind his irritation was clear.

"Lennon says your tracks are headed east," said Loretta. "You can walk with us, if you want."

Quickly, Nico finished gathering her things, slipped on her backpack, then stood and faced Lennon. Was it her imagination, or did he look a little ashamed?

"You were tracking me?" she asked.

"Not on purpose."

"How do you accidentally track someone?"

"I'm good at seeing where other people have been. And you're not very good at hiding it."

Nico's face flushed, and she whistled for Harry again (who'd snuck his way back over to the little kid). "I appreciate the offer. But we're going to continue alone."

Loretta took a step closer, and while part of Nico tensed, the other part of her felt a vibrancy emanating from the girl, as if they'd just stepped into a patch of warm sunshine. "Do you know what I think when I look at you, Nico?"

"What."

"I think, *Here's someone like us.*"

"Like you?"

Loretta smiled. "The world's leftovers."

In the back of the group, the little kid drew circles in the snow with a stick, his face like a plant someone had forgotten to water. Loretta seemed nice, but something sickly hovered in the whites of her eyes; the accuracy of Monty's ax-tossing made Nico nervous; and while she didn't hate the idea of traveling with Lennon, her mission to Manchester had cultivated a necessary isolation, a loneliness she couldn't help but lean into. Like her mother's old nesting dolls, she was a shell containing many Nicos, retreating deeper and deeper inside, constantly finding newer, tinier, tucked-away Nicos.

"No offense," she said, pulling out her compass. "But I'd really rather travel alone. Best of luck getting to Boston, though. And the coast." She tucked the compass away, looked at Lennon: "Please don't accidentally track me anymore."

She said goodbye to the group, and turned east, a mix of relief and sadness at the discovery of this new, tiniest of Nicos. Ten steps in, however, when she realized Harry wasn't beside her, she turned to find him in the middle of the group, the little kid having abandoned his snow-art in favor of hugging Harry around the neck.

Nico whistled.

This time Harry stayed where he was, didn't even pretend to hear.

All around, the trees of the forest seemed to sink into the ground, the earth turned to water, endless ocean miles in every direction, and where there once was a group of kids, Nico saw only an orca. *Why not tie your line to my dorsal fin, let me pull you to your destination?*

She walked back to the group. "You said the river's a day from here?"

Lennon shrugged. "Two, tops."

"All right. Let's go."

Reasons

She'd read enough to know that love was supposedly infinite, that the more you gave, the more you received, but she could not imagine this was true. Far more logical to think of love as the contents of a jug of water: the more people around your table, the smaller the portions. Some glasses would end up fuller than others, that was just the way it went. Only so much love to go around.

Harry's glass overflowed.

Convictions

For much of the morning, they walked in silence.

Harry kept to her side, mostly, though occasionally trotted beside the little kid.

Monty and Loretta were always together, whispering, holding hands.

Lennon seemed to be the group's navigator, leading the way up front.

There was a palpable energy among them, and she thought again of Lennon's words yesterday: *There were six in our group. And there are only four now.* Something had happened, some shared loss that made Nico an inherent outsider. Whether from this or something else, so far, being part of a group was not at all what she'd imagined.

That said, she hadn't spent much time imagining it. Her mind had been elsewhere, either on navigation or rations or fire or water or Flies, and behind it all, a persistent nagging doubt played like a single note over and over again: *What if this whole trip is for nothing?* What if the lines in her father's head had dissolved so completely that he could not tell the stories of his past from the realities of his present?

A different fear, too great to dwell on, but which seemed to grow with each step: What if her father died before the eight days were up? What if her worries about his lucidity were, in fact, unfounded, and his story was true, and she, like Voyager, would arrive in Manchester to find the legendary Waters of Kairos—only to discover they could not be activated because Bellringer had died during the intervening journey?

The prospect was a poetic injustice beyond her reckoning.

As if sensing Nico's anxiety, Harry nudged her knee. "Hey, bud," she said, stopping, kneeling to pull a bit of jerky from her bag. She fed some to him, ate a piece herself, scratched behind his ears, and wondered where in the world she'd be without him. And whether from this small dose of gratitude, or the revelatory insight that often comes from looking into the eyes of an animal you love, Nico understood that the doubt she'd felt since entering these woods was a mere offshoot of her family's evergreen conflict:

The conviction of her mother, to find hope and truth in ancient stories.

The conviction of her father, to find hope and truth in that which could be tested and observed.

"Lost," she said to Harry, who eyed the bag of jerky like it was prey. She gave him another piece. "That's where I'd be without you."

Footnotes

After a quick communal lunch, Nico found herself walking near the back of the group when the little kid asked, "Do you think tomatoes are a fruit or a vegetable?"

She'd been in the middle of observing Monty and Loretta. It was both sweet and strange to see romantic affection between two people who weren't your own parents (or characters in a novel), and Nico was surprised to find she was a little jealous. Not that she wanted to hold hands with Monty or Loretta. But Lennon—whose eyes gave her the same queasy feeling she used to get back home on the attic deck, looking out over miles of unknowable woods and thinking, *I might like to explore that one day*—Lennon was nice to look at.

Not just his eyes. His hair, too. Waves on waves.

These were the things Nico was thinking when the little kid asked her opinion regarding tomatoes.

"Um. I don't know?" she said.

"Have you ever *had* a really good tomato?"

"I don't think so," she said. "Maybe?"

"You don't forget something like that."

"It's Kit, right?"

"Yes."

She liked Kit immediately. However young he was, he seemed far older. For one, the stick he'd been using to draw shapes in the snow, he now used as a walking stick, a trait that somehow seemed old-mannish. There was also a cadence to his voice, a tone that suggested a soul much older than its shell. (Further confirmed by his tenderness toward Harry.) Whether this was due to the shared trauma of the group, or simply being a small kid in a world so devoid of small kids, she couldn't say.

"I have," said Kit.

"You have what?"

"I've had a *really* good tomato."

They walked and talked near the back of the group, their conversation accompanied by crunching snow underfoot, the sun painting the forest thick in a late-morning wash. Kit told her more about the town he was from (a place he referred to simply as Town), about the movie theater he was born and raised in. Apropos of nothing, he said, "I know I'm small. But I'm *lightning* quick," and then mentioned someone called Dakota, but immediately clammed up and put a hand on Harry's head as they walked.

"I like your dog."

"I think he likes you too."

"Maybe you guys can come to the Isles of Shoals with us. They're well stocked and organized. They have solar power and one hundred and eleven residents. According to Carl Meier, they're probably the only real community left in the whole godforsaken world. I don't know if they have any dogs there, but I'm sure they'd let in a good old boy like Harry."

Something else in Kit's voice: the ability to make one melt on the spot.

"Who's Carl Meier?"

"He's the radio and communications specialist on the Isles of Shoals. It was his voice we heard on Monty's radio." Kit went on to explain how crystal radios didn't require batteries or electrical power, and how this was similar to Lennon's watch. "He just has to wind it every night. Also, his watch has the city of Boston on it. Behind the hands, I mean. I wish he could come to the Isles of Shoals too, but I guess Boston is Lennon's destiny. That's a word I know. It means *fate* but sounds more dramatic."

The inner workings of Kit's brain reminded Nico of a picture she'd once seen in a book of a unicyclist juggling bowling pins while spinning a plate on his nose. It looked exhausting, but also—you couldn't help smiling.

As Kit kept talking (his brain spinning and spinning), she found herself looking toward the front of the group again, her mind wandering to those unknowable places just begging for exploration. From her books, she knew most people had "a type." She wondered what Lennon's type was, and also, if her face was as filthy as it felt, and if Manchester was on the way to Boston, would it be *assumed* that they would travel south together, or would one of them have to ask the other? He seemed nice. She hoped he was nice. Otherwise, she'd completely misread the eyes.

"Did you know octopuses have nine brains?"

"Really?"

Kit reached for something under the collar of his shirt. "One brain to control the nervous system. And one brain for each tentacle."

An image: an octopus, bright reddish orange, floating in the deep part of the ocean where the water was black. This happened sometimes, she'd imagine a thing she'd never seen, something she had no business knowing, and yet there it was in her head like she was part of the world's collective conscience.

"Have you seen one?" he asked, his voice barely above a whisper.

"An octopus?"

"A swarm."

Images of the buzzing whitetail, and the darkness of the Farmhouse cellar, her father's off-key singing as her mother read psalms. "I've seen one," she said.

"So you know."

"Know what?"

Time passed, there was no way of knowing how much, and when Kit spoke, it sounded muffled, the footnote of a whisper—

Nico wasn't even sure it was for her. "How they're bigger than mountains. How they operate as one, like they have nine brains. One brain for the central nervous system. One for each tentacle."

The swarm that had descended on that whitetail had seemed, in the moment, of mythical proportions. Only now did it occur to Nico that it might actually have been on the smaller side of the spectrum.

Beside her, Kit reached out to pet her dog. "Good, Harry. That's a good old boy."

Reincarnations

The day passed, and behind them the sun began its descent. Nico turned to catch a glimpse of its slow death in the west, and she wondered if a sunset was inherently beautiful, or if its beauty was found in this: that it would soon come back to life.

Loops

Bright tongues lapped wildly, the campfire in full form.

Nico added a fourth tally to her hand. The first three had begun to fade, so she traced over them, trying not to be too disappointed they hadn't reached the Merrimack today. She imagined her father back at the Farmhouse, sitting alone in the library, adding a fourth tally to his own hand (hopefully). Something she had not considered until now: being alone in the Farmhouse. Say what you will of the woods, its dangers and depths and infinite unknowns, but the wild was a place you got geared up for. Much harder, getting geared up to be alone in your own house.

"What's that?"

In the sleeping bag beside hers, Lennon was propped up on one elbow, winding his watch. Kit was right, and not only about the winding: in the firelight, Nico made out a polished silver band, and on its face, a city skyline.

He pointed to her hand, where she'd just been tracing the hash marks.

"Oh," she said. "It's . . . a long story."

"Oh, never mind, then. I've got places to be."

Nico knew there was some allotted amount of time in which it was socially acceptable for one person to look at another, but as to the length of the allotment she had no idea.

Done winding, Lennon strapped his watch back on. "You want to hear my theory?"

Everyone had gone to bed, wedged as close to the fire as they could without getting singed. Someone was snoring; the flames danced, the sky was open, and while it was possible others might hear them, it seemed unlikely they would keep anyone up so long as they spoke quietly.

"Your theory on what?"

"Loops," he said.

"Loops."

"Ever heard the term *eternal recurrence*?"

"No," she said.

"Okay, so. You know how everyone thinks this is the end of the world?"

Nico had overheard conversations between her parents about the way things used to be, watched them pick up a Metallyte pouch and stare at it, heard them talk about their last refrigerator like it was a beloved childhood pet. She'd heard enough to understand that those who'd had a life prior to the Flu, and those who hadn't, stood on opposite ends of an infinite chasm. For Nico, there was no How Things Used to Be; there was only How Things Are.

"Not everyone thinks that," she said.

"Okay, well, some people think these are the end-times."

"Are you one of those people?"

Lennon had a way of smiling without smiling. "One of the adults who raised me—Jean—she used to have this old television. Ran it off a generator until fuel gave out. I was young. I have vague memories of watching the thing, but there were certain shows and movies she'd seen so many times, she could basically recite them word for word. Sci-fi was her favorite."

"I know sci-fi."

"Oh yeah?"

Even though she hadn't cracked the book open in years, Nico could picture its exact place on the shelf of the Farmhouse library. "I had a book about a princess in space. It had these swords that lit up, and this—anxious golden robot."

"C-3PO. That's Star Wars. Classic series, according to Jean."

The fire was warm, the fire was comfort, and as Lennon spoke, Nico imagined their campsite from above, how they were splayed around the flames in a circular pattern like a fiery mosaic, and she thought, *This. This is what I had in mind.*

New people, new voices, new worlds.

"There was some show I can't remember the name of," he said. "About a planet where humans create machines that think for themselves, and eventually realize they don't really *need* the humans who created them. So they wipe out most of the planet, all but like—fifty thousand people, and those survivors load up on a fleet of spaceships and go cruising around the universe looking for a new home. The robots give chase, obviously."

"Obviously."

"Long story short, eventually the humans find some other hospitable planet, and they're like, 'Welp, good enough,' and basically set up shop. New planet. Fresh start. Happy ending."

"I'm guessing not?"

His almost-smile developed into its fullest form. "They fast-forward hundreds of thousands of years and show how humans do to *this* planet the same thing they'd done to the one before it. Create technology, the tech advances, the tech destroys most of us, and what few survivors are left go off in search of some other hospitable planet to torch."

"Ruin the ending for me."

"I figure the odds of you finding a working generator connected to a working television connected to a working disc player that happens to have that particular sci-fi disc are roughly one in a googolplex."

"That's a bleak outlook."

"I'm looking out, and it is bleak."

Nico waved an arm toward the stars. "Agree to disagree."

As if she'd reminded him what a beautiful sky it was, he shifted onto his back, stared up.

"We didn't get robots," she said.

"Hmm?"

"We didn't get robots. Or machines. Just Flies."

Lennon pinched the cinnamon on the ground by his bag. "At some point it occurred to me that I didn't know anything other than what Jean and Zadie told me."

It wasn't that Nico hadn't considered to question how things went down; it was that she hadn't considered to question how her parents said things had gone down. But maybe she should have. Maybe their downward spirals had started long before their illnesses. And Nico found herself telling this person she barely knew things she'd only ever thought. "Growing up, my dad and I were really close. We still are, but it's—different. At some point, around thirteen or fourteen, I'd catch him looking at me like . . . he'd seen me somewhere and was just trying to place my face. I'd be reading. And I'd look up and find him staring at me with that look. Like I was a stranger in his house, someone he recognized from someplace else."

She stopped talking, and suddenly wished she could suck the words back up, swallow them down, let them age and die in the place they were born.

"'All of this has happened before,'" Lennon said. "'And all of this will happen again.'"

"A little dramatic, but okay."

He tapped his skyline wristwatch. "Jean gave this to me. Said I had to keep it wound, keep it clean. She said time was like a distant lover—you take care of it, even though you can't see it. I think about that when I think about eternal recurrence. Like how maybe we don't live on a timeline. Maybe it's a time-ring. And at some point in the rotation, everything, everywhere, eventually falls apart. Doesn't matter whether the adults lied to us or not, really. Robots, diseases, asteroids, floods, Flies—it may end in different ways, but that shit *ends*. And just as sure as it does? Reboot. Rainbow. Start over. One of the quotes from that sci-fi show, this thing Jean always said when she told the story—'All of this has happened before, and all of this will happen again.'"

Yes, looking at Lennon was great. But as it turned out, listening to him was the real party.

"I've never really felt lonely," she said. "Not like Loretta said this morning, anyway. Like . . . one of the world's leftovers. But I think that's because I had books. I just really love books. I love them for story and character, I love them for language. I love the groundbreak as much as the trope. Twists and turns are fine, but give me the meandering, rambling dialogue. It's all documentation, right? Of how things were? Blow shit up if you must, but two people talking, one person thinking—I want *that* book."

"You're a bookworm."

"You were warned. But it's not just that. It's—sometimes I think about the people who wrote books, and the artists and their paintings, or songwriters, these people all over the world who created. And now those people are gone. And that's sad. But their art lived. I think the reason I'm not lonely is because when I read, I get to live those lives too."

That art breathes life into the lungs of a dying world was not a new idea. But sometimes Nico wondered: *If stories had the metaphorical power to save, might they also have the literal power?*

"You've got secrets," said Lennon, nodding toward her hand. "You're keeping track of something. Days or miles or . . . something."

"People have secrets."

"Ask me anything."

"Why Boston?"

He lifted his wrist so Nico saw the watch face clearly. Over the top of the city skyline, in small cursive font: *Boston*. "Jean and Zadie were good to us. Best moms you could ask for. That campground was our home, but it wasn't supposed to be. Growing up, I heard all about Fenway Park, Freedom Trail blossoming in the spring, the HarborWalk . . ."

A look came over his face just then, as if his mouth had been commandeered by his brain; clearly, there was more to this Boston story.

"See?" She smiled. "Secrets."

His face relaxed; the fire cracked. Beside her, Harry's rhythmic breathing brought comfort as always.

"You think they knew?" he asked. "The artists and writers. You think they tried to make something that would outlive them?"

"My dad used to say that for as long as people have grown old and died, there have been people looking for a way out of old age and death. Eternal life, the fountain of youth. Heaven. Loops."

"You're saying art is attempted immortality."

"*Achieved* immortality." Nico raised both arms in a firmamental hug. "Proof we were here."

Lennon got up to tend to the fire. "Are."

"What?"

"You said *were*." Quietly, almost to himself: "We're still here."

THE
DELIVERER

There are three Red Books: edges frayed, bindings loose, corners bent; pages upon pages of ink immortal; some writings are ancient, some new, all in my own hand, the Red Books are a written account of my many Lives, past, present, and future. On the back cover of the third Book, a single word is etched in the leather: LIVES.

Below that, four columns of numbers, from 1 to 160.

The first 159 are crossed out.

With each passing Life, the Books grow fuller, my evolutionary advantage grows stronger, my knowledge of land and time deepens, but only if I continue to understand the benefits of peripheral adjustments, and only if I continue to listen to the Books.

Right now the Books are saying, *We're close. Can you feel it?*

I can.

Entries range from lifesaving techniques to gardening tips, including various routes through towns and mountains, places to hide, people to help or avoid—but they rarely promote leisurely activities. Until these last few days . . .

DATE: October 30, 2043

ACTION ITEMS:

—*Enjoy the stars*

DATE: October 31, 2043

ACTION ITEMS:

—*Enjoy the wine*

DATE: November 1, 2043

ACTION ITEMS:

—*Soak in your alone time*
—*Prepare for a guest*

Years ago, those first weeks alone in the house, I would sit by the glass wall and devour the contents of all three Books in a day or two. It was an odd sensation, reading the years away, and time became pliable and nebulous, and I saw many futures, a map of the multiverse laid out before me, 159 versions of myself: decisions I'd made, for better or worse, paths I'd taken, people I'd tried to help. And while some entries are more memorable than others, some— *prepare for a guest*—are impossible to forget.

I smile, look around the house, try to imagine him here with me. "Echo," I say.

My first word in days.

KIT

sixteen million brains

Maybe *we don't live on a timeline. Maybe it's a time-ring.* Kit's body was tired but his mind was wired. He'd been restless last night, missing the genesis bedtime story, feeling embarrassed about missing a bedtime story, then feeling ashamed about feeling embarrassed about missing one. He hadn't *tried* to overhear Lennon and Nico. Their conversation had simply presented itself to his ears.

Maybe we don't live on a timeline. Maybe it's a time-ring.

Something about it reminded him of *Spacedog & Computer*, which took his spiraling insomnia in new directions: *Did any of my paintings survive the fire? Is Town still burning? I wonder if I'll ever paint again . . .*

It had been a long night. And night was when he missed his Dakota most.

Plus, when he finally *had* fallen asleep, he'd had the dream again. The bright-as-sun room where he sat with another person, speaking only in thoughts, followed by the all-consuming swarm. And because he'd only ever told Lakie about these dreams, the mornings after were when he missed *her* most.

He was tired of missing the people he loved. Missing people that much was like falling into a deep hole. It was like watching a breeze turn to dust, and if he thought any more about it, he was going to cry, and so he lagged near the back of the group and tried to stop thinking altogether.

They were all a little sluggish this morning, Loretta especially. Her cough seemed to have progressed overnight. He knew from *A Beginner's Guide to Infectious Diseases* that it could be a symptom of mononucleosis or whooping cough or pneumonia. It was freezing out here. Constant walking, gulping breaths of cold, thin air. Maybe it was just a cold, nothing more. A few times he'd looked into Loretta's eyes to see if he could find it: the thing that took his Dakota.

He couldn't tell.

"Hey." Nico slowed down until Kit caught up. "You good?"

"Yes." He reached down to pet Harry and, not for the first time, thought, *This looks like Spacedog.* He felt exhausted all over again. "Just need some time to think."

"I get that."

Cut from the same cloth was a phrase Kit knew, which meant the essence of one person was a lot like the essence of another. He'd suspected as much yesterday, but now felt certain: he and Nico were cut from the same cloth.

Harry too.

In his most secret heart, he'd daydreamed of running off with the dog. They could live together in the mountains, maybe, just a couple of lavish breezes, nothing to see here. Nico could join if she wanted. Same cloth and all.

"Sorry we basically pressured you into joining us," he said.

"No one pressured me to do anything. I have a soft spot for Harry is all. Anyway, I'm glad it worked out like this."

"You are?"

"Sure. Otherwise, I wouldn't have met you."

There were six ways to make people like you. Kit knew this, having found Dale Carnegie's *How to Win Friends and Influence People* tucked in the bottom of a Taft librarian's desk drawer. In addition to the promising title, the book's cover boasted sixteen million copies sold. As Kit understood it, there was a direct correlation between the inherent value of a thing and the number of people who bought it. And so he'd gone into the book with high hopes. In the end, he did learn a lesson, though it had less to do with winning and influencing, and more to do with herd behavior, which was a fancy term for when millions of people buy a book because millions of people bought the book.

Now, however, was the perfect opportunity to put Dale Carnegie and those sixteen million brains to the test. He could only remember a few of the methods. But it was better than nothing.

Kit looked up at her, put on the biggest smile his face could handle, and said, "Thank you, Nico. That means a lot to me. I'm glad to have met you too, Nico. I think you are very important. And I would like to hear more about your interests." He made eye contact for as long as he could—so long that he ended up tripping over a rock, falling face-first into snow.

Nico helped him up, a big smile on her face. "Would you like to be friends, Kit?"

Kit grabbed his necklace, careful to keep his eyes on the ground as they walked, lest his feet betray him again. "Okay," he said, glad to know Dale Carnegie hadn't duped sixteen million brains. "I would like that."

Sixteen million and one, he thought.

oh, love's contagious warmth!

They spotted the cabin that afternoon. From their position, maybe a hundred feet away, crouched behind a thicket, it looked small. Hard to imagine more than a single room inside.

To the left of the cabin, a firepit. Behind that, an animal carcass—deer, from the looks of it—had been cleaned, gutted, skinned, and hung from a tree. Lennon pointed out the pulley system, which kept the meat out of critters' reach. "We had one like it in Pin Oak. Doesn't need to freeze to keep. Just cold enough to slow down the bacterial microbes. Someone clearly lives here. We shouldn't linger."

Loretta put a finger to her lips. "You guys hear that?"

Moving water.

"Over there." She pointed beyond the cabin. "Guess we made it to the river."

Only now, here, on the cusp of saying goodbye to Lennon and Loretta and Nico and Harry did Kit really consider what it would feel like to finish the journey to the Isles of Shoals alone with Monty. Just the two of them.

"We'll go around it," said Lennon, pointing south. "Pick up the river down—" He stopped midsentence, eyeing Monty, who had dropped his backpack on the ground and was tucking his ax under his coat, eyes on the cabin. "Monty?"

"I'm going to knock on the door."

"The hell you are," said Loretta, immediately slipping into a fit of coughing.

"Dude." Lennon put a hand on his shoulder. "Not a good idea. There might be a whole group of people in there."

Monty pulled Loretta close, kissed her on the forehead, and whatever annoyance Kit had felt toward them, he officially took back. They lit up when they were together, like two lamps from the olden days.

Another reason why the impending split concerned him. He'd seen plenty of unplugged lamps during scavenges, sad and dusty and broken.

"You're not well." Monty spoke to Loretta in gentle tones, as if the rest of them weren't there. "And now we have a chance to get you inside, out of the cold. I'm not passing that up."

It was late afternoon, but it felt like evening, the sky an early winter gray. And even though this cabin in the woods gave Kit the creeps, and even though he could hardly feel his toes or tongue, his heart, strangely, was warm.

Maybe love seeped out of their hearts, through the air, and into my own!

Probably that wasn't how love worked.

"I'll go with you." Nico took off her backpack.

"What?" said Lennon. "Why?"

She pointed to Monty, who looked as determined as ever. "He's clearly not getting talked out of this. If there are people inside, I'd rather make nice now than have them hunt me down later."

She's lying, thought Kit. He wasn't sure how he knew, but whatever Nico's real motivations were, she didn't want them to know.

"Fine." Lennon stood, started taking off his own backpack. "You stay here with them. I'll go."

"Oh, okay, sure," said Nico. "Helpless women and children that we are . . ."

The air, which moments ago had been alive with love, now felt electric with something else.

"That's not what I meant," said Lennon.

Nico pulled a knife from her backpack, relocated it to her coat pocket.

"I just meant . . ." Lennon ran a hand through his hair; it was the first time Kit had seen him unsure of himself. "I *could* go. Instead."

She tossed her backpack to Lennon, kept her eyes *right* on him as she tied her hair back in a ponytail.

"If you'd rather *not* go, I mean." If a face could shrug, Lennon's just did.

Done getting ready, Nico stood still for a moment, calmly looking at him. Even in the cold, Lennon looked likely to melt.

And so it was that Kit learned of the powerful efficiency of silence.

When Nico finally did talk, it wasn't to Lennon. She bent down, whispered something in Harry's ear. And then, to Monty: "You ready?"

As Monty and Nico stepped out of the thicket and slowly approached the cabin, Kit put an arm around Harry. He felt big things: love and silence and impending goodbyes. He pulled the dog closer, tried to keep his psyche from leaking all over the place, and just then Kit wished more than anything for art supplies.

"You're a good old boy, Harry," he whispered. "I'd paint you right for sure now."

NIC

Welcomes

The trees thinned as they neared the cabin, but also seemed to grow taller, and connected at the top like a canopy high over their heads.

"Is it just me, or does it feel like night came early?" said Monty.

It wasn't just him; the sun felt very far away.

On the front porch, in campy font, a sign read WELCOME TO CABIN LEIBOWITZ, and as they climbed the rickety stairs, all of Nico—every shell of her, down to the tiniest, most tucked-away Nico, was flooded with a strange sensation . . .

"Can you imagine living here?" Monty asked, only she didn't answer.

The thing was, she *could* imagine it. It was why she'd volunteered to go with Monty in the first place.

From the moment she'd laid eyes on this cabin with its canopy-trees and far-off sun, she felt she knew the land, felt she'd lived here for years. Somewhere behind the cabin, the Merrimack River roared, drowning out the noises of the forest and filling her mind's edges and in-betweens with its full-tilt southern rush. The water was a reminder. She'd been given a job, something to do, something important, only she couldn't remember what, because she was here at last—

"You okay?" asked Monty.

They were on the porch now, the front door a foot away.

She said, "Yes," hoping the word sounded truer in her mouth than it felt in her head.

"Thanks for coming with, by the way." Monty looked at her. "I know this is . . . kind of weird."

"Sure." Nico looked at the sign again—WELCOME TO CABIN LEIBOWITZ—and before the déjà vu had a chance to kick back in, she reached out, knocked lightly on the door.

They waited.

No answer.

"Maybe we circle around back?" said Nico. "See if there's a window, or something." Because in her mind, she *saw* a window, a stack of mattresses, a coffee table.

"Huffl*fuck*."

Monty looked at her. "What?"

"Nothing." She reached out again, only this time she knocked harder, and the door swung open by inches.

Windows

There were mattresses, though not in a stack. Along the left wall, three twin-size, with crumpled quilts. In the opposite corner, a woodstove, a counter with overhead cabinets, a coffee table in the middle of the room.

An old map of New Hampshire hung on the wall beside a mounted blueprint of some kind of satellite tower. There was also a gun rack with three rifles.

Beside the mattresses, a bedside table with a gas lantern, and a framed kid's drawing of three stick figures holding hands: an adult woman with comically huge glasses; two kids, one taller than the other; the smaller kid held a stuffed elephant.

Each figure was labeled with arrows: *Mommy*; *Me*; *Elefint*; *Echo*.

There was a window in the back wall, exactly as Nico had pictured it. It was boarded up, but through a thin slit, she saw that the back of the cabin looked out over a steep hill, and at the bottom of the hill, running and alive as if it had skipped winter altogether: the Merrimack River.

After confirming the place was empty, the rest of the group joined them inside . . . Lennon, peering through the boarded-up window . . . Loretta's slow boots across the dusty wooden floor, the way she muffled her cough with the back of her fist . . . Monty, quietly combing through supplies in a cabinet . . . *They feel it too. It's why they're all so quiet.*

On a visceral level, something wasn't right. Not the cabin itself, but their presence in it.

Time to go, she thought. Whatever this cabin was, whatever the reason for its familiarity, she'd reached the river now. Manchester was due south, daylight was dwindling, and she was about to start saying goodbye when Lennon turned from the window and grabbed a rifle off the rack.

"Hey, Kit," he said.

Kit was staring at the stick-figure drawing. "What."

"Stay inside, okay?"

Before anyone could ask where Lennon was going, he walked out the door.

KIT

Marrowless bones were a dime a dozen, which was a phrase Kit knew that meant "nothing special."

But *these*—

These were marrowless bones like he'd never seen. These were at least a dollar a dozen, probably more.

At the base of a tree, lying on the ground like no big deal, were the bones of a hand and a head. The hand bones were wrapped around a gun. The skull lay on its side, a shattered chin, and a strange flap at the top like an open hatch. A pair of large broken glasses were on the ground, and scattered all around were teeth.

"She exploded," said Kit.

Lennon, taking it all in: "I thought I told you to stay inside."

"You're not the boss of me."

The tree itself was covered in what looked like dried blood; a large chunk of bark had been destroyed.

Monty joined them, bent down for a closer look. "He shot himself?"

"She," said Kit.

"How do you know?" asked Monty.

Lennon pointed to the large pair of glasses on the ground.

"They match the drawing inside. This was the mom." His eyes moved up the tree, the dried blood, the stripped bark and wood where the bullet hit. "It went up through the head, looks like. And then—"

"Flies got what was left," said Monty.

Sometimes Kit would look at the veins in his own hands and think, *All these little rivers flowing through my body, keeping me alive. Thank you, little rivers. Thank you.*

Only this woman had decided she was done with her rivers.

Up by the firepit, Loretta and Nico called them over, and when they got there, Kit wished they'd never stopped at this stupid cabin. He wished they'd just split up and gone their own stupid ways.

Stuck in the ground was a little homemade cross. In front of the cross, under a blanket of snow: a small, child-size mound. Kit's eyes burned. He felt Nico's arm on his shoulders, but not even the arm of a new friend could wash away purple-flower thoughts, grave thoughts, and this one so small, *like me.*

Lennon bent down, pulled something out of the snow. It looked like a miniature shovel. "Would have taken a while. Ground this hard, shovel this small."

"It's not a shovel." Kit wiped his eyes, heard his Dakota's voice answer a question from long ago. *What's that called?* he'd asked on the Paradise Twin rooftop . . . "It's a garden trowel."

They stood silently around the tiny grave. Out here in the death of things, so many ways for a kid to lose his rivers.

"Plenty of supplies inside," said Monty. "Dried meats, coffee. Old candy, even." He waved at the grave, and the bones back under the tree. "Given what we've found, I think we're in the clear. Three mattresses, plenty of room for whoever wants to stay. We'll crank the woodstove, roast up some of that deer. Kit, you're okay with staying the night, right?"

Kit said yes, knowing Monty had already made up his mind.

"Rett." Lennon nodded to the cabin. "Can we talk in private?"

After Lennon and Loretta were inside, Monty shook Nico's hand. "Thanks again for storming the cabin with me. You gonna stay the night, or . . . ?"

Nico said no, she wanted to cover more ground before sunset, and with this, Kit felt the sun of his own heart complete its descent.

"Feel free to restock some stuff from the cabin before you leave," said Monty.

Nico said she would, and then bent down and whispered in Kit's ear: "I'll be right back. This isn't goodbye yet, okay?"

Given the diagrams he'd seen of the human heart, and its relatively cramped quarters, it was amazing the sheer abundance of feelings a person could experience at once: grateful for his rivers; sad for his purple-flower thoughts; happy to have new friends; sad all over again that they were leaving.

"I miss her," said Monty, staring down at the little kid's grave.

Nico had gone inside. It was just the two of them now.

Kit opened his mouth to say, *Me too*, when it occurred to him, he wasn't sure who Monty was talking about. He had assumed Lakie, but it might just as easily have been Dakota or Monty's own mother. Or maybe he was thinking about tomorrow. Saying goodbye to Loretta.

There were simply too many *hers* to miss.

And so he said nothing, and they stood like that, looking at the little cross in the ground. He thought back to the stick-figure drawing, and wondered if *Elefint* was down there with the kid. He hoped so. Such terrible, unending darkness.

"I'm sorry," said Kit, still staring at the grave, only now realizing who he was apologizing to. He turned, looked up at Monty. "I'm really sorry."

Monty's eyes, no longer shells, were soft and full of sad light, and Kit found that he'd never meant anything more than this: "It was my fault. She was exhausted because of me. Because I was such a handful."

"Kit."

"Your parents are dead because my mom fell asleep. And she fell asleep because of me."

"Kit."

"I'm really sorry."

"Kit—*go inside*. Get the others."

Only then did Kit notice that Monty wasn't looking at him anymore, but at something over his shoulder.

Slowly, Kit turned around.

"Hi," said the boy in the trees. "I'm Echo."

NICO

Ethologies

When Nico was old enough to read on her own, when she'd grown too gangly to climb into her father's lap for a story, she took to sitting on the couch across the library, and even though they no longer read the same book at the same time, they read in the same room together, which was better than not.

"What?" she'd asked once, looking up from her book. She was halfway through her third reread of His Dark Materials, while her father was well into *East of Eden*.

"Hmm?" he said.

"You said . . . something about a wolf."

"Oh. Sorry. Didn't mean to say it out loud."

"Are there wolves in that one?" she asked.

He closed the book, held the spot with his thumb, and she saw that spark that always came when he'd found just the right words to explain a big thought. "Daemons . . ." He pointed to the book in her hands. "Patronuses . . ." He pointed to the well-read collection of Harry Potter on the bookshelf. "It says a lot about a human character, which animal they get paired with. Take Voldemort, for example. The guy's a snake."

"Well, technically, one-eighth, if you—"

"I mean, he has the *qualities* of a snake. He sort of looks like one, talks like one, thinks like one. I find certain characters in other books have animal-like tendencies too. Maybe not explicit. But they're there."

Nico considered how many daemons and Patronuses in some way resembled their respective characters. And while she'd conducted a few real-world applications from the Harry Potter universe (her favorite being what she called "unforgivable cursing," in which she created new curse words using Hogwarts terminology), she'd never thought to assign a Patronus or a daemon to characters from *other* books.

"Anyway." Her father leaned back, reopened the book where his thumb had been. "One of the characters in this book is very much a wolf."

"How can you tell?"

"You see it in the eyes, usually."

"It's a book, though."

"What," her dad said, smiling at the page. "You don't see eyes in a book?"

Meetings

Echo sat outside, in the clearing in front of the cabin, calmly stroking the head of an orange cat. The cat was in his arms when he'd emerged from the woods, and he'd yet to part with it.

Harry's hackles were through the roof.

"He says he lives here," said Monty, who'd been standing in the open door of the cabin since Echo's arrival, watching the boy like a hawk.

Loretta crouched beside the woodstove, looking like complete shit. "How do we know he's telling the truth?"

"I mean—" At the bedside table, Kit picked up the framed stick-figure drawing, turned it around: the tall woman with glasses labeled *Mommy*; the short kid with a stuffed elephant labeled *Me* and *Elefint*; and beside him, a slightly taller kid, clearly labeled *Echo*.

"Doesn't mean that's him," said Loretta. "He could be pretending."

"Guys. Come on." Nico turned from the slat in the boarded-up window. She'd been staring at the Merrimack, wondering how many more hours of ground she might cover tonight. "That kid lives here. We're not holding his house hostage."

"I agree," said Lennon. At the gun rack, he checked and removed all ammunition from the rifles. "We can talk about potential arrangements. Tell him about Loretta's situation, see if he lets us stay the night. But we're not demanding anything." He looked around the room, each face in turn. "Right?"

Once they'd all agreed, Monty called Echo inside.

The kid looked feral—there was no other word for it. About Nico's age, he was long and gaunt, pale white skin, a tangled mess of brown hair, and the hidey-hole face of a ferret. Monty explained their situation, told him about Loretta needing a night indoors, and apologized for barging into Echo's home. "We didn't know anyone was living here. Obviously, we wouldn't have helped ourselves."

Echo stood in the middle of the room, staring down at the cat in his hands, and said nothing. The silence was made even more uncomfortable by the extra bodies: six humans and two animals made the place feel like a medium-size closet.

"I like your cat," said Kit.

"She's not mine," said Echo, his first words since entering the cabin. "St. John belongs to the woods. But she stops by sometimes. For treats." Gently, he set the cat on the floor, watched with vague interest as the animal crept around the cabin, introducing its fur to everyone's shins.

Harry's eyes followed the cat's every move.

As it approached Monty, he bent down, pet it on the head. "We certainly don't want to be any trouble. But like I said, we'd really appreciate you letting us stay the night."

Echo looked at him for the first time, and Nico saw a flicker of something in the kid's eyes, a liveliness she couldn't quite place. "I don't really have a choice, do I?" he said.

Monty looked immediately to Loretta, and Nico could sense his internal struggle: How far was he willing to go to protect her?

"Of course you do," said Monty. "It's your place."

"Right." Echo looked around the room. "But there are five of you." He pointed to the gun rack on the wall, where Lennon had carefully replaced each rifle as it was before he removed the bullets. "You took my ammunition, which means you don't trust me. You made me wait outside my own house while you decided what to do with me. But right. Okay. It's my place. My choice."

"Should we trust you?" asked Loretta.

"The only reason you should is that I say you should. But what good is the word of someone you don't trust?" Echo lifted a single finger, made little circles in the air. "And round and round it goes."

Nico felt a new Vesuvius bubbling: later tonight she would draw a fifth tally on her hand, and it made no sense that she would draw that tally here, when she could be far south of here by day's end. She'd been waiting for a window to leave, a time to say goodbye to Kit, to let him say goodbye to Harry—and yes, maybe a quick goodbye with Lennon. But Echo's bizarre arrival now made that window seem impossible.

It was time to go.

She cleared her throat, was about to say as much, when Monty, who'd been studying the framed blueprint on the wall, said, "Is this some kind of satellite? If it's a radio tower, I've never seen one like it."

"Oh, that," said Echo, and that liveliness in his eyes landed on Nico. "That's the Cormorant."

Mythologies II

"Bellringer would climb to the top of the lighthouse, strike the Bell, and its toll would fly over the sea like a cormorant and then dive into the water . . ." It was out-of-body, impossible, but it was happening. Nico followed Echo around the back of the cabin as he spoke, the lilt of his voice like a sleepy-eyed storyteller: "Sky-keeper's job, supposedly, was *most* important. Without her, the sun, moon, and stars would fall from the sky . . ."

He was butchering the story, clearly, though in light of what was coming into view, it hardly mattered.

As they descended the hill toward the banks of the Merrimack, around a row of bushes and trees, Nico saw the outline of a towering device mere feet from the river. Echo's voice turned slow, his distilled rendition of *Voyager in the Water* grew silent, as if someone had turned down the volume of the world, and only when he was done did Nico realize she must have been logging the differences in her mind: *no mention of a blowfish, no mention of an orca, Voyager is a boy, no faceless witch . . .*

"What is this?" she asked.

"I told you," said Echo. "It's the Cormorant."

The mechanism resembled a tall steel tree with no branches. Wide at the base, it emerged from the ground by the edge of the water, gradually narrowing as it rose some forty feet into the air. Two devices had been affixed at the top: one looked like a large open book, angled toward the sky, as if offering a story to the cosmos; just below this, a circular satellite pointed downward, toward the middle of the Merrimack River. While it wasn't visible from the cabin, Nico recognized the outline of the device from the framed blueprint inside.

"Isn't a cormorant a bird?" Lennon asked.

So deeply submerged in her own mind, Nico hadn't noticed until now that Lennon and Kit and Harry were here too, nor had she noticed the old train tracks they were standing on, overgrown with weeds, running parallel to the river as far as she could see.

"Yes. A bird that flies and dives. At home in the sky and in the water." Echo reached out, placed a palm on the base of the steel mechanism. "My family has lived here since I was a baby. Mom told us the story. She said the Cormorant received Bellringer's toll, and then amplified it into the water"—he pointed to the middle of the river—"where it traveled to Manchester. Supposedly, the Cormorant operated on its own, but we were here to protect and maintain it. She even climbed up there a few times, said it needed work. Called herself Skykeeper . . ."

Echo's arm fell, and he looked back at them. "It's all bullshit, of course."

A weight sank like a stone in Nico's stomach. "What do you mean?"

"There's no *bell*. Whatever this used to do, it had nothing to do with activating some magical fountain. It was just another electric thing. Carrying power for a bunch of stupid people who didn't deserve it. It was a story. A way Mom could make the world feel less shitty."

It was one thing, having internal doubts; quite another, hearing those doubts spoken aloud as fact. Doubts aside, Nico felt a sudden urgency standing in the shadow of this towering device, an energy rekindled by questions: He'd said his mom had told him the story—did that mean their parents had worked together in Manchester? Why hadn't her father told her about the Cormorant, and why was Echo so sure it was all bullshit?

"That was your family," Kit said quietly. He pointed to the top of the hill. "Under the tree. And the little grave. That was your mom and brother, wasn't it?"

Echo's answer was a strange, sad simplicity: "They were sick when I went hunting. Only, there was a storm. And a couple bad swarms, and I got lost. Three days, maybe four. When I found my way back, they were like that."

The sadness of Echo's story was reflected in Kit's eyes, its scope multiplied by the kid's sweet innocence.

Daytime is dwindling, thought Nico. *Harry and I could still cover some ground if we leave now, only . . .*

Unable to take her eyes off Kit, she thought of the look Monty had given Loretta earlier, that young, wide love. It was a look she'd seen in her parents, and it always made her both glad and sad: *Yes, love like this exists; no, you will never experience it.* And while she was certain that was true, she wondered if the qualities of love were reserved for romance only, or if she might borrow a few.

She smiled at Kit.

He smiled back.

KIT

*the unrealized aspirations of
Echo Leibowitz*

After the *E.T.* debacle, it had been an unspoken agreement in the Paradise Twin that the projector would ruin no more reels.

Even so, those reels had provided hours of entertainment. When held in front of candlelight, each frame was visible. Kit and Monty and Lakie used to take turns making up stories to match these images. Their favorites had been full of comedy or romance, images that conjured laughter; their least favorites were the war movies. Young men getting shot and carried off on stretchers. Young men smoking cigarettes in bunkers. People shooting people for reasons none of them could understand. Sometimes these people survived, but even when they did, they wound up with a look in their eyes that said, *I'm just waiting my turn.*

Echo's face had a grime that would have made his Dakota's head spin, and the way he spoke was like the words were a food he hadn't chewed properly, but more than any of this: there was a look in his eyes that seemed to say, *I'm just waiting my turn.*

The group ate dinner inside the cabin, woodstove going strong. There were the usual suspects: Nico's freeze-dried strawberry granola, more dried meats (of which there seemed an endless supply in the cabin cupboards), and the last jar of his Dakota's peaches.

Echo had lowered the deer carcass from the tree, roasted a large chunk over the firepit. As he did this, he'd explained how his mother had taught him to carry the carcass at least a mile down-river, dress and clean the animal there, before hauling it back here. "Don't bleed where you eat, she used to say."

Echo ate like an animal.

Like it was his first and last meal.

Kit was a little scared of Echo. But when he thought of the bones under the tree, and the little grave, mostly, Kit felt sad for him.

"What do you do when a swarm comes?" asked Monty. "It's one thing, walking through the woods with nowhere to hide. Can't imagine living every day like that."

Echo calmly walked to the pantry, opened the door, got down on his knees, and began pulling up planks in the floorboards. They crowded around, looked over his shoulder to find a hole in the ground. Lined with tarp, it was maybe four feet deep, and about as wide as Kit's beanbag chair in the Taft library.

"I always wanted to live in a big house." Staring into this hole, Echo's voice seemed to take on the qualities of his name. "A house with many rooms. I tried to convince Mom that we should move. She always said, 'We can't evade Flies. But we can evade people.'"

Kit tried to imagine Echo in this hole with his mom and

brother, cramped and scared, waiting out a swarm. And it occurred to him then that there might be more than one kind of grave.

sleeping arrangements

One thing that was good: there had been no mention of Nico and Harry leaving. Kit wasn't sure what to make of that, or how long it would last, but he wasn't going to ask questions.

When they were done with dinner, Nico took Harry outside to pee, while everyone started claiming spots around the cabin, spreading out sleeping pads and settling in. Monty set up a mattress for Loretta beside the woodstove. "Thanks again for letting us stay," he said. "Lifesaver, no joke."

Echo lay down on a mattress in the corner, St. John curled by his feet. "If you say so."

Eyes on the cat, Kit wondered, "Don't you get lonely out here?" and only when he heard the room's collective inhale, as everyone paused the unfurling of sleeping bags and bedrolls, did he realize he'd said it out loud.

"My mom used to keep a journal," said Echo. As he spoke, he stared at the ceiling. "Not a diary, nothing too personal. Just a daily log. Our lives here in the cabin. Maintaining the Cormorant. Dumb shit like that. I read it after she did what she did. The last entry was from weeks ago, just as she was starting to lose it. You know what it said?" Echo paused, though no one was about to venture a guess. "'We started as make-believe, but now we're very real.'"

The line sounded familiar, like it was close to something Kit had read before, only not quite right.

"I don't blame Mom for pretending the Cormorant was part of some grand adventure," said Echo. "It gave us purpose. I guess I miss that. But you stop feeling lonely once you realize the truth."

"Which is what?" asked Monty.

"We're all alone to begin with."

Slowly, quietly, the room began to breathe again, and everyone went back to preparing bedrolls.

Nico and Harry returned and, looping her arms through her backpack, she announced that she and Harry were going to sleep by the river.

"Really?" asked Lennon.

"Is that okay with you?"

"Of course. I just meant—there's room here. It's warmer. And safer."

Kit thought he saw her eyes flit to Echo. "Maybe," she said. "But Harry gets up in the night, he'd step all over you guys. If a swarm comes, we're close."

As Kit worked on his own backpack, loosening the cord around his bedroll, his eyes landed on the stick-figure drawing of *Mommy* and *Me* and *Elefint*, and in his head, he saw the woman with the huge eyeglasses leaning over one of the mattresses, telling bedtime stories to her kids while the little one snuggled Elefint, and just as Kit was thinking how little he wanted to sleep here—

"You can join us if you want," said Nico.

Please be talking to me, please be talking to me . . .

He looked up.

She was looking at him. "Unless you'd rather keep near the woodstove, which I totally unders—"

"No." Kit rerolled his bedding, tucked it under one arm, and stood. "I'll come with you. To sleep by the Cormorant. With you and Harry."

revelation, a bedtime story

It was cold by the river, but Kit didn't care. He sprinkled cinnamon, which he no longer believed in, but he didn't care about that either.

He'd been *invited*.

Dale Carnegie and those sixteen million brains were coming through in a big way. Maybe they weren't full of *s-h-i-t*, as he'd originally suspected.

He sprinkled the pointless cinnamon, and watched Nico, who was supposed to be gathering kindling and firewood, but had gotten distracted. From here, he saw her outline in the light of the moon: hood up, wrapped in that long black coat, standing on the train tracks by the river, staring up at the Cormorant. Whatever piece of Kit compulsively painted the same thing over and over again knew that he would follow her anywhere. It wasn't love. It wasn't even friendship, though he was glad to have her as a friend. It was the same feeling he'd had back in that synthetic town, before the wave of Flies had washed over everything, when he'd stood in the middle of a road and known beyond all doubt, *I've been here before.*

What was troubling—what stirred the very depths of his psyche—was that this feeling, when applied to Nico, felt like fate. As if she and his Dakota stood at opposite ends of the same path. And while Kit couldn't see the path, he knew very well where his Dakota stood: at his beginning, the start of all things.

He continued shaking the stupid cinnamon, trying not to think about the logical conclusion of his little path analogy.

NICO

Words

"**M** *eta*," said Kit. "That's a good one. You know it?"

On her hands and knees, Nico blew into the tiny flame, watched it become a slightly bigger flame. "Refresh my memory?"

"*Meta* is something that refers to itself, but also feels sort of like an inside joke. Also, there's *irony*, which is a word I always think I understand until I don't. Like how you think you know yourself until you don't, like when my Dakota puts mushrooms in the primavera, seeing as how they're Lakie's favorite, and I always think I won't like them, but then they're delicious."

Dakota. Nico had heard the name once, though the last time Kit mentioned it, he'd quickly changed the subject.

Lakie. This was a new one.

Nico continued working on the fire as Kit discussed his favorite words—*ancient, doohickey, cerulean, balsamic, midwifery*—and she smiled and listened and did not ask about Dakota and Lakie, knowing there had been six in this group, that only four had survived, and how important it was to keep those you loved alive, even if only in your head.

Language was the giveaway: he'd used their names in the present tense.

He kept talking, and she kept working on the fire, her mind wandering. It probably said a lot that she found a night outdoors, under threat of Fly and stranger, as potentially safer than an overnight in a cabin with Echo. The kid was next-level sad, there was no doubt. Clearly, the Cormorant had once been a point of pride for him and for his family (as the Bell was for Nico and hers), and while she didn't envy his sadness, she did envy the liveliness she'd noticed in his eyes and voice earlier tonight.

Because she knew now what that liveliness was: *certainty*.

Echo had no questions. His family was gone, and that was horrible, but it was done. Whatever faith he'd had in the Cormorant, and his mother's stories, was gone too, and while also horrible, it was also *done*. If there were many versions of Nico, based on various forks in the road ahead, Echo was one of those versions played out to the end. She certainly did not want to end up like him, but part of her did envy that finality.

Regardless, she couldn't leave yet. Too many questions needed answering, and for now too many ears were around to hear. In the morning, she would find a way to get Echo alone.

"Hi." She looked up to find Lennon standing there, bedroll, sleeping bag, and backpack in his arms. "Yes, hello. I am here to protect the women and children, seeing as how they're so helpless and frail and whatnot." He smiled, looked at his feet, then back up. "That was a joke."

"Hilarious." Nico smiled a little and couldn't help wondering about his motives for wanting to sleep out here with them. "Well, come on, then."

Once the fire was going, they settled into their sleeping bags and took turns telling stories. Harry padded over to Kit, and rolled onto his back to participate in this most ancient and sacred of rituals: kid rubs dog's belly; dog gives kid joy; all is right in the world.

To be a dog.

Lennon told a story about a planet where it's never night because there are six suns—until one day, the moon eclipses them all, and nighttime falls, and the civilization, driven mad by the darkness, burns itself to the ground.

Kit told a story about a kind alien with healing powers who, being abandoned on Earth, forms a close friendship with a lonely boy.

As *Voyager in the Water* had gone through quite the transformation these past few days—from childhood favorite to her mission's supposed blueprint to an absolute enigma—she told a few stories from the oral collection her father had always called *Tales from Faraway Frozen Places*. As they spoke, St. John the cat—apparently too curious about the newcomers to stay inside the cabin—joined their circle, strutting around the fire, tail up. Harry held his position, but with ears perked, a low-key growl, and while Nico had no experience with cats, she was reasonably certain St. John knew exactly what she was doing to her poor dog.

Up on the hill, the cabin was silent. Smoke from the woodstove rose into the air, dissolving into the cold sky.

"Hey, Kit," said Nico.

"Yes?"

"What's a cat's favorite color?"

Kit sat up on his elbows. "I don't know."

"Purrrrrple."

Only when it appeared—that pure, little kid smile—did Nico realize it was exactly what she'd been trying to uncover.

She went for it again. "Where do generals keep their armies?"

"Where?"

"In their sleevies."

The smile broke into full-on laughter, and when Lennon asked what a corn on the cob calls its dad, Kit was primed for takeoff. "What *does* corn call its dad?" he asked.

"*Pop*corn," said Lennon.

Ultimate, life-giving laughter.

The three of them went on like this, until eventually Kit fell asleep midsentence. And for the second night in a row, Nico found herself beside a fire with Lennon.

She pulled out her pen, added the fifth tally to her hand.

"I really am sorry," Lennon said. "About earlier. I wasn't trying to suggest you couldn't take care of yourself."

Nico opened her mouth to say it was fine, that she knew she could take care of herself, and when you know something as truth, it takes a lot more than a suggestion of untruth to make it false— but instead what came out was, "Who's Dakota?"

Lennon looked over at Kit, his little sleeping bag slowly rising and falling. "That was his mother. I never met her. She died before our groups combined."

"And Lakie?"

A beat, a shadow across his eyes. "Monty's sister."

"But you knew her?"

"Yeah. Not for very long."

" 'They took two. And I watched it happen.' "

"What?"

"That day I saw you," said Nico. "Outside the station. You said you were a group of six. But the Flies took two."

Quietly, Lennon told her a story that took place on a baseball field, and Nico remembered what Kit had said about swarms, how they operated like giant octopuses, and all around her she felt the weight of the wild woods: trees that took a hundred years or more to shape, a river whose birth shared the same breath as the formation of the skies and mountains, and in the spirit of that ancient gasp, Nico uttered the most human of phrases: "I'm so sorry."

The fire popped; Kit rustled, turned on his side, snored.

"He's just a kid," said Lennon. "I hate that he had to see something like that."

"We're all kids." Even as she said it, she knew it was one of those things that should be true, and maybe once was. But in a world consumed by Flies, kids were adults and adults were nowhere. How long you'd been alive only meant something when life itself wasn't a luxury.

"Jean used to say, 'The Age of the Fly is the Age of no ages.'"

"Geez, Jean."

Lennon laughed. "Yeah, she was a thinker."

"I like it, though. *The Age of the Fly.*"

Lennon smiled and Nico felt like someone had built a little fire in her face.

Later, the last one awake, she thought about what Lennon had said: *The Age of the Fly is the Age of no ages.* Listening to the nearby river, feeling her own presence among the mountains and trees, it was comforting to think that all these ancient things had been here long before the Flies. They'd been here before technology, before the countless Electronics, before basic inventions and wars and even further back, to drawings on cave walls and first fire, and before the birth of the first human, whatever that looked like. Surely these things would be here long after the Flies too.

Surely.

Voices

In a dream, Nico stood in Kairos Castle by the fountain of spinning water, and she asked what she'd come to ask: *How can I fight this darkness?* A voice, both close by and out of reach, answered in muted words, and Nico tried to pull herself from sleep, that panicky sense of a nearby stranger, but she slept on, and by morning had no memory of the voice, or the four words it spoke: "We've been here before."

PART FIVE

IN
THE
WORLD
CONSUMED

NICO

Nephologies

S he'd always had a strong affection for clouds. From the attic deck, they seemed exotic, free. So many kinds of clouds, so many names and behaviors, some drifting endlessly, never changing, some blanketing the earth as if the sky *were* a cloud. Some moved fast, emptying themselves before disappearing into thin air, and these were the ones Nico was most interested in, the ones that revealed the true foundation of her affection: that even the biggest, darkest cloud had once been small and bright.

Fogs

The following morning, Echo had disappeared into thin air.

No one saw him leave, or if they had, they weren't saying so. There was some attempt at a search. They spread out around the cabin, called his name, and while they didn't find him, their search did turn up two unexpected things: a real shovel and a fresh grave.

"Doesn't make any sense," said Lennon.

They stood in a circle around the small grave, only now, there was a *second* mound of snow and dirt beside it, with a *second* home-made cross. After checking under the bloodied-up tree, Lennon confirmed that the hollow skull (and bony, gun-clutching hand) of Mrs. Leibowitz had disappeared too. "Still a few of her teeth, though."

"So in the middle of the night, Echo decides, *Hey, perfect time to bury Mom.*" Monty held the shovel in his hands, as if asking it for answers. "And then he takes off?"

"Could he have gone hunting?" asked Lennon.

"Again," said Monty. "In the middle of the night?"

Loretta said all the rifles were present and accounted for, not to mention Lennon had confiscated the bullets. Nico watched her as she talked, thought she looked a little better in the light of day, more refreshed, some color in her cheeks. "He came out of the woods," said Nico, feeling completely deflated, frustrated, mad at herself for not asking him questions when she'd had the chance. "Maybe he just went back in."

It was early still, a gunky fog hovered over the river, coating everything in dream-haze. This morning, Nico had been the first to rise, shaking the frost from her sleeping bag, refilling her filter bottle in the Merrimack. She'd dipped her hands in the ice-cold water, allowed herself a moment to feel its chill run up her arms and neck, closed her eyes, and thought, *I'd murder for a bath.* And when she'd turned around, Harry was right beside her, his eyes full of things to say.

He had that look now, here, by this new grave.

Whatever happened last night, you saw it, didn't you, bud?

Harry's eyes were too busy tracking a nearby squirrel to answer.

KIT

oh, wood's forgotten glory!

Kit sat on the dirty floor of the dead woman's cabin.

He listened to the others talk, feeling positive they'd forgotten he was even there, and so, becoming fixated on a knot in the floorboard.

Dark and circular, spiraling into itself, this knot had been part of the cabin from day one, had witnessed the rise and fall of the Leibowitz family, the birth and death of the Elefint-lover, the madness of Echo, the sadness of Echo's mother. *I know it hurts!* the knot had tried to tell them all. *I know you are sick or sad or both, and you want to go sit by that tree and put a gun under your chin, but that gun will only shatter your teeth and give you a weird flap on the top of your head, and the Flies will make off with what's left, and then you'll have nothing, no rivers of life. You'll be like me, a pitiful little knot in the floorboard that no one even knows exists.*

Kit brushed his hand against the grainy wood. *I see you,* he thought. *I know you exist.*

NIC

Reminders

"I'm staying," said Loretta, holding St. John in her lap. "Last night was good for me, I can feel it. I just need another night, maybe two."

In perhaps the least surprising news ever, Monty said he was staying too.

The two of them sat together on the mattress, holding hands, and again, Nico found herself in some jealous-adjacent land where you did more than love, you *fell in* love, where you did more than sing songs about holding hands, you actually held hands. She was glad Monty and Loretta had managed to find this elusive legend of a country, but glancing at Lennon—and then quickly away, as he was looking at her too—Nico wished they would report back with a route and map and appropriate list of snacks for what was surely a long and perilous journey.

Speaking of which . . .

"I need to get going," she said. "You think Echo would mind if I took some food?"

Monty waved toward the cupboard, and as Nico filled her backpack with dried meats, Lennon made the case for going to

Boston now. "You look better, Rett. And who knows what we might find once we get there. A community. Maybe even some kind of . . . medicine for you."

He was out on a limb and they all knew it. Shelf lives and expiration dates might once have been mere suggestions, but when every date you saw was a solid fifteen years prior, suggestion became law.

"You go on, Len."

"What?"

"I'm telling you," said Loretta. "Go without me."

"I'll wait on you if you need more time, I just—"

She coughed, fist to mouth, and when she stopped, she simply looked at him.

Lennon searched her face. "You don't *want* to go."

"I loved them," she said. "But for me, it was about getting out of Pin Oak."

Lennon stood, walked to the boarded-up window, said nothing.

"You were dead set on Boston," she continued. "I figured, sure, Boston, let's do it."

As Loretta explained her plan to join Monty and Kit on their passage to the Isles of Shoals, Nico felt Kit's eyes on her and she considered the clarity she'd had last night by the river, how she might enact certain qualities of love. She wondered what it would look like, inviting them to join her on the road south. Manchester, the Waters of Kairos, the geological anomaly, if it even existed, there were so many unknowns, she couldn't possibly be responsible for them, Kit, especially, so young, but maybe Lennon, if he was headed south to Boston alone, why not . . .

"I'm going to Manchester," she said.

They all looked at her.

"It's a city south of here." She looked at Lennon, and her stomach felt like a diving cormorant. "I'm pretty sure Boston is on the way. If you—"

Before Nico could finish, they were interrupted by a deep, distant rumble, like the earth was an apple whose core was trying to burst free. It lasted seconds, and then, as suddenly as it began, it receded, as if the swarm were simply reminding them of its presence, that while humankind might go on with their little plans, the Flies were there, purring, crouching in the long shadows where the dusk of humans met the dawn of Flies.

KIT

fantastic hugging

"**Y**ou're not the boss of me."

This was one thing Kit knew for sure. Once his Dakota was gone, and once Lakie got carried off by Flies, and once Monty fell all the way in love with Loretta, he had ceased having a boss.

Nico was saying things like "It's not that I don't want you to come," and "I can't be responsible for you," and "It could be dangerous," and other things Kit wasn't really listening to. He was his own man now. Proud owner of a psyche fully unleashed.

Monty bent down so they were at eye level, and Kit could see that he was also going to try to talk him out of it. "Kit—"

"You're not the boss of me either."

His words were close and quiet, and Kit felt himself about to cry. He wanted Monty to see in his eyes that he meant what he was saying, that his decision to go south with Nico and Harry and Lennon had not been made willy-nilly, which was a phrase he had been meaning to use.

"You're serious," said Monty.

Kit nodded. And the tears he'd been trying to hold off started to come, and because he couldn't speak, he leaned in for a hug. He put everything he had into this hug, hoping Monty might feel his heart, his apology, and yes, how much he meant this.

He hadn't expected to feel all those things back.

"I'm sorry," Monty whispered in his ear. "I should have been there to protect her."

And even though he couldn't see Monty's face, he could feel the hurt buried deep inside this boy he loved but had never quite understood how to say so.

"It wasn't your fault," said Kit, knowing he meant Lakie, and also knowing . . . "If you'd been there, the Flies would have taken you, too."

His relationship with Monty had never been affectionate. Only now, too late, did Kit realize this error. He'd hugged his Dakota a billion times of course, and Lakie, too. It wasn't like he loved Monty any less. Was it because they were boys? Did boys have a harder time hugging other boys? If this was true, it was stupid. And he'd been missing out.

Monty was a *fantastic* hugger.

"I want you to know"—Monty paused, and Kit suddenly felt that he was not ready for this conversation—"I don't blame you. For my parents."

The hug tightened, and Kit thought of the characters in books, who, after hearing some bit of good news, felt a "weight lifted off their shoulders." Monty said it again, said Kit was just a little kid, it wasn't his fault, and Kit realized just how tired his shoulders had been.

"I love you."

"I love you too."

As it turned out, the best way to tell someone you loved them was in a hug.

what he knew, and how long he knew it

There had once been a human for everything. Cleaning trash. Fighting battles. Keeping grass short and buildings tall. Driving large groups of small humans to school. There were doctors, not just for each human, but for *each human part*. A doctor for feet, a doctor for eyes, a doctor for privates and brains and colons.

There was a lot about the olden days that made little sense to Kit. But maybe the most baffling was the human inclination to say, *Yes, I will do that.*

"There used to be people whose entire job was to walk on a rope without falling off." Kit balanced himself on the steel railing of the train track. He'd made it a little challenge. See how many steps he could take without touching the ground. "People who dressed as clowns. People who got shot out of cannons."

Nico sat with her back against the Cormorant, Harry beside her, the two of them watching Kit balance and fall, balance and fall. "I guess when you're not worried about basic survival, you have to find ways to entertain yourself," she said.

Kit hopped off the railing. "Those are called crossties." He pointed to the slats of wood running perpendicular between the two rails. "In England, I think they call them sleepers. People had to build those. And then other people built trains. And then someone drove the trains while a bunch of other people rode them. And if this wasn't a people train, then it was a food train, probably, and people had to load the food onto the train." He sighed and shook his head. "I wish I could ride a train someday."

Kit left it at that, thinking he'd probably done a lot of talking, and he didn't want to overstay his welcome with Nico, which was a phrase he knew for when a person annoyed the ever-loving bejesus out of you.

"Maybe it was a circus train," said Nico, putting to rest his fears for now.

"Maybe."

He joined her at the base of the Cormorant; warmth from the morning sun mixed with the chill of wind off the river. Up on the hill, Lennon was saying goodbye to Loretta. It seemed to be lasting a while. But Kit understood.

"She looks better," said Nico. "Loretta, I mean."

Kit thought so too, though he didn't want to jinx it. Even for a Knower of Things of his stature, these sicknesses made no sense. *Maybe it's me. Maybe I'm sick, only I don't know it, so I'm just passing it around.*

"You feel okay?" he asked.

"What?"

"You don't feel, like . . . sick?"

"I feel good," said Nico. "You?"

"I feel fine."

Harry drank from a section of the river that had somehow isolated itself. Like a little pond. A little pond river.

"You have a plan," he said. "Right?"

Nico put an arm around his shoulders. "I have a plan."

"And I'm part of it."

"I didn't really know until now," said Nico. "But yes, I think so."

Kit thought of last night, how he'd watched her here by the river, and how he'd realized then that he'd known her for a very long time. He and Nico were part of something. He didn't know what yet, but it felt like the pyramids in Egypt, which, according to the nonfiction shelf in the Taft Elementary library, had been built around five thousand years ago.

"I knew," Kit said quietly.

"Hmm?"

He looked at Nico. "I knew I was part of the plan."

"Yeah?"

"Yeah. I've known for a super-long time."

NICO

Assurances

"**B**efore we get too far, I need to know if Kit can come with you to Boston."

Fifty yards downriver, Kit and Harry played fetch. Lennon walked beside her, the cabin a mile or more behind. "What's in Manchester?" he asked.

"Right now. Before he can hear. I need an answer."

Lennon looked at her. "Of course he can."

"Promise it."

"I promise."

Beside her, the river seemed louder than it had last night, wild and lawless. The haze had cleared, the morning sun shone bright, and in the water's reflection, she saw cold trees and sky, and she wondered if the Merrimack was a siren calling her south, or a snake chasing her there. She was glad to have Lennon and Kit with her; but she was concerned, and not just about Kit's fate. Echo's version of the story still rang in her head, and in light of his disappearing act, her decision to wait until morning to ask questions now seemed grossly irresponsible.

Surely there were other scientists at Kairos, which made it

plausible for Echo to be one of those scientists' children. So what else had his mother told him? Whatever Echo knew, he seemed positive it was bullshit, but didn't the mere fact of the Cormorant's existence corroborate her father's story? For that matter, did she even *want* her father's story corroborated? So far, she'd been more preoccupied with the validity of his claims, but what of the claims themselves? Say she got to Manchester, found the Waters of Kairos spinning, what then?

In you go, my dear.

With no clue what was on the other side, did she have it in her?

Maybe that was why she'd put off asking Echo questions: A small and timid part of her had *hoped* he would prove her father wrong. That some fact had been passed to him, which could be passed to her, and which she could use as evidence to turn back, give up, and go home.

"Nico. What's in Manchester?"

"Nothing, Len."

He had Boston. Kit, too, if it came to it. Whatever her story's validity, it belonged to her. She would only share it with them if the need arose.

"I like that," he said. "In case you were wondering."

She turned to find Lennon looking at her with that almost-smile, and suddenly the possibilities of what, *exactly*, he liked seemed endless. A timely gust of wind blew his hair in a way that felt downright boastful— *Look what I get to do,* said the wind.

And Nico wondered if this slightly nauseating, overly exhilarating, entirely new feeling she had was what the characters in her books meant when they claimed their hearts had skipped a beat.

"You like what?" she asked.

The almost-smile flowered; he looked away. "When you call me *Len*."

KIT

hands & feet

Squad was a word Kit knew, which denoted a group of cool kids who talked in shorthand and mostly walked around towns causing nonviolent shenanigans.

Kit, Nico, Lennon, and Harry (an honest-to-goodness "squad") followed the Merrimack south. The river was an easy enough go, winding in some places, occasionally cutting through fields or smaller towns, but mostly keeping to the woods. There were riverside houses and buildings, and occasionally a wide bridge would cross the river to the east bank. They would walk underneath these bridges, and Kit would imagine how cars had once passed overhead.

One of the main roads from the olden days ran alongside the river, disappearing for long stretches and then reappearing around bends when they least expected it. They avoided the road where they could, hoping to remain unseen, keeping close to the water and the old train tracks (which continued their parallel route beside the river).

As they walked, they talked about histories and hopes. About their parents. About their lives before they'd met.

Nico said she'd been raised in a boarded-up farmhouse in the middle of the woods, which had a deck on the upstairs attic. When she was little, she said, she would sit up there and pretend her farmhouse in the middle of the woods was a lighthouse in the middle of the ocean. "I used to think Dad saved his best stories for the attic deck, but now I think maybe the deck brought those stories out of him."

Kit liked watching Nico talk, all these soft words blossoming in the air in front of her face, disappearing as new ones came. And when Lennon described their circle of campers in Pin Oak Forest, Kit watched his words blossom and disappear too, and he thought, *Maybe words are the origins of a breeze*, and he found he wanted to contribute.

"Before I was born, my Dakota practiced midwifery, which is a fancy word for helping pregnant women have babies, which means she was there at the genesis of hundreds of lives. She was my beginning, and she was a dancer and a runner before the world went dark, and I've seen pictures of her twirling a baton in high school, and she liked to move her hands when she talked. She used to live in a commune in the mountains. And since she helped so many other people have babies, she was scared to have one herself. But one night in the commune, an angel spoke to her in her dreams. The angel told her not to be afraid, and then, when she woke up, she had this key in her hand"—he pulled the necklace out from under his shirt and coat, showed them the silver key attached to it—"and then she got pregnant with me and saw a sign that she remembered from before the world went dark, and that sign reminded her of Town, and then she moved into an old cinema, which is where I was born, and where I lived my whole life, in the projection room upstairs. My Dakota spent most of her days in a garden, where she grew vegetables, and tomatoes were her favorite. And they were my favorite too, and I just really love her. Loved her. I miss her. And Lakie. I miss them both a lot."

Kit felt every ounce of the silence that followed. *I went overboard, they don't want to be friends anymore, I knew I would annoy the bejesus out of them.*

Nico reached out a hand. "Dakota sounds lovely."

He took her hand in his, and felt his Dakota's key around his neck, and it was like a perfect circle with no beginning or end.

"Nico?"

"Yes, Kit."

"Why do you draw marks on your hand?"

He'd noticed them before but hadn't wanted to pry. Now, holding that marked-up hand, seemed a good time to ask.

"See how there are five?" she said. "When there are eight, I have to be in Manchester."

"How come?"

Nico smiled but in a way that made Kit wish he hadn't asked. "My dad sent me to find something. And I need to be there on a certain day to find it."

"Can I help you look?"

"I was hoping you would."

"Is your mom dead?" he asked, immediately regretting it. "Sorry."

"It's okay. Yes, she died."

Somewhere a bird chirped, and he thought maybe it was a finch from the sound of it, and he said, "My mom died too," as he looked at his feet, such weird little feet, and he wished they were wings. "That's who I was talking about. She called me *her Kit* and I called her *my Dakota* because we belonged to each other." But his feet were just feet, sadly, not the flying kind, and so he tossed his thoughts into the air instead, watched them glide around, blossom into breezes, little *I-see-you*s floating this way and that, landing like a soft quilt on all the world's small forgotten things.

"It's okay if you don't want to answer," Nico said. "But do you mind if I ask how she died? Was it recent?"

He felt like climbing a tree, and just living there forever. "Yes, it was recent. I don't know how."

"Did she sweat a lot?" Lennon's voice, quietly, behind them. "Bad cough?"

"Yes," said Kit.

"Start getting confused, mumbling? Seeing things that weren't there?"

I see you, little knot, little Elefint.

I see you, beautiful purple flower.

"Yes," Kit said.

"It was the same with Jean and Zadie," said Lennon.

And suddenly Nico's blossoms weren't so pretty as she explained her father's theory that they all had Fly Flu, but that in some, for whatever reason, the virus was dormant. "It's called a latent virus, and a person can have it for years and not know it, until something reactivates it. Could be another sickness, wholly unrelated. Could be physiological changes. So maybe . . . age? I've seen a few other people but can't be sure any were adults."

"You've seen other people?" asked Lennon.

Nico said, "Before you guys," and her tone made it clear: whoever she'd seen, she didn't want to talk about it.

"Carl Meier sounded super old," said Kit. "The voice from Monty's radio. He's still alive."

"Was the recording date-stamped?" asked Nico. "That could have been years ago."

Kit thought about this for a second; he couldn't be sure, but he didn't think it was. "You said the Flu could be reactivated by another sickness?"

"That was one of Dad's theories."

In his mind, Kit could still see the cover of Humphries and Howard's *A Beginner's Guide to Infectious Diseases*. "Do you know how easy it is to get pneumonia out here? Tuberculosis, mononucleosis, whooping cough, Hodgkin's lymphoma, scurvy—"

"*Scurvy?*"

"Micronutrient deficiencies are a serious matter," said Kit. "Which, given how we eat, seems *not* impossible."

Beside him, Harry whined.

This was quickly becoming Kit's superpower: bringing every conversation within a ten-mile radius to a grinding halt.

Lennon threw a stick, and they watched Harry run after it.

"Dad could have been wrong," said Nico. "He even admitted it. It may not be reactivating at all. Might just as easily have found its way into our food and water, so now people are contracting it years later for the first time."

Lennon, who'd been quiet for the last few minutes, laughed under his breath.

"What?"

"Nothing, just—for some reason, I started thinking . . ."

"Yes?"

"Zadie kept this old calendar on the wall. I used to flip through it. Everything from friends' birthdays to dinner parties to oil change reminders. It was all so . . . mathematical. Mapped out, all the things she was going to do. And here, we're headed to two different cities, which, for all we know, are nothing more than holes in the ground. Swarms around every corner, eating meals out of bags, maybe we're carrying the virus that wiped out humanity, maybe not." He shook his head, the laughter long dead in his throat. "A *calendar*. Can you imagine?"

It was silent for a long time after that.

At least I'm not the only one who shuts down a conversation, thought Kit, whose hand had grown considerably sweaty in Nico's grip, but whose heart was too full to let go.

the art of language

The book was hard to forget for two reasons: first, the front had a photograph of a lion's head bursting through the cover, as if attempting to escape the pages inside; and second, it was called *Language Arts*, which, at the time, Kit found highly intriguing.

The book was totally boring, of course.

Kit could only assume that the brains inside the heads of those kids who'd lived in the olden days had been dulled by the luxuries of their soft lives, a time when growing old was expected, and one's heart didn't jump out of one's chest at the sight of small flying bugs.

Language Arts was a sham.

(And nary a lion to be found, though Kit liked to think this was because it had succeeded in its pursuit of emancipation. He wished that lion all the best.)

The book did, however, prod Kit into a Time of Intense Thought. He'd sit in that orange beanbag in the corner of the Taft library, let his mind go where it needed going. And he decided then that while *Language Arts* was a sham, the language *of* arts was not.

His paintings talked to him.

But only if he was listening.

Once, in a very different (far more interesting) book, he'd read about the importance of "finding your voice" as an artist.

"Voice" was, apparently, a highly desirable, exceedingly elusive commodity. If this book was to be believed, artists had climbed mountains, crossed oceans, plummeted mines, drank very old liquids made of corn and grapes until they'd forgotten not only their names and problems, but also how to breathe (in, out, repeat), all in hopes of finding their "voice."

But Kit thought maybe it was easier than all that. His paintings only spoke when he was listening, so maybe you just had to be super quiet. Maybe to *find* it, you just had to *hear* it.

Maybe that's why it was called *voice*.

NICO

Electrics

Late in the afternoon, they came to a place where a small arm of land split the water in two: while the river continued on one side, an inlet had formed on the other. They stuck to the mainland of the west bank, circling the inlet south through thick brush and high grass, before their way opened into a long, wide field. On their right, the high wooded mountains. On their left, a symmetrical row of tree-poles, stripped of bark and branches, connected by long wires running between them. Nico had seen these poles before, by the station, and a few places between the cabin and here. But these seemed newer, in better shape.

"Power lines," said Lennon. "These are pretty intact."

"We had some in Town," said Kit. "I've never seen them with cables like that."

Lennon said there was a time when they'd all had cables, when these wires had delivered electricity to every house, every building, everywhere. Light. Heat. Televisions and computers and ovens and refrigerators. Staring up at the power lines, Nico thought of the words of the nameless, faceless witch: *A darkness has chased away the sky. It has erased the Kingdom of Manchester, and all great*

Kingdoms of the world. In reality, the kingdoms of the old world had been great because they'd been electric. It felt strange, then—or not strange, but significant—to now walk near, around, underneath the instruments that had granted this greatness.

At the southern tip of the inlet, they were reunited with the river and the train tracks, and the new addition of power lines added a sense of communal direction, as if their path had been laid out before them by water, power, transport. And in a way, it had. People had built the tracks, power had surged south, and those untold beings who called the river home had blazed this trail long before Nico and Kit and Lennon got here.

And Nico found herself thinking, *Sometimes it's nice to feel small, to know you are far from the first.*

Beside her, Lennon tripped over a root. "Why won't you walk on the tracks?" she asked, only now noticing that he actively avoided them.

"The slats don't line up with my stride," he said, and Nico wondered if it was possible for a string of benign words to sound charged by nothing more than the mouth from which they came.

"Crossties," she said.

"Hmm?"

She looked at him, and it seemed he was smiling now, or maybe it was just her smile had extended its reach. Regardless, she felt giddy for no apparent reason, and suddenly found herself wanting to tackle him. Like, headfirst. Land right on top of him, just—bam. Like that. She pushed her hair back out of her eyes, which, had she ever done that before? Surely this was not a new move, though now that she thought of it, normally, her hair fell where it fell, and that was the fucking end of things, *what in the world?*

"They're called crossties," she said.

"Or sleepers!" yelled Kit, some twenty paces ahead. "If you're British!"

Harry barked.

"Crossties," said Lennon. "Okay then."

Overhead, the power lines led the way south, and Nico couldn't help wondering if maybe some of their electricity had hung around.

Hopes

Conversation ebbed and flowed with the water, and when the power lines veered east, away from the river, they each waved a fond farewell.

"Coke," said Lennon. "From a can."

"Really?" she asked.

"Yeah. I mean, it's probably gross by now, but still. Wanna see what all the fuss is about."

"You can have your Coke. Give me a real library. Unspoiled. Undamaged. A wordy heaven."

"*Nerdy* heaven, more like."

"Compliment registered and accepted."

They'd been playing this game for a while now. Things We'd Like to Find in Manchester. The list had grown considerably since they'd started an hour ago.

Kit said, "Paint. And paper, obviously."

"Wouldn't paint be spoiled by now?" asked Lennon.

"Oil-based paint is made of natural pigments," Kit said. "They only go bad if the solvent evaporates. If the containers are well sealed, they can last just about forever. Or decades, at least. Same basic thing."

"How do you know so much?" asked Nico.

"I read a lot."

"*I* read a lot. I don't remember things the way you do."

"My Dakota used to say I had"—Kit held up his non-walking-stick hand to gesture an air quote—" 'unusually extended eidetic memory.' "

"Eidetic memory," said Lennon. "Like photographic memory?"

"Sort of," said Kit. "Actually, no, not really. Photographic memory would be like, you see a painting hanging on that tree right there, and then three days from now, you remember every tiny thing about it. Eidetic memory is like, you see a painting hanging on that tree, and three minutes later, you can *still* see it. Like—physically. But it's more of a short-term thing."

"Only yours is"—Nico air-quoted as well—" 'unusually extended'?"

Kit shrugged. "I can see things long after they're gone."

As the sun descended, the river seemed to curl in on itself, and while the woods were still thick and present, they found themselves walking over more paved areas, and behind larger beige buildings, not dwellings, but old stores and businesses.

"Could be Concord," said Lennon, tapping a spot on the map where the river twisted to the east. "See?" He pointed to a bridge in the distance, then found a correlating bridge on the map.

"There's a boat." Kit pointed to a riverside house with a dock, and a little boat tied up.

No one said anything; the question didn't need asking.

"I mean—it would probably be quicker," said Nico. "But I have no experience with boats."

"Me either," said Lennon.

They stood in silence for what felt like a very long time; Nico had no idea what the others were thinking, but all she could imagine were three kids and a dog capsizing in the middle of the river.

"Sun's almost down," said Lennon, folding up the map. "We're not going much farther tonight anyway."

Nico turned from the river to face the backs of the buildings. "What are the chances one of these shops used to sell mattresses?"

They left the riverbank, walked around to the front side of the building. It was an L-shaped strip of old businesses and stores, a giant parking lot in the middle with more run-down cars and trucks and piles of bones than any of them had ever seen. Most of the stores were locked, a few had such a strong stench coming from within that they didn't need locking. If it weren't so cold, if they hadn't already gotten their hopes up for a night indoors, they would have turned around before they saw it: a store with a sign that read BAM! BOOKS, TOYS, TECH, MORE.

"Okay," said Nico.

They stood in the parking lot, wide-eyed, staring up at the sign.

Kit swallowed audibly. "Yeah."

A brief pause; Nico continued. "So, here's the thing."

"Right," said Lennon.

"I'm not going to get my hopes up, is what I'm saying."

"Yes," said Kit.

"I'm going to walk up there *assuming* the door is locked."

"That's good," said Lennon.

"Or that the books and toys and tech and more have been completely ransacked."

"Most likely," said Kit.

"Or that it smells like the rotting intestinal tract of a large river rat."

Harry barked.

"Okay," she said. "Well."

Out of words, heart well past her throat, now making its way into her own intestinal tract, Nico stepped toward this mythical store called BAM!

At the front door, she turned, gave a thumbs-up, and mouthed, *No smell.*

Still in the parking lot, Kit looked up at Lennon beside him. "Is she whispering?"

Lennon shrugged.

There was no protocol for hope of this magnitude.

Nico turned back to the door, reached out a hand, felt the cold metal against her fingers—and pulled.

KIT

oh, magical Books-A-Million!

Not since before his Dakota got sick had Kit felt such pure, reckless joy.

Rows and rows of it.

As it happened, BAM! was an acronym for "Books-A-Million," and while he never got around to counting, it sure felt like the store delivered on its promise.

Yes, it had been somewhat rifled through. But barely, as if the looters' hearts weren't really in it.

Unlike most shops, these windows were not broken, the space was warm enough. Outside, the moon was too low to offer much light, so they divvied up lighters, quickly checked for people-bits (none) and straggling strangers (none). Given these enviable qualities, and not having a lot of experience sleeping in one of the old buildings, they decided to barricade the doors.

They shifted four bookshelves of BARGAIN BUYS in place, and then turned to face this wild, untamed land called BAM!

Harry trotted up and down each aisle, nose to the ground.

In a matter of minutes, Nico had basically built herself *into* a book-fort in the corner, the walls comprising a sensible combination of hardback and paperback, classics and young adult novels.

As opposed to Nico's rabid hunger to consume as many books in as short amount of time as possible, Lennon approached the sci-fi section with cold calculation. He pulled a few books from the shelves, opened them with a timid, almost religious respect.

Unsure what was appropriate or expected given this radical turn of events, Kit had decided to wait and watch his friends first before jumping in. Apparently, the spectrum of appropriate and expected ranged from "starved wolf" to "zealous monk."

Okay then.

He knew what he was here for. And even though he'd never been in this store, per se, his feet seemed to know the way.

In the art section, he grabbed five boxes of colored pencils— three, he put in his bag; two for tonight; plenty more were here, if needed—and then found a sharpener and a sketch pad on the next shelf over. In the gift section, he found boxes of scented candles advertising an "authentic old book smell" (i.e., musky rain and dried paint and orange beanbag chairs).

He spread the candles around the middle of the open floor, well away from the aisles of books and toys and tech and more, and then rolled out his sleeping bag, climbed in, and opened his sketch pad.

"In the beginning, there was nothing," he whispered. "Then the world. Then people, but no art. Then people made art. Then people died. Now there is art, but no people. And that's how it went."

Even now, even here, when presented with a blank page, he stewed in the adrenaline of artistic possibility. He touched the pencil to paper—only this time, instead of drawing what he knew he would draw, the pencil stopped.

He pulled it back.

"That's how it went." Kit stared at the whiteness of the page, the possibility . . . "But only for a little while." He let the pencil fall again, let it create. "Years passed. The old died and the young grew. And some became artists." Whereas before, he had created different versions of the same thing, this was wholly new. He wasn't sure if he liked it. But he thought it was good, maybe. "And now there are people again. And art. There are people and art together, the way it's supposed to be."

At some point—there was no telling exactly when, as time seemed irrelevant in the land of BAM!—Nico and Lennon joined him in the center of the floor, rolled out their own sleeping bags, each having brought their stacks of favorites.

"Trying to figure out how many I can justify bringing with," said Nico, opening her bag.

"Same. I can bring this"—Lennon held up a brick of a book called *The Complete Stories: Volume 1*, by a man named Isaac Asimov, which Kit thought was perhaps the awesomest name he'd ever heard—"or the first three Harry Potter books," said Lennon.

"I mean, as far as rereads go, I have to think HP holds up better than—"

"I've never read Harry Potter."

Nico froze, slowly looked up. "Expelliarmus?"

"What?"

"Excuse me?"

"I've never read Harry Potter."

Nico looked to Kit. "A little help?"

Kit went back to his sketch pad. "I only got to *Q* in fiction."

"Muggle-fucking son of a Squib." Nico looked around the shop, as if the ghosts of booksellers past might come to her aid. "A slumber party—*in a bookstore*—and I'm stuck with a couple of HP virgins."

"Yeah, I'm going with Asimov." Lennon tossed the Harry Potter books aside.

"Wait—" Nico pointed to two books already in his bag. "What about those? You can replace those."

"Uh, no. Those are Ted Chiang's short stories. Those are what you call *non*-negotiables? Yeah. I bring them with me or I stay here forever."

"Respect. That's me, with these—" Nico held up two books: *The Secret History* by someone called Tartt, and *I Am the Messenger* by someone called Zusak.

Kit made a mental note: If he ever got a pet, he would name the animal Tartt-Asimov Zusak. His Dakota had always loved interesting names. She would most definitely approve.

"What about this?" asked Lennon, pulling a third book from Nico's bag.

"It's nothing."

"*Leaves of Grass*, huh?"

"What."

"Nothing, I just—didn't peg you as a poetry person."

"First off, I don't know what that means. And second, I reject any literary criticism from someone who hasn't called Hogwarts home."

"I mean—I get the *gist* of Hogwarts."

"The *gist*?"

"Yeah. Jean told me the story. You've got the kid wizard—"

"Oh my God."

"Whatshisname."

"He is literally the title."

"Harry, right. You've got Harry. And then he goes to the magic school with Gandalf—"

"Stop." Nico raised a hand, palm outward, took a deep breath. "Kit. My beloved friend, pray tell. What spoils will you be bringing with you?"

"Three boxes of colored pencils, already packed." Kit pointed to his bag. "And then I'll probably bring another one of these." He tapped his sketch pad.

It wasn't that Kit didn't like reading. He loved it, truly, and very often missed his library. But the books had always been intermission.

Art was the show.

Later, once everyone had packed what books and art supplies they could fit, they ate dried meats from Echo's cabin, a few servings of Nico's strawberry granola, and talked more about the notion of traveling by boat.

"In places where the river's widest, we'd be visible for miles," said Nico. "Nowhere to hide if the Flies come. And God knows who else is in these woods. I'd rather not announce our presence to the world."

"I agree," said Lennon. "We'd be sitting ducks out there."

"Plus, the water gets fast in places," said Kit. "And there are rocks. Big ones."

After they all agreed it was best to continue on foot, they settled into their sleeping bags. Harry nestled beside Nico as she pulled a pen out of her bag, added another tally to her hand. And Kit wondered what it would feel like if his Dakota had given him a mission before she died. Good, because he'd still have a connection to her. But not good, because what if he failed?

"Hey—" He propped himself up on one elbow, having just noticed something. "Why are you guys so far apart?"

Lennon said, "Who?" and Nico said, "What?" at exactly the same time.

"Yeah, see"—Kit pointed to Lennon, who was in his sleeping bag by the endcap labeled STRONG WOMEN—"you're there. And then Nico's, like"—he pointed to Nico, six aisles down by an endcap called BODY, MIND, SPIRIT—"*waaaaay* over there."

A solid four seconds of silence before Lennon said, "You got any more of those hilarious jokes, Nico?"

"I mean, there's all this *space* between you." Kit threw both arms wide open. "It's a little weird, is all I'm—"

Nico interrupted with a loud clearing of her throat. "So this alpaca walks into a fancy restaurant and asks if they serve potato chips."

Lennon chuckled. "Ha. Good one. Alpaca. Classic."

"It's not over, bud. So the alpaca asks if they serve potato chips, and the waiter is like, 'No, we don't have potato chips. Also, we don't serve alpacas, now get out.' So the alpaca leaves. Next day, the alpaca comes back to the same fancy restaurant. 'Hey, you guys serve potato chips?' The waiter is like, 'No, now *get out*.' Day after that, same thing. Alpaca is back, asking for potato chips. Waiter says, 'We don't have potato chips, we don't serve alpacas, and if you come back again, I'm going to staple that fluffy tail to the wall.' Alpaca leaves. Next day, he comes back to the same restaurant, only this time, he asks to borrow some staples. The waiter says they don't have any. The alpaca says, 'Awesome. Do you guys serve potato chips?' "

Laughing with your friends in the magical land of BAM! was Kit's new favorite thing.

faces in the tendrils

Later, long after their laughter had died and the soft flickering (old book) candlelight had taken Kit by the hand, ushered him to the edge of a deep, promising sleep—

"Nothing is as strong as the absence of itself," Lennon whispered.

Kit lifted his suddenly weighty head to inquire just how long it would be before Lennon stopped talking. It was one thing, laughing with your friends in a magical bookstore. Quite another, trying to decipher their late-night musings.

But when he looked across the room, he saw on Lennon's face the faraway kind of sad, and so said nothing.

"Jean used to say that," Lennon continued. "She had all sorts of wise little nuggets."

Kit was suddenly reminded of his own mother's nugget of wisdom. "When the majority of the world has been wiped out, you don't kill what's left." He turned over onto his back, stared up at the ceiling. "My Dakota used to say that. I eat meat all the time now."

Lennon, quietly: "We are completely different people than we're supposed to be. In a completely different world."

"Hey—" Nico was interrupted by her own massive yawn, which made Lennon yawn, which made Kit yawn. And by the time they'd all finished yawning, they slipped into a fit of giggles at the orchestra of yawns. Finally, when the yawns and giggles had come to an end, Nico completed the thought she'd started like an hour ago: "Did you guys know that Flies aren't really flies?"

"Sure," said Lennon. "I mean, no one really knows what they are."

They lay in the dark and listened to Nico explain how her father had told her that Russian scientists had used a virus to genetically modify the honeybee. "Only it went wrong—"

"You think?"

"The virus and bee mutated, and now . . . here we are. Yawning in an empty old bookstore, in the middle of a destroyed world."

Kit thought of the homemade sign in the Taft library, how it had theorized that the Flies were not a product of nature, but a failed experiment.

"If that's true," said Lennon, "it's next-level poetic justice."

"You mean that the world ended at the hands of human hubris?"

"You fuck with nature, it fucks you back."

O bedtime stories of old! How Kit missed those tender-hearted tuck-ins. Even so, his eyelids felt weighted, and just when he thought he could no longer keep them open . . .

"What did she mean?" asked Nico.

Lennon rustled, turned onto his side. "Hmm?"

" 'Nothing is as strong as the absence of itself.' What does that mean?"

The question hung in the air a few seconds, and then Lennon said, "I used to think it meant, like—the normal things people did that I'll never do. Drive a car. Go to college. Change a light bulb."

"And now?"

Her voice sounded as tired as Kit felt, and as he let himself plunge into the glorious free fall of sleep, he heard Lennon say, "You can't feel the absence of something that was never there to begin with," and Kit was vaguely aware of his friend's words spiraling up into the bookstore rafters, another tendril among a thousand *authentic old book* plumes, where together, words and smoke took the shape of the saddest boy Kit had ever met, someone who surely understood absence in a way he never would.

"I wonder what happened to Echo," said Kit, and then he fell asleep.

THE DELIVERER

I follow the Merrimack north, shovel over shoulder, as it is written in the Red Books.

As I walk, I imagine others out there like me, roaming hillsides and ruined cities, foraging for supplies, operating on the fringes, trying to put their little piece of the world back together again. Maybe they have biosuits too. Maybe the biosuits were a military thing, in which case, who knows how many there are? Maybe after the completion of the Books, I will explore and investigate these matters. And if I do find others like me, we could compare notes, laugh over shared experiences, and I'll look back on it all through rose-colored glasses. *Ah, the good old days*, we'll say, and we'll toast each other over raucous rounds of "Auld Lang Syne."

Shake the thought.

Life after the Red Books is a distant, fragile bird. Quiet, or you might scare it off.

I arrive at the appointed place, keep to the banks of the river, quiet now, behind thickets and bramble. There, in a clearing: the group sleeps soundly around a fire.

It is not uncommon to develop a sense of where I'm going before I get there. *Transport imprints*, I call them. Like harvested images from someone else's life. The sallow-green tint of the visor turns their campfire strange pinks and purples, only amplifying the effect. The image bleeds into my head, I feel it now, not someone else's story, but my own.

"We've been here before," I say softly.

One member rustles from sleep. I duck behind the brush, wait until all is quiet, and I cannot help myself from thinking how easy it would be for me to tell him.

He's right there. I could wake him up and tell him.

I could stop it from ever happening.

According to the Red Books, I have tried. Not once. Not twice. Four times.

In my 152nd Life, I came here with no shovel and a different agenda. Upon arriving, I crept over to where he slept, and I told him what would happen. Ensuing panic, according to the Red Books. I was shot and barely made it back to my house alive.

In my 153rd Life, I tried again, only when I got here, I had a completely different idea. Things went much better, though I wished I'd brought a shovel (which I recorded in the Books).

Apparently, Lives 154, 155, and 156 had decided to forgo the plan that worked for the plan that did not. All three attempted the same actions as my 152nd Life, and all three were remarkably unsuccessful.

Even so, it is tempting to try again.

Maybe this time would be different . . .

I close my eyes and see his face. And as much as I wish it weren't true, I know . . . there's nothing I can do.

For now, I follow the code. I stay put. And when all is quiet, I carry my shovel up the hill, not toward the cabin, but toward the appointed tree. It is an old tree, and it has witnessed many things, but none so tragic as the death of the woman who painted it red.

At the foot of the blood-tree, I collect what little of this woman is left, carry her to her small son's grave. And beside *that* grave, I dig a new one.

Under the snow, the earth is hard.

That's okay. This is not my first dig in hard earth.

The cat joins me first; the dog comes next, as it is written. They sniff my legs, I offer my hands, and when they seem satisfied that I am not here to hurt them, or anyone else, I pet their heads, feel them calm to my touch.

Under the gaze of animals, I go back to my digging.

When the hole is deep enough, I place the woman's remains in the bottom, begin the process of filling it in. Eternal rest is only as good as the company you keep; at least she will be buried beside her little boy.

When the job is done, I set the shovel on the ground. Under the blood-tree, I find two twigs, and pull a spool of thread from my pocket. When the cross is done, I stick it in the ground at the head of the new grave.

"Rest in peace."

I take a breath.

And when I look up, the other one is standing there as I knew he would be, watching my every move, light from the moon glinting in his sad-star eyes.

Echo is a mess, the product of accidental survival.

I raise a finger to my mouth. *Shh*.

He nods. *Okay*.

Only on the rarest of occasions have the Red Books instructed me to intercede fully on behalf of a person's fate (the weeks of gastric lavage practice and the incident in the Pin Oak forest being the most obvious). These brief interludes in the Law of Peripheral Adjustments provide an opportunity to flex a little, to use the full extent of my knowledge and skill. And while experience reminds me of the inevitable comedown afterward, it makes little difference in the moment: deep inside, a flame ignites; there is light in my Life.

I motion for Echo to follow.

He looks at the two little graves. Then he looks at me, and nods. *Okay*.

The cat is already gone, disappeared into the woods.

The dog follows us for a while, tail wagging as we walk the Merrimack south. I let this go for a half mile, then stop, take a knee. I pet the dog's head. "Time to go back now," I say, and the dog obeys.

Reality is a meticulously calibrated machine: a single turn of the dial in the wrong direction, and everything goes to shit. New turns are possible. I went 152 Lives before bringing Echo to the house, and so far, that turn seems to work out fine.

Some turns of the dial don't work so well.

Like the one currently asleep in the shadow of the Cormorant. That dial I've tried turning many times, and every time, a disaster.

Echo and I walk alone.

"Where are we going?" he asks.

"I'm giving you what you always wanted."

"And what's that?"

I consider how many memories I've lost and found, transport imprints from various Lives bleeding together, and already I feel the comedown, like I've fallen into a hole only to discover there is no bottom.

"A big house," I say.

KIT
things look different in the morning

Morning people, as Kit understood them, belonged to a breed
of humans who derived unending joy from the horrors of
emerging from one's bed.

Monty and Dakota were "morning people." Most mornings,
Lakie and Kit would stumble down the stairs of the Paradise Twin
to find their counterparts in the kitchenette, having finished breakfast, already discussing the day's plans. Inevitably, either Monty or
Dakota would make a snide comment about early worms or the day
being half over, et cetera and so forth.

The only thing "morning people" enjoyed more than morning
was telling everyone else about it. It was a badge of honor, apparently, to be a "morning person."

Kit wore no such badge.

As such, when he woke the following morning to find he was
the first one up, his initial thought was that something had gone
horribly wrong. This was immediately followed by relief that nothing had, which was then followed by four quick realizations:

One. For the first time since departing the Paradise Twin, he'd
slept through the night without his recurring dream. No bright-as-
sun room. No person on the other side of the table. No speaking in

thoughts. No buzzing-black fog rolling in like a storm. Nothing but deep, peaceful sleep.

Two. Harry was right beside him. Thinking back, Kit was sure the dog had fallen asleep beside Nico.

Three. The sunshine through the windows seemed quite a bit brighter than usual. Closer to an afternoon sun than a morning one.

And four. When Kit had fallen asleep, Nico and Lennon had been separated by six aisles of floor space. Now, still asleep in their respective sleeping bags, there was only a few feet between them. Each had a single arm outstretched toward the other, and in the middle, their hands met, fingers interlocked.

Beside him, Harry yawned, and looked at him like, *Can you believe this?*

Kit smiled, scratched behind the dog's ears. "It's all very healthy and normal, according to Emil Johansson, MD."

the language of art

By the time everyone was awake and packed, and breakfast had been had, the sun was much higher in the sky than they would have liked. Still, it seemed their evening in BAM! had bonded them to the point where *squad* was hardly the right word.

Family seemed more appropriate.

A quick perusal of the map correlated against the roads running through and around the BAM! parking lot confirmed what they'd suspected last night: they were in the city of Concord. And because the river took a few detours through the city, Lennon decided it would be more direct to simply follow the compass south and slightly east for a while, before picking back up with the Merrimack.

Concord, as a city, was beautiful; a unique mix of wildlife and civilization, as if the humans of old—or the Concordians of old, at least—had figured out how to grow and thrive without destroying the natural beauty around them.

Somewhere south of the city, they found an enormous movie theater tucked back in the woods. It was nothing at all like the Paradise Twin. Probably had a dozen screens or more.

"I once read a book about the early days of movies," said Kit. "It said one of the first films ever made was called *The Horse in Motion*, which was three seconds of nothing but a horse running. Another was called *Roundhay Garden Scene*, and it was two seconds of people walking around a garden. And there was a third one called *Arrival of a Train at La Ciotat*, which was literally fifty seconds of a train pulling into a station. This was back in the 1800s. But according to the book, the people who saw these movies were shocked and amazed. Unleashed psyches all over the place."

"Unleashed psyches," said Lennon.

"When that down-deep part of your soul feels free and easy."

Nico and Lennon smiled at each other. They thought he couldn't see them, but he could. Normally it annoyed the ever-loving bejesus out of him when people treated him like a little kid. But this particular smile seemed like something else, maybe.

"Anyway," he said. "The book made it seem like those people were silly for thinking how amazing it was to watch a train pull into a station, or a horse run for three seconds, or people walk in a garden. But I get it. If I saw a photograph *move*—"

"My psyche would unleash so fast," said Nico.

"Hard same," said Lennon. "A little magic is better than no magic at all."

Nico glared at him. "Says the boy who's never read Harry Potter."

"I mean, he has to get the ring to Mordor before Voldemort turns him to stone."

"Oh my God, enough with the talking."

Later, when Lennon and Harry had started a game of fetch, Kit dug around in his bag and pulled out the best of last night's sketches. He was never able to get the room quite right, but that was the way it went. His art never felt "good" or "done." It was always just . . . *enough*.

"Here," he said, handing the folded-up paper to Nico.

"What's this?"

"I drew something for you. Last night."

She started to open it.

"Not yet," he said.

"What?"

"Just—don't open it in front of me."

"Got it."

"It's probably not very good. But it's part of me. My beginning. Anyway. Maybe someday you'll find the perfect spot to hang it."

"I'm sure I will." Nico tucked it away. "Thank you, Kit."

Eventually they were reunited with the river and the old train tracks, as with old friends. And even though they tried to avoid roads (thereby avoiding the possibility of others), there were sections of the river that ran *right beside* the road, and still other sections where houses lined the water, and they found themselves walking through the high grasses of what had once been maintained yards.

"You guys hear that?" asked Nico.

They stopped and listened: a thrumming drone in the distance.

"A waterfall," said Lennon.

Farther south, the rushing sound intensified, and they saw the outline of a wooden structure built across the river like a bridge, but fenced off, clearly meant for some other purpose. Approaching it, a sign read DANGER: NO TRESPASSING, and a tall barbed-wire fence ran between them and the Merrimack.

And then the waterfall came into view.

Having never seen one in real life, Kit walked right up to the fence. "Look at that."

Behind him, silence. Turning, he found Lennon and Nico had continued walking, only to stop at a bend in the path some twenty paces ahead. At first, after catching up with them, he thought they were staring at the large brick warehouse by the riverbank. But as he rounded the corner, he saw what had stopped them in their tracks: adjacent to that warehouse, probably the size of *two* Paradise Twins stacked on top of each other, was a steel cage-like construction, with cables and antennae and power lines running in every direction.

"What is it?" he asked.

Lennon shook his head. "No idea."

"Garvin Falls Hydroelectric Station," said Nico.

They both looked at her.

"How in the world would you know that?" asked Lennon.

"Oh, I'm quite brilliant." She rolled her eyes, pointed to a sign posted nearby.

"So the water . . . made electricity?" Kit turned a slow, full 360 degrees, taking it all in. The power lines, the electrical station, the train tracks, the warehouse, the waterfall, the structure built like a bridge over the river.

"I won't pretend to understand how," said Lennon. "But yes."

A constant enigma, these humans of old. To build things like this. To invent things like a smartphone and a room with two machines, one for washing clothes, one for drying. To lay miles of train tracks so people and food could get from one place to the next.

He would never understand how humans could be so entirely smart and so entirely stupid at the same time.

Not 50 percent one and 50 percent the other.

They were 100 percent smart and stupid.

He turned back to the waterfall. *Existential* was a word he knew, which he found a bit confusing, but which he thought was in the same family as the unleashed psyche. When you feel deep things you can't explain or see something that makes you wonder at the meaning of life.

The river was wide, the water fell fast and hard. And even though the drop wasn't nearly as steep as it sounded, Kit watched the spray at the bottom as water hit rock, and he felt like he was standing in a second-story window staring at mountains, wondering of breezes from far-off places.

He wanted to paint this place. He wanted to have a conversation with it. *Hi. My name is Kit. Where are you from? How were you made? Tell me all about your genesis . . .*

And if finding your voice as an artist meant listening to your art, then maybe feeling existential was like that too.

Hi, Kit. We are the waterfall. We were made at the beginning of all things, by the Master of Breezes. What about you? Where are you from? How were you made? Tell us your genesis . . .

Kit turned, found Nico and Lennon staring at the waterfall too. Maybe they were having their own conversations with it. Maybe there were other languages, not just of art.

The language of loss, which sounded like a hollow breeze through a dead tree.

The language of sacrifice, which sounded like tying a red bandanna in your hair or buttoning a yellow plaid shirt.

The language of friendship, which sounded like a steady river, and soft footsteps at your side.

One thing was for sure.

"Good thing we decided against a boat," he said.

there is no there

Late in the afternoon, somewhere north of Manchester and south of Garvin Falls Hydroelectric Station, they passed a sign welcoming them to the town of Waterford.

WELCOME TO WATERFORD, NEW HAMPSHIRE

FOUNDED IN 1822

POPULATION 2,023

The first thing they noticed about Waterford were the murals. They were everywhere. Colorful images plastered across storefronts and signs, walls of brick and stone, the sides of houses and banks, and, yes, even a movie theater.

It was real mural mania.

Some of the images depicted in these murals were strange but harmless: a car at the bottom of the ocean; a rabbit on top of a cannon; a house in the shape of a man's face. Others were far more frightening: an enormous empty eye socket; humans with animal heads dancing around a fire; a woman giving birth to a smartphone.

"This town is unpleasant," Kit said.

Lennon shook his head. "You are *not* wrong."

The main road had no name, or the sign had long since been torn down. It felt like an old place, but not old like Town, where the streets smelled of nostalgia and hugs.

Here, the streets just smelled like street. No fancy shoes, no fancy cars or dresses. Aside from the murals, it was all crumbly and forgotten, either side of the road lined with ramshackle shops, unreadable signs, and a thin layer of snowy rust. Even the trees grew at haphazard angles, twisty and turny in all the wrong places. Overhead, clouds filled the sky, and suddenly late afternoon felt like early evening.

Waterford was the kind of place where a person might believe there were no other places. *When you're here, there is no there.*

"Where are all the marrowless bones?" asked Kit.

"The whats?"

"You know. People-bits."

Every other town they'd cut through: people-bits everywhere. But not here. Which meant the town had been completely cleared out prior to the Flu, or else someone had moved them since. They shifted to the center of the road, as if the missing marrowless bones might jump out at them from one of these abandoned shops.

A faded sign in a bookstore advertised a local author event.

A pub. A bakery.

No windows, just gaping holes of darkness.

In the front yard of an old church, a sign read:

BLESSED CHURCH OF THE RISEN SAVIOR

BE FRUITFUL, AND MULTIPLY, AND REPLENISH THE EARTH.

——GENESIS 1:28

Lennon mumbled something about it being a weird thing to put on a sign, when—

"*Stop!*" The word rang through the street, the gaping shop windows, the twisty trees. "*Just the three of you?*"

The Blessed Church of the Risen Savior was on their right, a run-down mess, with cloudy stained glass, chipped white paint, and heavy-looking wooden front doors; on their left, a row of equally dilapidated houses.

"Yes!" said Nico, turning in a slow circle. The voice had been too echoey to be sure which side of the road it had come from. "Plus the dog."

Lennon yelled, "Just passing through!"

The *clunk* of a lock being turned, and the heavy doors of the church swung open, and two men—one old, one young, identical aside from age—stood in its frame.

The younger one held something like a gun, pointed right at them.

"Tell you what," said the older one. "Come on inside, and we'll have a nice chat about who's going where."

NICO

Phonologies

Some people said a lot in quiet voices, some said nothing in loud ones. And some, she was learning, simply loved the sound of their own voice.

Stages

"We're the last survivors of Waterford, proud descendants of the town's first fucking settlers."

Bruno and Gabe Rainer looked like they'd been eaten, digested, and passed through the bowels of an adult moose. Small but sinewy, white, with oil-black hair pulled back into tight ponytails, the dirt on their faces had moved into whatever stage came after *caked on*.

Bruno was older, probably in his fifties (calling into question Nico's theory that age reactivated the virus), with a chunk missing from one ear. He'd introduced himself first, and then, with a flourish, "And *this* is my son, Gabe." The bravado in his voice was off-putting, as if Nico and Lennon and Kit had crossed mountain, canyon, swarm unending with the sole aim of meeting his offspring, Gabe Rainer, the Chosen One.

Gabe was a bit older, maybe early twenties, with perpetually watery eyes and the face of an empty sack. He walked with a limp and carried an object about the size of a rifle, made of wood and metal and a kind of cord. Clearly a gun-like weapon—Nico could only guess at its function.

The way they carried themselves, Bruno's tone of voice, Gabe's weapon, both sets of eyes dim as could be—*these two would've fit right in with the Metal Masks*, thought Nico.

Bruno, especially, whose dramatic shift into consummate host was clearly an act.

Inside the church, he rattled on about its history while they took in its bizarre architecture. It reminded Nico of a photograph she'd once seen of an old town after it had been bombed, buildings where one side remained intact, while the other was demolished.

The entire back wall of the church, and part of the ceiling, was gone. And since the church backed up to the woods, she found herself staring out into a thick-forested darkness. In the middle of the floor, an enormous firepit with flames kicking around, smoke funneling up through the hole in the ceiling. What walls were still intact had hanging torches, which, when combined with the size of the firepit, accounted for the relative warmth in the room, as well as the damp floors.

"What's that sound?" Lennon looked at the floor.

Nico had noticed it too, a low frequency humming under their feet.

"Catacombs." Bruno walked to the corner, stomped his foot

on a trapdoor with a giant padlock. "Run the length of the church underneath. With the falls upriver, certain times of year, water rattles the ground, you can actually *feel* it here." He fell back into his regional history lesson, how this was the first structure built in Waterford. "Should have seen it in its heyday, long before the businesses arrived."

"Businesses?" asked Lennon.

"He means Flies." From the moment they'd entered the church, Kit had stood like a statue, facing the interior of the front wall, less interested in catacombs and gaping holes, more interested in the strange mural looming over them. "*Business* is the technical term for a swarm," he said quietly.

Bruno smiled. "Little man knows his shit."

This mural was done in the same style as the ones they'd seen outside, though it was bigger and more elaborate. In the top corner of the wall, a big moon, and in the sky around it, instead of stars, bright red computers and telephones, blue light bulbs and televisions, neon outlets and keyboards, a thousand twinkling technologies wild and alive in the dancing firelight.

Nico put an arm on Kit's shoulder. "You okay?"

He didn't say anything, just stared up at the strange image.

"Our very own drawings on the cave wall." Bruno pointed to Gabe, who'd been sitting quietly in the corner, wooden weapon on one shoulder, watery-eyed and silent. "Man of few words, my son, but quite the talent. Now see, you got me rambling on about history, and I've forgotten my fucking manners. Who's hungry?"

Operations

The only real furniture in the church was a long wooden table with chairs on each side. *Surely, somewhere in Waterford, they have a building with four walls and a ceiling*, thought Nico. Even for their strange hosts, dining in the ruins of an old church seemed bizarre. But the firepit and torches made it feasible, temperature-wise, and she thought it best not to question.

Eager to get back on the road, they wouldn't have accepted the dinner invite had it been presented as an invitation. As it was, Gabe's rifle-like weapon was never far from use, always on his shoulder or in his hands or beside him as he tended the fire.

The food was fine: a salted lettuce with tomatoes and some sort of corn relish. Bruno sat at the head; Nico and Lennon sat by each other on one side, while Kit sat across from them, staring up at the mural over their heads. Seemingly uninterested in food, Gabe remained preoccupied with the fire. Under the table, Harry's wet snout rested in Nico's lap.

"So you're an artist," said Bruno, chewing as he talked.

"Not really," said Nico.

"Actually"—Bruno pointed to Kit—"I was talking to Little Man."

Kit turned from the mural, looking genuinely shocked to be addressed.

"Some people see my son's art and it sort of—freaks them

out." Bruno turned in his chair, looked up at the wall. "But the way you've been staring at it makes me think, *There's an artist who gets it.* You saw the ones coming into town, I assume. What'd you think of the empty eye socket? Mark of genius, am I right?"

Kit took a well-timed bite.

"We've got a whole setup of art supplies in an underground bunker out back." Bruno pointed through the back of the church, into the forest.

"Sorry." Lennon gazed out into the woods. "Underground bunker?"

"Good place to hide, when the need arises. Thoroughly designed and fucking fortified. But it's primarily a space for Gabe to store his supplies. My boy would've had quite the life for himself in the old world. Big studio in New York City, the whole nine. As it is, he's got a bunch of brick walls and a hatch in the ground. But so be it."

Bruno's smile was the opposite of a smile; even the way he ate his salad—slowly, methodically, planning the next bite while chewing the current one—felt scripted. And yet somehow, each topic bled into the next, so that now he was talking about some period of time in which America was in jeopardy of being bombed by the Russians. "1960s, I think. Underground bomb shelters were all the rage. Of course, they never attacked, but we got pretty good and wiped out anyway, didn't we?"

Under their feet, the river's dull roar took the reins of the conversation for a moment.

Harry had disappeared, gone out for dinner, no doubt.

"So"—Bruno gulped his water, wiped his mouth with the back of his hand—"what brings you three to Waterford?"

"We're headed to the coast." Like that, Nico was in the lie, espousing Monty's motivations as her own, explaining how they'd had a radio in their old town, how they'd heard a recorded loop, and were now making their way to an island off the coast. She was careful to omit specific names and timelines, not wanting to get caught in the lie, but mostly, wanting to keep her friends safe. If the Isles of Shoals really was some safe haven, she had a feeling it wouldn't be for long once Bruno and Gabe got there.

"Interesting." Bruno looked up at his son. "Isn't that interesting, Gabe?"

The room was well lit, warm. But apparently not warm or bright enough for Gabe, who'd been piling wood and prodding the fire while they ate. *Like he's a servant or something, preparing the room for his guests.*

"Yes. Interesting." Gabe's first words of the evening. He followed them up with a few more. "If you'll excuse me, I need to use the facilities."

They watched him leave, then ate in awkward silence. Eventually, as much to break the silence as anything, Lennon commented on the freshness of the salad.

"Gave up meat for obvious reasons," said Bruno. "Thought I'd miss it, but we've gotten creative with the vegetables. You like the relish?"

"Obvious reasons?"

"Hmm?"

"You said you quit eating meat for obvious reasons."

"Right." Bruno stopped chewing as he looked around the table. "Oh. You don't know?"

"Know what?" asked Nico.

Bruno leaned back in his chair, rubbed his hands together slowly, as if savoring the moment. "Okay, well. Let's start here. Did you know sharks can smell blood in the water from hundreds of meters away? Doesn't take much either. One part blood for every one million parts water. Roughly"—he picked up his cup, held it out, and tipped a few drops of water onto the floor—"*that*. In a room like this. Resilient creatures, sharks. And still. No match for Flies."

"Hard to imagine a shark being deterred by cinnamon," said Nico.

"Cinnamon doesn't do anything." Kit sank a little in his chair. Until now he'd managed to go the whole dinner without saying a word. "Our friends got carried off by Flies. We had cinnamon all over the place."

Bruno took a sip of water. "Au contraire, Little Man. Cinnamon is pretty effective against smaller swarms. Larger ones, not so much. Now, I wasn't there when your friends got carried off, but I bet you guys killed some kind of animal that night. Lots of blood, yeah?"

"The wild turkey," said Lennon.

Bruno nodded. "We Rainer boys don't put too much stock

in theories. We put our faith in God and in ourselves. Outside of that, faith becomes fantasy. For example, if I said I knew how the Flu operated, how it killed—that'd be fantasy. But, now, if I said I knew the Flies, understood what made them tick, how to control them, how they operated . . ."

He stood, crossed the floor to a small closet beside one of the torches on the wall, pulled a key from his pocket, and unlocked the door.

They heard the Flies first: in diminutive form, like a small sampling. Appropriate, considering that's exactly what it was. From the closet, Bruno pulled out one end of a broom. On the other end, a clear plastic bag had been applied with a hefty amount of tape. The bag was alive, expanding and contracting, pushing and pulling, flailing in furious punches. "No need to worry," said Bruno, eyeing the end of the broom as if it were a beloved pet. "I've spent time with this little business—and many before it—studying them, getting to know them. Another month or two, they'll outgrow the bag. For now, you're safe."

Outside, the forest was alive with invisible things, nighttime critters and near-winter winds and tree-siblings breathing staccato breaths, reaching out for one another, seeking touch. Nico listened for their words of comfort . . . *We are here. You are not alone.* She felt her place among them, felt them calling her home.

We have to get out of here.

"When we ran the planet, we went where we pleased, and *whenever* we damn well pleased, and not always with some urgent purpose." Bruno spoke with a quiet resolution, as if talking himself off a ledge. "Flies enjoy that same privilege now. You might see giant swarms roaming aimlessly, you might not see one for weeks. Maybe you're in the wrong place at the wrong time, and now you're dead. But there is one way to up those chances. Like sharks, Flies are drawn to blood. The smell alone is enough to make them crazy. You can roll the dice, hunt smaller animals. Might go days hunting without seeing a swarm. But it just takes once. And so no—we don't fuck with meat in Waterford. We don't fuck with blood any more than we have to."

With great care, as with some ancient relic of the church, Bruno gently placed the broom back in the closet with a soft "Amen." And as he inserted the key into the padlock, turned it with a metallic *click*, Nico noticed it was the same lock used on the trapdoor in the corner, the one leading down into the catacombs. And suddenly, the low frequency humming under her feet took on frightening new possibilities.

Theologies

If one were to crawl under the Farmhouse, strike a match, and look around, that person would see that the roots of the house were sunk deep into the intersection of science and faith. "I'm not saying I definitely *don't* believe in God," her father said one night. "Just that there's no empirical evidence to support the theory."

Nico remembered it clearly. It was a Delivery Day. They'd

taken four Metallyte pouches of chili mac, tossed in boiled corn and a packet of something called taco seasoning. So far as Nico was concerned, if it was empirical evidence of God her father was looking for, he need look no further than his own plate.

"Okay, two things. First"—her mom paused; whereas her dad let loose every word that came to mind, content to sift and reorder afterward, her mother let words build up inside, carefully choosing the ones best suited to her purposes—"if there were empirical evidence of God, it wouldn't be called *faith*. I see God in the starry sky. The snow and rain, the books in our library. I see God in my snowstorm girl. In our survival."

This particular conversation was more like a very long book, which her parents never finished, only dog-eared when they were tired of reading. It rarely felt like an argument; the further in they got, the wider their smiles became. Their tones were calm, loving, tender—sometimes to a fault, in Nico's opinion. Her mother would talk of God, her father would talk of science, and the looks in their eyes would turn to a fervent sort of hunger, just as the nausea in her own stomach roiled.

Her parents were the only two people in the history of the world for whom debating the existence of God conjured romantic sparks.

"And second?" asked her father, eyes alight.

Her mother's smile grew, and at first Nico thought it was for all the usual nauseating reasons. "If not God," said her mom, "then where did *it* come from?"

Under the table, Harriet whined.

"Where did *what* come from?" Nico asked.

Her mother continued, as if Nico hadn't said a word. "Have you considered the possibility—"

"No."

"—that God put it there? As a way out? That maybe He placed each and every Tollbooth strategically around the world to save humanity from itself? Maybe *Tollbooth* is the wrong nomenclature. Maybe . . . *Ark* . . . would be better."

"Uh, okay." Even the miracle of taco seasoning took a back seat to whatever was going on. "What are you guys talking about?" asked Nico. "What *tollbooth*? Like from the book?"

Her father wiped his mouth, set down his napkin, stared at her mother across the table. "There was a time when humans looked at the aurora borealis and thought it was a window to heaven," he said. "Throughout history, ambiguous elements of fantasy are eventually proven to be anything but fantastic. Science wins the day, every time."

Ambiguous elements of fantasy? Aside from his stories, Nico had never heard her father speak like this.

"You call it ambiguous," said her mother. "I call it divine."

"The Tollbooth has nothing to do with divinity, believe me."

"Careful. That sounded dangerously close to an absolute."

"Okay." Nico dropped her fork on her plate. "You guys are freaking me out."

The silence that followed drowned out everything. And then:

"Believe it or not," said her mom, "the idea of *houseflies* wiping out the world's population once sounded like pure fantasy. But that's not the only fantasy that—"

A throat clear from across the table; that was all it took to put a stopper in the sentence. Carefully chosen words or not, her dad clearly didn't approve.

But the stopper didn't hold.

"Before the Flies came, your father and a group of scientists—"

"Honey."

"—found something."

"Not yet. Please."

Her mother's eyes dimmed; she returned to her food.

"Well, you can't stop there," Nico said. "What did they find?"

The dinner table, the library, the attic deck, hunched over the radio in the cellar: through the years, every corner of the Farmhouse had played host to mysterious conversations. Sometimes her parents would hand her a piece of the puzzle, though it was rarely a corner or edge; and so she was left with a splotchy and incomplete view of her own world.

The older she got, the more questions she had: What had her father found? Had fantasy and reality somehow evolved to coexist? Were the secrets of the universe bound up by God or science, and did it have to be binary? In arguing for one over the other, weren't her parents reducing the size of their own respective faiths? Nico often asked these questions, and many others, alone on the attic deck, her back to the panoramic view.

The Bell was stable, present, loyal. In its shadow, she felt understood.

That night, over chili mac with corn and taco seasoning, Nico didn't care about feeling understood—she wanted to *understand*. But she was years away from her eighteenth birthday; Harriet was alive, Harry not yet born, her mother was a spiritual sprite with cheeks the color of the rainbow. Nico's life was small but intact.

"I want to know," she said, wishing for a bigger world.

Her father put a hand on her arm. "I'm not saying *never*. I'm saying *not yet*."

Being treated like an outsider was bad enough. But that it should come from this man who'd never babied her, always trusted her, only made it worse. As she got older, and the *not yet*s piled up, she was better able to articulate this incongruence. *For a rational man*, she would think, *it's his most irrational belief: that survival is only possible when the kid is kept in the dark.*

THE
DELIVERER

If my math is right, I've experienced just under three thousand winters.

Summers, falls, springs, just as many of those. But winter, when the year reaches a crotchety old age, bitter and cold and too tired to care—what a fucking headache.

I stand in the middle of the street, staring at the church, feeling this particular winter in the deeper parts of my soul. "I could do something."

I really could.

According to the Red Books, I have tried.

In my 11th Life, I completely ignored the task at hand. Instead of giving the rifle away, I carried it across the street, opened the door to the church, and took fate into my own hands.

Fate, as it turned out, would not be handled.

The following Life, I was a little smarter. I arrived in town a day early, set up in the woods, and waited. Something about that decision changed their course; the group never showed.

I tried again in my 13th Life. Smarter. Earlier. More prepared. Again, they never showed.

I've broken every rule, taken every turn, told them everything, told them nothing. Sixteen times, I've tried to stop tonight's events from happening, and sixteen times I have failed, each failure further confirmation that to live by the Law of Peripheral Adjustments is to accept the curse of the middle domino: you are a means to an end you will never see.

I turn away from the church to face the saddest-looking house on the block. All chipped paint and rotted wood, heavy locks on doors, bars on every window. Eager to be rid of the rifle in my hands, I walk to the front door, set to work picking the lock. I remind myself that this is action, and while the middle domino may cause little destruction, the final domino is nothing without it.

KIT

goliath

The broom changed things.

Bruno took his seat at the table, asked if they would like a refill of water, like he hadn't just wielded death itself. Lennon said no,
they were fine, thank you, but they weren't fine. And even as they
tried to hide it, Kit felt a new weight in the air. Things were heavier,
slowed down, as if the whole church had been immersed in a lake.

It was Lennon who finally broke the silence. "We should get
going. Don't want to overstay our welcome. Thanks for the food,
it was—"

"*Lennon.*" What little light had lived in Bruno's face was gone.
He was the unplugged lamp, sad and dusty and broken. "*Len-non,*"
he said again, as if chewing the name, debating its taste and tex-
ture. "You know—ever since you introduced yourself, I've been
thinking about your name. I have to say, I would have pegged you
as more of a *Rashid.* Or *Samir,* maybe."

Kit had read of superheroes who could shoot bolts of lightning
from their eyes, which he'd always found sort of silly. But there
was nothing silly about the bolts of lightning in Lennon's eyes
right now.

Bruno continued: "I assume your parents had a deep respect for the greatest American band of all time, it's just—difficult to imagine respect for the Beatles coming from . . . Pakistan? Lebanon?"

Voices came to Kit from miles and days away: in a sad, dusty nursery, *So long as there are people on Earth, there will be willful ignorance and hatred*; on a baseball field, searching for the perfect stick, *Doors had been closed to them based on who they were, where they'd come from.*

"Not like you picked the name," said Bruno. "Or like you could be expected to know anything about the Beatles. I just think a parent has a duty to consider their own history—"

"Winston," said Lennon.

A beat.

"Sorry?"

"John Lennon's middle name. But you probably already knew that."

Bruno's smile was still there, but it was different, strained.

Lennon went on. "After Yoko came along, he tried to change it to Ono, but something about the law wouldn't let him drop the Winston, so he just wound up adding Ono to the mix. John Winston Ono Lennon. Born October 9, 1940, with three names. Shot and killed December 8, 1980, with four. But again, I'm sure you already knew all this. The children's book he wanted to write, the UFO he claimed to have seen, how he signed an autograph for his assassin the morning of his assassination. I'm sure you've read about how dissatisfied he was with his own work, how of all the songs he wrote, he was only happy with a single lyric. I'm sure, given your *deep respect* for the Beatles, you know which lyric I'm referring to . . . ?"

Lennon waited a beat; Bruno said nothing.

"My parents—not that it's any of your business—were Jordanian immigrants. The women who raised me told me my mom made a killer mansaf, that my dad preferred his knafeh with ground pistachios, that they'd rigged a camping trailer to the back of their Subaru, and that they *loved* the Beatles. I have no way of knowing how deep their respect was, but I'm guessing it was deep enough to know the Beatles were a British band, not American, you smug motherfucker."

Kit knew *of* the word. Which is to say, he knew it existed. He had no idea how it could burst from the mouth like a little explosion, lighting up the room with thunder and muscle.

"We're leaving now." Lennon stood—and just as he did, there was a *zip*, a loud crack against the mural wall behind him, little chunks of painted stone crumbling to the ground.

"Gabe must be feeling generous," said Bruno. "He doesn't miss unless he means to, and he never means to twice. I would sit down now."

Slowly, eyes on the woods, Lennon sat.

"That was a real nice little speech you just gave," said Bruno.

"Left me all warm and fuzzy inside. Allow me to return the favor. You know the Bible story of David and Goliath? Kid takes down a giant with nothing but a slingshot. I always found that hard to swallow. But I get it now." Bruno turned, gazed into the dark woods. "I never was much of a shot. But Gabe always liked the sport of it. Real determination, even when he was little. Once we learned about the Flies' thirst for blood, we ditched the rifles. Mostly ate what we grew. I figured, weapon-wise, we were left with our bare hands, but—my boy had other ideas. Started with a little Y-shaped stick and a thin rubber band. Before long, the stick got thicker, the band got wider, and the rocks flew faster. He tinkered with different designs before finding the right one. Named it Goliath. Very clever, my boy. See, unlike a bullet, a rock isn't aerodynamically designed to tear through flesh. Oh, it'll enter the body easily enough, but depending on where you hit"—he leaned back, put both hands on his lower abdomen—"gut shots, namely—it's rare for the rock to exit the other side. You'll bleed some, sure. But in the right spot, with no exit wound, it's minimal."

"What do you want?" asked Nico.

"The answer to that is a different Bible story." Bruno took a sip; afterward, he kept his eyes on the glass, as if talking to the water. " 'Be fruitful and multiply.' It is our sacred duty to repopulate the earth," and as he spoke, Kit heard the words in his head before they came out of Bruno's mouth, so the man seemed only an echo of himself.

Nico will stay here . . .

"Nico will stay here . . ."

. . . to help my son accomplish this.

". . . to help my son accomplish this."

He heard Lennon's words in his head too: *Fuck you, no one's staying . . .* "Fuck you, no one's staying in this madhouse."

Bruno reached behind his head, removed the band holding his ponytail in place, and let his hair fall in sheets around him. " 'Replenish the earth, and subdue it,' " he said, digging both hands into his head, scratching like an animal. " 'Have dominion over the fish of the sea, and over the fowl of the air, and over every living thing that moveth upon the earth.' " As he pulled his hair back into a ponytail again, for the first time, it seemed the man's face was his own, a mask removed. He pointed to the locked closet. "For all the shit we pin on Flu-flies, no living thing has been more fruitful, or multiplied at such phenomenal rates. We can learn from them, but only when we realize we have nothing to fear. They are doing what God created them to do. As are we."

"I'm not staying here." Nico's voice was a quiet-fierce. "None of us are. We each have somewhere to be because of someone we love."

"We're not staying here," said Lennon.

"We're not staying here," said Kit.

Bruno laughed. "You guys are cute. Sticking together, power of friendship."

"We're family," said Kit.

"Yes, we are." Nico pulled a large knife out from under the table, turned it to Bruno. "And we're not staying here."

Bruno pointed to the knife. "That's a big fucking mistake, right there."

"Funny, I thought it was a big fucking knife."

"I don't think you know how to use that."

"Tell Gabe to stand down, or you're going to find out."

He looked from the knife to Nico. "Lineage is *everything*—"

"You're creepy as hell. Tell Gabe to stand down."

"—without it, the world becomes a dark place."

"The earth is 4.54 billion years old," said Kit. "Humans have been around for 200,000 years. The planet could blink and miss us. Our extinction would be a return to the status quo."

Across the table, Nico winked at him; he winked back, and he felt tears coming on, as if his heart was too full of heart-juice, so now it was leaking from his eyes.

"I've been around my own kid too long," said Bruno. "Forgot how goddamn arrogant you guys are."

"Last chance," said Nico. "Tell Gabe to stand down."

"You think you're the first eligible bachelorette to stumble into town? Don't get me wrong, given all the things that have to go right in the baby-making department, a second option is not without value. But we already have a primary candidate. You're expendable."

The knife held steady in Nico's hand. "You're lying."

"He's not," said Kit, and in his mind, he saw the town from an aerial view, as if watching from the window in his projection room:

the sign welcoming them to Waterford, the street they'd entered it on, little murals all over, and run-down houses . . .

"What's the reload time on a slingshot?" Nico asked.

Suddenly Kit knew what she was about to do. And if the panicky look on Bruno's face was any indication, he knew too.

Lennon reached out, put a hand on her shoulder. "Nico—"

Time slowed, and when Kit closed his eyes, he saw his Dakota's final hours, saw himself at her bedside, watching sweat pour out of her, wishing he could give his life for hers, as the Mackenzies had done for them. *Just sit there*, said his Dakota, over and over. *Just stay where you are*. And he held her hand, told her he wasn't going anywhere. And now, eyes still closed, he saw himself at this table, saw Nico take a breath, knew she was about to lunge for Bruno, and like so many words this evening, Kit saw the path of the rock before it arrived: from the woods, *zip*, through the hole in the back of the church, it would pass over his shoulder, *zip*, across the table, and Nico, mid-lunge, would be hit in the gut. Unless . . .

Just sit there, Kit.

From the open window of his art classroom, he saw his Dakota across the street, on the roof of the Paradise Twin.

Please. Just stay where you are.

That face he loved, in a world so impossibly big.

Please.

In her hands, a potted flower, still growing.

Just sit there.

He smiled at her.

And then stood up.

the brightest room

The church dissolved, melted like snow in spring. The mural, too, everything gone, washed in light, an infinite vacuum of blinding brightness in every direction . . .

In the middle of it all, Kit sat at a table.

A woman sat across from him.

This is from my dream, said Kit, looking around.

The woman put her arm on the table, pulled up a sleeve to reveal a tattoo: *Dreams are memories from past lives*, it read.

He tried to shield the light behind the woman to get a better look at her face. At first he thought she might have been his Dakota, but she was too young. Then he thought she was Nico, but she was too old. She seemed both strange and familiar, like walking into the Paradise Twin only to find it filled with someone else's stuff.

I think I've lived many times, he said. *The same life, over and over.*

The woman did not move. She did not speak.

Only—everyone dreams. So why am I the only one who remembers?

She raised her other arm to reveal a second tattoo, this one an image of concentric circles, too thin and too many to count. She pointed to the smaller circles in the middle of the tattoo—and then pointed to Kit.

I'm a small circle, he said.

She lowered both arms, said nothing.

Like eidetic memory. The smaller the circle, the easier it is to remember each lap. So then . . . they remember things too, just not as well.

Still, she was silent.

Where are we?

Slowly, the woman reached across the table, took Kit's hand in hers. On the back of her hand was a tattoo of an old cinema marquee. Her other hand reached across the table now, and on it, a tattoo of a road winding up into the mountains. Kit looked into the woman's eyes, and there he saw his beginning and his end, not Nico *or* his Dakota, but the two combined. The opening and closing of his circle.

Around them, the brightness imploded, broke into pieces as color flooded in.

I'm scared, he said.

As the woman began to dissolve, she smiled at him, turned her hand over, and just before she and the room both melted away, he saw in her palm one last tattoo: a small purple flower.

the completion of spacedog & computer

There was no pain.

Or it was something else altogether: his body was thunder, a radiant shock of *I'm here* and then *I'm there*, back and forth. Nico was leaning over him now, he was on the ground, *I don't remember falling*. She lifted him into her lap, and when she pulled her hand back, he saw blood, *cadmium red*. "It's a natural pigment," he said. "It lasts forever," and Nico was crying, told him not to talk, not to worry, and he felt like laughing—he wasn't worried at all.

Behind Nico, the mural loomed large. That big bright moon lighting up the sky, technology from the olden days shining like stars, and out of nowhere, Harry trotted up, sniffed Kit's face. "Good boy, Spacedog," said Kit, the thunder receding in his chest. Harry turned, looked up at the mural, and Kit thought how he'd always loved painting the dog best.

Just like this.

Nico cried, held him in her lap like his Dakota had held him before bed, telling him his genesis story, her dangling necklace brushing his face. "She was on a bad date," he said. "She was a midwife, and she was there for the baby."

"Shhh," Nico said. "Don't talk."

From under his shirt, he pulled out her necklace with its bright silver key. "Oh," he said, lifting his hand, holding the key between the painted moon and the boxy computer and the black dog at the bottom. He closed one eye so the key was part of the mural, giant and shimmery. And he wished Nico would stop crying. He wanted to tell her how wonderful it was, how perfect that it had taken a piece of his Dakota to finally complete his painting. *It's okay*, he tried to tell her, but when he opened his mouth, a thick flower bloomed, not purple but red, and he died, the first and only artist to ever truly finish anything.

NICO

Birthrights

In the Age of the Fly, there are many laws. Love, but do not fall in love. Sing songs, read books of lives fulfilled, but do not wish to fill your own. The world is large, the mile long, and time stands still. Here, in the ancient gasp of trees, rocks, rivers, sky, the young are left to their own devices. Their cities are ruin. Their families are dust. Their histories lost. And in the dark woods of the world, they find a parasitic element embedded in their most basic code: *You will hurt others, and others will hurt you.*

It has always been this way.

And while Nico's brain had long accepted her birthright, her heart had not—until now.

Faces

She watched Kit's eyes pass, blood on her arms and hands, the feeling of owing somebody your life and watching the death that paid for it.

He knew where he'd been sitting. He knew exactly what he was doing.

"*Goddammit.*" Bruno stood from the table, walked around to where Nico and Lennon had crawled to be with Kit. "Now see, if you'd listened to me, this wouldn't have happened." He turned to the woods, yelled for Gabe to open the hatch. "We need to get underground, a swarm will be here soon. And this mess is on you, you're cleaning up whatever the Flies don't get." He pointed to the pool of blood still spreading on the floor.

Through tears, Nico saw the key in Kit's hand; she took it, tucked it into her side pocket, unsure why, but knowing he'd kept it safe for a reason, and so now she would too.

Harry whined, licked Kit's face, as if the love of a dog might bring him back.

"We need to get out of here," said Bruno, but before he could say anything else, a gunshot echoed in the woods.

Not a *zip.*

A *bang.*

Beside her, Harry tensed, growled. And while all eyes were drawn to the woods, hers were drawn to Bruno. "Gabriel!" he shouted, and she stared at him as he scanned the trees, his eyes full of fear. Again, he shouted his son's name, and ever so gently, she shifted Kit's head out of her lap, laid him on the stone floor, never taking her eyes off Bruno . . .

Now.

Do it.

She'd dropped the knife when Kit went down—

You don't need the knife.

"Gabe!" Bruno yelled again, not noticing Nico begin to stand.
You are the only weapon you need.

"Gabriel!"

She made no noise.

Go.

He inhaled to call out again—and she went. Lunging fast, she grabbed his ponytail, jerked his head back—a split second of confusion in his eyes, a veiny pulsing throat—and then she punched it, hard, the base of her palm sinking into his Adam's apple like a loose leathery-skinned drum. His body tried to fall, but she held his hair tight, and Harry was barking, trying to attack, Lennon beside her now, pulling the man back up, and Nico watched Bruno's eyes become two dark moons. Vaguely, she wondered if she would hear the bullet or the rock from the woods before it would hit her, and when a second shot *did* ring out, she braced herself for pain, but felt nothing, only the anticipation of her birthright. As Bruno coughed for air, she leaned in close to his healthy ear, whispered, "Stronger than I look, motherfucker," and when she bit, she found the muscle of the neck to be tough, stringy, raw, and something about the salty mess made her bite harder. She felt Bruno try to scream, but all she could hear was a sweet voice asking if she'd ever had a really good tomato. She bit harder, and now, another voice, new and closer and real . . .

"Hey." A hand on her shoulder . . .

The touch of another person pulled her out of things; Nico unclamped her jaw, watched Bruno fall to the ground, hand on the side of his throat, eyes wide, body convulsing. What pieces of him were still in her mouth, she spat on the floor.

"It's okay," said this new voice.

When Nico turned, she found a girl with a red bandanna tied around her face: one eye was completely covered; the other stared at her with the look of someone well acquainted with pitch-dark places.

Dominions

In the dwindling flames of the firepit, light reflected off Kit's blood, his body lit in strange ways. Across the floor, in the corner, Bruno lay in a pool of his own blood, one hand against the gash in his neck, the other against the wound in his leg, spewing raspy, animal-like noises.

That explains the second gunshot. The reason Nico had felt no pain: the bullet hadn't come for her; it had come for him.

The new girl leaned over Kit's body, pushed his hair off his forehead, tried to rub some of the dirt from his face. "We need to go," she said quietly.

Her tenderness toward Kit, the way she touched his head . . .

"You're Lakie," said Nico.

A heaviness seemed to weigh this girl down, the unmistakable sign of having a hole where a person used to be. And Nico thought of her father: If he could see her now, would he regret his decision to send her to Manchester? How far had the un-blossoming progressed? Was he even still alive? She'd considered the inside-out darkness of living alone in the Farmhouse, but it was certainly better than dying there alone.

"We need to go, *right now*." Lakie stood, wiped her eyes, pulled a torch off the wall. Then, to Lennon: "Can you carry Kit?"

"What about the other one?" Lennon pointed to the woods. "Gabe—"

"I shot him," said Lakie. "Gabe's dead."

And that explains the first gunshot.

In the corner where Bruno bled, he gave a gurgling cough, his eyes glassy and wide at the news of his son's death.

Gently, Lennon picked up Kit's body, but when he started for the door, Lakie said, "Not that way," and proceeded to lead them to the blown-out hole in the back wall. Harry ran ahead, jumped through first; the rest of them followed, and just as their feet stepped from stone to dirt and snow, behind them, those raspy, animal-like noises turned into a voice . . .

"'Have dominion . . .'"

In the far corner, Bruno was on all fours, half dead, soaked in sweat, blood, urine, every ounce of his insides in a mad rush to escape. *"'. . . Over the fowl of the air . . .'"*

A deafening boom went off beside her, and in the church, a bullet whizzed by Bruno's head, cracking the mural behind him.

Mere feet away, Lakie had sunk the bottom end of the torch

in the ground, and was aiming her rifle, steadying herself, and even though Nico didn't know anything about guns, she could spot the stance of someone who did. "He's going for it," Lakie muttered into the rifle.

Going for it?

Lakie shot again. This time, the bullet caught Bruno in the shoulder, flinging him backward onto the ground. He groaned— and pushed himself back up.

"This fucking guy." Lakie cocked the rifle, tried to pull the trigger, but nothing happened. "Shitty four-round magazine."

In the church, Bruno fumbled with something on the floor.

"Okay." Lakie pulled the torch from the snow. "Now we run." She turned for the woods, and in the receding light, Nico saw the look on Bruno's bloody face, heard the turn of a key in the trapdoor—a familiar metallic *click*—and she understood what he was going for.

Turning, she ran, Lennon just ahead of her, Kit's little body flopping around in his arms, and in the lead, the bobbing light of Lakie's torch cut their path through trees. On the ground, the quick image of a passing body sprawled at unnatural angles, Gabe's head opened up, and in his hands, Goliath had fallen.

Behind them, a whirring . . .

Lakie's torch stopped on a dime, and when Nico caught up, she found Lennon and Kit descending into earth, Lakie holding open the hatch door of the underground bomb shelter.

"I'll go," said Lakie. "You lower the dog."

She scurried down the ladder as Nico picked up Harry. It was awkward, getting a good hold on him, but he tucked his tail and let it happen, and she said, "It's okay," and promised double-rationed granola as she lowered him into Lakie's waiting arms belowground.

"Okay, come on!"

And now the whirring exploded; Nico was about to climb down into safety, but over the top of the hatch door, she caught a glimpse of the swarm fully released from its tomb, and she could not look away. It was what had happened to the whitetail, multiplied beyond measure, as Flies poured out of the catacombs in a feverish upward spiral, flailing all over the place but never too far from its core. *Like an octopus*, she thought, *one brain to control the nervous system, and one for each tentacle*, the swarm operated as one, with more noise, more rage, more organization than she'd ever imagined. Untold years of breeding with each other, eating each other, in the darkness of the catacombs, they'd patiently waited for a chance at resurrection. Now they had it, they were wasting no time.

Somewhere buried under all the sound, the voices of Lakie and Lennon, telling her to climb down . . .

The swarm spun in cylindrical fury, forming shapes around Bruno: a giant arch over his head; a revolving waist-high hoop; occasionally it broke apart, each to its own, a freestyle fly, before reshaping itself into a tornado with Bruno in its eye. She could see him in outline only, as if the Flies had formed a full-body suit, covered every inch of his skin. And his dark, pulsating form raised its arms to the sky, opened its mouth as if to speak, but before words came, the Flies found this curious new opening. They filled his mouth, descended into the hell of Bruno, his body twisted into odd, alien shapes as the Flies filled him up like a balloon. And when he began to lift off the ground, Nico's first thought was of some divine miracle, an ascension to heaven, that God had seen fit to spare him.

It happened slowly at first—as if the Flies needed a running start—but once they'd filled him substantially, it didn't take long. The swarm carried Bruno straight up into the air, past the mural of twinkling technologies, through the hole in the ceiling, and his body became like the Flies, melted into its hive mind. Up and up the swarm carried him into the sky, and together, this nightmarish creation painted the night darker than it had been moments ago. Behind her now, in the distance, a second swarm on its way, drawn like sharks to blood, *the smell alone is enough to make them crazy.* Nico climbed down into the shelter, closed the hatch, and it occurred to her that she *had* witnessed an ascension, though not to heaven, and certainly not by the business of God. Wherever Bruno had gone, he'd been dragged there by his own fucking business.

PART SIX

IN

THE

GREAT

GLASS

DOME

NICO

Tombs

The shelter was cold and musty but clean, shelves stocked full of paints and brushes, a first aid kit, tents and gear, a few jugs of fresh water, jars of vegetables, even a few Metallyte pouches. There was a cot in the corner, which currently held Kit's featherweight body.

Aboveground, the on-again-off-again sound of swarms, varying factions drawn to the blood of Bruno, Gabe, Kit. Nico lit some candles; Lakie passed around bottles of water, downed her own, and opened another. Lennon quickly caught her up on all that had happened since they'd last seen each other: finding Nico, the cabin, Echo, the parting of ways with Monty and Loretta.

"So he's okay?" asked Lakie, ripping open a pouch of cereal. "Monty's okay?"

"Yeah," said Lennon. "Hopelessly in love. But yeah."

Lakie looked down at Kit, a small, fleeting smile. "He saw that coming a mile away."

After they'd all eaten something, they sat on the cement floor and waited for the swarms to pass. And here, surrounded by the paints Gabe had used to tell one story, they listened to Lakie tell another. "That night on the baseball field, Monty and Loretta made some excuse to go off into the woods together. You and Kit were gone, I don't remember why now."

"He wanted a new stick."

Harry was nestled in Lennon's lap, and Nico felt both glad and sad at the ease of their companionship.

"I don't understand," said Lennon. "The Flies carried you off. How are you alive?"

Lakie's face softened, not a smile, but in the family of one. "Big Alma," she said under her breath.

"No."

"Who?" asked Nico.

"Seventy-five-denier ripstop nylon shell," said Lakie. "With Insotect Tubic construction. Big Alma saved my life."

Nico looked from one to the other. "I'm lost."

"Her sleeping bag," said Lennon.

Nico's father once said there was no kind of magic like nonfiction magic: things too impossible, too inconceivable, to *not* be true. She thought of this as she listened to Lakie describe how fast the Flies were on them, the sound of Pringles's animal-like screams, thoroughly *in*human, and how she'd done the first thing that came to mind: zipped herself into her sleeping bag. "Like being buried alive. Just the weight of them on me. And then I felt myself being lifted, like—a giant hand scooping me into the air." Lakie looked at Kit as she spoke. "Bruno never shut up about the Flies. Blood this, blood that. Fucking fanatical, that man. But I think he was right about blood. I'd just butchered that turkey. Pringles's elbow was in bad shape. If it was blood the Flies were after, they found plenty of it on that baseball field."

"I'm sorry"—Nico leaned forward—"how long were you *inside* a sleeping bag?"

"I don't know. An hour maybe? Felt like days. And then eventually they just—dropped me."

Lennon cursed under his breath as Nico imagined the whitetail falling from the sky.

"I hit something on the way down." Lakie let go of Kit's hand, lifted her red bandanna to show them a pretty gruesome cut, diagonal from eyebrow to cheek. The eye itself was a mess of popped vessels and blood sores, almost completely red. "And then I hit water. By the time I got out of the sleeping bag and swam to the surface, I was pretty light-headed. Could only see out of one eye. So when I first saw it, I figured I was hallucinating."

"First saw . . ."

"The city."

Lakie said she'd landed in a river, surrounded by enormous buildings, roads and bridges, gray skies, fog and a smoggy cold.

"Which city?" asked Nico.

"There were a few different signs. But I think it was Manchester."

"How far away? From here to there?"

"Took me almost two days, but it's a lot closer. I was freezing, in shock, couldn't walk right at first. I can still barely see anything out of this eye; otherwise, I would have hit Bruno in more than the leg and shoulder."

"How'd you wind up here?"

"I knew our group had been headed east to a river. Figured there was a chance this was that river. Only question then was whether I should follow it north or south. I tried to visualize the maps we'd used. I was pretty sure Manchester was south of us, so—I warmed up inside a house, hung my clothes to dry, got some sleep—and then started walking north."

Lennon counted on his fingers. "So you've been here—four days? Five?"

"Feels like a month."

"Where'd they keep you?"

"This little house across the street, converted into a prison. Bars on windows, locks on doors. I got a chunk of Bruno's ear one night. Pretty sure I busted Gabe's testicle. They could have killed me, I guess, but that would have defeated their little plan."

" 'Be fruitful and multiply,' " said Nico.

Lakie looked at her, and in that one, piercing eye, Nico saw another life where they might have been good friends. "They had this whole system. One meal a day. Barely any water. No fire."

"Trying to wear you down."

"Get me to break."

"So you couldn't fight back."

There was more Nico wanted to know. *How* Lakie had been caught, for one, and if she'd spent five days here, surely there had been other altercations. But her own curiosity was nothing compared to the level of trauma Lakie had been through. *There's plenty she's not saying*, thought Nico, immediately followed by: *Can't fucking blame her.*

Quietly, in a voice thin and faraway, Lakie said, "We've been here before," and while Nico felt she'd heard the phrase recently, she couldn't place where. "That's what it felt like, locked in that house. Like I'd been there for ages."

"How'd you escape?" asked Lennon.

She took a long sip of water, and then, very calmly: "The spaceman. Just like Pringles said."

Stunned, Lennon told Nico the story of how Pringles had accidentally served poisonous berries only to have someone in a spacesuit appear out of thin air and save their lives. "I always pretended I didn't see him," said Lennon. "I don't know why I did that."

"A couple months ago Kit said he saw somebody walking in the woods, dressed like an astronaut, only in all black." Lakie looked at his small hand in hers as if it might come alive at any moment. "I've known the kid his whole life and he never lied, not once. The shit he knew, he had no business knowing. But I didn't believe him."

Nico hadn't given much thought to someone not believing in the existence of the Deliverer, just as she hadn't given much thought to someone not believing in the existence of Harry. Only now, in the company of others, did she understand that her eyes had grown used to the light of the Farmhouse, that her entire perspective of the outside world had, like a prolonged womb, developed within.

Down here, in the new light of Lennon and Lakie, she saw how truly insular her life had been. "We called him the Deliverer," she said, and she described the slat in the door of the Farmhouse, the regular deliveries of goods, and how she'd once thought the hands of the Deliverer were magical little birds.

"Earlier tonight. I'm locked up in that prison-house," said Lakie, "when I hear the lock click, and I think, *Here we go*. And then the door opens, and this person in a spacesuit's just standing there, staring at me. Sets a bolt-action rifle on the floor, nods once, then turns and walks away. Not a word. Leaves the door wide open. I run out of the house just in time to see the—Deliverer or spaceman or whatever—walking out of town— with *him*."

She nodded toward Lennon.

"Me?"

"The dog," said Lakie.

Harry kept his snout on Lennon's outstretched legs, but his ears perked, his tail wagged. *He knows we're talking about him.* Nico recalled his absence during dinner. Now she knew *where* he'd gone; she just had no idea *why*.

They sat quietly a moment, and Nico looked at the paints along the wall, imagined Gabe down here with an image in his head, gathering supplies for his murals. And she wondered if Lennon was right, if this had all happened before, and would all happen again. Maybe one day, she and Harry, Kit and Lennon and Lakie would star in their own mural, and some other person thousands of years from now might stare up and wonder who these people were, where they'd come from, what Vesuvius things they'd done.

"Lakie," she said, suddenly grateful to be alive.

"Yeah."

"Thank you. And I'm sorry."

Aboveground, the woods seemed to have returned to their normal wintersong, the swarms passed. Staring at Kit, she could almost hear that sweet voice explaining how paint made from natural pigments could last forever, and Nico thought, *Maybe here, in this little room, that's exactly what will happen.*

Eulogies

It was late, the darkness full.

Nico and Lennon and Harry walked south together, exiting Waterford on the same nameless road they'd used to enter it. The derelict buildings loomed darker, the murals more disturbing. At the southern tip of town, they found a sign identical to the one they'd passed on the northern end . . .

WELCOME TO WATERFORD, NEW HAMPSHIRE

FOUNDED IN 1822

POPULATION 2,023

Nico set down her bag, pulled out the can of red spray paint she'd brought from the shelter for just this purpose. She shook it, walked up to the sign, and when she was done, it read:

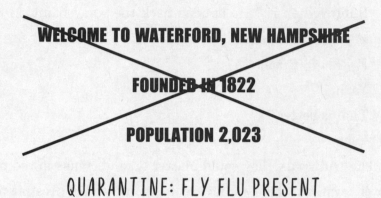

WELCOME TO WATERFORD, NEW HAMPSHIRE

FOUNDED IN 1822

POPULATION 2,023

QUARANTINE: FLY FLU PRESENT

Lennon held out a hand. "Let me see it a sec?"

She handed it to him, watched him run north up the road, back the way they'd come. Sometimes talking felt as possible as thinking a mountain into existence; it was a great comfort to have someone who understood things without her having to say them.

As she waited, her mind wandered back to Lakie. Whatever bond Nico had with Kit was nothing compared to his relationship with her. It was obvious in the way she looked at Kit, talked about him, held his hand. "I'll spend tonight with him," Lakie had told them as they'd left the shelter. "Tomorrow I'll pack a bag and head north."

They'd described the Cormorant, an unmistakable landmark. If Monty and Loretta were still at the cabin, she would find them easily enough. And if not, she would turn east from there, follow them to the coast and the Isles of Shoals.

"You steal my idea?" asked Nico when Lennon returned.

"Improved on it." He handed back the spray paint. "I used *imminent* instead of *present*."

"*Fly Flu imminent*."

"Yeah."

"That is better."

"Yeah."

The truth was, they could plaster fake warnings in red paint all over town, but there was no way to guarantee Kit's resting place would go undisturbed.

I never should have let him come. As they walked south, the words played like a chorus in her head, over and over until it was all she could hear, *I never should have let him come, I never should have let him come, I never should have let him come—*

"Hey." Lennon nudged her shoulder.

"I never should have let him come."

"You have a short memory, don't you?"

"What?"

"You *told* him not to. You said it could be dangerous and that you couldn't be responsible for him. You remember what he told you?"

But she couldn't talk through her tears, and so Lennon answered for her. "He said, *You're not the boss of me.* And you weren't. And neither was I. We could have tried to restrain him, I guess, but good luck with that. He was small, but—"

"*Lightning* quick."

Two brief smiles in the dark.

"What happened to him isn't your fault, Nico. It's not mine, and it's not his. What happened to Kit is the fault of two *fervently* fucked-up, fanatical Fly-lovers."

Unconvinced, but with zero emotional bandwidth for words, she kept quiet as they walked, avoiding the math of their dwindling footsteps.

Swears

They crossed the place where the road cut through saplings and ancients rather than bricks and built-things, a dusting of snow, light and patchy. Overhead, the trees were thick, each side joining forces until it felt like walking through a wooded tunnel. Nico and Lennon and Harry veered off-road, into the forest again, toward the sounds of the Merrimack, each with a silent oath never to return to Waterford, and yet Nico felt, deep down in a place she could not explain, that this would be a difficult promise to keep.

Studies

An hour south of Waterford, they came upon a row of houses with docks lining the river. They found a house that was in decent shape—windows and doors intact, air free of the smell of decay—and camped there for the night.

Judging from the map, they hoped to be in Manchester by late tomorrow morning, leaving them with most of the day to find Kairos (if it existed). As neither of them knew what to expect, they took comfort in the tedium of evening routines: Lennon gathered wood for the fireplace while Nico spread cinnamon in a circle around the house.

After they'd washed their faces and hands in the river, they went inside and set up in the middle of an old living room. Dusty furniture and photo albums everywhere, remnants of people living happy lives—were it not for Lennon's enthusiasm about sleeping indoors, she would have preferred a fire by the river. As it was, they were surrounded by sad relics, a darkness due not to lack of light, but lack of life.

Harry scratched at the door, eager to get out and let loose his newfound primordial hunting instincts. Nico debated letting him go, given what they now knew of blood.

For a moment she stood at the door, stared through the dark window, the moonlight off the river, and she considered that long lineage of logic: Her parents had been right to be cautious of blood. She wondered now if they'd known, or simply suspected. And how many other theories, shots in the dark, were right? How many far-fetched notions of survival, homemade Flu remedies, how many implausible methods of warding off contraction were actually effective?

Days ago she'd wondered what to do when someone handed

you a fiction and called it fact. Now she wondered, in a world where truth and lore looked so alike, how was anyone expected to tell them apart?

"Not tonight, bud." She reached out, turned the dead bolt.

On the floor of the living room, surrounded by dancing shadows on the walls, the flames in the fireplace waltzing and whirring, they ate a few Metallyte pouches (having replenished their supply from the shelves of the underground shelter) and a jar of mixed vegetables. Even Harry was content with the meatless dinner. And when, once again, he seemed to prefer Lennon's company to hers, she said nothing.

Later, however, as they crawled inside sleeping bags, she gave a quick whistle and held out a strip of her father's jerky, the last bit left. It was one thing, watching Harry prefer Lennon during waking hours, but Nico would sooner surrender to the Flies than watch the two of them curl up by the fire for the night. She rubbed behind the dog's ears, savoring the success of her bribe, knowing things were about to change and there was nothing she could do about it. And Nico thought of a different night, when Kit had sprinkled cinnamon around their campsite, talking about the word *meta* . . .

"Tell me more about Jean and Zadie," she said.

"What about them?"

"Anything. I need to get out of my own head."

"Okay." For a moment it was quiet as Lennon thought, the only sound the popping of the fire. "Zadie always made this noise after taking the first bite of every meal. Like a cross between a grunt and a purr. Like *that* motherfucking bite was *exactly* what she'd been looking for."

Nico laughed. "My dad did this thing where, after he took the first bite, he'd slap the table with his palm, and then roll his eyes back in his head."

"What is that? Like, is there some parenting handbook that says, *After the first bite, we strongly suggest you lose your mind?*"

It was a snowball laughter, the kind where one person ramps up the other until you've got a nice, rumbling avalanche. And Nico felt a weight lifted off her shoulders, if only a little.

"Hey, what was the lyric?" she asked. "The one John Lennon was proud of?"

" 'All you need is love.' "

Nico considered this. "You think he was right?"

"I don't know. Sometimes I worry it's one of the things that was only true before."

Nico propped herself up on one elbow, looked at him in the firelight. When they'd first gotten here, she'd pretended not to notice how quickly he'd unrolled his sleeping bag, leaving their proximity up to her. Of course, there was also the fire to be considered. She tried to remember how it had gone last night, in the darkness of BAM! They hadn't said much, and she couldn't be sure who'd made the first move, but somehow their hands had found each other.

Tonight she'd positioned her bag thoughtfully, close to him, yes, but close enough to the fire to maintain plausible deniability. *Oh, are we close? Sorry. The fire, you know.* Now, surrounded by these dancing flame-shadows, she was closer to him than she would have guessed, and couldn't help feeling her deniability was less plausible than she'd originally thought.

"Nico? You okay?"

"So you know how sometimes you don't know how to say what you want to say? So you just say it, and that's how you know?"

"Okay."

"I want you to know, I like your birthmark."

"Okay."

"I mean, I have no idea how you feel about it, and I'm not saying *you* should like it or not like it, I just wanted you to know what I thought about it. Which is that I like it."

Even as the words were coming out of her mouth, she wondered not why she was speaking, but *why these words in particular?*

"I have no idea what to expect tomorrow," she said, words like a runaway train. "But I'm glad you're with me. I miss my mom and my dad, and I miss Kit, and I'm tired of missing people, but I'm glad I don't have to miss you."

"I'm glad I'm—"

"You're the first person I ever talked to who wasn't related to me." Nico thought back to that day at the station when she'd seen the boy with the Alaska-shaped birthmark standing in the road. "Earlier that day, I'd almost—"

Her close encounter with the Metal Masks never felt far away. The image of what they'd done to the blue-lipped family in the back room of the station, and just as Nico had burned the place down so as to wipe clean those images, she found she did not want to bring them here.

"You almost . . . ?"

"Nothing," she said. "I'm just glad you're—you know—*you*."

"I'm glad you're you too."

Nico wanted to spill herself: *I spent the first eighteen years of my life in a boarded-up Farmhouse*, she would say. *I'd like to spend the next eighteen letting some light in.* She would tell Lennon of her search for the ageless love, the kind that doesn't leave. And if not lovers, let them be trees, bursting from the ground, branches swaying, growing toward each other, a dendrochronology intertwined, as if they'd spent many lives together, born in different places around the world at different times, but always finding their way back to each other.

"You wanna know what I thought?" he asked. "The first time I saw you?"

"How dumb I was for setting that station on fire?"

"After that."

Had he gotten closer? They seemed closer.

"I don't really know how to explain it," he said. "I guess it's like—you know how we look at stars from Earth and we think they're beautiful? But we don't *really* know what they look like, or how they behave. All we know is how they look from here, or what we've read. But there are some people who actually went up there. *Into* space, I mean."

"You're kind of a space nerd, aren't you?"

"As such, I know that there have been a select few humans who have gotten close enough to a star to either confirm or deny its beauty. Seeing you felt like that."

Nico pretended not to know what he meant. "You're saying I'm a *star*."

"Oh my God, you're going to make me say it, aren't you?"

"I'm just having a little trouble decoding your space metaphor."

He *was* closer. Though she wasn't sure how, was the thing.

Also, Harry had abandoned them for a dusty couch in the corner, something about their changing proximity scaring him off. *Bye, dog.*

"It wasn't just that I thought you were beautiful, or whatever," said Lennon. "It was like—you confirmed that kind of beauty existed."

There were times when Nico wondered if feelings could sense an opening, and that was why the strongest ones came all at once: disappointment at Harry's disinterest led to a longing to hear the wafer-thin pages of her mother's Bible, which led to the aftertaste of her father's stale tea, and maybe more than anything, unending sadness at Kit's absence. And yet, for all these feelings, there was a simpler one at play: a desire to feel Lennon's face in her hands. Right or wrong, there it was—she could hardly ignore it.

"Kalology."

"Was that a word?" he asked. She could hear the sound of his lips as they moved, which, she didn't know that was a thing. And now she realized how he was getting closer without moving: *she* was moving.

"My dad loved *ologies*," she said. "*The studies of*, you know? Geology, theology, anthropology, zoology. Rarer ones too, ones I never saw in books."

"Kalology being the study of . . ."

"Human beauty."

A weight like a blanket fell over them, a rare moment in which Nico felt tied to the old world by some ancient, built-in thing. And when they kissed it felt explosive and microscopic, warm and cold; she was a river and a mountain, a young child, a wise and aged woman. He asked if it was okay, as if she hadn't been edging closer to him this whole time, but she said, "Yes," because she loved that he asked.

They spent much of the night studying each other, these new masters of kalology. Time turned in on itself, and the lifeless dark of the room turned bright, and later, sharing a sleeping bag, Nico brushed her hand across Lennon's face, felt his hair in her hands, finally.

"What?" he asked.

"Nothing."

"That look on your face is not nothing."

She was lost in him, and wanted to stay there, but out came

the words. "The first day I met Kit, he said he wished you could come with him to the Isles of Shoals."

The glow in Lennon's eyes changed. "Really?"

"He told me you couldn't, though, because Boston was your destiny." This close to each other, eyes locked, for a second, she forgot they weren't the same person. And she wondered if he could read her mind: *Was Kit right? Is Boston your destiny? And are destinies chiseled in stone?*

But he kissed her again, and her questions melted right along with everything else.

Years later Nico would turn this night over in her mind, inspect it from all angles, wonder if it ever really existed. She would daydream of coming back to this moment in this random riverside house where she'd discovered love, her first and only visit to that elusive legend of a country. And there, finding the ghost of her younger self tucked beside a boy, she would tap them both on their blushing-bare shoulders, and whisper, *Even in a world where Fly exterminates Human, this has not changed: that one person might find beauty in another.*

THE DELIVERER

By the time I get home, it's almost two a.m.

Echo is asleep on the couch.

In the kitchen, on the island counter, a half-finished jigsaw puzzle, fragments of Van Gogh's *The Starry Night* spread all over the place. I guess he found the puzzle stash in the upstairs closet.

At least he's done a *little* exploring.

Yesterday Echo got the grand tour: I started with the solar panels, then moved on to the ten-thousand-gallon harvesting tank; I showed him the garden, the chickens in their fortress-coop, and told him the whens and hows of my maintenance schedule, the calendar outlining feedings and plantings, harvestings and all necessary upkeeps. "This is just my system, though. You may come up with your own."

Echo said nothing. Just stood there, looking around, a statue barely come to life.

I showed him how to work the stove and refrigerator. "Light begets light," I said, flipping the kitchen light off, then back on.

Not a word.

We moved to the living room, the glass wall, and I pulled a record off the shelf, Miles Davis, showed him where to place the stylus, how to turn on the receiver. I showed him the water-filtration system. "This is the most important thing in the house," I said, and told him the only way to survive was to stay healthy. "I consume only the water that comes through this filter. And I eat no meat. When the house is yours, you can do what you want. But I'm thirty-six and I'm alive."

I took him downstairs, showed him the cavernous storehouse. We walked up and down the aisles of freeze-dried foods, lighters, medical supplies, cinnamon. I handed him the spreadsheets, showed him how to keep track of everything so it lasted. "You have three years of rations, if you're smart about it."

He never said a word.

And I began to see my house through new eyes: the bathroom was filthy, the water pressure not nearly what it once was; the cellar storehouse looked like a ransacked shell; and my circle in the rock wall—countless hours spent chiseling, creating—Echo didn't even notice.

I watch him now, asleep on the couch.

The notes under most entries assure me that his silence is normal. A few Lives even theorize about the *levity* of the house, and how, even if we'd had someone to talk to in the early days, we most likely would have chosen silence too. Echo seems to prefer solitude, which, if not a prerequisite for living here, will surely work in his favor. And while my House by the Solar Cliffs cannot give him his old life back, it may, perhaps, give him *a* life back.

I should go to bed.

I should change out of the biosuit, shower, and sleep.

But I don't. Instead I set my helmet on the counter beside a thousand pieces of *Starry Night*, pull out a bottle of wine, uncork, and drink deeply. Straight from the bottle. Seize the fucking day, for tomorrow I say goodbye—to the wine, the showers, the eggs, all of it.

I pull out the third Red Book, flip it over. On the back cover, using a kitchen knife, I etch a line through the number 160.

Over and out.

"Godspeed, 161."

I shut the Book, drink, stare up at the spot where the Architect had hung himself; I still see him clearly, his body in the late stages of decomposition. I think of the hours it took to get him down, to bury him in the backyard, and I think that word— *decompose*—lacks the proper gravity. A long, deep drink as it occurs to me that I will never know who he was, where he came from, why, how, or if he built this place. Was this his Noah's Ark? He'd killed himself before the Flies hit North America, which made the Ark theory seem a bit extreme. But then he'd also produced a biosuit to withstand a swarm attack, so maybe. Probably, I'm overthinking it. Probably, he was just one in a long line of paranoid survivalists.

"You're only paranoid until you're right."

Gulp the wine now, and whether it's the presence of Echo, the knowledge of what tomorrow will bring, or the not-knowing what comes after, the essence of my eternal memory feels like a thread on a spool spinning in the wrong direction.

For years I've daydreamed of life after the Red Books; now it's almost here, I can't seem to summon those dreams, day or otherwise.

I sit at the kitchen counter, try to finish the puzzle.

I can't finish the puzzle.

Fuck the puzzle.

Finish the bottle instead.

I should go to bed. But then, who would drink this second bottle of wine, which magicked itself from the cabinet? Uncorked now, down the hatch she goes. Almost three a.m., no matter. *If there was ever a reason to get sloshed . . .*

A sudden need for air, and so I take the bottle out the back door, and as I drink, I let the cold night drink me, and I wonder if nighttime fosters brooding, or if brooding brings the night. I pass the tank, and the Architect's grave, a little trickle of wine on the snow, not too much. "You're dead," I mumble, "and the dead don't thirst," and I must be stepping all over Echo's spring harvest, but c'est la vie, life goes on, Life after Life, and just a few more steps to the cliff now, that sheer drop, the tip of the upside-down *V*, the open air begging for someone to show the birds a thing or two—

Stop at the edge.

Drink, and drink the view.

Miles of uninhabited winter-white and dark green, a thousand-piece puzzle connecting the sky and stars and moon. *Wine seriously tastes better from the bottle*, but no matter how much I drink, I cannot shake the image of them jumping from this very spot, memories from one Life bleeding into another, and the more Lives I live, the sharper these transport imprints become, images from the early Lives, even, of gruesome survival before the house, and what's the fucking point? Why am I here? Just a pawn in some elaborate orchestrated reality, doomed to live over and over again, and in so doing, never really live at all? I can't stop the Flies, I can't stop the Flu, all I have are my peripheral adjustments and this bottle of wine. Maybe the world is a record, and I'm a scratch on the vinyl, a cut in the concentric circles, doomed to play the same seven notes over and over again. Maybe the world needs to be picked up, let down in another place. Maybe it needs to move on from *me*, to be traded for something without so many scratches. There are times when I feel everything, and times when I feel nothing, and both seem equally painful, so which is it now, which is this, and shit, I'm drunk.

I look down at the multitude of solar panels, such great lengths the Architect had taken in the name of self-preservation—only to decide his self wasn't worth preserving. And here, at the edge of the world, my kingdom in the clouds, I understand his final motivation. His untold want had been the same achievement of all creatures great and small: a proper ending. I throw my arms open, let the cold air have me, and I scream, wondering how many more numbers will be carved into the back of the Red Books before I achieve my own ending.

"Hey."

It takes a second for the voice to register.

I turn to find Echo standing there, wind blowing through his hair, lips blue. Between the biosuit insulation and the second bottle of wine, I hadn't realized how cold it was.

"You're not going to jump, are you?" he asks.

I drink. Look from the view, back to him—shake my head.

A few seconds pass, then he says, "I have a question." Our eyes connect and just when I think it's coming, the question I've been dreading ever since first removing my helmet in front of him—*Do I know you from somewhere?*—his eyes lighten, and he says, "I need help finishing the puzzle."

I take another drink, look up at the stars, and then back at him. "Not really a question. But okay."

Inside, he puts on a pot of water for coffee. We piece Van Gogh back together, swirly stars, the moon like an eye, and I think how glad I am that my 153rd Life had thought to bring Echo here, how suited he is to this place.

"I've never done one of these before," he says, wedging two pieces together. "How's it feel once it's finished?"

I open my mouth to say something—clip one piece of star into another—and smile. "It's not really about the finished thing. More about the process of putting it together."

I have asked the stars many questions; this is the first time they've answered.

NICO

Tracks

They'd gotten an early start, hoping to hit Manchester by midmorning. Seven tallies on her hand now. Tonight there would be eight, and her father would ring the Bell, and for better or worse, she would finally know the full extent of his un-blossoming.

Most of the walk so far had been spent in silence. Little more than *how'd you sleep* followed by *good, you?* It wasn't shame or embarrassment that kept the pleasantries artificial; it was the light of day—the light of *this* day—that painted the events of last night in hazy shades.

They came to a place where three clustered bridges crossed to the east bank of the Merrimack: one, a paved road, clearly meant for cars; one, rotted wood, and narrower, most likely for people; and one for the train tracks. Nico and Lennon stood for a moment in front of this last bridge, watching the tracks disappear over the water into unknown lands on the other side. They held hands as Lennon said a few words, but all Nico could hear was Kit explaining crossties, and how there were people to build trains, people to drive trains, people to ride them, people to load them. *I wish I could ride a train someday,* he'd said that morning, in the shadow of the Cormorant.

"Maybe now you can," she whispered.

Illuminations

Nico walked alone.

Twenty yards up, Harry trotted beside Lennon, two peas in a pod. She watched with mixed emotions and a bag devoid of jerky, bribery no longer an option. They began to play the Game, and when Harry ran ahead, Lennon turned, half smiled; her mixed emotions reunited, and she dreamed of a world where destinations were people instead of places.

Ahead, Lennon stopped walking, pointed at something to the west. "Look."

Either this particular section of the river had brought them closer to the road, or vice versa, because when Nico looked where Lennon was pointing, she saw a large billboard between a gap in the trees:

NEXT EXIT

~~BLESSED CHURCH OF THE RISEN~~ SAVIOR

NOW VOYAGER

"SEEK AND YE SHALL FIND"

"Like from Echo's story," he said, once Nico caught up to him.

"When Voyager goes to Manchester, remember? The Bellringer, or whatever. He says that."

Nico imagined her father, one hand through the railing of the attic deck, as if reaching for the trees. *The untold want by life and land ne'er granted*, he would say. *Now, Voyager, sail thou forth to seek and find.*

"It's Whitman," she said.

"What?"

Tell him.

And just when she thought she couldn't, she opened her mouth and the truth fell out. As they walked, she told Lennon everything: how Echo's story was one version of a story she'd heard her whole life; how her father had once been a geophysicist and, according to him, had worked for the government under the pretext of a company called Kairos to study a geological anomaly in a riverside mill; how, like Voyager, she had been sent to Manchester to find this anomaly; and how scared she was that it didn't exist.

Lennon didn't say anything at first. When he finally did speak, it wasn't at all what she was expecting. "Did you know the ancient Greeks had two words for *time*?"

"How in the world do you know that?"

"I told you." He held up his Boston skyline wristwatch. "Jean was obsessed with this stuff."

"Okay."

"So one of those words was *chronos*. Where we get the word *chronological*, a timeline the way we think of it. The other was *kairos*," and Nico felt her face warm as Lennon explained how Kairos was the god of opportunity, how the word had evolved, how archers had begun using it to denote the exact moment in which an arrow should be fired in order to pierce its target with maximum force. "The opportune moment," he said. "The *kairotic* moment. An opening in time."

"What's your point?"

"We just saw a sign that has a phrase from your dad's story *painted on it*. We already know the Cormorant is real, and Echo's mom told him the *same* story, so at the very least we know your dad wasn't making it all up. I guess my point is—maybe it *had* to be this way. Maybe, if your dad told you the truth years ago, you would have tried to leave then, only it wouldn't have been the right time. Maybe this is your kairotic moment."

Her face now felt like fire, not only at the seemingly endless pile of things her father hadn't told her, but because whatever part of her wanted to believe her dad was the very part she would lose if his story *wasn't* true: the knowledge that she, above all others, knew him best.

"Maybe," she said.

Downriver, Harry ran ahead, attempting to play the Game again, but neither of them was in the mood. Minutes passed in the relative silence of footsteps and the gently running river, and then Lennon stopped, eyes faraway. On his face, that same constricted look she'd seen days ago, by the fire as he spoke of Boston, his mouth having been commandeered by his brain.

It had stopped him short then. But not this time.

"Every minute of every day," he said. "Do you know what I think about?"

And then the look broke apart, and his eyes welled, and something about seeing him on the verge of tears brought her there too.

"It's awful"—the well overflowed, a few tears fell down his cheek—

"Lennon." She reached out but he pulled away.

"I wonder what would have happened if my birth parents had survived instead of—" He looked away, wiped his eyes. "Jean and Zadie gave me everything, and I loved them, and I wouldn't trade that. But there were two people before them who sang songs to me at night, took pictures I'll never see, made plans I'll never know, because the *only* things I know are what they told a couple of strangers over dinner at a campsite hours before the Flies hit. So it's hard for me when I hear you . . ."

It took everything in her not to reach out again. "I'm sorry," she whispered.

Harry returned, ears perked, head tilted, and whereas before his eyes had asked, *Why no Game?*, they now said, *If you are sad, I can make things better.*

"You don't need to apologize." Lennon bent down to pet Harry; Nico knelt too, scratched behind the dog's ears. "I just wish I'd had a chance to know them," he said. "And I worry—*all the time*, I worry that Boston is a mirage. Another sad consolation."

Nico had heard a thousand stories in her life, understood their call and response: *Once upon a time*, her father would say; *I am listening*, she would say. But listening was about more than hearing; it was about when and where you put yourself in the story.

"I've lost everyone," said Lennon. "I have memories, that's what I have. Memories and a wristwatch with a skyline."

For the first time Nico saw herself, not as Voyager, but as a trusty blowfish. And the old story was made new, its truths richer and more complex.

"Dad trusted me with his stories because he knew I'd take care of them," she said. "I'm guessing Jean gave you that watch for the same reason." One hand on Harry, she took Lennon's hand in the other, and this time he did not pull away. "That skyline's not nothing, Len. And you haven't lost everyone."

Between them, Harry soaked up the attention: tongue out, King of Dogs, *There now, that's better, isn't it?* The three of them stayed like that for a few minutes, content in this new and fascinating consolidation.

Lines

Farther south, somewhere in the distance: the low, familiar drone of a waterfall, steadily louder with each step. The closer they got to Manchester, the more houses and apartments lined both sides of the river. There were empty hotels and restaurants, overturned cars in streets, and it wasn't that they hadn't witnessed these things before now, but there was a feeling of magnitude, as if all towns prior to Manchester were little more than dry runs.

It began to sleet. The air chilled, emptiness filled their moods, the grayness of the sky so visceral, Nico felt it in her teeth.

"Well," said Lennon. "Welcome to Manchester, I guess."

They took cover under a small gazebo between apartment complexes, ate a quick bite before formulating a plan. Harry kept his nose in the air, sniffing the sleet as if gathering intel.

"So what are we looking for?" Lennon pulled out his map.

"In the story, Bellringer says Kairos is surrounded by a cluster of mills."

Nico pulled out her own map, pointed to the red circles on the bank of the river. "Dad circled these. It's been years, and with so many mills, and with his—memory—who knows how accurate this is. Could take hours to find."

Lennon looked up—then back at the map. "We should have crossed."

"What?"

He pointed to the red circles on her map. "They're all on the east bank. We should have crossed the river north of here. One of those bridges . . ."

He was right. The train tracks, the pedestrian bridge, any number of bridges they'd passed.

"Looks like there's a bridge here." He pointed to the map, just south of where they were. "And another here. We'll find a way across."

When the sleet let up, they tucked their maps away, slung

on their bags, and within an hour they came to the first bridge, a paved four-lane road. As Lennon led the way across, it wasn't hard to imagine the bridge as a once-impressive thoroughfare, four lanes of city traffic, the hustle and bustle of it all. Now it was little more than a crumbling monument to a dead city. The road felt wobbly beneath her feet, the sky grayer, and with each step forward, she wanted more and more to turn back.

Just when she was about to say so, Lennon stopped abruptly, arms out.

"What?"

He pointed ahead, where the road succumbed entirely, went from crumbling to obliterated. It picked up again closer to the east bank, but there was a solid twenty- or thirty-yard gap where the middle section of the bridge had collapsed, resting somewhere at the bottom of the Merrimack.

And just as frustration was about to boil over—at herself, for not thinking to cross when they'd had the chance, and at her dad, for the piecemeal directions—she turned south and saw all of Manchester spread out before her, like the city had been hiding, and only here, from the middle of a half-collapsed bridge, high over the Merrimack River, would it reveal itself.

The entire city was built on, or around, the Merrimack River. Massive brick structures lined the water's edge, bigger than anything Nico had ever imagined, impressive even in their various states of deterioration. The wide rocky river led down into a proper panorama, power lines and industry, a landscape Nico had only dreamed of. It was a different kind of awe up here than the view offered by the attic deck. Both provided wonder, but where the endless horizon of treetops and mountains was pure potential, the gray Manchester skyline was a product of potential wasted. Little craters everywhere, massive holes where natural-gas lines had sprouted leaks and, ultimately, exploded. *Rusty pipes and leaky tanks and no one there to repair them*, her father used to say. *Whole cities going up in flames, craters where buildings once stood, ash-snow, mountainous piles of soot—*

"A darkness has chased away the sky," Lennon said, his hand weaving into hers, and she took a breath to say something, but nothing came out. Here, this relic of a city spread before her, Nico understood the world that she had missed, knew that she'd been cheated by time itself. But even as this injustice threatened to wreck her, she felt some small seedling of hope wriggling to the surface: that whatever part of her still doubted her father, a larger part must trust him to have come so far.

Ruins

After retracing their steps back to the west side of the river, they continued south in hopes that the next bridge was intact. The sound of water intensified, and they came to another hydroelectric station, with its huge cage-like construction of rusted metal or steel, and tall cone chimneys reaching up to the sky. As before, various sections of the cage were connected to power lines, maybe even the same ones that had followed them here.

Beyond that, they came to the spot where the river reached its widest, and a waterfall plunged some fifty feet before crashing and continuing its path south. In that old shoebox in the attic, there was a photograph of her parents when they were young, on a boat at the foot of a waterfall that seemed to come straight out of the clouds. In the pictures, they'd had to wear special ponchos so they wouldn't get soaked. The waterfall in front of Nico and Lennon was nothing like that, though the sheer breadth of it—from one side of the bank to the other—was its own kind of impressive.

Even with the city in their sights, the walk got harder before it got easier. The brush thickened, as if the rural could sense the urban just around the corner. *Now or never*, it seemed to say, growing and blooming until they had to turn back in places. It was a frustrating go-the-long-way-around situation, especially this near to the end, and by the time the next bridge was in sight, it felt like hours had passed.

"What time is it?" she asked, the overcast sky making it difficult to get a read on the sun.

Lennon looked at his watch. "Almost four. What time is he ringing the Bell?"

"He said a couple hours after sunset."

She tried to calculate what time of day the sun normally went down, but as time had always been relative to meals or sleeping—

dinnertime, lunchtime, naptime, bedtime—it was difficult to say. Nearing the second bridge, Nico tried to think. "Knowing what time he rings the Bell won't help us get there any faster."

"True," he said. "Still. Maybe we . . . ?"

"Yeah."

Without another word, they broke into a light jog.

The second bridge was more elevated than the first one, closer to the heart of the city. They would be visible for miles up there, exposed to any and all lurking Brunos or Metal Masked mobs.

"We'll go fast," said Lennon, reading her mind.

Hands in pockets, breathing into the front collars of their shirts, they started across this new bridge, chasing after Harry. What had been cold on the streets of Manchester was now, out over the Merrimack, downright frigid. Below them, the river had outgrown its shores, spilling into the ground floors of the mills lining the water's edge. Farther downstream the land dipped, and the flood line looked significantly higher, two or three stories completely submerged. Nico had read books where the world had been wiped out, whether by pandemic, nuclear fallout, alien invasion, or, according to Lennon's stories, robot uprisings. Now, looking out over the foggy skyline, she tried to reconcile those fictions with the realities of this city: its decaying infrastructure and smoking craters, its cables leading nowhere; empty streets, empty cars, empty houses; a river that had risen, reached out, and devoured the nearest buildings; and all under a sky of ashen chaos only made possible by nobody being alive to give a fuck.

They made it across without incident.

If you can call that without incident, she thought.

Floods

Most of the mills had names on the outside, signs etched into stone or brick. It was a considerable amount of running around, trying to find each sign, but at least they weren't forced to inspect every mill inside and out. A good thing, given Nico had never seen so many buildings in her life, not just mills but stores and stations and restaurants. After searching for any sign of Kairos, consulting the little red circles on her dad's map, holding it at different angles, they wound up in a parking lot by a sign that read AMERICA RUNS ON DUNKIN'.

So far they'd seen three just like it.

"Maybe Dunkin is the guy who makes the doughnuts," said Nico.

"What's a doughnut again?"

"Like a cake, I think?" She shrugged. "I don't know."

"Look." Lennon pointed farther west. "There's another one over there."

The sky was the color just before evening snow, when the whole world looked like one big cloud. Some twenty feet away, a rusted-out car was parked in the lot. Inside, the skeletal remains of a person in the driver's seat.

Lennon pointed to one of the mills they'd already checked,

which had been converted into a museum. "Why don't we try in there? Maybe find a more detailed map of the town or something."

Walking into the museum was like walking into another dimension. Everything was surprisingly intact, organized, aesthetically pleasing, and small enough to not feel overwhelming. Photos on walls depicted canals from years ago, captions explaining how many of the paved streets they'd just walked on had once *been* canals. A huge display of the Merrimack River showed how it all worked: from the Upper Canal to the Lower Canal, water ran through each mill, spinning a turbine under the floor that powered textile machines throughout the building. There was a whole section about the "Manchester renaissance," a period that began in the early 2000s, when tech companies and restaurants and coffee shops and high-end lofts turned the run-down mills into valuable property.

Another display outlined the many floods through the years, the most destructive of which occurred in 1896, submerging buildings and taking out bridges. The 2020s saw a slew of floods, one after the next until the final one—which Nico could only assume was the one outside now—stuck around. As if the Merrimack River were a giant battering ram, each flood an attempt to break down the castle door. Now that it had, it wasn't going anywhere.

They walked through a hallway with closet-size dioramas of Manchester through the years: the Manchester News, city hall, a soda shoppe, a stylish little bookstore called Bookery, and at the end, a reconstructed movie theater with a marquee that read COMING SOON: "MANCHESTER AND THE GREAT WAR."

The whole thing was an immersive and curious experience, a time capsule of the old world. On any other day, Nico would have loved it.

But today was today.

They exited the museum with nothing to show for it; outside, the snow had started, big thick flakes in a steady stream, and the sky had deepened to a darker shade of evening.

"Hey," said Lennon.

"What."

He pointed to the mill across the street. It was enormous, probably four stories high, a hundred yards long. Earlier, when they'd checked the entrance of this mill, the ground floor was completely underwater. What they hadn't noticed until now was that the mill was built on an incline, so what was the ground floor of the south entrance was apparently the basement of the north entrance.

In front of them now, a walkway led to a set of double doors, with a small sign beside it reading KAIROS, INC.

Characters

It was dry under the awning, but she felt shivery, the cold and wet having seeped into her bones.

A heavy chain had been wrapped through the handles and then padlocked together. Stenciled across the top of the door, in bold white lettering: AUTHORIZED PERSONNEL ONLY. Lennon pointed to a broken camera up under the awning. "Video surveillance. Though this . . ." He ran his hand over a small black box attached to the wall. It was hard plastic, with a blank screen and a few small round nodes. "I have no idea what this is."

"Some sort of digital lock?"

He bent down for a closer look at the screen. "Zadie used to travel for work. She told stories about airports that scanned your retinas for identification." From one end to the other, the width of the box was almost exactly the width of Lennon's face. "I bet that's what this was."

Nico thought of the blue-lipped family in the back of the station, and the crowbar that locked them inside. "I guess the geological anomaly needed protection from the outside world."

"Or the outside world needed protection from it."

Nico blew into her hands to warm them. "A retina scan. So futuristic and yet—"

"A thing of the past."

"Maybe."

Braving the elements, Lennon ran to the nearest window to see if it was locked. "You think retina scans will make a comeback?"

"Like you said. Reboot. Rainbow. Start over."

Nico bent to pet Harry. He, too, was wet with sleet, and she had a sudden memory of bath days in the Farmhouse, how sheepish he looked while being bathed, but then, once done, how he'd run around in circles, barking at nothing, just happy to be clean and alive. She could almost hear her father now: *The most compelling evidence of intelligent design is the joyous stupidity of dogs.*

"Why put up a sign?"

"What do you mean?" asked Lennon, back under the awning again.

She pointed to the sign by the door. KAIROS, INC. "If it's a secret government thing. Why even have a sign?"

Lennon thought for a second. "Can you think of a better way to draw attention to your company than a giant unnamed, unmarked building?"

He had a point. Still, Nico couldn't help wondering if maybe her father *had* worked for a company called Kairos, only instead of studying some vague geological anomaly, he'd been nothing more than a cog in an office, pushing papers around, sipping coffee, wondering what was for dinner.

"So. All the windows are barred. Guess we should circle the building, see if there's another way in?" Lennon grabbed the giant padlock, shook the chain around. "Unless you have a key."

Slowly, she stood and stared at the padlock.

"What?" said Lennon. "That was a joke, I don't expect you to actually have—"

From her pocket, Nico pulled out a silver key attached to a chain necklace.

"What is that?"

"A key," she said.

"Well, I know it's a key. I'm saying—"

"It was Kit's."

"Is that the one he said—like, an angel supposedly gave it to his mom, right?"

"Yeah."

"Nico. There are a billion keys in the world. I think I've found half of them on scavenges."

Ignoring him, she stepped forward, and it felt as though the crushing weight of Kit's absence had been reallocated to this light-weight object in her hand. Nico took a breath, inserted the key into the lock, felt a smooth *click* as she turned it, and a small part of a much larger wound began to heal in ways she could not explain.

"*Holy shit,*" said Lennon.

In no time, the padlock was tossed aside, and as they pulled the thick chain out of the door handles, Nico felt Lennon's eyes on her. "I don't know," she said.

"I mean."

She smiled, shrugged. "I don't know."

"Those chances are astronomical. I'm just saying—that can't be a coincidence."

"I know." She shook her head. "I'm just saying—I don't know."

Inside, Nico pulled a lighter from her backpack, flicked it on. They were in a small entryway with a split stairwell; going up was the only option, as downstairs was entirely flooded.

On the wall, they found a directory of the building showing four floors: the bottom floor of suites was labeled 1001–1040; the second floor was 2001–2040, and so on with the third and fourth floors. Some of the numbers had worn off, and there was not a single business or store name to be found, each suite entirely unoccupied, with a single exception.

"There." Nico pointed to the last suite on the fourth floor, number 4040.

Beside it, a single character: O.

She thought back to the morning Echo disappeared, how disappointed she'd been that she'd waited to ask questions, not in hopes of finding answers, but in hopes that Echo might prove her father wrong. This, she knew, was who she was at her weakest.

"Is that the letter *O* or a zero?" asked Lennon.

Nico turned, started up the stairs, feeling strong for the first time in days. "Neither," she said, confident that even if the father who'd raised her had lost his mind, the story he'd raised her on was all heart. "It's a circle."

Doors

The fourth floor greeted them with an eerie quiet. A single hallway ran the entire length of the building, right down the middle, with doors to offices on either side. Direct access to these offices meant no access to windows, and total darkness. From where they stood, looking down the hallway felt more like staring into a horizontal abyss.

Nico held up the lighter to the nearest door. "Suite 4001."

"Of course we're on the wrong end."

Guided by the miniature flame, they started down the hall. The floors were an old wood, every step a creak or snap. Lining the walls between the office doors were black-and-white photographs of the mills in the early days, pictures that oozed industry and smoke and large iron tools, images of ghostly faces staring out at them as if they'd been caught in the act of living.

The lighter flickered out.

"*Shit.* Hold up." Nico dug another lighter out of her bag, was about to flick it on when Lennon grabbed her arm.

"You hear that?"

At first all she could hear was Harry's panting. Gradually, though, something else: a humming or whirring, but different than the one in the catacombs of Bruno's church, more fluid. It wasn't an instrument, but there was musicality to it, a single note buried in the orchestra, pure and sad and you don't notice it at first, and then once you do, you know the orchestra would be lost without it. And whether because of this humming, or because the Deliverer made no noise at all, Nico and Lennon did not hear a footstep, did not sense a presence, until an electric light at the far end of the hall clicked on, and they saw the black helmet and synthetic suit, the tinted visor, the gloved hands that were not exotic birds—they saw the Deliverer standing there, as if waiting for them.

"*Harry,*" said Nico, her dog calmly disappearing into the darkness of the hallway before reappearing in the light of the Deliverer's torch.

Nico whistled him back; he did not come.

The Deliverer bent down, rubbed behind Harry's ears, and Nico could not deny the sense of relief at finally seeing this person who, for so long, had meant so much to her family. All those

Delivery Days, the taco seasoning, the Metallyte chili macs, more pounds of cinnamon than she could count. It was like coming face-to-face with the Wizard of Oz, or Aslan from Narnia. So yes, relief, but also—as she would be if confronted by the Wizard or Aslan—terror.

As they watched from the middle of the hallway, the Deliverer turned, opened a door, and, together with Harry, disappeared through it.

Lennon grabbed her hand before she could start for the door. "Hey," he said, and Nico thought, *Here it is, he's done, shit has gotten too weird.* She couldn't blame him. Shit *had* gotten weird, and he didn't owe her a thing, and Boston awaited, and how was she supposed to say goodbye to him at all, much less like this—

"Your boots are untied."

"What?"

He pointed down at her feet. "Your laces."

It was less a hug, more a gentle tackle, a tight wrapping of the arms around the neck, pulling him close. "Thank you," she whispered.

"I mean—it's dark. I didn't want you to trip."

"That's not what I meant."

"I know what you meant."

Maybe it was ridiculous, having this moment now, but as they let go of each other, turned toward suite 4040, Nico couldn't help feeling that opening this door would somehow close others, more quixotic ones, doors to places where two people got lost in each other beside a fireplace, where wild joy could be found in nothing but the sound of your name on their lips.

"More cameras." Lennon motioned toward the broken camera hanging from the ceiling. And again, stenciled in frosted glass, the words AUTHORIZED PERSONNEL ONLY with the video camera icon.

Nico put a hand on the knob. "You ready?"

"Nico."

"What."

He pointed to her boots, and she handed him the lighter, and maybe because her mind was on doors, but as she bent to tie her laces, it occurred to her that this was true friendship: a person in your life who was willing to walk through strange doors into dark places, so long as they could walk there with you.

Controls

The few times she'd imagined a professional office, Nico had pictured a soporific flood of beige carpets and walls, dusty computers and desks with nameplates, neck-high partitions divvying up the room.

This was not that.

The showstopping centerpiece of the room was the ceiling. Though *ceiling* seemed the wrong word, as the entire thing had been replaced by a great glass dome. Outside, the gray sky had ripened into navy, deep and unending, boasting stars and moon so bright they shone through the clouds, lighting up the room. Snow was coming fast now, an onslaught of flakes hitting the outside of the curved glass and sliding away.

The dome reached its highest in the center of the room, at least six or seven times taller than the outer walls of the suite. The room was large enough on its own, but the glass dome made it feel cavernous.

Harry, she thought, looking around. She was about to whistle when she spotted him sniffing the base of another door, this one leading into a smaller room within the room, an entire corner partitioned behind glass. Inside, what looked like a wall of computers and panels.

Beside her, Lennon muttered, "Control room."

"Controlling what?"

The larger room was mostly empty. There were no desks or tables; instead four wrought iron posts were positioned in the center of the floor, each as tall as a person, each with a thick chain running between them, roping off the area. Over a dozen video cameras were set up all over the place, each pointed toward this roped-off space.

The Deliverer stood by one of these posts, staring down at the floor, and as Nico and Lennon stepped forward, hand in hand, Nico felt as if they'd slipped into a painting, a feeling that only enhanced when she noticed the Deliverer wasn't staring *at* the floor, but *through* it. The posts and chain were roping off a square hole, some ten feet by ten feet, that had been surgically cut into the floor directly below the apex of the glass dome. As they neared, the Deliverer pointed down, and Nico's wonderings evolved and multiplied: through the hole, she saw another surgical square had been cut into the floor of the room directly below them, suite 3040, and another square cut into the floor of suite 2040, so that there, four stories down, having flooded the first floor years ago, was a ten-foot-square view of the Merrimack River.

"What time is it?" Nico asked.

Lennon said nothing, just stared through the hole.

"Lennon."

He looked at his wrist. "Eight twenty." As he said this, Nico noticed that the Deliverer, in an instinctive reaction to her question, had also looked at a wristwatch: a polished silver band and a face with a skyline . . .

Exactly like Lennon's.

Before she could process how it was possible a world like theirs might contain two of the same unusual watches, Harry barked behind them. Fully upright, he had both front paws propped against the door to the control room, tail wagging wildly.

She looked at the Deliverer.

A slight nod. *Go ahead.*

Together with Lennon, she joined Harry at the control room and pushed open the door. Inside, Harry assumed his usual posture, nose to the ground, covering the small square footage in no time. A couple lockers lined the back wall of the room. Everything was coated in layers of dust, a few stacks of papers and files, coffee cups, and a panel of computers and technological equipment with buttons and screens and switches whose functions Nico could only dream of.

"So the geological anomaly happens out there," said Lennon. "And they monitor it in here."

On the panel, under a computer screen, Nico spotted a small framed photograph, and when she picked it up, the air rushed out of her as her heart filled, all the physiological comings and goings of the body at once.

"Who's that?" Lennon looked over her shoulder.

They looked happy in the photo. Somewhere she didn't recognize. *Like that's really saying something.* Probably, it was a restaurant or a movie theater or some friend's house, one of a hundred places people used to go when people still did things like that. "It's them," she said. Her dad was midsentence, talking to someone off camera. Her mom was looking at him, a smile like she knew he was hers. "It's my parents." She allowed herself another moment to stare, and then tucked the photo into her bag.

Wherever she was about to go she would want them with her.

Lennon picked up a case of silver pens. Engraved across the front were the words *Property of Helen Leibowitz.*

"Echo's mom," said Lennon.

From a random file, Nico pulled out a chart with four columns: across the top, from left to right, they were marked *Tollbooth Entry*

Date, Name, Destination (hypothesized), Tollbooth Return Date. The first three columns were completely filled with names, dates, places. The last one—*Tollbooth Return Date*—was empty.

"You figure most of their documentation was digital." Lennon put a hand on the nearest computer. "Videos, information, years of footage and work. People stored their lives in these. Now they're just . . . little tombs."

More files containing pages of transcripts, mostly scientific and difficult to make sense of. More references to "Tollbooth," which seemed to be used interchangeably with the geological anomaly, and Nico remembered conversations about God and science, Tollbooths and Arks. Ways out.

"'What had started as make-believe was now very real,'" said Lennon.

"You're quoting *The Phantom Tollbooth* now?"

"The what? No, look." He pointed to the window, where someone had taped a napkin with those handwritten words. "Echo quoted that. Or something close. Said it was in his mom's journal."

"When?"

"In the cabin. You'd taken Harry outside to pee, I think. What's *The Phantom Tollbooth*?"

Quickly, Nico summarized the story of a boy called Milo who assembled a mysterious tollbooth, which turned out to be a portal to an entirely other world. "Dad used to read it to me all the time."

"Look at this." Lennon held out a file with a piece of paper containing a list of cities in which other geological anomalies had been documented: Madrid, Alexandria, Bend, Seoul, Lima, Missoula, Asheville. The document also outlined concern regarding military interference, and a brief debate over the origins of the anomalies, whether they were earthly or alien. "'Wherever it originates,'" Lennon read, "'whatever its biological makeup, however far down it goes, when one considers the cities in which anomalies have been documented, it is relatively safe to assume they manifest themselves through, or near, water. If harnessing the Tollbooth is priority, sound is key.' Signed 'EA.'"

A sudden memory, sitting with her father on the attic deck, drenched to the bone. He raised his face to the sky to drink the rain . . . "Sound travels through water much faster than it does through air."

"Really?"

Through the glass, Nico saw the Deliverer watching them, and when Harry exited the control room, Nico followed. "When water moves, sound feels it," she said, still in the memory, walking toward the Deliverer, Lennon behind her. "When sound changes, water is affected," and somewhere in the building the humming sound returned, same as before only amplified, and the floor under their feet groaned, and all went abruptly quiet.

Overhead, thousands of shadows danced, white snow against the bright moon, and Nico knew it was more than just the Deliverer that had been waiting for her: it was this time, and this place.

"It's happening."

The humming crescendoed, whirring and sonorous, a deafening drone that sunk its claws into the room, and when it rose
to meet them, it came slowly, as if ashamed of its own volume:
it started with only a few drops of water floating up through the
square hole, and then a dozen drops became hundreds, a slow-
motion rain in reverse. The bass of the drone dropped out, the
sound now a freestyle glissando, the most beautiful musical noise
Nico had ever heard. She could see it clearly: the note of the Bell
flying over miles of treetops, and the Cormorant catching that
note, amplifying it, aiming it toward the river. She looked down
at her hands, then at Lennon and Harry, a need to confirm some
anchor of reality, that the laws of physics were still in play. But it
was only the water breaking these laws, the Merrimack River floating upward in pieces. Drops of water poured in by the thousands
now, well organized and of one mind, flying around the room in a
massive formation like some miraculous flock of tiny birds.

Like the Flies.

And then—as one—the flock connected, the waterdrops combined into a single shape in midair: the bottom of the circle hovered
inches over the carpet; the top reached the apex of the glass dome;
and the great circle of water began to spin, slowly at first, then
faster, then much faster until Nico felt mist on her face. And here,
in a place called Kairos, in the presence of the nameless, faceless
Deliverer, she stared into the center of the spinning water and saw
a second night sky, a second snow, a second woods. "How can I

fight this darkness?" she asked, knowing the answer before the Deliverer said it. Little details of the story changed with each telling, but the ending was always the same.

"In you go, my dear."

Watches

The Deliverer stepped forward, held out a handful of books. "You'll need these."

Nico thought it was the voice of a woman, though the helmet and visor made it hard to say for sure.

"Go on," said the Deliverer. There were three books, thick and red. "Take them."

As soon as they were in Nico's hands, she felt their age. Old leather wound together by a black cord. The edges of the journals were brown and worn, the black cord had clearly been wrapped and unwrapped thousands of times.

"Wait. Where did you get that watch?" Lennon looked down at his own, confirming it hadn't been stolen.

The Deliverer ignored Lennon, pointed to the middle of the spinning water, the second night and snow, the second bright moon. "Jump."

"*You* jump," said Lennon. "I want to know where you got that watch."

Staring into the water-circle, Nico felt two emotions at once: relief that her father was still alive to ring the Bell and curiosity as to where this thing led. The truth was, it didn't really matter where it led or how it got here. Whether alien or machine or black hole on Earth, Nico felt planted in a new light of love: that she knew her father, and he knew her.

She was going to jump. She hadn't come all this way for nothing.

Harry was beside her now, and as she bent down, pulled him into a tight hug, her heart outgrew her insides, and she cried, whispering promises of triple-rationed strawberry granola. She tucked the red journals into her bag—and her eyes landed on the drawing Kit had given her.

It's probably not very good, he'd said. *But it's part of me.*

He'd asked her not to open it in front of him. And she heard his sweet voice . . . *Maybe someday you'll find the perfect spot to hang it . . .*

"Nico."

She tucked the drawing safely under the red journals, closed her bag, and stood. "Harry is going to *love* Boston," she said, wiping tears with the sleeve of her coat, trying to smile.

"You're really doing this."

"Like I said. Dad gave me his story. This is me, taking care of it."

She put a hand on Lennon's cheek, and she knew why this goodbye felt different. Lennon was the only person she'd ever considered in the full context of time: not only past and present, but future, too. "So you know how everyone thinks this is the end of the world?" she asked, feeling those years slip between their hands.

"Not everyone thinks that."

As their foreheads touched, images swam from one mind to the other, pictures of lives unlived, loves unloved, a host of possibilities beyond what might be offered to two people raised in the fucked-up Age of the Fly. Lennon reached down, pulled off his wristwatch, and Nico pretended she didn't know this would happen, pretended she couldn't hear his voice in his eyes.

Here. Take this . . . "Here," he said, handing her the watch. "Take this."

"Lennon."

This is me, taking care of it . . . "This is me, taking care of it."

Nico strapped on the watch, already feeling the years of missing him, of staring into the little skyline framed in the silver circle of the watch face and thinking of Lennon and Harry on the streets of Boston. She wished she could put herself in that picture.

Lennon opened his mouth, and she heard what was coming, and she wanted it, wanted so badly for him to come with her. And while there were a million reasons for him *not* to come—she didn't know how it would work, where it would go, what would happen, and on and on—only one reason really mattered: "This is what he gave me," she said. "Jean gave you . . . your own destiny. Which is a word I know that means fate but sounds more dramatic."

They both smiled, a sweet memory soured by loss. And when they kissed, it was new and wondrous, a book by the fire, a cormorant in the sea, both understanding and feeling understood. Their kiss was a blinding purity of one empath colliding with another, until her thoughts were his, and his were hers, and this collision dovetailed into something even more beautiful than before. It would be over too soon no matter when it ended, but behind her, the water beckoned, its humming so intense she felt the sound in her bones, and so she willed herself to step away from Lennon, turn toward the Deliverer.

"Will you go back to the Farmhouse?" she asked. "I don't want him dying alone."

The Deliverer nodded once.

"Good," said Nico. "I assume there's . . . a place for me?"

The Deliverer pointed to Nico's bag. "It's all in the Red Books."

A slight nod passed between them. *Talk about a consolidated pulse.*

And now she answered the water's call. It would take a running jump to clear the hole in the floor. She secured her bag, wrapped herself in her coat, and took a few steps back. A last look at Lennon—"This has all happened before," she said—and then she ran, eyes on the spinning circle, right for it, intensely aware of her own senses, as if her life to this point had been one long sleep, and now, finally, she was awake. In the light of the moon, under shadows of snow, she felt colder as the circle drew near. Harry barked, and she thought, *How much I'll miss that dog,* and then she heard her father's voice, the great eye in the sky, *Some people are more ancient than others, Nic. All those growth rings inside,* and she knew that he was the water and she was the sound: when one moved, the other felt it; when one changed, the other was affected. And now the shine of her mother was inside her too. *My snowstorm girl*, her mother said, and Nico understood that she was the product not of faith *or* science, but of both, that there was truth and hope to be found in even the most unlikely of fictions.

Inside the spinning circle, mist turned to snow, thick flakes on her face and chest, and all these words in her mind chatted like old friends, speaking of birth and death and birth again, of life after life—and Nico jumped, disappearing through the water-circle.

Chronologies

"We're a little like trees, don't you think?" her father had asked years ago.

They sat like that, perched on the attic deck, staring out over miles of treetops at night, the Great Green and Navy Unknown.

"How so?" asked Nico.

And he explained how trees have growth rings inside, smaller circles in the middle, larger as the tree expands, each ring representing the age of the tree. "Dendrochronology, it's called. Someone specializing in dendrochronology could point to one of those rings and tell you how old the tree was at *that* point in time, or what the atmospheric conditions were at *that* point in time. Yes," he said. "We used to be quite good at things."

Nico looked out over the land and chewed on this. "How are *people* like trees, though?"

Somewhere an owl hooted; a wolf howled. It started raining, and it seemed the seasons were changing before their very eyes, the Great Unknown bursting oranges and yellows more than greens and navies.

"Some people are more ancient than others, Nic. All those growth rings inside."

Soon they were both soaked to the bone, content to sit in the rain if it meant they could keep sitting together. Her father raised his face to the sky, opened his mouth, drank it in. "We may be like trees, but we're made of water."

Nico joined him, opened her mouth to the sky, and couldn't help smiling.

"Pretty weird when you think about it," said her dad. "But then, water is weird."

Sometimes Nico thought life with her father was composed of nothing but a single question, over and over and over: "How so?"

"Its relationship with sound, for one," and he explained the intimate connection between water and sound, how when one moves, the other feels it; when one changes, the other is affected. "Certain frequencies can actually change the physical shape of water. Given the right circumstances, a note can travel through water like a fish."

"Really?"

"Sure. How do you think Bellringer's toll made its way to

Manchester? Actually, sound travels through water much faster than it does through air."

Nico suddenly saw herself as a cormorant gliding through the night sky, searching for the moon and stars, and, finding only darkness, plummeting into water. It was just a vision, but she suddenly felt delirious, looked down at her feet dangling over the edge of the attic deck, the ground far below, and she began to cry.

"It's okay, Nic. Let it out."

Their talks often went like this, starting in theoretical places, ending in inexplicably personal ones. Vivid images. Like she'd *been* in the places they'd only talked about. And while she'd never given this feeling a name, she thought maybe it could be called *ancient*, as if she'd lived not one, but a hundred lives.

Her many growth rings.

Openings

The forward motion of Nico's jump had carried her a few steps, but now she stood in blinding snow, a cold so deep it burned. She looked back the way she'd come, half expecting to see Lennon and Harry and the Deliverer standing in suite 4040—but it was only more snow.

Looking around, it seemed she was in the middle of nothing, some frozen planet, a universe in a patchwork quilt of white snow, black sky, white snow . . .

There was sound, something new. Faint at first but growing louder. In the distance, small lights became larger, closer . . . Nico turned and ran. The ground changed. Not visually—everything was still white. But the feeling of it, a softness she recognized.

Behind her, those sounds exploded, but she did not look back, not yet. Through the heavy snow, she made out a line of trees ahead. *The woods*, and she felt enormous relief at the presence of the familiar. At the first tree, she ducked behind its trunk, turned, and looked back the way she'd come.

A vehicle was on its side, smoke billowing out of it, drifting up into the night sky. Two others behind it now, sliding on ice before stopping.

Cars.

Actual moving cars with engines and foggy windows. From behind the tree, Nico watched more cars approach, tires rolling slowly before stopping altogether. People came out of their cars, ran to the one that had tipped on its side, and more cars came to a standstill, lights everywhere, smoke and sound unending.

She turned back to face the woods, slid down to the base of the tree, blew into her hands.

Think, Nic.

From her bag, she pulled out the three red journals, slowly unwrapping the black cord that wound them together. As she did, a folded paper fell into her lap; she opened it and found the faded greens and grays of roads and towns, a map of mountainous terrain. In the bottom corner, someone had drawn a circle in red ink around the word *billboard*. In the same ink, a line ran between the billboard and the top corner of the map, where a phrase was written: *This house will save your life*.

Something gave Nico pause.

She put the map away, opened one of the journals. A chunk of pages had been torn from the beginning of the book, and the first few after that were crossed through. She kept flipping until finally landing on the first cleanly written page . . .

DATE: October 28, 2025

ACTION ITEMS*:*

—*Billboard first.*
—*Then get to the house. (See: map.)*

A sudden urge to vomit.

October 28, 2025. The day she was born.

Pulling herself from the journal, she was about to turn her attention back to the map when she saw the old photograph of her young parents, the one from the control room.

You got this, they seemed to say. *Be the Listener.*

She stuffed the books and the photo back into her bag, turned to look around the tree again. The footprints she'd made getting here had already filled with fresh snow. Up by the road, a small crowd was attempting to pull someone from the crashed vehicle.

Behind them, the line of cars had grown. And there, maybe a hundred yards away, rising high into the snowy sky, was the back of a billboard.

Ten minutes later Nico stood on the ledge of that billboard, higher than the tallest tree. Using a can of spray paint taken from the underground shelter behind the Blessed Church of the Risen Savior, she added two words to a billboard advertising that very church. "*Now*," she said, her breath like smoke as she sprayed the giant letters right where she knew they belonged. "*Voyager*."

When she was done, she turned slowly, wind whipping her hair around in the freezing air. "I was born in a snowstorm," she whispered, and this high up it felt trancelike, dizzy and out of body. Far below, the line of cars was endless, alive with exhaust and lights, and like a mental checklist, she ran through the details of the last real conversation she'd had with her dad. *In the back seat of a car . . .* There were so *many* cars, though. *Stuck in traffic on the highway . . .* It was dark, everything wet with snow, but she kept looking. "You saw me on a billboard ledge, and you couldn't explain it . . ."

Looking, looking . . .

"But it gave you hope."

There.

His eyes were brighter and younger. But it was him.

They stared at each other, and Nico smiled. "That we would see each other again."

PART SEVEN

IN

THE

AFTER-LIFE

THE
<u>DELIVERER</u>

I stand on the bridge and watch Lennon and Harry head south out of Manchester. Part of me wants to chase after them, tell him everything, go with them to Boston. Seeing Lennon like this— I can't help but think back to a time when I imagined us together, all those images of love and life with him, knowing they were impossible, dreaming them anyway.

The sure sign of youth.

But I am no longer young. And so I offer a quiet goodbye, turn north—not because the Books say so, but because *I* say so—and take the first few steps of a walk I could do with my eyes closed.

NIC●

She found the man hanging over the table, neck in a rope, his head large and on the gray side of purple.

It was the second shock in as many minutes, the first being far more pleasant: that when, out of shivering curiosity, she flipped a switch, a light came on. It felt like something that should be written in history books. *There once was a house on top of a mountain, and this house had working electricity.*

All through the house, Nico found herself losing track of time, staring at a thing and realizing she had no idea how long she'd been standing there: a faucet of running water; a cold refrigerator; everywhere, the small hum of electric things. *Nothing is as strong as the absence of itself*, Lennon had said. Nico felt the absence of her wits in abundance, and nowhere was this truer than the upstairs bedroom closet, in which she found a dark gray synthetic suit and helmet, or the basement, in which she found a warehouse full of canned goods, buckets of freeze-dried meals, medical supplies, tubs of cinnamon, seeds, rice. Taco seasoning.

She wandered out back into an unkempt garden, found an enormous tank, and a steel-reinforced coop, in which chicken bones were scattered suspiciously among a few well-fed chickens. She walked to the edge of the cliff and was met with a view rivaled by nothing: not the woods from the attic deck, or the sweeping Manchester landscape from a crumbling bridge. And when she looked down, she had the answer to the question that had been running through her mind since she'd first arrived in this place. *How is this possible?*

She had never seen so many solar panels in one place.

Back inside, three packs of Metallyte chili mac later, Nico sat on the couch by the glass wall, and pulled the red journals from her bag.

THE DELIVERER

My House by the Solar Cliffs may have had hot showers and Miles Davis, but the Farmhouse has my childhood.

I walk up the porch and, for the first time in eighteen years, open the front door. Inside I take off my helmet, set it at the foot of the stairs, and listen. Flames crackle in the library fireplace.

The door was unlocked.

He's expecting me.

Such a thing, the smell of a house: here is old wood, a good book, rabbit furs, beard balm. (As a kid, I always thought it was just the way Dad smelled. Only later, taking inventory in the basement stores, did I put two and two together.) The dining room and kitchen, the woodstove, the mudroom—these memories bleed too, but not like transport imprints. These aren't memories from other timelines. These are my own memories.

Harriet—and then Harry—begging for scraps.

Mom quoting Scripture.

Dad telling stories.

The first floor is vacant, as I knew it would be.

Take the steps two at a time, now upstairs, across the

cluttered attic, I open the door to the deck—and there he is. In the corner, sitting on the ledge, sipping tea from a mug like I'd never left. "You should taste the sludge I've been brewing this week." He turns, looks up at me, and smiles. "Barely drinkable."

NICO

Considering the relatively compact size and weight of the journals, Nico was astounded at their capacity to pack a punch. For starters: she'd been a mother.

"Huffle*fuck*?"

Or—not really a mother? But sort of.

She flipped to the beginning of the first journal, determined to understand.

The opening pages were missing, and the next twenty were full of scribbling and cross-throughs, a madness transcribed. What little she could make out looked like dates and underlined warnings, fragments outlining strange methods of survival followed by joy at finding this house. The first *clean* entry was the one she'd read two days ago, which brought her here, and it felt like a storm inside the book had cleared, clouds rolled away, pages of blue skies.

All told, the journals covered eighteen years, beginning October 28, 2025—the day Nico was born—and ending November 5, 2043, the day she'd jumped through the water-circle. But if she was reading this right, this wasn't her first time through that particular cycle. The journals referred to these cycles as "Lives," each Life beginning with her painting the highway billboard, and ending when,

at thirty-six years of age, she would hand the journals to the next
Nico, who would jump through the water-circle and . . .

Reboot. Rainbow. Start over.

"Lennon would flip his shit."

She willed away the lump in her throat and went on.

Most of this week's entries read like an intro to the house, detailing the best way to cut down the man who'd hanged himself,
where to bury him; explaining the importance of maintaining the
ten-thousand-gallon rainwater-harvesting tank; how to clean the
closet filter and take care of the chickens so they didn't wind up
eating *more* of each other. It outlined a schedule for Deliveries. And
it explained the significance of the biosuit, its protective devices,
how to trigger the metal hooks on the boots so they anchored the
wearer to the ground.

She wasn't sure how many cycles she'd been through (Lives
she'd lived?), but if the notes under the entries were any indication,
it was into the hundreds.

The notes under the entries. This was where things got *really*
interesting.

Today's entry, specifically. October 30. The action item was
nothing surprising (cut down and bury the dead man). But underneath, her 7th Life—the "founder of the house"—had written a
note of warning. A quick perusal of the pages offered two insights
on this note: it was by far the longest, and it was the only one with
a signature at the end.

Nico had skimmed it the first time, but now, having gotten

the lay of the journal-land, was ready to reread this note exactly as her 7th Life requested: carefully, with an open mind and open eyes. After reading it three times, she looked up, stared through the glass wall across miles of untamed woods, her kingdom forever. Literally.

"Huffle*fuck*."

THE DELIVERER

We spend most of our time in his room, and life proves again to be nothing if not circular: I pull a few favorites from the library, and then sit in a chair by his bed and read excerpts aloud.

From *East of Eden*, "A child may ask, 'What is the world's story about?' And a grown man or woman may wonder, 'What way will the world go? How does it end . . . ?'"

We taste Morrison's *Song of Solomon* . . . "She was the third beer. Not the first one, which the throat receives with almost tearful gratitude . . ."

We climb Mount Doom, travel with Billy Pilgrim, and when we follow Dumbledore into a cave full of Inferi, and the aging headmaster says, "I am not worried, Harry. I am with you," my father raises his hand a few inches, says, "I know how he feels."

While I am grateful for this time together, an invisible clock hovers over our heads, an incessant ticking, and I toggle between the Harry who loves Dumbledore for his goodness, and the Harry who hates him for his elusiveness.

"Dad."

"You were born at the hands of an angel," he says. "I saw your

face that night, and I remembered it. Eyes like fire. I remember—"
He taps his brain, as if to say, *Steel trap*.

"I know, Dad. I saw you too."

"Did you see the angel?"

"You should really get some sleep, you know."

But he doesn't. He says those fiery eyes stayed with him through the years, says he watched them blossom slowly, right in front of him, day after day. "I knew it was time to send you when your mother . . ."

I have often wondered what it would be like to devote my entire life to a single person. To hand them my heart, and to hold theirs in return. As my father's eyes fill with tears, I think of my photo from when they were young—Mom's smile captured in time, a look that said she knew he belonged to her—and it hits me that while I've had eighteen years to cope with losing my mother, her death is still fresh for him. I kiss his hand as the maddening logic of loss rages silently in his eyes, and while I may never experience such pure devotion, in front of me now, I see what happens when the person you give your heart to is no longer there to hold it.

A few minutes pass, and he asks how I feel, and I tell him of my life in the House by the Solar Cliffs, how I ate only what I grew or what was in the basement stores, how my water was filtered. "Whether it's another virus, or water or food—I don't know. But my house saved me."

"Good." He smiles. "So, you'll go back there. After."

After.

I tell him what he wants to hear, and I smile, but a thought has been turning in my mind, something I need to ask while he's lucid, and before his *after* is here.

"The other portals," I say, recalling the cities in the file at Kairos. "Madrid, Seoul, Missoula—"

"Alexandria, Bend, Lima, Asheville."

Like a switch, I think. His brain turns on and off and on again.

"So I've been thinking . . ."

And I tell a story. *There once was a plague that wiped out the world*. My story is bare bones, no jokes, not nearly the detailed depictions of his imaginative tales. But the gist is this: an apocalyptic world where the mass exodus of humanity occurs, while at the same time, a number of mysterious portals appear. "At the end of the world, what could be more convenient than a way out?" I ask.

"You sound like your mother."

We smile, tinges of the maddening loss still lingering.

"Even if you're right," he says, "the portals aren't ways *out*. They're ways *back*."

"Maybe instead of portals to other worlds, all we needed were portals to other times. Maybe it's not alien or cosmic or some divine modern-day Noah's Ark. Maybe it's just the next step in evolution. Single-cell organisms, fish, birds, dinos, apes, upright, freethinking humans, followed by—"

"The same humans. Living over and over again." He smiles. "Your evolutionary timeline needs some work, but it's . . . an exciting thought."

Silence for a moment, and when I try to fill it by reading again, he stops me. "Let's just be," he says, and so we do. We sit there, just being together, not speaking or even looking at each other, and it feels quietly tectonic, the kind of moment that might move a mountain if it were let outside.

"I knew it was you," he says, breaking the silence. "Figured it out years ago."

I don't know what to say to this. The thought of so many years passing between us, each knowing the other is alive—like standing on opposite sides of a closed door, not being able to walk through.

"There's a reason we couldn't live together?" he asks.

I've memorized those particular entries in the Red Books. The transport imprints of them jumping off the cliff are burned in my mind, the nightmare those Lives became. I could tell him. And I almost do. But when I look at him, eager and frail and so close to the end, all I can say is, "Yes. There was a reason."

He slips into a fit of coughing, which turns to blood in his mouth, and out of the blue, the verbal spiral descends: the angel from heaven, my mother's sweaty hands, "Your sweet mother," he says, and I hold him, tell him not to talk, just rest.

Later that evening, after he's had a heavy nap, I help him eat some bone broth, and he asks questions about how the Tollbooth worked. I explain what it feels like, the mist of the spinning water, and my theory that going through so many times has left a mark on my soul.

"Like a tree ring," I say. "Dendrochronology, remember?"

His smile is mechanical; I can't tell if he remembers, so I go on, explain the concept of transport imprints, how I'd begun having memories of things from other timelines, other Nicos, earlier Lives.

"How many Lives?" he asks, his face an expectant sunrise. "How many times have you gone through?"

"I'm number 160."

He laughs out loud. "My Nico," he says, and my heart warms at the affection in his voice, until he follows that up with—"Number 161."

That night after he's asleep, I go up on the attic deck and stay awake into the early hours of the morning. As a child, when this treetop sea whispered possibilities and freedoms beyond my reckoning, I listened with eyes wide and ears open. Eighteen years of the Red Books have made the prospect of freedom dizzying. And so I turn from the view to face the Bell, try to recall a transport imprint from my last Life, but it doesn't work that way. Instead I close my eyes and imagine how it might have gone, a time when, laughing, my father had called *me* his Nico.

My Nico, he would say. *Number 160.*

NIC●

DATE: *October 30, 2025*

ACTION ITEMS:

*—The man hanging from the walkway needs cutting down
(obviously). We can use our knife, but there's a machete in the
upstairs closet that works better. It takes a while, so that's it for
today. Enjoy the bed.*

INCIDENTAL NOTES

Hello, Nico.

*Welcome to the House by the Solar Cliffs. I am Life 7, the
founder of the house, and as an older, wiser you, I do hope you
will read this note carefully, with an open mind and open eyes.*

*First, an apology for the incomplete nature of these Books.
The early pages detailed our six Lives prior to the house. They
were full of darkness and desperation and so I tore most of them
out. It was impulsive and on my worst days, I wish I hadn't—
perspective can be a balm. But it's done, so let's move on.*

After eighteen years, the end of my time in this house looms, and I am compelled to return to the beginning of these Books, not to apologize, but to warn. As I've already spoken with our 8th Life (more on this in a minute), I write this warning for the benefit of our many Lives to come.

Your instinct, upon arriving in this place, will be to fill it with those you love. I know, because I am you. Whatever number you are, it has probably already occurred to you that your parents are young, alive and well. The house is clearly a miracle, an embarrassment of riches, beautiful and bountiful in many ways, and so why not bring them here?

Let me tell you why.

In bringing your parents here, you bring yourself also— as a very young child.

I admit, the idea was so bizarre, it had not occurred to me until I'd already arrived at the Farmhouse with the invitation, only to find Youngself asleep by the fire with Harriet. And while I could fill these Books with details of the traumatic experiences that followed, there are only so many pages, and who knows how many years of notes ahead, and so for the sake of concision, here are the details that truly matter:

I brought Mom and Dad and Youngself to live with me. Each of us were inclined to see the House by the Solar Cliffs as a ticket to a better, safer life—if not for us, then for Youngself.

Nico, listen.

This living arrangement is unnatural to the point of nightmarish. It drives our parents to the edge of the cliff, and eventually, hand in hand, over it. And while their joint death ends the nightmare for them, it is only the beginning for Youngself and me.

For years now I have been left alone in this house to raise myself as my own.

Nightmare is the only word for it.

Imagine: You change your diapers, teach yourself to walk. You watch yourself lose your first tooth. You teach yourself to read, listen to yourself learn to sing. Small tics, growing pains, secret thoughts (not so secret), awkward limbs, puberty, sexual awakening, and through it all, you watch and feel yourself become yourself, and I promise you, it is lonelier than being alone.

Maybe it wouldn't be like this for you. Maybe you'd bring them here and Mom and Dad would be happy, and you'd be like an older sister to Youngself, or a live-in aunt. But I doubt it. And if things go for you as they did for me, bringing them here only robs Youngself of a life in the Farmhouse: all the stories on the attic deck, the Bell, the books by the fire, Mom, Dad, faith, science, songs, brittle pages, stale tea, all of it, gone.

For lack of a better word, our 8th Life has been my daughter, and I, her mother. And yet, she is not my child.

She is me. My Youngself.

This life—this Life—has been a waking nightmare.

Please listen.

—Nico

LIFE 8 HERE—

My life fucking sucked. I was raised in this stupid fucking house by my own fucking self. And now I'm here alone, which, I guess, is minimally better. Listen to Momself. Leave it the fuck alone.

LIFE 9—

I had a great life in the Farmhouse. Life 8 left it the fuck alone. I highly recommend you do the same.

LIFE 10—

Use the machete to cut the guy down. It's way easier. Also, the ground is super hard outside, but there's a softer spot behind the rainwater-harvesting tank. You should get going; it's about to snow again.

LIFE 23—

Listen to Lives 7 and 8. I tried to bring them here. Thought it might be different, seeing as how I knew what to expect this time. It isn't different. It is a waking nightmare.

LIFE 100 HERE—

It takes living in a circle to think in one. That's the long and short of it. Apparently, this is only possible alone. Tried bringing them again. Failed again. Listen to 7, 8, and 23. Stick to the Law of Peripheral Adjustments and learn to love your own company. It's all you have.

LIFE 160—

When you get both drunk and existential—and you will—I recommend the stash of jigsaw puzzles in the upstairs closet.

Still on the couch, Nico sat in shock, staring through the window. She knew what she needed to do: go upstairs, get the machete, cut the guy down, bury him behind the harvesting tank, but all of that was presupposed by her getting up off this couch, which, for the moment, was not happening.

From the minute she'd flipped the first switch in the house—*and there was light*—all she'd been thinking was how and when to get her parents here. But okay, fine. Clearly that wasn't possible. Her next thought was of Lennon and Kit, immediately followed by the realization that Kit was years away from being born, and Lennon was probably a baby.

Surely there was something more she could do.

Considering not just where she was, but *when*, the implications were mind-boggling: October 2025. Four months, give or take, before the Flies hit North America. Theoretically, what was to stop her from pinpointing the moment of the outbreak and stopping it? Her father had said the failed experiment had occurred in Russia. "My God," she said aloud, and immediately turned back to the journals to see if any other Lives had thought to do this.

She had no idea where the nearest airport was. Manchester, probably. Though where in Russia would she even begin? Four months wasn't a ton of time, and even if by some great skill or luck she *was* able to pinpoint the exact location of the outbreak, what then? This wasn't a button someone pushed to launch a missile, or a phial of some airborne disease busted open in a largely populated area (which she could theoretically prevent?), and as she was thinking these things, she landed on a few entries from her 9th Life detailing an attempted trip . . .

INCIDENTAL NOTES

LIFE 9 HERE—

Considering saving the world? Forget it.
I made it to the airport, but apparently, you need a passport
for international travel, and apparently, this takes months

*to obtain, and apparently requires not only a lengthy and
detailed interview process, but documentation proving, among
other things, a place and date of birth. We have no such
documentation, and even if we did, we are technically, currently,
an infant.*

And a few pages later, this note from her 10th Life:

INCIDENTAL NOTES

LIFE 10 HERE—

*In lieu of Russia, I used the months prior to the arrival of the
Flies attempting to warn a federal agency called the Centers
for Disease Control and Prevention. As it turns out, it's pretty
difficult getting a government employee to take anyone seriously,
much less a teenage girl from the fucking future.*

Aside from these few entries, most of the pages outlined
fairly small-minded ventures: delivering food and goods, saving
a few people here and there, mostly regional Good Samaritan
stuff. No family, fine. Can't save the planet, got it. But Nico was
currently in possession of some real Time Turner–level shit. Surely
there was something *bigger* she could do, some task equal to this
godlike power.

Kit. If he was still years away from being born, she had years to find Town. Forget bringing him to the house; all she had to do was find Dakota, warn her about what would happen in Waterford. Although—if she accomplished this, there was the potential he would never *leave* Town, which would change the entire timeline of her next Life. Maybe she could find him in the days leading up to Waterford, warn him that way.

A quick perusal of the journals informed her of all the ways she'd tried to save him, all the ways it never worked, and while Nico took some comfort in living in a world where the reality of Kit was still ahead, not behind, she couldn't help feeling cheated.

Outside, it began to snow.

She stood from the couch, fully intending to get the machete and do the job that needed doing. Instead she found herself standing by the shelves full of records, vague memories of warbly music from her father's old radio, the occasional Farmhouse a capella session. She reached up, pulled a record off the shelf. It was called *Pet Sounds* by a band called the Beach Boys. It took a while to figure out how the turntable worked, but eventually she managed, and as the music played, she looked around the house, felt its light and warmth, things like miracles around every corner. She could already sense how the house would grow on her, how she would come to rely on it, and maybe one day, even love it. But for now its sounds and lights weren't miracles so much as reminders of her own quiet, dark world.

She turned the volume up until her ears hurt.

THE DELIVERER

I bury him in the cellar beside Mom.

After that, it's hard to remember. I stay in the Farmhouse for a while. Days, weeks, it might have been a month.

Time is nothing now, time is wind. I feel it, but barely, and it passes in a gust.

Outside, there is quite a bit of snow. January, then. Maybe February.

However long I stay, it is too long. This transition happens quickly, or at least covertly: one minute, the Farmhouse feels like home, the squeaky floorboards of my childhood like a loving, arthritic old woman; the next minute, I am an orphan.

There are simply too many echoes.

It takes less than an hour to pack. Metallyte pouches from the cellar, maps, lighters, et cetera. Before I know it, I'm in the biosuit again, walking the woods, feeling more at home with my tree-siblings than at any point in the last few weeks.

Days. Months. Whatever.

Something about being in the woods again calls to mind the poem I'd read over Dad's grave. Covered in dirt, having just dug the hole and trying to read through tears, I read Dad's old copy of *Leaves of Grass*, which felt expected, but I was at a loss for originality. And though I'd buried Mom years ago, the freshness of her grave in this Life made the missing that much stronger. And so I'd read over both graves, wondering at the virtue of peripheral adjustments, of spending years keeping my own family alive in a world where to do so cost me a place with them . . .

"'The untold want by life and land ne'er granted. Now, voyager, sail thou forth to seek and find.'"

And that was when I saw it.

The next poem in the book. I'd read it before, years ago, my first night in the House, alone and looking for company in pages.

"'What are those of the known,'" I say now to my treesiblings, "'but to ascend and enter the Unknown?'"

NIC●

"'And what are those of life but for Death?'"

Her first night in the house, after the sun had set—after a long and difficult process in which she'd cut down the Architect with a machete, made a mess of the floor downstairs where he fell, and then buried him in the grounds out back—after she'd gone to the basement for a snack, only to stare at the rock wall so long, she began to see the outline of the circle that brought her here—after taking the first hot shower of her life, and thinking, *Music, sex, hot showers, and time travel, it's been a week*—Nico lay in what must have been the most comfortable bed in the world, and stared at this poem.

How had she never read this before? Had her dad mentioned it? She thought she'd remember, as it was one of those rare compositions that forced the reader to believe the author was nothing short of an oracle, listening to your secret thoughts, walking into the corners of your soul, taking your ugliness and turning it to beauty on the page.

"'. . . ascend and enter the Unknown,'" she read aloud, as pieces of her final conversation with her father came back to her:

*The unknown can be scary. But when the known is death itself, you
enter the unknown.*

She stared at the poem's title, big block letters, as if willing her
to defy their truth:

"PORTALS."

Gently, Nico closed the book, one of her treasures from Books-
a-Million, in what felt like a lifetime ago (and in a way, she supposed, it *was* a lifetime ago). She set it on the bedside table beside
the photograph of her young parents, which she'd arranged in a
way that allowed her to see them from any given point in the room.

Exhausted but wired, she flipped through one of the red journals at random, landing on this entry, still years away:

DATE: May 7, 2033

ACTION ITEMS:

*—Farmhouse delivery. Last time, we found a note on the door
requesting more taco seasoning.*

She remembered putting in that request. And the joy she'd felt
on the day it arrived.

After reading a few more entries, something occurred to her.
A trend. The more ambitious Lives—the ones that stretched the
boundaries of their power—generally ended in trauma, disaster,
or grief. Whereas those Lives who understood and respected their
power were generally fulfilled.

She shut the journal, was about to set it down for the night when she noticed something else. There, on the back cover, a single word etched into leather: LIVES.

Below that, four columns of tiny numbers carved from top to bottom, beginning with number 1, ending with number 160.

Each number had been crossed through.

Up here, in this house on top of a mountain, the moon seemed closer, its shine through the window a light she'd never known. In that light, Nico stared at the crossed-through numbers and considered the chickens in the fortress-coop, the eggs she would have tomorrow morning. The refrigerator and stove, the showers and sinks, the records and lights and *life* that was possible here, and she wondered why the Architect had denied himself survival in a place so well-equipped to survive. Maybe one day she would have more than theories, she would have certainty. Maybe the Farmhouse would seem a distant memory, and she would think, *Surely that was some other person.* But on that first night, she stared at her own two hands and considered those two little birds that had once brought her family exotic foods from far-off lands, and she thought, *How strange that we should ever think we know anything at all.*

Reaching down, on the floor by her bed, Nico pulled her knife from her bag. Very carefully, she etched a new number into the back of the Red Book.

THE
DELIVERER

I f I could wear a city like a sweater, I would wear Boston.

I stand behind a statue, staring up into the second-story window of an old stone apartment, and even now, hyper-focused on the window, the feathery wintertime beauty of the city is distracting. Every city looks better buried in snow, no amount of destruction outside its reach: ruins and craters where buildings once stood, overturned cars and piles of bones, the beauty of snow does not discriminate.

And, if timed right, can make an easy job of tracking.

They'd been a tough pair to miss: one set of boot prints, one set of loyal-to-the-bone paw prints.

I wonder if their pulses have consolidated yet.

At one point, the tracks multiplied, the comings and goings of a small group, all from the same stone apartment. Every window in this apartment is dark or damaged, save one.

From behind my statue, I stare up at this window with its small flickering light, and I wait. *To what end? Do I plan to talk to him? Will I tell him who I am?* Back at the Farmhouse, when I'd first had the idea to come find him, the question of purpose seemed insignificant.

Once I get there, I'll know why I came.

Now I'm here and the same voice is saying, *Once you see him, you'll know why you came,* and I can only hope that voice is right.

I wait.

I don't know how long. Because time is wind.

And then it happens. It's quick, and so I stretch the moment to my liking . . .

His face in the window, looking up at the night sky, the boy I loved, now half my age. And in this stretched-out instant, my pulse quickens as Harry jumps up beside him, puts two paws on the window. A second person appears now, and Lennon turns, says something to her—

They smile, and the window is empty again.

The voice was right: I know why I came. And where else I need to go.

NICO

The commune was tucked in the pocket of a mountain, exactly as the Red Books described. Tents were positioned like a little village, well-worn paths running this way and that. It was the middle of the night; the moon was young, a sliver in the sky.

A few of the tents were lit from the inside, a single flame flickering through canvas, but most were dark.

"Quiet now, okay?" Nico handed the little boy an applesauce packet, which he readily accepted.

After miles and days together, she still wasn't sure if he could talk. Probably around three years old, he was the kind of quiet that made her wonder how much he really understood. She picked him up, and together, they circled the settlement, headed toward the sprawling oak near the back where they would find the appointed tent.

Already, Nico felt the cadence and calls of the woods were her own, the roots of her knowledge sunk deep in its soil. And so the guards on duty did not see her, nor did the man who, mere feet away, had thrown open his tent flap and stumbled outside to relieve himself.

Nico was a ghost when she needed to be.

They reached the tent in question. She stopped, took a breath, opened the flap, and entered. In the corner, a low candle burned; its light shone green through her tinted visor, and in that light, she saw the woman on the ground wrapped in heavy blankets, breathing peaceful rhythms of sleep.

Nico set the little boy down, motioned again for him to keep quiet. He held up a tiny hand, displaying the empty packet, eyes begging for more. She pulled another applesauce from her biosuit pocket, handed it to him, and knelt beside the sleeping woman.

Dakota Sherouse was younger than Nico imagined, her face kind and careworn. And whether because Nico saw only what she wanted to see, or because the traits were actually there, she saw in this face the shades and brushstrokes of the face to come.

"Don't be afraid," she whispered, and just as Dakota had been the angel for Nico's birth, Nico became the angel for Kit's. "One day you will have a son." Tears caught in her throat; she pushed them down, went on. "And he will be one of a kind, a pure soul, and a friend to those in need."

The rhythms of sleep stopped abruptly.

Nico held her breath, waited for them to begin again. When they did, she pulled the key from her pocket, reached out, and placed it gently in Dakota's outstretched palm. "Do not be afraid," she whispered again. "This time, I've taken care of everything."

Nico turned and, before leaving the tent, knelt beside the little boy. The key was written in the Red Books; bringing it here was a necessary step, one that had proven to work time and again.

The boy, on the other hand, was a gamble. No other Life had brought him here.

There was no telling how it would go.

"This is your home now," she whispered. "This woman will take care of you."

Only later, alone again, a ghost in the woods, would Nico have time to begin processing what she'd done. She would remind herself that other Lives had tried similar things, but while theirs had ended in total disaster, hers had, at the very least, given this little boy a better life. For years she would wonder if it worked, if the pieces she'd broken of her own soul had been for nothing. She would sit on the edge of her cliff at night, and plead with God, the Red Books, the stars, anyone who would listen, to let Kit live a full life. She would write it all down in the Red Books, in hopes that it worked, in hopes that future Lives would do the same, and that Kit would live again and again.

"I'm sorry for what I had to do," Nico whispered to the little boy in the tent. "I hope you don't remember what you saw."

He held out his hand for another applesauce.

Nico pulled the last one from the pack and opened it. Handing it to him, she smiled and lightly rubbed his cheek. "Goodbye, Gabe."

She left the tent without looking back, eager to get home and wash Bruno's blood from her suit.

THE DELIVERER

In a bobbing kayak, seven miles off the coast of Rye, New Hampshire. From the mainland, the Isles of Shoals had appeared as little rocks on the horizon; once I got out here, it was clear which island I would find him on.

I keep close to the rocks, low and unseen. The wind and ocean are freezing, but my suit is warm, my mind clear.

I hold binoculars to my eyes. This particular island is clearly the tech hub of the community; I'm not even sure what I'm looking at. There are solar panels, yes, but also what appear to be miniature versions of the hydroelectric stations along the Merrimack, little steel cage-like structures linked by wires and antennae, and all of it connected to a lighthouse.

And then I see him. In the lighthouse, either adjusting or affixing an antenna. It is the first time I've seen Monty since the cabin in the woods: eighteen years ago for me, only a few months for him. Someone joins him now, and I adjust the binoculars to find Lakie beside him, rifle over one shoulder, and together they look . . . happy? Maybe.

Content.

They look content.

I don't see Loretta, but she could easily be on any number of these little islands. Given the look of contentment on Monty's face, if she is alive, she is in this place.

And I know why I came to the Isles of Shoals.

It's the same reason I went to Boston.

I needed to know my friends had people in their lives willing to walk through strange doors into dark places, so long as they could walk there together.

Binoculars packed, I hold the paddle in my lap, let the rhythms of the ocean take me. All around, the sounds of the sea undulate, roll in softly, flow out loudly; I look up at the sky, and when I ask the question, it feels new because I am new.

"How can I fight this darkness?"

The stars seem a little less cold than usual, a little more caring. And whether from seeing Monty for the first time in years, or a directive from the stars themselves, I think of that cabin in the woods, how I'd first approached it with a sense of having been there before.

Can you imagine living here? Monty had asked so long ago.

I never answered him, because yes, I *could* imagine it. It had seemed impossible at the time, a memory from another life . . .

9 YEARS LATER

NICO

"**H**alfway there," said Nico, passing the crooked birch she'd long ago marked as the halfway point between her House by the Solar Cliffs and the Farmhouse. Winter deliveries always took longer, the contents of the pushcart weighed down in snow—five-pound tubs of cinnamon felt like ten, candles and freeze-dried meals seemed twice their size.

Last time, after dropping everything through the slat in the door, she'd felt someone watching her as she walked away. In the nearby brush, she'd quickly turned to find the curious eyes of her younger self peering through the cracks in the boards of her old bedroom window. *There it is*, she'd thought. *The realization that the Deliverer is a person, not a couple of magical birds.*

All around, the woods were white with snow, a new-bright blanket. There was no green left in the trees, no yellows or maroons, just old brown trunks and twigs hanging around. Her years in the woods had instilled a deep respect for trees. So many things to love about them, not the least of which was their determination to exist.

We're a little like trees, don't you think?

Memories of her father's words came often, like excerpts from her favorite books. And anyway, wasn't that exactly what she'd been given? Her Lives were imperfect like a book, unexpected like a book, and as books were made from trees, perhaps her father was right in more ways than he knew. He'd done more than give her a story—he'd given her life *inside* the story.

She stopped, suddenly—

Be the Listener.

There. The low hum.

It could be nothing else.

Nico set down the handles of the pushcart, unzipped a pocket of her biosuit, and pulled out a compact plastic tarp. Quickly, she spread the tarp across the top of the pushcart, wrapped it underneath, and tied the corners together. Once done, she dug the metal hooks of her boots deep under the snow, into the hard earth below, and waited.

THE DELIVERER

I t is the kind of warm night that makes the cold ones seem far away. In my lap, St. John looks up at me, her eyes alight, inquisitive, and slightly judgmental: *Who are you again?*

Years together, and still, she treats me like a stranger, only wants my attention until she's got it. I'll be occupied in the garden, chopping wood, or working on the jury-rigged water filter, and she'll paw and mew until I set down what I'm doing, carry her here, let her sit in my lap. This usually lasts about four minutes before she gives me this exact look, and then off she goes, back into the woods, tail held high in smug victory. After a whole childhood with a dog, nine years with a cat has been a daily mindfuck. But her eyes are turning older, the fur around her nose and ears grayer, and I cannot deny that when St. John is gone for good, I will miss her.

"I am Nico," I say, gently rubbing her back. "A person in three acts."

Early April now, the trees are breathing and alive. Not alive like plants but like people, talking, loving, laughing. I gave them a good trim years ago, reshaped their relationship with the sun, and now the air is full of their chatter, their hands stretching toward one another, toward me, and how could I ever feel alone? Behind the cabin, the Merrimack flows wild and free, louder at night, it seems, or maybe louder in April.

Seasons: the earth's rhythms, to which all things march in time.

"Act One, in a Farmhouse with people I love."

A Farmhouse now emptied, its goods long since relocated and dwindled: Metallyte buckets, candles, lighters, soap and salt and sugar. What filter bottles were left, I'd gutted, reconstructing their insides into a few food-grade buckets to create a large-scale filter.

The Cabin Leibowitz is no afterlife, but it often feels like my life after. It is smaller than I remember, but cozier, too. Three mattresses stacked in one corner, my biosuit hanging by the door. On the bedside table, where there once was a child's drawing of a family, there is now a different portrait: an old photograph of my young parents. And on the wall, where once hung a blueprint of the Cormorant, now hangs the most perfect sketch I've ever seen, given to me long ago by the most perfect soul I've ever known: in the drawing, a woman sits in an old cinema projection room, a silver key dangling from her necklace, brushing the forehead of her young sweet-faced son.

It took years, but I finally found the perfect spot to hang it.

"Act Two, alone in a house of electric light."

My gardens are coming along nicely, flowers around the graves and blood-tree, vegetables and fruits and herbs in the clearing out front. Among the books I'd hauled from the Farmhouse were a few on the practices of gardening: which vegetables to grow and when, how and where, best for protein, most versatile.

No hunting. No meat. Whether it's the killing that draws the Fly, or the meat that causes the Flu—or both, or neither—I am content. I have had a really good tomato. I have had good friends, and I have known love, and if this is life after the Red Books, then I can live with that.

Occasionally I consider going back to my House by the Solar Cliffs, but the notion never sticks. The house was a product of the Books, which I am done with, and a necessity for the Deliverer, who is no longer me, and so in a sense—and for lack of a better term—I outgrew my enormous home.

Anyway, it belongs to Echo now. I do hope it has treated him well.

"And Act Three"—I look the cat right in her old eyes—"in a cabin by a river with an ungrateful cat."

St. John hops off my lap, disappears around the corner of the cabin, and I have a sudden memory of playing the Game with Harry.

God, I miss that dog.

I'm lost in thought when St. John reappears at the corner of the cabin, looks at me, and then looks back the way she came.

"Yeah, but what are you gonna do once I get over there?" I stand, smiling, and step down off the porch. "Some cunning plan to make me look stupid, I'm sure."

When I reach her, she trots a few more steps along the side of the cabin, toward the back, and then stops at the top of the hill, staring down at the Merrimack.

I bend down to pet her when I see what's got her attention.

At the bottom of the hill—by the river and the Cormorant, and partially hidden in brush—an old woman stands beside a dog. The woman's hair is long and silver, her skin a watery white; she wears odd clothes, like a cross between a biosuit and a nightgown made of some reflective material I don't recognize. She holds a large book in both hands, and even from here I see the firm but gentle grasp: the book is clearly precious to her.

The dog looks nothing like Harry. It is bigger, more wolflike, with gray fur and eyes the color of ice. And I'm suddenly reminded of those times with Harry when his eyes seemed like a deep well, and, looking into them, I found the soul of his mother at the bottom, staring up at me.

There is a well in this dog's eyes too: it is deep and occupied and it takes my breath away.

We stand like that, staring at each other, as if someone had painted the moment into being. And then the old woman smiles, wind from the river whips her hair around—and I know who she is.

Slowly, she sets the book on the ground; and together, she and the dog turn north and are gone.

NIC●

Nico waited patiently beside the pushcart. And when the swarm came, she did not run, did not take cover. Arms and face raised to the sky, she watched through the tinted visor as the bright winter sun turned black, as the mountains flooded in darkness, and the gently falling snow became an angry, buzzing army. The Flies brought the night, and they brought it eagerly. Arms outstretched, she let them come, let them cover her from head to toe, let them shroud her so completely that she could see and hear nothing but them. For a time it went like this, her boots hooked into the ground as if anchored to the bottom of the sea, the powerful current of Flies bearing down on her, and under it all, Nico smiled, knowing this swarm that was the death of all things would not be the death of her.

THE
DELIVERER

At the river's edge, I inspect the book left behind by the old woman. Its color is a relief: not red but worn gray. Leather-bound, it's at least three times the size of a Red Book, and I know it will be heavy before I pick it up (though its heaviness seems less to do with weight and more to do with gravity). Embedded in the cover is a large circle, and inside the circle, a title: *Atlas of Ages*.

The sun is gone now, and in the rusty shine of a patina moon, I sit with my back against the Cormorant and begin to read: here are firsthand accounts of numerous geological anomalies separated by state lines, ruined cities, swarms great and small; here are methods of mastering the travel of time through water; here are maps and vivid details of families living in a secret place as older generations pass down truths hidden in tales. There are no dates, no action items, no incidental notes. This isn't that kind of Book.

This is a story. And as the truth of the old woman sinks in—as beside me, the river calls my name—I understand that this *Atlas of Ages* is more than *a* story.

It is my story.

It just hasn't happened yet.

ACKNOWLEDGMENTS

've spent most of my writing career exploring the metaphorical ways in which art and story can save us, so I suppose it was only a matter of time before I explored their literal saving graces as well. And not just for my characters. In many ways, *The Electric Kingdom* was born in the fray, a child of pandemics and wildfires and systemic collapses—of the economy, of politics, of decency in leadership. On a personal note, while writing this book, I found myself in and out of the hospital with a number of medical issues. Some days, it felt like this book was trying to kill me. But then I would feel that magnetic pull to the light, and, as Nico and Kit and Lennon drew closer to their own versions of redemption *in* story, I felt myself being redeemed *by* story. But never alone. To that end . . .

Thanks to my agent, Dan Lazar, for his wisdom in asking the right questions, and his patience when I answered with deafening silence. To the whole Writers House team, including Victoria Doherty-Munro, Cecilia de la Campa, Alessandra Birch, and Jessica Berger—and to Josie Freeman and the film/TV team at ICM—a dramatic doff-of-the-cap to each and every one of you.

Thanks to friend and publisher Ken Wright, and to my brilliant editor, Dana Leydig, without whom this book would be a shadow of itself. A million thanks to my Penguin family: Elyse Marshall, Lathea Mondesir, Jen Loja, Felicity Vallence, Felicia Frazier, Carmela Iaria, Venessa Carson, Emily Romero, Alex Garber, Brianna Lockhart, Christina Colangelo, Rachel Wease, Kara Brammer; and those second-to-none sales reps on the ground, fighting the good fight, including (but not limited to) John, Allan, Doni, Jill, Colleen, and Sheila; to Theresa Evangelista, for yet another stunner of a cover; to copyeditors extraordinaire, Kaitlin Severini, Krista Ahlberg, Marinda Valenti, Nicole Wayland, and Abigail Powers; and to Opal Roengchai for the gorgeous internal design.

Many thanks to my early readers: Court Stevens, Becky Albertalli, Jasmine Warga, Justin Reynolds, Melissa Albert, Julian Winters, Kyle V. Hiller, Emily Henry, Bri Cavallaro, and Greg Weidman; Mindy McGinnis, whose knowledge of outdoor survivalist tactics saved the life of this book, and in the event of nuclear fallout, perhaps someday, the life of this author (I am both honored and terrified to call you friend); Jeff Zentner, for pushing me to create a fuller, more realized postapocalyptic world, and for his strange arsenal of bee-related knowledge; Ashley Couse and Margaret Buxton for their midwifery expertise; Brian Armentrout for virus-related terminology; Dan Garcia and Taylor Tracy for all things art related. Any errors or miscalculations in any and all of these areas are mine alone.

Thanks also to: Adam Silvera, less for Book Reasons, more for Heart ones; David Levithan, Victoria Schwab, Alex London, Silas

House, and Brendan Kiely, each of whom, at various points in the life of this book, offered much-needed direction and wisdom; the OG crit group—Erica, Ashley, and Josh—for listening to a story about a bell tower in a farmhouse and not laughing it off; Shiloh, for making research way more fun than it has any business being; Beverly Peters, Daniel Peters, and everyone at the Millyard Museum in Manchester, but especially John Clayton, for his in-depth tour and exhilarating history lesson; George and Diane, whose view from the top of a mountain at Moosehead Lake sparked an idea; my brother, AJ, for feedback regarding MREs and "gun bullets"; Fred Mills and Greg Cason for the tour of Kentucky Theater (which is, literally, my favorite place in the world); the Nomads and the Lexington Writers Room, for local community; the good people at the Bookery in Manchester, especially Erynn and Jasmin; everyone at Joseph-Beth Booksellers and Parnassus Books; and all the booksellers, librarians, teachers, bloggers, and readers who've supported me all these years.

Thanks to the following artists and storytellers whose work inspired and, in a million small ways, saved me: Slow Meadow, Hammock, Hildur Guðnadóttir, Ryuichi Sakamoto, Max Richter, and the late, great Jóhann Jóhannsson; Carl Sagan, Emily St. John Mandel, and Ted Chiang; Yves Tanguy, René Magritte, and Helen Lundeberg.

Last but not least: Stephanie and Wingate. From the Big Plan to a galaxy far, far away, you guys are my team. Love you both so much. (Plus one.)

AUTHOR INTERVIEW

1. THIS BOOK WAS YEARS IN THE MAKING. WHAT INITIALLY SPARKED THE IDEA FOR *THE ELECTRIC KINGDOM* AND FROM WHERE DID YOU PULL INSPIRATION?

I first had the idea back in the fall of 2013. I was a stay-at-home dad of our one-year-old, putting the finishing touches on my first novel, when the image of a family in a boarded-up farmhouse popped into my head. It was years before I understood who that family was or what their world looked like. For a long time, the book was just called *Nico*, and it was a file on my computer where I stuffed ideas I didn't know what to do with, like a messy closet you're too afraid to open. There were countless inspirations along the way: the work of Helen Lundeberg, Ted Chiang, Emily St. John Mandel, Cormac McCarthy, Jóhann Jóhannsson, Hildur Guðnadóttir, and Christopher Nolan; the view from the top of a mountain in Maine; a wooden board in my office with a painting of a ship at sea. Some ideas sprout wings overnight, while others need years in a cocoon, developing gangly limbs in the dark, fumbling around, never quite sure when or how to be born. This was definitely one of those gangly ideas that evolved over a long period of time.

2. YOU OFTEN CITE TED CHIANG AND EMILY ST. JOHN MANDEL AS WRITERS WHOSE WORK YOU ADMIRE. HOW DID THEIR WRITING MOTIVATE YOUR CHOICES WHILE WORKING ON *THE ELECTRIC KINGDOM*?

In 2016, I walked into a movie theater to see what I thought was an alien movie, and when I walked out, I was a changed person. Like so many, I came to Ted Chiang through the movie *Arrival*, brilliantly adapted by Eric Heisserer from Chiang's original short story "Story of Your Life." I just remember thinking, "That. I need more of that." Both of Chiang's books—*Stories of Your Life and Others* and *Exhalation*—are those rare short story collections where your favorite story is whichever one you happen to be reading at the moment. It's heady, twisty stuff, and you may not connect every thread, but you never doubt that Chiang has. That idea was a north star for me with *The Electric Kingdom*: I don't expect every reader to connect every thread in the book, but I do hope it's written in a way that allows the reader to trust that I have. And obviously, *Station Eleven* was another huge influence, the way Emily St. John Mandel built this brilliant postapocalyptic backdrop of enormous scope, and then told these more intimate, character-driven stories right in the middle of everything. But I think that's why I prefer *post* apocalyptic fiction to *apocalyptic* fiction: the latter asks the question, *How did the world end?* whereas the former asks, *Who survived?* This inherently shifts the focus from plot to character, while also injecting an element of hope into the story. And let's be honest, postapocalyptic worlds are often bleak. Whether you're reading Octavia Butler's *Parable of the Sower*, Ling Ma's *Severance*, or Cormac McCarthy's *The Road*, a little hope goes a long way.

3. THE NOVEL RUNS ON A NONLINEAR/CIRCULAR TIMELINE. CAN YOU DESCRIBE A LITTLE ABOUT THE WRITING PROCESS AND HOW THE PLOT CAME TOGETHER?

As a writer, if you decide to construct a story with four nonlinear timelines, you better have some smart people in your corner. Luckily for me, I do! I spent a lot of time on the phone with my editor, Dana Leydig, trying to piece together the story like a giant jigsaw. In its earliest form, the manuscript was actually a series of interlinked but distinctly separate narratives, which I'd decided to nest into one another (à la *Cloud Atlas* by David Mitchell). After finishing a draft that way, I realized I was sacrificing story at the altar of format, so I scrapped it and just told the story in its most natural form, which ultimately meant alternating between three separate POVs (plus a fourth in the prologue). I don't outline a ton, but I do keep timelines going for each of my books; for my first three novels, this consisted of a single sheet of paper and took all of an hour. For *The Electric Kingdom*, I wound up unrolling a few feet of brown wrapping paper on the dining room table and spent a week mapping it all out. I came so close to quitting this novel a number of times, but it's like anything that feels too big or too impossible to tackle—you find one small thing, and you focus on that. Then, once that's done, you find another small thing, and so on, and that's how you trick yourself into thinking the thing you're working on isn't so big. It's the only way I ever get anything done.

4. THE SETTINGS OF YOUR BOOKS ARE OFTEN AS VIVID AND THREE-DIMENSIONAL AS YOUR CHARACTERS. EXPLAIN THE SIGNIFICANCE OF SETTING IN *THE ELECTRIC KINGDOM*, AND WHAT KIND OF RESEARCH WENT INTO WRITING THESE LOCATIONS?

For my first novel, I had a character before anything else. My second started with a feeling, and my third began with a concept. Seeds can come from anywhere, and so it was only a matter of time until I wrote a book where that seed was setting. As I mentioned above, *The Electric Kingdom* began with an image of a farmhouse in the woods; also, my wife has family in Maine, so we've taken a few trips to that part of the country, and I think rural New England has been simmering in my mind for a while. In addition to those family visits, during the years it took to write the book, I went on two dedicated research trips to Manchester, New Hampshire, and the surrounding areas. During one of those trips, while hiking Nico's path along the Merrimack River, I stumbled across a Books-A-Million, and was like, "Oh, this is too good." I went inside the store, walked around, imagined what the place might look like in a postapocalyptic world. Pretty quickly, I knew my characters were going to spend the night in this abandoned bookstore, and it wound up being one of my favorite scenes to write. Also, the theater where Kit grows up is based on an old cinema in my hometown called the Kentucky Theater. The owners were kind enough to give me a behind-the-scenes tour of the place, which made writing Kit's early sections feel more alive, like I'd actually been there. Google Earth is helpful when writing, but there's no substitute for experiencing a place for yourself. At the very least, this kind of research confirms and enriches what I already know, but there are always one or two instances when I find something entirely new.

5. *THE ELECTRIC KINGDOM* ORIGINALLY PUBLISHED IN EARLY 2021. GIVEN THE TIMING OF COVID-19, WAS THERE ANY CONCERN ABOUT PUBLISHING A NOVEL THAT CENTERS THE AFTERMATH OF A GLOBAL PANDEMIC?

I think if I'd written a book *about* a pandemic, I probably would have asked to push back the publication date. But like I mentioned above, part of why I love postapocalyptic fiction is that the story isn't *about* the apocalypse—it's about what comes after. *The Electric Kingdom* takes place roughly twenty years after the apocalypse, so it doesn't spend a lot of time on *how* the world ended, instead centering those who survived and how they navigate the new world. In that sense, the book offers quite a bit of hope (I hope), which I think the world can use right now.

6. THERE ARE FOUR SEPARATE POVS IN *THE ELECTRIC KINGDOM* AND ONLY ONE OF THEM IS A TEENAGER. LIKEWISE, WHILE MANY OF THE THEMES ARE CERTAINLY RELATABLE TO TEENS, THERE ARE TIMES WHEN THE BOOK READS LIKE AN ADULT NOVEL, AND TIMES WHEN IT READS LIKE A MIDDLE GRADE NOVEL. HOW OFTEN DO YOU CONSIDER YOUR AUDIENCE WHILE WRITING, AND WHO WOULD YOU SAY IS THIS BOOK'S IDEAL READER?

My answer to this question has evolved through the years, and there's no reason to think it will stop evolving anytime soon, but here's where I am at the moment: My goal is to write the best book I can. It takes years for me to write a novel, and I don't generally think about the audience until much later in the process; even then, I'm thinking about things like accuracy and research, representation, authenticity, and even a satisfying resolution. Maybe I should consider age, but the truth is, I don't. I think this partially stems from a pet peeve of mine, which is when I feel an author writing down to their audience, or not giving it their all, based on the presumed age of the reader. I'm not saying every book has to challenge the structure of storytelling or shake the foundations of literature—some of the more brilliant novels are brilliant in their simplicity. But I do try to put my best, my fullest, my most into each book, and then trust the experts—publishers and librarians, booksellers and teachers, bloggers and parents, heroes all—to know which book goes with which reader.

7. *THE ELECTRIC KINGDOM* HAS A LOT TO SAY ABOUT THE PARENT-CHILD BOND, THE POTENTIAL FOR LOVE AND LOSS IN THOSE RELATIONSHIPS, AND THE WAYS CHILDREN TRUST THEIR PARENTS (AND VICE VERSA). AS A PARENT YOURSELF, DID YOU FIND THESE SECTIONS PARTICULARLY DIFFICULT TO WRITE?

I think being a parent is a lot like being a storyteller: you've literally created a character; you see a lot of yourself in them, for better or worse; you send them on their way, hoping for the best as they make one questionable choice after another. I said before that I rarely (if ever) consider the age of my audience, and that's true—but I do consider the age of my characters, and when writing teenagers, there's no way around it: a fundamental tenet of the teen experience is impulsivity. This is often fun to write, but it can be challenging when those impulsive decisions go sideways, a not altogether rare occurrence in the world of this book. I will say, distilled to its purest, *The Electric Kingdom* is about one father's attempt to spare his child pain and suffering and maybe even death itself. In that sense, I don't think it's a coincidence that the initial idea for this book came to me while I was a stay-at-home dad of our newborn son.

RESEARCH COLLAGE

A SELECTION OF PHOTOS FROM DAVID'S RESEARCH TRIPS
FOR *THE ELECTRIC KINGDOM*

Nico's route along the
Merrimack River, some-
where in the woods of
New Hampshire.

North of Manchester, first glimpses of the city.

The Merrimack River in Manchester.

The repurposed mill in Manchester, which Kairos is based on.

One of my favorite places on earth, the Kentucky Theater, which Paradise Twin is based on.